A Time to Laugh

★ NUMBER THREE IN THE AMERICAN ODYSSEY SERIES ★

A Time to Laugh

GILBERT MORRIS

Fleming H. Revell
A Division of Baker Book House Co
Grand Rapids, Michigan 49516

© 1995 by Gilbert Morris

Published by Fleming H. Revell
a division of Baker Book House Company
P.O. Box 6287, Grand Rapids, MI 49516-6287

Printed in the United States of America

Library of Congress Cataloging-in-Publication Data

Morris, Gilbert.
    A time to laugh / by Gilbert Morris.
        p.   cm. — (The American odyssey ; no. 3)
    ISBN 0-8007-5566-9
        1. United States—History—20th century—Fiction. 2. Family—United States—Fiction. I. Title. II. Series.
    PS3563.08742T566   1995
    813'.54—dc20   95-14699

Scripture taken from the King James Version of the Bible.

To Holly Sarver

The best little tater-grubber in the whole state of
Louisiana!
(And a real sweetheart, too!)

CONTENTS

PART ONE   The Silver Screen

1 A Circus and a Service *13*
2 Christie's Man *26*
3 Sometimes the World Falls Apart *39*
4 A Nanny for Adam *52*
5 "I've Got to Do It!" *64*
6 Running Wild *76*

PART TWO   Wings

7 Lenora *89*
8 Jerry Takes a Walk *102*
9 A Job in Fort Smith *114*
10 Lylah and the Burglar *127*
11 Jerry to the Rescue *140*
12 "He Doesn't Look Like a Gangster—" *152*

PART THREE   Airmail

13 Mario *167*
14 Snowbound *180*
15 Into the Darkness *192*
16 Jerry Gets a Warning *204*
17 Last Passage *216*
18 A Gathering of Stuarts *224*

PART FOUR   Chicago

19   A Little Warning   *235*

20   Capone Strikes   *247*

21   A Family Argument   *258*

22   "It's What I've Been Looking For
     All My Life!"   *269*

23   The Answer   *279*

24   Love and Ice Cream   *287*

THE STUART FAMILY

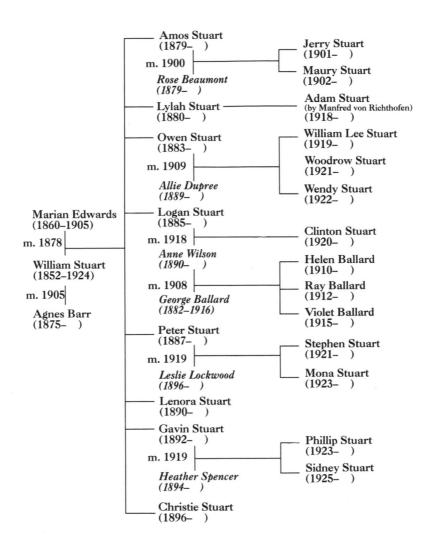

Marian Edwards
(1860–1905)

m. 1878

William Stuart
(1852–1924)

m. 1905

Agnes Barr
(1875–)

Amos Stuart
(1879–)

m. 1900

Rose Beaumont
(1879–)

Jerry Stuart
(1901–)

Maury Stuart
(1902–)

Lylah Stuart
(1880–)

Adam Stuart
(by Manfred von Richthofen)
(1918–)

Owen Stuart
(1883–)

m. 1909

Allie Dupree
(1889–)

William Lee Stuart
(1919–)

Woodrow Stuart
(1921–)

Wendy Stuart
(1922–)

Logan Stuart
(1885–)

m. 1918

Anne Wilson
(1890–)

Clinton Stuart
(1920–)

m. 1908

George Ballard
(1882–1916)

Helen Ballard
(1910–)

Ray Ballard
(1912–)

Violet Ballard
(1915–)

Peter Stuart
(1887–)

m. 1919

Leslie Lockwood
(1896–)

Stephen Stuart
(1921–)

Mona Stuart
(1923–)

Lenora Stuart
(1890–)

Gavin Stuart
(1892–)

m. 1919

Heather Spencer
(1894–)

Phillip Stuart
(1923–)

Sidney Stuart
(1925–)

Christie Stuart
(1896–)

A Time to Be Born   A Time to Die   A Time to Laugh

1900	1910	1920	1930	1940	1

Spanish-American War	Woodrow Wilson elected president	Lindbergh makes solo flight across Atlantic	The Great Depression	Polio epidemic ravages country
Boxer Rebellion in China	World War I		Franklin Roosevelt elected president	Japanese attack Pearl Harbor
		Stock Market crash		

Part 1

THE SILVER SCREEN

1960	1970	1980	1990	2000
Billy Graham launches major campaigns	Vietnam War	Jesus People revival among youth	Ronald Reagan elected president	Bill Clinton elected president
Racial segregation of schools declared unconstitutional	Martin Luther King Jr. assassinated	Watergate scandal causes Nixon's downfall	Scandals involving TV evangelists	AIDS crisis worsens

1

A CIRCUS AND A SERVICE

A green flare rose from the grandstand below, bursting into fragments. At the signal Gavin Stuart nodded at Tony Pasco, whose wing tip was no less than a foot from his own, and put his Standard biplane into a steep dive. The two planes seemed to be linked together by invisible wires, and the sound of their engines changed from a gentle purr to a heavy throbbing.

"Oh, the daring young *m-a-a-an* on the flying trapeze . . ."

Gavin saw in the cockpit a few inches ahead of him Cara Gilmore's helmeted head bobbing crazily as she sang at the top of her lungs. She turned and gave him a lascivious wink, then turned back and began beating the side of the Standard with the flat of her hand. Gavin shook his head, wondering what went on inside the girl's head. He could never quite understand how Cara could get such pleasure out of risking her life, and for one fleeting instant memories came to him of being raked by bullets in his Sopwith Camel by a scarlet triplane. It was not a pleasant memory, and he shook it off, concentrating on the maneuver.

Beyond Cara's head, through the blur of his propeller, he caught a glimpse of the crowd below. He could tell how fast he was flying by the trilling of the wind on the wires. Shooting a quick glance at Tony, he aimed at the crowd, grinning as many of the people made a frantic dive to get away from the two ships that seemed determined to plunge into their midst.

Pulling the stick back in exact harmony with Tony, he felt his cheeks sag as the two planes flattened out, then zoomed upward together. The wires were singing a low vibrato as he brought the Standard over on its back. Now the crowd was above him and the clouds below him. As he hung on his seat belt he heard Cara singing, ". . . he flies through the air with the greatest of e-e-e-ase!"

Finally he righted the Standard, glanced at Tony, then shouted, "All right, Cara!"

As the two planes slowly turned fifteen hundred feet over the earth, Cara climbed out of the front cockpit and stood on the lower wing. The wind tore at her pink overalls as she put one hand on the cowling in front of Gavin. When he looked at her, he saw that her dark blue eyes were laughing as they always did. She reached forward and touched his cheek playfully, then moved forward. Grasping a bar set into the leading edge of the upper wing, she swung herself upward to the top wing. Still singing at the top of her voice, she freed the four thin wires that held the belt and strapped it on. Then she set her feet in the leather stirrups and stood up. Bending her knees, she waved her arms at Gus Tomlin, who was directly above her. He was hanging by his knees from between the wheels of the Travelaire, waiting to make the pickup.

Gavin gauged the position of the stands, aware of the distaste that had come to him for this stunt. The crowd would not be displeased if Cara or Gus should be killed. They were watching now for something to go wrong, and if a tragedy occurred, there would be no tears. It was what people came to see, just as they went to see auto races or the high fliers at the circus.

The two pilots brought their ships together in a precise movement. Cara freed the straps, and Gus reached out, their fingertips touching. As they swept by the bleachers the air was smooth. When the pair sensed the time, Gus's strong hands closed on Cara's wrists. Instantly Gavin let the Standard fall away.

Gus grinned at Cara, saying, "You're getting fat, honey!" He lifted her within reach of the bar and swung himself to a seated position. He patted her on the rump and laughed when she slapped at his hand playfully. "Ready?"

"I was born ready," Cara shouted into the wind. She took the parachute, fastened it, then lowered herself until she hung by both hands. Looking up she shouted, "How about we do the town tonight?"

"Sounds good!"

Cara loosed her grip and shot down toward the earth. She heard the crowd cry out, and she laughed with delight. Then after the parachute popped open, she began to swing back and forth singing, "Oh, the daring young man on the flying trapeze . . ."

Almost as soon as Gavin stepped to the ground he saw Lylah. Blinking with astonishment, he broke into a run, and when he got to her, he grabbed her and spun her around in a wild spin. She gasped but clung to him, and when he set her on her feet, she laughed, "You wild Indian!"

"Never mind that," Gavin interrupted. "Where's that nephew of mine?"

Lylah reached down to pick up the small boy wearing a sailor suit with a wide collar who, with a pair of bright blue eyes, was watching the tall aviator. When he found himself suddenly plucked up and tossed into the air, he didn't cry with alarm as most two-year-olds would have done but instead grinned suddenly and chortled with glee.

"He's grown a foot." Gavin shook his head. He held the child in the crook of his arm, examined his features, then nodded. "You're going to be as good looking as your uncle Gavin!" Then he turned to Lylah and gave her a quick once-over.

What he saw was one of those women who is beautiful in youth but who grows more so as she ages. Lylah Stuart's face was familiar to many, for she had been an actress since running away from Bethany Bible Institute in Fort Smith,

Arkansas, at the age of seventeen. She was not tall, but her figure at the age of forty was the despair of women half her age. She had a wealth of auburn hair, a rich complexion, and full, well-shaped lips. But her best feature was her eyes, large, well-shaped, and violet. She wore a white chiffon blouse with flutter sleeves, an apple green and white chiffon skirt, and a wide-brimmed hat.

"You look good," Gavin nodded. "Never get a day older."

"Yes, I do." Lylah's reply was somewhat short, and when Gavin gave her a surprised look, she shook her head. "Sometimes I feel like I'm an old woman," she murmured. Her eyes touched on the face of Adam, and for one instant sadness marked her eyes. "It's hard to raise a son in my business," she added.

"Sure. But you're doing a fine job, Sis," Gavin said quickly. He thought of the time when he had stood with his brothers Owen and Amos looking down at Lylah and her newborn son. It had been in Paris at the end of the Great War. Lylah had been defenseless and afraid—perhaps for the first time in her life. Gavin remembered how she'd held the tiny, red-faced boy to her bosom, looking up at them. Adam's father was dead—Baron Manfred von Richthofen, the famous Red Baron.

As if reading her brother's thoughts, Lylah murmured, "It seems like a hundred years since Adam was born." Putting out her hand she tucked a lock of fine blond hair in place on the boy's forehead, then shook off her thoughts, saying, "Come on, Gavin, we've got a lot to do."

They turned to go, but a woman's voice caught their attention. "Gavin!" The young woman that came to stand beside Gavin was dressed in a pair of whipcord riding pants, a thin, blue silk blouse that revealed a full figure, and a pair of glossy, black, high boots. She took Gavin's arm with a possessive gesture, her eyes on Lylah. When she smiled her teeth were gleaming white between red lips, and there was a feline quality about her that Lylah noted instantly. "You're not running off, are you?"

"Yes, I am." Gavin shrugged free from the young woman's grasp, then nodded. "This is my sister Lylah—and her son Adam. Lylah, this is Cara Gilmore. You just saw her do her stuff."

"The actress?" Cara's eyes widened with a new interest. "Do you know Douglas Fairbanks?"

"I've met him," Lylah nodded. Her eyes were heavy lidded, and she seemed to take in the young woman in one glance. As Gavin proceeded to give Cara instructions about the next day's performance, Lylah said nothing, but as she and Gavin left, she whispered, "A real man-eater! Does Heather know you've got her on the payroll?"

"Sure—and she said the same thing about Cara." He grinned, looking very young in the April sunlight. "Don't worry. I've got the best woman in the world. Just an old married man, that's me."

Gavin carried Adam easily, and eyes turned to him as he walked off the field beside Lylah. He was tall and lean, with handsome features, including dark hair and eyes. "When did you get in, Lylah?" he asked.

"Yesterday. And I hope I never have to ride a train from New York to Chicago again! I caught a cab to your show."

"Did your play close?"

"Yes, finally." They moved across the field to where cars were parked until Gavin stopped beside a tall black car. "Just bought this." Lylah eyed it carefully, then nodded. "One of the new T Fords. They're tough as a boot, Lylah." He helped her in through the left-hand door, shaking his head. "Wonder why Henry Ford didn't put in a *right*-hand door to these cars?"

"I suppose he saved a dollar or two on every car," Lylah shrugged. She took Adam from Gavin and set him in her lap carefully. "He's made his millions doing things like that."

Gavin reached over the wheel, set the spark and throttle

levers in position, picked up the crank from the floorboard, and moved to the front of the car. With the crank in his right hand, he put his left forefinger through the loop of wire controlling the choke. He pulled the wire, turned the crank vigorously, and as the engine broke into a roar, jumped on the running board and adjusted the spark and the throttle.

Leaping into the seat, he grinned, "Here we go!" As the car swept out of the parking area onto the dirt road, Adam laughed and cried out, "Faster! Go faster!"

"Hey, he's a speedster!" Gavin said, delighted with the boy. He ruffled the fine blond hair, thinking again how much the boy resembled his famous German father, then asked, "Where to? My apartment?"

"I guess so." Lylah held on to Adam as the car sped down the road, lifting a spiral of dust in its wake. She fell silent, watching the cars and wagons that vied for space on the dusty road. She listened as Gavin talked to Adam, her face cast into a sober mold. Finally when they had moved onto a hard-surface road, she said abruptly, "I have a big decision to make, Gavin."

"Not thinking of getting married, are you, Sis?"

"No!" The answer came sharply—so abruptly that she at once realized she had given something away. For a moment she sat quietly, wondering how to put what was in her heart. Finally she shook her head, saying, "I don't think I'll ever marry, Gavin."

Skillfully Gavin swung out, passed a large black touring car, then said diffidently, "Well, you've got time to think about that, I guess. Be good for Adam to have . . ." He glanced down and saw the boy looking up at him, listening carefully. "Well, anyway, you're young enough to have time. What's the decision?"

"I've got an offer to go to Hollywood."

"Not surprised. You'd be great in the movies, Lylah."

"I don't think so." The car struck a deep pothole, causing Lylah to grab Adam and utter a gasp. When she recovered, she shook her head gloomily. "The theater is hard enough, Gavin, but the idea of making films—well, I don't like it."

"Why not?"

"When I'm on the stage, there are people out there. I can hear them, see them. They're part of the play, in a way. It's *alive* is what I guess I'm trying to say."

"And movies aren't?"

"No, they're not. I visited one of the sets last year. John Barrymore asked me to come."

"Hey, that's great! And if *he's* in the movies, I guess that's pretty high recommendation. What was the movie?"

"It was *Dr. Jekyll and Mr. Hyde.*"

"Hey, I *saw* that movie! It was great!"

"I haven't seen it," Lylah answered. "But *making* the film was terrible, Gavin." She wrinkled up her nose with distaste, then shook her head. "Remember the scene when Jekyll realizes he's turned into a monster? Well, they shot that scene *sixteen* times! Barrymore did it over and over and over again. I'd go crazy if I had to do that!"

"Well, he got it right," Gavin shrugged. "And the movies have one advantage, and that's getting the view up close. In the theater, the people in the audience, except for those in the first few rows, can't see the details of an actor's face. But I could see every line in Barrymore's face. It was pretty good, I thought."

The two spoke of the new art form, the motion picture, until Gavin pulled up in front of a brownstone house, one in a line of many, and stopped the car. "Come on," he said, reaching up to take Adam. "Heather will be tickled to see you."

When they went inside, Heather at once came to hug Lylah, saying, "My dear! How wonderful to see you!" She was an attractive Englishwoman with blond hair and blue eyes. Her parents were impoverished nobility, but she never spoke of their title to anyone. She and Gavin had met when he was flying in the Lafayette Escadrille; they had fallen in love and married as soon as the war ended. They had come to America, and she had encouraged Gavin to begin a risky career. The two of them were deeply in love, Lylah saw, and smiled as she said, "You two are still holding hands. I wish marriages always did as well as yours."

"When the husband is as handsome, charming, and thoughtful as I am, they always do," Gavin said loftily.

"Just for that, you can wash the dishes tonight!" Heather sniffed. Then she bent over and looked Adam in the eye. "How's the old man?" she whispered. When he nodded, she asked, "You don't like cookies, do you?"

"Yes!"

The three adults laughed at the energy of the child's reply, and Gavin said, "Well, you and I will eat cookies, then we'll play until dinner is ready—and then we'll eat it. Will that be all right, Adam?"

"Yes!"

The two women went into the kitchen, where Heather said at once, "Dinner's almost ready. You sit down and tell me all about what you've been doing. How's the play?"

Lylah had become very fond of her sister-in-law, and she sat drinking real English tea while speaking of the play. She stopped once, hearing something falling in the living room, and smiled wryly. "Sounds like they're breaking the furniture. Adam's very rough."

"Gavin loves children," Heather said. She was wearing a white apron, and as she sliced celery into small sticks, she smiled suddenly at Lylah. "He wants six boys," she said. "Not all at once, I should hope!"

Lylah glanced at Heather in a way that gave away her question. "Are you expecting?" she demanded.

"No, but I will be as soon as possible." She put down the knife and leaned forward to say, "I love children, too." She rose to take the bread from the oven and paused to enjoy its aroma. "If you ever need any help taking care of Adam, please let us have him."

A thin line creased Lylah's smooth brow. She drummed

her fingers on the table, then nodded. "I may take you up on that, Heather. It's very hard to raise a son in my business."

"We'd love to have him, of course." Heather opened the lower oven door and took out a pie. "Did you see the lovely Miss Cara Gilmore?" she asked suddenly. When Lylah hesitated, she turned and saw the look on her face. A merry laugh came from her lips, and she put the pie down, saying, "Oh, I know all about her, Lylah. She chases anything in pants!"

"Even Gavin?"

"Oh, she plastered herself all over him from the first," Heather shrugged. Then astonishingly she giggled. "Gavin treats her like a bomb about to go off! He tried to fire her, but I talked him out of it."

Lylah stared at Heather doubtfully. "That's not what most wives would do. Aren't you just a little afraid that—" She halted, then added, "Well, Gavin is a man—and she is a sexy little baggage."

Heather shook her head. "Gavin loves me. I know that much. And we've talked about things like this, Lylah. Both of us have pledged to be true—and if we can't trust each other, what's left of a marriage?"

Lylah was fascinated by her sister-in-law. The English girl had a calmness that most American women lacked. Finally she said, "Well, I'm glad Gavin got a wife like you, Heather. You two are so happy!"

Heather would have responded, but at that instant the door burst open. Gavin galloped in, Adam clinging to his back and yelling like a banshee. They circled the table, then Gavin gasped, "Help! This kid is wearing me down!"

"He never gets enough playing, Gavin," Lylah said ruefully. Then she took Adam from Gavin, ignoring his protests. "You can play after supper," she promised.

"No, we're going to meet'n after supper," Gavin announced. When he saw the surprise on Lylah's face, he asked, "Didn't you know that Owen's here in Chicago for a revival?"

"I guess I forgot," Lylah exclaimed. "But I'd love to go."

She grinned wickedly at Gavin, adding, "Give him something to shoot for—getting his ornery sister right."

"He'll do his best," Gavin nodded. "He's doing well, Lylah. The churches of Chicago built a special tabernacle just for Owen's meeting. There'll be ten thousand people there tonight."

"Don't you dare warn him we're coming!" Lylah was fiercely proud of her preacher brother, though she herself had no faith. "He'd make me stand up in front of all those people."

"He might tell about how you and Amos and him smoked behind the barn the morning you left the farm to go to Bible school," Gavin teased. "He loves to tell about that!"

Lylah shook her head but insisted that Gavin not call Owen. They ate a fine dinner, then left for the tabernacle. When they arrived, she was astonished at the size of the building. "Why, it's bigger than a stadium!" she exclaimed. "And look at the mob going in! I wish this many people would come to see me in a play!"

"Come on," Gavin nodded. "I used my pull to get us some good seats. Come on, Adam," he added, picking the boy up in his arms. "You're going to hear some mighty good preaching from your uncle Owen tonight!"

Lylah and Heather followed Gavin to four seats ten rows from the front. They sat down and watched the place fill up. Lylah had last been to one of Owen's services in Oklahoma, where the crowd had been no larger than three hundred people gathered under a big tent. Now she watched the seats fill up, making a sea of faces that seemed to blur toward the back.

Ten minutes after their arrival, a huge choir entered to fill a section behind the platform, and soon the tabernacle resounded with the sound of ten thousand voices singing "Amazing Grace." Lylah sang along, remembering her days in Bethany Institute when, despite her poor attitude, she'd sung in the school choir. Now as song after song wafted from the crowd, she found herself thinking of those days, and a thought came to her: *I never should have left this behind!*

Finally the platform was filled by a group of pastors, many of them poorly dressed. And then Owen came to mount the platform, and Lylah's heart swelled at the sight of him. He was tall and muscular, his chestnut hair gleaming under the glow of thousands of lights. When he lifted his right arm, she saw the polished steel hook, a reminder of the battle in which he'd lost his hand—and had won the Congressional Medal of Honor.

She sat stiffly, hearing little, until he got up to preach. *He looks so young!* she thought, and as he began to preach, she thought back to the days when he'd come in from the fields, tired to the bone. She'd rubbed the back of his neck, and he'd grinned at her wearily, saying, "I sure put a good mule out of work today, Sis!"

Lylah never remembered much of that sermon, except that over and over again Owen had quoted his text: "Ye must be born again!" It was a sermon she'd heard often, but now as Owen Stuart preached, it became more potent somehow. She felt the power of God flow over the crowd, and when Owen gave the invitation, hundreds got up and moved forward.

"Where dey going?" Adam asked loudly. Snuggled on Gavin's lap, he had slept through most of the sermon, but now his eyes were bright with interest. "Can we go wif' dem?" he demanded.

"Not now, but later we'll go see your uncle Owen," Lylah whispered.

They waited until most of the crowd left and then got up stiffly. When they had made their way almost to the platform, Owen lifted his head and spotted them. He came at once to embrace Lylah, who held to him, whispering, "I'm so *proud* of you, Owen!"

Owen drew back, his eyes fixed on Lylah. "I'm glad to see you." Then he turned his eyes on the boy. Seeing Adam's eyes on the steel hook, he held it out. "Give me a shake, Adam," he smiled.

Adam stared at the hook for a long moment, then reached out and took it firmly. Owen laughed, then picked him up. "Come on, let's go find Allie. And I've got a new addition you've got to meet—William Lee Stuart!"

They found Allie with her new baby, and after Lylah had made the proper remarks, Owen took them all out to a restaurant to eat hamburgers. While the others were talking, Gavin found time to have a brief conversation with Lylah. He listened as she told him about the play closing, then added that she was going back to the farm to visit for a time.

"Good! Wish I could go with you, Lylah," Gavin said. "Pa needs all the encouragement he can get. Don't see how he's endured all the years with Agnes." He shook his head, thinking of the woman their father had married after the death of his first wife. She was a crude, loose woman who managed to make the visits of the children miserable. "Maybe I'll take Heather for a visit after the show in Rochester."

"Have you seen Amos lately?"

"About a month ago. He's worried about Jerry. That young man is a handful!" He looked over at Adam who was stuffing himself joyfully and shook his head. "That's the easy time— when they're his age. After they get to be twelve, it's a battle."

Lylah gave Gavin a strange look. "I've thought about how much grief I caused our folks. They didn't get any pleasure out of raising me. All I did was break Ma's heart." She lowered her head to stare at the table. "I wish I could go back and do it all over again . . . but I'd probably do it the same way."

"Hey, now, that's no way to talk!" Gavin reached over and put his hand on hers. "You've got a fine son, and you're young enough to make a good life for him. I wish you'd find a good man, quit this acting, and become a wife and mother."

Lylah summoned a smile and squeezed his hand. "All the good men I know are named Stuart. If I could find one like

you or Owen or Amos, I'd take a chance, but I haven't seen
any."

The party broke up, and after Lylah and Adam were in
their hotel room they went to bed at once. When Adam was
almost asleep beside her, he mumbled, "Mommy, I like Uncle
Gavin and Uncle Owen."

"That's good, darling." She touched his head gently, whispering, "I hope you grow up to be as good as they are."

2

CHRISTIE'S MAN

Will Stuart drew the bow across the battered fiddle, and as the tune of "Sweet Betsy from Pike" drifted across the afternoon air, his eyes grew soft. *I was playing this tune the night I met Marian,* he thought. *And it was just this time of the year.*

The recollection disturbed him, and he began to play "Greensleeves." He'd noticed recently that when he thought of his first wife and the love they'd had, it made life as he now had it almost miserable. *Can't no man ever go back to what was . . . but I'd like to. She was a wonderful woman, Marian was.* The image of Agnes invaded his thoughts, and his lips drew together into a thin line. *Never should have married her . . . been nothing but misery for me and the kids.*

His thoughts were diverted as the sound of hoofbeats came faintly from his left. Resting the fiddle in his lap, he turned to see a fine chestnut stallion come out of the woods. He was taking the ground in giant strides, and Will smiled to see the figure of the young woman astride the big horse. When they reached the rail fence that zigzagged around the pasture, he heard the woman cry, "Come on, Buck!" and the horse took the fence in stride.

"You're gonna break your neck, Lenora, jumpin' fences like that!" he called out.

Lenora Stuart laughed aloud and slid down from the steaming horse. She was thirty years old but looked no more than twenty. She was not pretty, for her features were too strong for that, but Will admired her tall straight figure and the ash-blond hair that she allowed to fall down her back. She had hazel eyes, and as she tied the horse to the rail and came up the porch with a graceful movement, there was a peace in her face that Will loved to see.

"You stop worrying about me, Pa," she said, bending over to kiss his cheek. "I never fell off a horse in my life."

"No, you never did," Will admitted. She was an enigma to him, for most girls married young in the mountains of Arkansas. But Lenora had never shown a great deal of interest in men, choosing instead to put her energies into the farm. That and church. She was a fervent Christian, and now as Will looked at her, he thought she should have been a boy. *She would have been a good preacher,* he thought fondly. *Maybe as good as Owen.*

The door opened, and Will demanded, "Well, Christie, you've spent enough time on that dress—lemme' take a look at it."

Christie Stuart was another daughter who'd put off marriage. At the age of twenty-four, she was termed an old maid by the locals. She had the good looks that Lenora lacked, with a wealth of honey-blond hair and enormous dark blue eyes. She blushed at her father's greeting, saying, "I needed a new dress, Pa."

Will winked at Lenora. "Looks like a man-catchin' dress to me." He saw that his words embarrassed Christie and regretted them. This youngest daughter of his was as sensitive as any girl could be, and he changed the subject. "Well, it's a pretty dress. Your ma couldn't have done no better."

Lenora had not missed the expression on her sister's face and said, "I wish I could sew like you, Christie. All I can do is plow and grub taters."

The three of them sat on the porch, enjoying the late afternoon breeze. They were close, these three, and it was only when Agnes Stuart came out that they fell silent. She gave them a sharp look, then said, "Well, what time is she supposed to be here?"

The telegram had come the previous day stating that Lylah and Adam would be arriving for a short visit. Will and the young women had been excited, but none of them had missed the sour expression that the news brought to Agnes's face. She'd said little, but her attitude was clear, for she'd never made any secret of her dislike for Lylah.

"I guess sometime this afternoon," Will answered quietly. "Train gets into Fort Smith about noon. Guess she'll get somebody to bring her in a car."

Agnes Stuart had been an attractive young woman, in a sensual way. It had been this sensuality that had enabled her to catch Will Stuart in a weak moment after the death of his first wife. But the years had not been kind to her; time had swelled her until she was overweight, and her face was no longer pretty. She longed for town life, for she hated the country. Any affection that Will or the children had felt for her she'd forfeited by her excesses and her sharp temper.

It was this cutting temper that surfaced now, for she saw that the three of them were excited about the arrival of Lylah and the boy. Her eyes drew half shut, and she shook her head sharply. "Looks like she'd have more sense than to come home dragging that baby that ain't got no daddy!"

Will Stuart was a mild-mannered man, seldom lifting his voice, but at Agnes's words he abruptly came out of the cane-bottomed chair, sending it to the floor with a rattle that startled the others. He was a tall man, though now at the age of sixty-eight he was slightly stooped. His hair was gray, except for one streak of pure white on the left side. A minié ball had plowed a crease there at the Battle of Five Forks in the Civil War.

"Don't you ever say one word agin' that child—or agin' Lylah! You hear me talk?"

Agnes Stuart had never seen Will so angry—nor had his daughters. His mild eyes were blazing, and his fists were clenched. He had been a weak man, unable to say no to liquor—or to women—in his youth. But now a dangerous quality leaped out of him, and Agnes was afraid of him for the first time.

"Why, Will . . ." she stammered, taking a step backward. "I didn't mean! . . ."

Will cut her off sharply, "Say what you want to about me, Agnes, but if you even *look* crossways at my daughter or my grandson, I'll kick you off this place so fast it'll make your head swim!" He kept his eyes fixed on her steadily, then demanded, "You understand that, Agnes?"

"Y-yes."

"That's good, because I won't say it twice."

Agnes ducked her head, swallowed, then mumbled, "I'll go see to dinner."

As soon as she was out of hearing, Lenora suddenly gave her father a hard hug. "Good! I'm so happy I could scream!"

Christie had been wide-eyed with astonishment, but now she giggled. "I didn't know you had it in you, Pa. She's been talking mean about Lylah and Adam for a long time."

Lenora nudged Will in the side. "If she doesn't behave, give her a good one, Pa!"

Will forced himself to relax and gave Lenora a curious glance. "I thought you'd tell me to turn the other cheek," he murmured.

"That's if she gave *you* a slap, Pa," Lenora nodded firmly. "When she hurts Lylah or Adam, she needs a stick taken to her. Want me to go cut one off the peach tree—like the one you used to use on me?"

"Don't guess so," Will shook his head. "I've plumb lost the knack of it." He looked out over the hills that lifted themselves to the north of the farm, and a fond look came into his eyes. "Sure will be good to see Lylah and the boy!"

"They're here, Pa!"

Christie had been searching for guinea eggs near the barn

as a car appeared over the rise. She ran toward the road, and when the big gray touring car pulled to a stop, she was the first to grab the woman who stepped to the ground.

"Lylah!" she exclaimed, stepping back. "Where's that nephew of mine?"

"Right here." Don Satterfield got out of the Essex, reached up, and lifted Adam out of the car. "Another addition to the Stuart line. How do you like him?"

Satterfield was the pastor of a church in Fort Smith. He smiled as Will and Lenora came running down the path to greet the newcomers—and noted that Agnes stood on the porch. *Poor soul! I wish she'd lose that hateful spirit. She's her own worst enemy.* Then he turned to Will, who was holding the small boy in his arms. "I think he looks like you, Will," he smiled.

"I wasn't never as good lookin' as this young'un," Will protested. He smiled at Lylah, then said quietly, "He's a fine boy, Daughter."

"Thanks, Pa," Lylah smiled. "I hope he gets some of your musical talent."

Will turned to look at Satterfield, saying, "Never knowed a preacher to come when a meal wasn't on the table. Come in and set."

"Don't mind if I do, Will," Satterfield nodded. "I want to hear about what all Lylah's been up to."

"Better ask Christie what *she's* been up to," Lenora said. "She's got a fellow, Reverend."

"Is that so? Who's the lucky fellow, Christie?"

Christie flushed and mumbled, "Mel Tolliver."

Surprise washed across Satterfield's face, but he quickly smiled and remarked, "Why, Mel's getting to be quite an up-coming businessman in Fort Smith. He has to come a long way to do his courting, doesn't he?"

Christie disliked being the center of attention. "He doesn't come too often."

"But he's coming for supper tonight," Lenora put in. "You

can look him over, Lylah," she added slyly. "Talk to him and
find out if his intentions are honorable."

"Don't . . . don't you dare!" Christie burst out, then turned
and walked into the house.

"Lenora, you stop teasing her about her man," Will ad-
monished. "She's real shy. Calls herself an old maid."

"All right, Pa," Lenora agreed. "Come on, Lylah, I want
to show you the new foal."

"She can see that hoss tomorrow," Will said. "Come on,
let's see about this here grandson of mine."

Lylah allowed them to make over her. She was tired from
her long journey and was glad to sit down in the parlor and
listen to the busy talk that went on. Don Satterfield came to
sit beside her, asking, "What's new with you, Lylah?"

Lylah began to tell Don about her activities, but she could
not forget that he had once been in love with her. He was
middle-aged now and had gained weight—and was still not
handsome. However there was a kindness in his face that
she'd always been drawn to, so that she wondered, *What if I'd
have married him?* Instantly she knew that it would not have
worked. *I'd have ruined his life. If there's one thing I'm not cut out
for it's being a preacher's wife.*

"I gave you a hard time when I was in Bible school, didn't
I, Don?"

Satterfield was taken off guard by her sudden remark. He
shot a quick glance at her, taking in the classic features, then
grinned. "You sure did! Every time I tried to get you involved
in some sort of Christian work, you were out smoking behind
the church!"

"I was terrible!"

"You weren't ready for Bible school," Don agreed. He
wanted to say something to this beautiful woman but somehow could never find the right approach. He stared up at the
calendar on the wall, noting that it was dated 1919, a year
old, then said gently, "I pray for you and Adam every day,

Lylah. I know it must be hard for you to raise a son in your profession."

Lylah's eyes grew soft. "That's like you, Don. If everyone were as kind as you . . ." she broke off, for Christie entered the room accompanied by a large young man. "We'll talk later," she whispered, then rose to greet the two.

"This is my sister Lylah, and this is Mel Tolliver, Lylah," Christie said. She was nervous, and as soon as she had made the introduction, she said, "I'll go help Lenora and Agnes with the dinner. It's almost ready."

Mel Tolliver, Lylah saw, was a tall man, about thirty, and somewhat overweight. He had blue eyes, thinning blond hair, and a mustache that was a mistake. *He grows that thing to cover a weak mouth*, Lylah decided, but this was her sister's first beau, so she set out to charm him. "Don, go help set the table," she said. "Mel and I need to get acquainted. Sit down, Mel, and tell me about your business."

Tolliver was overwhelmed by the beauty of the woman who smiled at him. He'd seen pictures of Lylah, of course, but no photograph could have the power that she had in person. And she had touched on the one thing that was close to his heart—his business.

"Why, it's not a big business, Miss Lylah, not yet that is—but I've got plans. I don't see why Tolliver Hardware stores couldn't be strung out all over the state—or even further!"

Lylah listened carefully. This man was important to her, for she knew that Christie was not wise where men were concerned. Her sister was the sweetest woman in the world, but vulnerable. Lylah herself was a shrewd judge of men, and by the time she'd listened to Tolliver for ten minutes, she had formed a judgment. *He'd bore me to death with all his talk about nails and bolts—but Christie may not be so hard to please.*

Finally Christie came to say, "Dinner's ready," and Lylah rose and went with Tolliver to the dining room.

The table was loaded down with food, and Lylah exclaimed, "Why, I'd be as fat as that hog you're so proud of if I ate this, Pa!"

"Don't care how fat *I* get," Lenora grinned. "Brother Satterfield, I hope you've got a short blessing in you."

Don Satterfield did indeed have a brief blessing, and after it was finished, the food disappeared at an alarming rate. Don noted that Agnes Stuart said almost nothing, and he wondered at it. When he complimented her on the food, she looked nervously toward her husband, saying only, "Thank you, Brother Satterfield."

The woman's reticence puzzled the minister, and he whispered to Lenora, who sat close to him, "What's wrong with Agnes?"

"Pa beat her." Lenora had a humorous streak and giggled at the shocked look on Satterfield's face. "Well, he didn't actually—but he threatened to."

"Should have done it a long time ago. She's almost pleasant tonight."

"How are Logan and Pete doing?" Lylah inquired about her brothers. "I haven't heard from either of them for ages."

"Logan's working himself to death on that hill he calls a farm over near Stone River," Will Stuart frowned. "Just had a new baby. Named him Clinton. Don't see how he feeds them four kids on that scratch farm!"

"Pete's doing better," Lenora inserted. "Got a job working in the oil fields in Oklahoma."

"Have he and Leslie produced any Stuarts?" Lylah asked.

"Not yet."

"Don't see why people like Logan and Pete bring children into the world." Mel Tolliver had put food away at an enormous rate. His face was red with the effort, and he grunted as he downed a massive forkful of sweet potato pie. "If they can't feed them, why do they have them?"

An awkward silence fell over the table, and it was Christie who said gently, "Why, I think poor people need children—maybe more than rich people, Mel."

Tolliver gave her an impatient look. "Can't feed kids on love," he said sharply. "I say people who don't have the ability to take care of a family shouldn't have one."

"Some at this table wouldn't be here if I'd thought like that, Mel," Will said gently. He smiled and winked at Lylah, adding, "I didn't have a pot to plant a petunia in when your mother and me got married. But we made out."

"You did better than that, Will," Don Satterfield said. "You've got one son who's going to win a Pulitzer for his reporting, one who's the greatest evangelist in America, and one daughter who's the greatest actress in . . . in . . ."

When Satterfield groped for a word, Lylah laughed, her eyes sparkling. "In this room?" she jibed. Then she turned to her father and nodded, "You should be proud, Pa. You've got a fine family."

The meal ended, and after a long evening Lylah shooed Christie out of the kitchen. "Mel didn't come here to see you wash dishes," she chided. "Go for a walk with the man. Go on now!"

Christie went to the parlor where Mel was giving his view of prohibition to her father. He was smoking a large cigar and punctuated his sentences by poking it toward Will. "Going to be trouble, Will," he insisted. "The Volstead Act, making it illegal to sell alcoholic beverages, went in on January 16, and there's trouble already. Why, I read that it'll take 250,000 police in New York alone to enforce it."

Will shrugged his shoulders, saying, "Don't know about New York, but folks in these hills been makin' whiskey for a hundred years. Guess a law passed in Washington won't change that."

Christie listened to the men talk, then said, "Mel, would you like to see the new calf?"

Tolliver rose and went out of the house with her. They walked along the path to the barn, and after he had dutifully admired the calf, they strolled back toward the house. He stopped beside the oak tree and glanced toward the house. "Makes things awkward, your sister being here."

"Awkward? How is that?"

"Why, her bringing that baby here. Folks don't take to that sort of thing, Christie. I'd think she'd be ashamed to bring her illegitimate child back home."

Christie wanted to argue, but she had learned that Tolliver was not a man to change his views. "Pa wanted to see his grandson," she offered mildly.

"Well, them actors and actresses got no morals." Tolliver shrugged. "Just like animals, everybody knows that. Anyways, she and the kid won't hang around here." He frowned, adding, "I've got a reputation to maintain in Fort Smith, Christie. A man has to be careful about things like this."

The moonlight laid a silver gleam on Christie's face, and Tolliver suddenly reached out and pulled her close. His lips were loose and wet, and Christie endured his kiss, giving nothing of herself.

"What's wrong with you, Christie?" Tolliver demanded, displeased with her. "Don't you feel anything for me?"

"I . . . I just don't have any experience, Mel," Christie pleaded. "You'll have to be patient with me."

Tolliver shifted his feet, then laughed. "Why, sure," he nodded. "You just need a teacher, that's all. After we're married, you'll warm up. Come on now, give me a *real* kiss. I've got to get back to Fort Smith. Got a big sale starting tomorrow."

At the same time that the pair were talking, Lylah had come down after putting Adam to bed to find her father staring into space. He was sitting in the living room alone, and when she sat down and put her hand on his, he started. "Oh, Lylah, guess I must be gettin' old."

"You're still the best looking fella in the county, Pa." Lylah leaned back and asked abruptly, "Why is Christie going with this Mel Tolliver?"

"Nothing wrong with Mel," Will said defensively. "He's an up-and-coming young man."

"And dull as dishwater!"

"He may not be as excitin' as some of them actor fellows you run with," Will said stiffly, "but if he suits Christie, ain't no business of yours to criticize him!"

Lylah sat silently, disturbed by what was happening. She knew that her father had a terrible life, and it was likely that Agnes made life hard for Christie and Lenora as well. She felt a streak of guilt, not for the first time, of leaving them to cope with the hardships of farm life—and with Agnes. "I'm sorry, Pa," she said contritely. "It's just that I want Christie to have a good life. She doesn't know much about men, and I'm just not sure Tolliver's the man to make her happy."

"What's wrong with him?"

"For one thing—he's a lecher."

"A *what?*"

"Pa, he's not to be trusted where women are concerned."

Will stared at his daughter, then shook his head. "He's got a good reputation with women. If he hadn't, we'd know about it. Can't keep a thing like that secret in a town this small. He's late marryin', but he's got his mother to take care of."

"Pa, you know the minute you take up a fiddle if it's true or not, don't you?"

"Why—sure!"

"Well, I'm not proud of it, but I'm the same way about men." A bitterness crept into Lylah's tone, and she shook her head sadly. "I learned the hard way, Pa, and I wish I hadn't. A woman alone—especially an actress—meets all kinds. It gets so you can just *look* at a man and know what he is, and I'm telling you that Mel Tolliver is a womanizer!"

"But he's never been one to chase women!"

"It's in him, Pa," Lylah nodded emphatically. "You ever see one of those little dogs who like to bite ankles?"

"Sure I have!"

"Well, you can put a muzzle on one of those dogs. He won't bite anyone—but you can bet he's lusting after an ankle! Tolliver keeps it all up tight, but sooner or later he's going to bust loose—and I just hate to see Christie tied to a man like that."

Will shook his head, and he seemed to age as he sat there before her. "I don't worry about Lenora. Don't reckon she'll ever marry. I look for her to go for a missionary someday. It's what she's always wanted. She's a tough one—like you in a lot of ways, Lylah. But Christie—she's tender. She's ashamed of not bein' married."

"Why didn't she marry, Pa? She's pretty enough."

"I think she had a bad experience when she was about sixteen. She ain't never spoke of it, but before that she was a laughin' girl. Went to the dances, and the boys liked her. But that summer when she turned sixteen—somethin' happened. I tried to talk to her, but it wasn't no use. She lost somethin'— and it wasn't until six months ago she started courtin' again."

"You think some man misused her?"

"Don't like to think that—but it's happened." He heaved himself to his feet and turned to her as she rose. "A man don't know much about women. There's a little world in them that no man can quite get into." He thought hard, then shook his head. "I wish she'd not chosen Tolliver, but she wants a home, and that takes a man."

Lylah wanted to protest that the wrong man was worse than no man at all, but she felt that her own record gave her no right to speak. She pulled his head down, kissed him on the cheek, then whispered, "I've got a mighty fine pa!"

Will blinked in surprise, then said, "Wish your ma could hear you say that." He turned and left the room heavily, leaving Lylah alone. She moved to the window and looked out at the moon that was wreathed with a thin veil of silvery clouds. They moved quickly, cloaking the silver disk until it was hidden. Then she turned and went to her room. And there was a heaviness in her that she knew no night's sleep would lighten.

She had one short conversation with Lenora the next day. The two of them were walking along the small creek where

Lylah had caught sunfish when she was a girl. They talked about Christie, and when Lylah expressed her doubts about Tolliver, Lenora agreed. "Nothing to be done, except to pray for her." Then she took Lylah by the arm and said, "What about you, Lylah? Are you ever going to let God have his way with you?"

Lylah expected such an approach from Lenora. There was a directness in this sister of hers that she would have resented in anyone else, but she knew the sweetness of her heart.

"I've got to take care of my son, Lenora. I'm forty, which means my time is almost gone for leading roles. I've got to have a quick break, make it big. That's why I finally decided to go to Hollywood. In that place, crazy as it is, just one good picture can make me rich enough to take care of Adam—get him raised and through college."

Lenora said no more, so Lylah asked, "What about you, Lenora?"

"I've given my life to God. He's called me to serve him— as a missionary, I hope." She abruptly embraced this willful sister of hers, kissed her on the cheek, then whispered, "I know God is going to catch up with you, Lylah, but he may have to cripple you first—so you don't run so fast!"

3

SOMETIMES THE WORLD FALLS APART

Although Christie enjoyed visiting with her brother Logan and his family, she was grieved by the hardness of their lives. The forty-acre hill farm Logan scratched with mule-drawn plow had been worn out before he bought it, and the first months of 1920 had been bad. The year had started out wet, so that Logan was late breaking the land and planting. Water stood in the middles and washed gullies across the fields. Flies bred in the wetness, and seed ticks hatched on weed tips in clumps heavy enough to bend them over.

Christie had learned to tie strings soaked in coal oil around her wrists and legs to ward them off, but every time she visited the fields, she came home clawing at the tiny insects. She had come to be of help with the new baby, Clinton, and had found herself working around the house a great deal of the time. Anne, Logan's wife, had not recovered well from the birth, and Christie took it on herself to do as much of the hard work as she could.

Just outside the house Logan had put an ash hopper big enough to hold the ashes from a year's fire in the cookstove and the fireplaces. All the ashes went into the hopper, and a trough was set so that with every rain some water trickled down on the ashes and was caught in a wooden keg at the bottom. This was the lye water for making soap and for husking hominy.

One hot morning Christie came to a pot of soap in the second day of boiling. It bubbled in an iron washtub with its three legs set on three flat rocks. Christie built up the fire, humming, "What a Friend We Have in Jesus" under her breath. The trick was to keep the soap boiling, but not enough to run over. It had started out as a layer of hog grease on lye water, but now the lye had worked, she saw. There was only one liquid needing now to be boiled down to a thickness of soap.

Logan appeared, his thin chambray shirt darkened with sweat. "You don't have to work yourself to death, Christie," he remarked. He was a tall man of thirty-five but looked ten years older. Wrestling the bare necessities of life out of the rocky hill farm had drained him. Taking off his straw hat, he wiped the sweat from his face and smiled at her. "I remember when you were just a little thing, when we were picking cotton. I used to have to tie you with a string to a stake to keep you from wandering off into the woods."

Christie laughed, her eyes crinkling in a way that was characteristic of her, something she alone of the children had gotten from her mother's side of the family. "And once I got loose, and everyone had to quit picking and hunt for me."

"You were up to your ears in the creek, having a fine time." Logan's eyes grew thoughtful, and he shook his head. "Those seem like good times to me, Christie." He looked around at the fields, at the lanky mules hitched to the plow, then added, "Don't mean to complain, but it's been a hard couple of years."

"Maybe you could get a better farm in the lowlands, Logan. This place is worn out."

"Takes money for that."

"Amos said he offered to help you."

"He's got a family of his own." Logan's face turned stubborn, and Christie said no more. She was well aware of the independence of her brother. They were all like that, as were Lenora and Lylah. Logan, she knew, would starve before taking help from anyone, even his own brother. To change the subject, he said, "Let's go catch a fish before it gets hot. This blamed old garden will wait."

"I'd like that."

Thirty minutes later the pair were sitting on the grassy bank of a creek that bubbled whitely over water-smoothed stones. Christie lifted her ten-foot-long cane pole and captured the small hook. Reaching into an old syrup bucket, she extracted a huge worm that wiggled frantically. "Night crawlers are the best bait," she said, then stuck her tongue out as she threaded the worm carefully on the hook.

"You're gonna' bite your tongue off one of these days," Logan grinned. "Never knew a body's tongue had to be out to bait a hook."

Christie completed the operation, studied the worm, then spit on it. "That's the reason I catch more fish than you do," she nodded. "If you'd listen to me more, you'd know more."

Logan watched lazily, leaning back against the bank at their backs. He was tired to the bone, as always, and the hot sun made him sleepy. He studied Christie, admiring the long blond hair and the trim figure. She was wearing a pair of ancient overalls that had belonged to him, and he thought suddenly, *She'd be a beaut, Christie would, if she had some pretty clothes. Maybe that feller that's courtin' her will dress her up when they get married.*

Christie swung her bait out, let it drop into the smooth water, then set her eyes on the red-and-white cork. "Sure would like a mess of goggle-eye perch," she remarked. "Anne can cook fish better than anybody I know."

"Yep, reckon that's right."

The sky was an azure blue, hard enough to scratch a match on, and the white clouds that drifted over their heads formed huge billows. Looking up, Logan observed them through half-shut eyes and said idly, "When you and Mel going to tie the knot, Christie?"

"Oh, he hasn't even asked me yet." The question seemed to disturb Christie, for she turned her head away, studying five buzzards that were making their fatal circle over a field a mile away. "Buzzards sure do fly pretty for such ugly things," she remarked.

Logan gave her a careful look, knowing that she was avoiding the question. He had worried about this younger sister of his, for most girls in the mountains had started their families at her age. He wished he could help her, for though he was not an educated man, Logan was what many call "country smart." He had an uncanny ability to judge people, and his impression of Mel Tolliver had been that Tolliver was a selfish man. He struggled to find some way to put what was in his mind before Christie, but he was not good with words. Finally he gave it up. "Going to be a hot day," he said, letting the moment pass.

Even as he spoke, Christie's cork disappeared with a loud *plop,* and she lifted her pole sharply. The line zigzagged frantically, cutting through the dark water. "You got 'im, Chris!" Logan shouted, as she came to her feet. "Hold 'im tight, don't give 'im no slack!"

"Teach your grandmother to suck eggs!" Christie cried. Her eyes were bright as she played the fish skillfully, not yanking the hook from his mouth by pulling too hard and not giving any slack to let him shake it free. Finally she worked him to the bank and with one swift, firm gesture lifted the pole.

"It's the dad-gummed biggest perch I ever seen!" Logan said, watching with admiration as Christie grabbed the fish by the back, avoiding the dorsal fin. "He'd make a mess all by himself!"

Christie admired the beautifully colored pumpkin seed perch, all blue and green and silver. He was thicker through the body than any she'd ever caught, and she laughed, saying, "He'll look good in a frying pan, won't he, Logan?"

Removing the hook, she pulled up a small, loosely woven feed sack from the ground and slipped the fish inside. Pulling the neck tight with a drawstring, she tossed it into the water, tied the string to a projecting root, then proceeded to bait her hook again. "Wish everything was as much fun as fishing, Logan," she observed, swinging the line back so that the cork fell into the same position.

The casual observation seemed to strike Logan with force, for he gave her a quick glance, then nodded. "Reckon I wish the same, but it ain't so, is it?" He stared moodily at his cork, then shook his head with a gesture of infinite sadness. "Guess most of us just have to eat our peck of dirt."

"Logan, are you sure you can't find a better farm than this?"

"Don't have the money."

The simple statement was a credo for most of the hill people. They rose early, worked late, and fell into bed exhausted, then rose again to repeat the operation. Their lives were measured out by minor pleasures and major tragedies. Women had their children in an endless succession, many of them dying young in the process. It was a common saying of men, "He done wore out three wives already."

Christie said nothing, for she had no answers. She knew that it hurt Logan that Anne had no pretty store-bought dresses, and the children had none of the pleasures of town children. She determined at that instant, *I'm going to see that Anne and the children have some nice things. When I get married, I'll get Mel to help. I can come and visit and take the kids places, maybe to town to a circus . . .*

But even as she thought of this, a doubt rose in her mind. She had heard enough of Mel's philosophy to understand that he grudged every penny that was not put back into his business. Her face grew sober, and she wondered again if she was doing the right thing by marrying. She felt keenly the shame of being an old maid and now asked herself, *Am I marrying because I'm afraid of what people will think if I don't?*

She thrust the thought away, and for the next two hours, she and Logan enjoyed themselves. They caught sixteen fish large enough to keep, then Logan said regretfully, "Guess I've got to get back to the fields, Chris. You can stay though."

"No, I'll go clean these fish. We'll have hush puppies and fried potatoes with them. My favorite supper!"

They went back to the farm, and after Logan returned to plowing, Christie took the fish to the back of the house and got a sharp knife and a spoon from the kitchen. The children came to watch. As she took the knife and prepared to take the head off, Violet, aged five, inquired, "Does it hurt a fish to get his head cut off?"

Ray, three years older, gave her a look of infinite disgust. "Course not," he pontificated. "They ain't got no feelings, fish ain't!"

"How do you know, smartie?" Helen, aged ten, with red hair and blue eyes, challenged. "You'd have to be a fish to know a thing like that!"

"Would not!"

"Would too!"

The argument went on as Christie took the knife and, holding the fish firmly with her left hand, sliced downward just in back of the two small fins behind the eye. Then putting the knife down, she took the head in her left hand and grasped the body of the fish in her right. With one sharp motion she snapped the head off and pulled the entrails free. Tossing the offal into a bucket, she handed the decapitated body to the oldest girl, saying, "You want to scale this fish for me, Helen?"

Helen started to say no, but Ray grabbed it, saying, "No, *I'll* do it, Aunt Christie!"

Hearing Ray call her Aunt Christie, she thought, *I'm so glad Anne's allowed these three to become a part of our family. Logan is wonderful with them. He treats them like they were his own kids, just like he will treat Clinton.*

Logan had married Anne Wilson Ballard two years earlier, after she had lost her first husband, George Ballard, to pneumonia in 1916. Logan's love for Anne had taken in her three children as well, and the children were hardly aware of any father but Logan.

Christie's thought was broken by the three children squabbling over the fish.

Helen snatched the fish back, saying, "She asked *me* to do it!" A quarrel started, and Christie stopped it by saying, "All three of you can scale. There are plenty of fish." She showed them how to pull the edge of the spoon against the scales, and soon all three of them were taking turns at making scales fly. When the fish were clean, she washed them in water and threw the offal out into the edge of the woods where the coons and possums would have a feast.

Putting the dressed fish into a flat pan, she went into the house where she found Anne in the kitchen churning butter. "Oh, those are *nice* ones!" Anne Stuart was a small, plain woman, but she had nice brown eyes and was as loved by her husband as if she were a beauty queen. "Put them in the pie safe so the flies won't get them, Christie." When she saw that done, she said, "Sit down and tell me all about the family."

The two women talked as Anne churned, and finally Christie said, "That soap ought to be about done, Anne. I'll go take it up."

Making her way to the hopper, she looked into the depths of the kettle, then nodded with approval. She pulled away the fire to let it cool, then covered it with boards. While it cooled, she worked in the garden, answering the multitude of questions the children asked her. They were very lonesome, and when visitors came, they swarmed them, hungry for attention.

Finally Christie said, "Let's go get the soap." She led the three of them to the soap, dipped some of it into a bucket, then took it in for Anne's approval.

Anne sniffed at it and nodded. "Just right, Christie. You done good." The soap was thicker and darker than sorghum molasses and smelled of wet ashes. They carried the soap to a barrel in the small storehouse, and then Christie took a gourd and dipped some into a pan of hot water. She watched as the water turned milky white, and she stirred some foam to the top. "Turned out good," she murmured. She liked to do things well, and even such a simple thing as making lye soap gave her pleasure. She set one gourdful by the dishpan and another on the wash shelf on the back porch.

When Logan came in at dusk, hot and worn, he sat down and washed his feet in a basin. Covering them with the soap, he groaned with pleasure, saying to Christie who came to watch, "Just right. You get it too strong, it burns. But this just feels plumb good, Christie!"

By the time he had finished washing, Anne called, "Come and eat!"

They all hurried to the table, and when they sat down, Logan asked a simple blessing. Looking up he shook his head, "Don't reckon the king of England and all his dukes got a supper like this!"

Anne had felt better that day, and the table seemed bowed with food. A heaping platter of fresh fish, another of fried potatoes, and a third of hush puppies formed the heart of the meal, but there was yellow squash, fried okra that crunched between the teeth, purple-hull peas that smoked in their white bowl, and fresh-baked bread.

Christie gave Violet a lesson in eating a whole perch. "Look, hold it like this and pull this top fin out," she demonstrated. The entire fin came out, exposing white meat that gave off steam. "Now, don't burn yourself—put your teeth against the top, see? Like eating corn on the cob. This way you don't get any bones in your throat."

They ate while Anne nursed the baby, then Christie rose and said, "Got a surprise for you, Logan." Going to the top of the cookstove, she opened the warming door at the top and took out a pie. Turning to Logan she smiled, "Don't guess you'd like a piece of fresh pecan pie, would you, Brother?"

"My, oh, my!" Logan said, very reverently. He took the pie, holding it as if it were the crown jewels of England. "Why didn't you tell me you made a pecan pie? I'd of ate it first!" He grinned and looked around, asking innocently, "Didn't

you make one for the rest of you, Christie? I shore don't aim
to share *my* pie with anyone!"

At this the children began pestering him, but he teased
them for a long time. "No, siree, I'll share anything I got—
except pecan pie. You'll jest have to eat more fish!"

Finally he reluctantly agreed to let them have "just a lee-
tle taste" of the pie, and Christie began to cut it into wedge-
shaped slices. As she did, Logan lifted his head, a puzzled
look on his face. "Somebody's comin'," he announced. "In
an automobile."

At once they went outside, Logan picking up a lamp. The
yellow glare of twin automobile headlights broke the darkness. The cone-shaped lights juggled up and down violently
as a car came bobbing over the rough dirt road.

"Don't rightly know who it could be," Logan said. He
waited until the noisy vehicle came to a stop in front of the
yard, then when the engine cut off, he called out, "Who is
it?"

"Don Satterfield."

"Why, Preacher, whut you doin' way out here this time of
the night?" Logan lifted the lamp, and when the tall figure
emerged from the darkness, he said, "Come inside . . . you
young'uns get back and let Brother Satterfield in."

Christie had a premonition as soon as she saw the face of
the minister. Before he could speak, she asked, "Is somebody
sick, Brother Don?"

Satterfield's face was etched with lines of fatigue. He
clamped his jaws together, then nodded. "It's Lenora," he
said grimly. "She was thrown by a horse—going over a fence."

Fear surged through Christie, and she swallowed, then
asked, "Is . . . is she hurt bad?"

"I'm afraid she is. I came to get you, Christie."

"I'll get my things."

As Christie moved swiftly out of the room to get her few
belongings, Logan asked, "Is she dying?"

"No, she'll live, Logan." Satterfield noticed the instant re-

lief in the farmer's face and added quickly, "But she's paralyzed from the waist down."

"Can't they do something, the doctors?"

"They say not. I'm afraid she'll be crippled the rest of her
life."

Anne began to cry, and this frightened the older children.
They drew close to her, staring almost angrily at the tall minister. He was the bearer of evil tidings, and they had only him
to blame.

Logan got the details from Satterfield, and when Christie
came out, her face pale, he moved to give her a hug. "You go
see to Lenora. Tell her we'll be there soon as we can."

Christie nodded, hugged him, then each of the children.
She kissed the soft cheek of Clinton, the newborn, then Anne.
"I'll write and tell you. I'm sorry I have to leave you with all
the work."

"We'll make out," Anne nodded. "Tell Lenora we'll be
praying for her."

Christie moved out into the darkness and got into the car.
Soon they were bumping over the rocky road. "A dog frightened the horse just as he was jumping," Satterfield told her.
"He swerved, and Lenora was thrown. Wouldn't have been
hurt, but she landed right on a sapling stump. It caught her
right on the back of the neck . . . ."

Christie listened as the minister related the story. Her
throat was thick, and she wanted to weep, but she knew she
had to keep herself strong. Finally she said, "She won't ever
walk again?"

"The doctors say she won't."

"But we can pray for her to walk!"

"I'll do that," Satterfield said. "God can do it . . . and *he'll*
have to. The doctors say that they can't do anything for her."

The ancient Essex bounced over the road, finally turning
onto a better highway. As they headed toward the hospital in
Fort Smith, Christie broke the silence. "I'll take care of her—
as long as she lives!"

Satterfield was startled at the defiant tone in Christie's voice. He twisted his head, caught a quick glimpse of the young woman's profile. "That's a hard thing, Christie. She'll need a lot of care."

"I can do it." Christie's voice was even, and she added, "She'd do it for me."

Satterfield swerved to dodge a possum with a cluster of babies clinging to her tail. The ratlike beast had red eyes, and he missed her by only a fraction. When Satterfield got the car under control, he nodded, then said in a whisper, "Yes, she would, Christie. Lenora's that kind of woman."

"Well, time for you to come home, Daughter."

Will Stuart came into the hospital room, a piece of paper in his hand. He paused before the wheelchair, then added, "Don's getting the car around to the front. You had enough of this place, I reckon?"

Lenora's face was thin, and she had lost her healthy color. The days at the hospital had been torture for her, though she had kept up a good spirit. Now she smiled, saying, "I'm ready, Pa."

"Well, let's get goin'." Will moved to the back of the chair, saying, "Christie, you get her things, will you?"

"Yes, Pa. They're all packed."

As her father shoved the chair out of the room and down the hall, Christie followed. She'd already said good-bye to the orderlies and the nurses, but they all greeted her. Several of them stopped the progress to say good-bye to Lenora. The whole hospital staff had taken a vital interest in her, and when they came to the front door, they were greeted by Doctor Henry Miles, the chief of staff. He was a tall man of fifty with fine gray eyes and a cheerful manner.

"Well, we're losing our star patient," he smiled down at Lenora. He took her hand, saying, "I'll expect to hear from you."

"I'll miss you, Doctor," Lenora smiled back. "And I'm not giving up on you. You need Jesus Christ as your savior."

The physician hesitated, then gave a despairing look at Will. "This girl of yours won't give up on me, Mr. Stuart. I've told her I'm too hard a case, but she just won't quit."

"No, I won't—and neither will God."

Lenora had been a faithful witness to the hospital staff—from Doctor Miles to the maintenance crew. In the midst of a life-wrecking tragedy, she told all who came into her sphere of their need for Christ. Doctor Miles had come in once to find his most hard-bitten nurse sitting beside the stricken woman, stroking her arm gently. Nurse Biddle had given the doctor a defiant look, stating, "Whatever she's got—I need it!"

Now the doctor lost his smile and said gently, "I'm sorry we couldn't do more for you, my dear. We doctors can't really do much."

"All things are in God's hand," Lenora said evenly. "It's more important that you find peace with God than for me to walk. I'll be praying for you, every day."

"I can use it!"

And then the doctor turned and left abruptly. "He's a nice sort of feller," Will observed, then pushed the chair down the hall. When they reached the door, Christie saw Mel Tolliver entering. He had been to the hospital twice, and now she saw that he was startled to see them.

"Had to get somebody to work for me," he excused himself. "Sorry not to be here sooner." He followed them outside, and as Satterfield and Will carefully put Lenora in the seat of the car and loaded the wheelchair, he asked, "She not going to get better?"

"No, I don't think so."

"How'll she make out?" Tolliver asked.

Christie knew he was asking her how much time she herself would give to her stricken sister. She had prepared herself for this moment and now said, "I'm going to take care of her, Mel."

Tolliver gave her a startled glance. "But what about . . ." He broke off, but his thoughts were clear. He glanced at Lenora and shook his head. "A shame," he muttered. "Young woman like that. Never have a home now, except with her folks."

"She'll have me."

Tolliver stared at her, then shook his head. "We'll talk about it. There are nursing homes, things like that."

Christie said, "They're ready to go, Mel." She left him, and when she got into the car, she saw that he was staring at her in a peculiar way. When the car moved away, Satterfield inquired, "Mel feeling bad about something? Guess he's upset about Lenora."

"I don't think so."

Satterfield exchanged a glance with Will, and the two men fell silent. Each of them knew the tragedy that had brought Lenora down might still have potent effects.

Christie sat beside Lenora, keeping up a cheerful flow of talk as the car moved along. She held her older sister's hand, stroking it from time to time. And she wondered what would come of this. One thing she was determined about. *I'll take care of Lenora—no matter what it takes!*

4

A NANNY FOR ADAM

C ut!"

Lylah was so mesmerized by the making of the motion picture that she jerked with surprise as a balding man who looked as if he were dressed for a polo match shot out of his chair and came to stand before a woman in a nurse's uniform. "That was *excellent*, Mary! Just the right expression."

The actress was tiny, almost diminutive. She looked up, smiled sweetly, then said, "Thank you, Mr. DeMille."

"America's Sweetheart, that's Mary Pickford."

Lylah felt her arm seized and turned to look into the face of Howard Duncan. "She's a fine actress," she murmured, then managed to retrieve her arm from Duncan's grasp— without making an issue of it. Duncan was the male star of *Over the Top* and had been at her side since she'd come to the set of the picture. "Has she ever done anything on the stage?"

"No, nothing." Duncan was aware that he had been rebuffed and was amused. A million women would have been delirious at the chance to have an arm squeezed by one of the foremost matinee idols from Hollywood, but Lylah Stuart was not one of them. He was wearing the uniform of a lieutenant and looked spotlessly handsome as he stood beside her. "She's only done one role in Hollywood. I suppose you know that?"

"No, I don't know much about films."

Duncan liked her honesty. "She's made a dozen or so films playing young girls. She and her new husband, Doug Fairbanks, along with Charlie Chaplin, are the hottest stars in town. Can name any figure they like and get it."

"That must be nice."

Howard Duncan shrugged. "I'd like to find out, but I'm just one of the spear carriers."

Lylah gave the actor a startled look. "But you're costarring with Miss Pickford!"

Duncan pulled a silver cigarette case from his pocket. He offered her one, and when she declined, he extracted a cigarette, snapping the case shut. He seemed to be amused at her innocence and took his time lighting the cigarette. "It doesn't work that way, Lylah," he said slowly. "There are half a dozen big names in pictures, and they get the lion's share of the money. The rest of us toil and wait for the big break." He studied her carefully, then said, "You don't know this world, do you?"

"No, not at all. I've been on the stage since I was seventeen—and for the past few years in Europe." She looked around at the set, shook her head, and said doubtfully, "I'd never learn to do this sort of acting."

"Sure you would. If Cecil B. DeMille says you can do it, you've got the goods."

"He liked me on the stage, but I don't know if I could do that scene as Miss Pickford just did." Her eyes widened with disbelief, and she said, "She showed that expression ten times, and I couldn't see any difference. On the stage, you get one chance, and that's it." She smiled suddenly, then laughed aloud. "I can just see a director of a stage play calling out, 'Just a minute, Lylah, you didn't smile right. Run through it again.'"

Duncan found this woman very exciting. He was bored with empty-headed starlets who came to him willing for anything, for he knew they were tigresses ready to kill for a career in the movies. He had been surprised when DeMille had told him how much he admired Lylah Stuart. "She's *theater*, Howard," the bald-headed director had insisted. "We need

•
talent like that in Hollywood. I'm going to sign her—if I can get her."

DeMille was a power in Hollywood, and when he had asked Duncan to entertain the visitor, he had agreed. He had been surprised to discover that Lylah Stuart was not as young as most aspiring actresses and had commented on the fact to the director. DeMille had given him a knowing smile. "She has maturity, Howard, and *real* beauty, not the cheap prettiness we see so much of. Look at her bone structure when you meet her. You're a woman's man, you'll see what I mean."

And now as he chatted with Lylah, Howard Duncan understood what DeMille had meant. *She's got the same features as Bernhardt,* he thought, *and it'll come across on the screen.* He had been surprised to discover that she seemed to be immune to his charms, but he was pleased in some perverse way. Easy success with women had been exciting when he was younger, but somehow the regal beauty and the ease with which she refused his approaches made her more attractive.

"Well, tonight we'll have more time to talk. Did DeMille tell you I'd be taking you to the premier?"

"Premier?"

"Why, you *are* naive, aren't you?" Duncan said. "It's the world premier of *The Mark of Zorro,* starring Douglas Fairbanks. You'll find it exciting. I understand Doug does everything but turn himself inside out." He heard his name called and looked up to see DeMille waving him to the set. "I'll pick you up at seven, all right?"

"I'd like it very much."

Howard Duncan paused long enough to smile at her, and he was charming at such times. "I even promise not to squeeze your arm, Lylah."

"And I'll promise you the same, Howard."

Duncan laughed in delight. "Fair enough—but I may change the rules later. What will you do this afternoon? Watch me win the Great War?"

"No, I've got to find a nanny."

Duncan gave her a bewildered stare. "A . . . goat?"

Lylah laughed again, making a charming picture. "No, that's what the English call a lady who cares for small children. I have a two-year-old son, and I've had a terrible time finding someone to keep him."

"Well, I'll volunteer for anything but that, Lylah. I'd like to meet your son, though."

He left, and as the crew went into action for the next scene, Lylah left the set and made her way to the exit. Mr. DeMille had assigned her a car, and the driver opened the door, asking, "Yes, Miss Stuart?"

"Take me to my apartment."

"Yes, Miss Stuart."

On the way to the apartment building, Lylah thought hard about what Hollywood had proved to be. She had discovered that there was no Hollywood in the sense of a movie capital, only villages set in orange groves and onion fields with dusty roads to connect them. Scattered over the area were studios, usually barnlike structures with no charm or beauty. Inside them she had been amazed at the skill with which carpenters and plasterers could change a set. One day the actors were in a Louis XIV French palace, the next they might well be in a slum of Chicago.

Since the pictures were silent, as the scenes were shot the director would constantly shout instructions such as, "Scowl, Madeline! Look like you're going to bite him!" Or, "For Pete's sake, Howard, you're supposed to be in love! *Look* like it!"

She had met William S. Hart, the cowboy star, and Pola Negri, the most sensuous woman on the screen, so Howard had informed her, Charlie Chaplin, and a host of minor actors and actresses she could not remember now. It was a confusing world, and she dreaded the thought of leaving the theater, which she had learned to love.

She stepped out of the car in front of her apartment, saying, "I won't need you any more today, Steven. Pick me up at eight in the morning, please."

"Yes, I'll be here, Miss Stuart."

Lylah took the greeting of the doorman, walked across the Italian marble floor, and rode the elevator to the sixth floor. The elevator operator, a young woman wearing too much makeup, made her usual plea. Her name, or so she claimed, was Gloria Starr, and she would have killed her grandmother to get into the movies. "Did you mention my name to Mr. DeMille, Miss Stuart?"

"I didn't talk to him, Gloria."

A pout appeared on the girl's full lower lip, and she retorted, "I guess you're too busy to pay any attention to me!" As she brought the elevator to a stop, she maneuvered the car until it was six inches short of the floor. "Or too jealous of us young ones," she snapped nastily, glaring at Lylah.

Lylah gave the girl a look of disbelief, but said only, "I don't have any influence with Mr. DeMille or anyone else." She stepped up to the level of the floor and made her way to the door of her apartment. It was an expensive hotel room, but DeMille had insisted that it was rented full-time by the studio and would be empty if she didn't stay there.

When she stepped inside she was almost knocked off her feet as Adam lunged into her, grabbing her legs in a tackle. "Adam!" she cried, catching her balance. "What in the world!—"

"Playing football!" he said, looking up at her. He was a sturdy child with handsome features. He was also a willful child who would allow himself to be pulled to pieces rather than give up an idea that lodged in his round blond head. "Come and see," he said suddenly, and grabbing her arm, he pulled her into the living room—where she saw Miss Potter asleep on the couch.

"She sleeping," Adam announced. "Won't wake up and play with me."

Even as Lylah leaned over the woman, she smelled the

strong scent of liquor, and her eyes fell on the empty bottle
that had fallen to the floor. Anger exploded in her, and she
jerked the woman upright.

A nasty scene followed, one that she wished Adam hadn't
seen. The woman, who had been sent by a "reliable" agency,
was argumentative, profane, and abusive—totally unlike the
personality she'd shown Lylah earlier. When Lylah finally got
the woman outside, Adam came to her asking, "She sick?"

"Yes, sweetheart, she was sick."

"I don't like her. You stay with me, Mum."

Lylah reached out and hugged the boy, holding him tight.
"I wish I could, Adam, but Mum has to work."

"Why?"

"Because I need money so I can take you out to eat. Come
on, let's go."

"Can I have ice cream?"

"Yes."

"And candy?"

"All you want!"

Adam laughed, and the two left as soon as possible. As they
walked toward the restaurant, Lylah asked herself, *What am
I going to do? How can I leave him alone with strangers?*

Getting a contract from Triangle Pictures proved to be
the simplest of the goals that faced Lylah. Cecil B. DeMille
was so ardent in his praises of her after a series of tests that
the owner of Triangle, Thomas H. Ince, offered her a lu-
crative deal for three pictures. When Lylah accepted his
contract, she received a healthy advance and found a small
house on the same side of town as the studio. For three
weeks she worked hard on the new picture, while at the
same time fighting to give Adam as much of her time as
possible.

But finding a woman to serve as housekeeper and nursemaid proved to be a formidable task. She tried four women,
one after another, but none of them came anywhere close to

suiting her. Finally in despair she said to Howard Duncan—
her costar in the film she was making for Ince—"I don't think
I can go on, Howard. It's driving me crazy!"

The two of them were sitting in her living room, where
they had come after a hard day at the studio. The picture was
called *Desert Love*, and much of it was shot outdoors in the
desert surrounding Hollywood. The July sun furnished plenty
of light for the cameras, but it also scorched the skins of the
actors. Duncan had been sunburned so badly he almost quit,
and despite all her care, Lylah had suffered almost as much.

She picked up a tall glass of iced tea, swallowed it thirstily,
then lay back against the overstuffed pillows on the couch
and closed her eyes. "How many incompetent, lazy, drunken,
slovenly women are there in this town?" she said. "I can't go
through them all until I find one good one!"

Duncan reached over and took her hand. She opened her
eyes at once and looked at him. He laughed and released it.
"You're like a set trap, Lylah. Can't I touch you without having you give me that look?" He opened his eyes wide, mim-
icking her, adding, "Not every man you meet is out to get
you into bed."

"But you are, aren't you, Howard?"

Duncan stared at her nonplused, then threw back his head
and laughed. "Yes," he admitted, shaking his head. "I've
never deceived you about that."

"Why don't you give up and start chasing those starlets
who stare at you so longingly?"

"They bore me. They've got brains of oatmeal!" He leaned
back and studied her closely, then said abruptly, "You don't
suppose I'm falling in love with you, do you?"

"Would that be so bad?" Lylah smiled at the shocked look
on the handsome face. "You're really good with children.
Adam adores you. Wouldn't you like to have some of your
own?"

"Good heavens! Think of it—six or so miniature Howard
Duncans set loose on the world!" His expression amused her,

and he laughed at himself. "That would be rich, wouldn't it, Lylah? As many young ladies as I've managed to escape from—and now to think you may lead me to the altar."

"I'm too old for you."

But Duncan grew serious. The thought of marriage, having been far from his thoughts for years, now seemed rather close. "You know, it might not be too bad. If Fairbanks and Pickford can do it, why not us?"

"Because I don't want to come between you and the person you love," Lylah said quickly.

"What's that?" Duncan demanded.

"I'd hate to break up the romance of Duncan and Duncan." Lylah rose, laughing at the expression on Howard's face. "If you ever fall out of love with yourself, we'll talk about it, Howard. Now, get out of here. I've got to get on the phone and try to find another nursemaid for Adam."

"Are you offering enough money?"

"Yes, that's not it." Lylah handed Howard his hat and shoved him toward the door. When she opened it, she suddenly pulled him close and kissed him on the lips. Then she pushed him away as he reached for her. "For an actor, you're not a bad fellow, Howard. Good night. I'll see you tomorrow— if I can find a nanny."

But she didn't find a nanny that week, and the succession of part-time women was not suitable. She came home time after time to find Adam in poor shape. Some were too lax, letting the child do whatever he wanted, while others were so strict that they drove him to tears.

When the cameras rolled, there was no excuse. Every actor and actress was in place. This was especially true of DeMille's pictures, and Lylah understood that she had no choice. Finally a day came when she was not in any of the scenes, and she determined to spend the whole day with Adam. She rose early, cooked a good breakfast, and then got on the phone. She arranged with the employment company to interview two applicants after four o'clock, but she had little faith in the results. She determined to place an ad in the paper, hoping that she would strike gold, but that approach, too, seemed doubtful.

She and Adam had a fine morning. They walked down the streets, and when Adam spotted some ponies for rent on a vacant lot, she stood there as he rode all six of them. "Can I have a pony?" he demanded as she lifted him off.

"Someday, when we have a house in the country," she promised. She led him to a small cafe where they ate ham sandwiches, then ice cream, and then he was ready for more sight-seeing.

Lylah asked a cab driver what was in the city that a child might like, and he said, "Why, the zoo, ma'am." He had a thick southern accent, and he took the two of them to a nice zoo on the outskirts. Lylah gave the cabbie a healthy tip, saying, "If you'll come back in two hours, I'd like to go home."

"Yes, ma'am!" He nodded happily. "Be right here!"

Adam had a fine time, and so did Lylah. They walked through the zoo, and Adam was amazed at the animals. Finally, however, he grew tired, and the two of them found a grassy bank close to a pond where pink flamingos waded in the still water. Adam watched for a time, then he came to sit beside her. His eyes were heavy, and when Lylah lay back and pulled him to her, he quickly dropped off to sleep in the fashion of a two-year-old.

Lylah herself was exhausted, and as she held his head on her shoulder, became drowsy. She looked down at Adam's face and seemed to see the face of his father, Baron Manfred von Richthofen. And then she fell asleep and dreamed of the time back in the dim recesses of the war when she had fallen in love with the famous German ace. It was one of those dreams when she seemed to see herself from a far distance, as if she were watching herself in a play:

The snow was on the ground, and Manfred took her into the woods. They stopped close to a small creek, and he said, "Quiet now. A stag may come to drink."

And finally a beautiful doe stepped out, and Lylah could not shoot. Manfred lifted his gun, and two shots rang out. He ran forward, put his gun down, and pulling a knife, slit the throat. The blood made a crimson fountain, and when he came back to stand beside her, his hands were bloody. He wiped them clean, then asked, "Why didn't you shoot?"

"I don't know. She was so beautiful."

"Yes, but deer are put here by God for us to use as food." And then he asked abruptly, "What about the war? Do you hate every German?"

"No, of course not! I don't hate you—how could I ever hate you?" The flier looked at Lylah. Silence was thick in the forest, and finally he said, "We cannot be lovers. We are on different sides."

But at these words, Lylah put her arms around him, kissing him passionately. When she drew back, she whispered, "Love isn't a matter of politics, Manfred."

They kissed again, and finally he said, "Lylah, we're making a mistake to let ourselves be drawn together."

And Lylah whispered, "I know, my dear. But I've been making mistakes all my life, and I can't help it." And she drew his head down—

Lylah awakened with a convulsive shock. She had dreamed that scene many times in the months that followed Manfred's death, but she had thought it was over. Now she felt a bitterness, for she often felt guilt over bringing a fatherless child into the world—especially with such a father. The war was over, but many Americans had lost sons and brothers and husbands—and had strong feelings about Germans.

She sat up, abruptly aware that Adam was not at her side. Fear ran through her, but then she saw him down the slope. He was playing some game with a young woman, and Lylah drew a sigh of relief. She sat there, watching the two for a long time. The woman seemed very young, no more than fifteen or so. She had straight black hair, dark blue eyes, and an olive complexion—a very attractive girl. She was wearing a pale blue dress, and her dark eyes seemed to sparkle as she spoke to Adam. She laughed at something Adam said, and her laughter seemed to tinkle on the afternoon air.

Finally Adam caught her hand and drew her to where his mother sat. "Bonnie, Mum," he announced. "She's fun!"

"You two were having a good time," Lylah smiled. "You're very good with children. What's your name?"

"Bonnie Hart," the girl smiled. "You have a fine boy. I hope someday I have about six like him."

"Well, to tell the truth, I have trouble keeping up with *one* like him."

"He's lively, but such a darling."

"Mum, we take her home?"

Lylah laughed aloud and picked Adam up in her arms. "She's not a stray cat, Adam," she said. Then she sighed, "I wish I *could* take you home, Bonnie. To take care of Adam, I mean."

"Take care of him?"

"Yes." Adam squirmed, and she set him down. As he ran down the slope whooping at the top of his lungs, she explained. "I work, and I have no husband. I've been trying to hire a nanny for weeks now."

"A nanny?"

"That's what the English people call a woman who cares for children."

"I didn't know that," Bonnie said thoughtfully. "I'd be good at it, though."

A thought leaped into Lylah's mind, and she asked impulsively, "I don't suppose you'd consider being a housekeeper and nanny for Adam and me?" Even as she spoke her mind was saying, *She's too young, and she's had no training*—

A thoughtful light touched the dark blue eyes, and the answer was slow. "I never worked for anyone. But I could keep a boy like Adam. And I'm a good housekeeper."

Lylah asked cautiously, "Do you live with your family, Bonnie? They might not want you to work for an actress—some people don't like them."

Bonnie's eyes opened wide, and then she laughed aloud. "I live with my brother—but he's gone most of the time. He wouldn't care, though." She looked at Adam who was throwing stones at the dignified pink flamingos and then said thoughtfully, "I get lonesome sometimes. Do you think I could do it?"

Lylah took a deep breath, then nodded. "I don't know if you can cook—but you can play with Adam. My name is Lylah Stuart. Why don't you come along with me, to my house. We can talk about it. Then both of us can make up our minds."

"All right."

By the time Bonnie left the house, Lylah knew the girl was capable. The two had talked long, and Bonnie had made cheese omelets for them all—a dish that Lylah had never mastered. Adam had clung to Bonnie's hand much of the time, and Lylah observed that the girl knew how to be firm with the child.

"Let's try it for a few days, Bonnie," she said finally. "If at the end of the week you want to leave, that's fine."

"And if I don't suit you, you can fire me," Bonnie smiled. "Do you want me to come in the morning?"

"We have an extra bedroom," Lylah said. "Why don't you come and stay with us for the trial period. That way we can see the worst of each other."

Bonnie studied the face of the older woman, then said simply, "I don't think you have a worst side—and I know Adam hasn't!"

"That's what you think—but I'm glad you think so."

After Bonnie left, promising to be back at seven the next day, Lylah put Adam to bed.

"She coming back?" he asked sleepily. "She's nice!"

"Yes, she'll come back." Lylah tucked him in and kissed him on the cheek. "And I hope she'll stay!"

"Me, too!" The two words were mumbled, and as Lylah looked down on him, she thought again of the man who had fathered him—and tears came to her eyes as she turned away.

5

"I'VE GOT TO DO IT!"

My mother would have cut a peach tree switch to any of her daughters who went out in public dressed like that!"

Amos Stuart and his wife, Rose, had gone out for a rare evening on the town. They decided on impulse to treat themselves to a dinner at an expensive restaurant. But they had no sooner been seated in the restaurant of the Biltmore Hotel than they had been shocked by the dress of the young women in the room.

Rose, who kept up with fashions more than her husband, took in the dancers on the floor and frowned. "I'd heard about how bad this sort of thing was getting, but I didn't know it was so . . . so raw!"

The women on the floor were a part of what would be known as "flaming youth." They were part of a revolt that exploded after the end of the Great War. Before the turn of the century there was a "code," unwritten, but commonly agreed on by conservatives all over the country. Roughly, it held that women were the guardians of morality, made of finer stuff than men. They were to remain pure and innocent until the right man came along, allowing no male to kiss them. It was assumed that no decent young woman would smoke. And as for drinking, that was unthinkable!

But now as Amos and Rose stared at the young women in the room, they saw that the code was no longer in effect. The dresses that the women were wearing were all of nine inches above the ground, were made of thin material, and in some cases were sleeveless. Most of the young women had rolled their stockings below the knee, and the spectators were treated to glimpses of shinbones and kneecaps. When they were not dancing, the "flappers," as they were already being called, wore rouge liberally applied to their faces, and most of them were smoking as they talked.

"What have they done to their hair?" Amos demanded.

"I think they've 'shingled' it," Rose said. "Some women even go to men's barber shops to get their hair cut. Looks frightful, doesn't it?"

Amos made a close inspection of the men and growled, "Look at the hair on those fellows! Black and slicked down with brilliantine—all parted in the middle."

"They got that from that movie star Rudolph Valentino," Rose informed him. She was appalled by the sight, but a gleam of humor that she could never suppress for long surfaced as she murmured, "If a fly lit on a slick head like that, he'd slip and break his neck."

"Look at that girl," Amos broke in. "Why, she's got on enough makeup to be a clown in the circus!" He indicated a young woman who was no more than seventeen. She had shaved her eyebrows into pencil-thin lines, made her lips up into a pouting cupid's bow, and outlined her eyes with dark eye makeup. "She needs a good whipping," Amos said, shaking his head in disgust.

The waiter appeared, and they ordered, but as they waited for their meal, both of them were disturbed. Amos toyed with the glass of water in front of him, watching the crowd with a puzzled look. "What's happened to this country, Rose? Before the war, no decent girl would let herself be seen cavorting like those out there. There ought to be laws to stop them!"

"That's been tried, don't you remember, dear?" Rose shook her head and looked away from the dancers, adding, "A bill passed the Virginia legislature that forbade any woman from wearing shirtwaists or evening gowns that displayed more than three inches of her throat, and Ohio went even further. They made it illegal to sell any garment that displays or accentuates the lines of the female figure. But passing laws won't change this, will it?"

"No, it goes deeper than I'd thought. And we've already begun to see that prohibition won't keep people from drinking."

They ate their dinner with some distaste, for they saw many instances of drinking that violated the law. Many men pulled flasks from their inside pockets and offered them to their female companions—who drank readily enough. Amos said moodily, "The big thing in men's fashions now is to have a pocket to conceal a bottle of booze. And some men are starting to wear Russian boots because they can stuff several flasks of liquor inside."

They finished their meal and left the restaurant feeling depressed. When they arrived at their home, they found that Maury, their eighteen-year-old, had left a note that said,

> I just wanted to remind you that you said I could stay with Sally Stevens tonight. I'll see you tomorrow. I love you.

Amos stared at the brief message, then grimaced. "I guess we're lucky to have a daughter who's thoughtful enough to leave us a note."

"Maury's very responsible, Amos." Rose took off her coat, then said, "Let's sit and talk."

"All right—and next time let's go to a better restaurant."

"I think they're all about the same."

Rose made coffee, and when she took the tray into the room, she found Amos fiddling with the new wireless set. He had gotten it to listen to the returns of the presidential election between Harding and Cox, but they had scarcely been able to make out the words of the announcer who was broadcasting such a thing for the first time. Now the sound of music filled the room, but it was so distorted and scratchy that Amos turned the machine off in disgust.

"That thing will never work," he said moodily. "They're

supposed to broadcast the championship bout between Jack Dempsey and this French boxer, Carpentier, but that won't work either."

"Jerry says it will work," Rose murmured, pouring coffee into his cup. "He's very interested in things like that. I think he could be an engineer."

"Well, he didn't get that sort of thing from me. I guess he got his brains and his good looks from you, Rose."

"He's very much like you, Amos."

"Jerry? Why, Rose, we're *nothing* alike! We can't be in the same room for ten minutes without an argument."

Rose sipped her coffee and regarded Amos over the cup. He was still trim and athletic at the age of forty-one, with the same ash-blond hair and dark blue eyes that had attracted her when they first met. They had been poor, but their courtship had been very romantic. Rose had fallen into disgrace, and only the ministry of the Salvation Army had brought her out of it. She had gone as a mission volunteer to China, and when the Boxer Rebellion had broken out, Amos had been trapped there with her. It had taken a miracle to get them out of China alive, but when they returned, they had married. Amos had become a highly respected newspaperman, the star reporter for William Randolph Hearst, owner of the most powerful newspaper in the country, the *New York Journal*.

Their marriage had been blissful, and their two children were becoming fine adults. But whereas Maury seemed to accept her parents' way of life, Jerry had been a problem ever since he was old enough to say "No!" For some reason that neither Amos nor Rose could ever fathom, he had a built-in "no" that seemed to fly from his lips as soon as any command or request came from his parents.

This surfaced when he was a mere baby, and at first it was only a minor thing. But when he was two years old, he threw a fit in a restaurant that made Amos and Rose realize that he had a serious problem. It occurred when they sat down to eat, and Rose attempted to put a bib on Jerry. He immediately said, "No bip!" Rose had cajoled him, saying, "Now, Jerry, you don't want to get your food all over your nice new sailor suit, do you?" But a mulish look appeared on the youthful lips, and he said louder, "No bip!" Rose had attempted to put the bib on by force but a major war had ensued. Amos had joined in and by brute force had held the child while Rose struggled to get the bib in place—and all the while Jerry was shouting at the top of his lungs, "No bip! No bip!" He had won the battle, for his parents were so embarrassed by his display of rebellion they left the restaurant without eating.

As the two sat drinking coffee, Amos thought of that scene and said, "Remember when Jerry threw that fit over his bib? He must not have been over two years old." He turned the coffee cup slowly in his hand, thinking of the many struggles that he had endured with his son since that time, and finally gave Rose an odd look. "I don't know where he gets it from, Rose. We Stuarts are a pretty stubborn bunch, but Jerry is downright rebellious."

"From me, I suppose."

"Don't be silly!" Amos said, reaching over and pulling her close. "You're the sweetest person I've ever known." He kissed her cheek, then repeated an old joke. "I got the pick of the litter when I got you!"

Rose took his hand, kissed it, then smiled. "I *was* the litter, if you'll remember."

The two of them sat close together, speaking quietly for some time, but Amos was still troubled over Jerry. "I'm going to take Jerry with me next week when I go home to see Pa. Why don't you come, too?"

"Oh, I'd love to—but I agreed to be a sponsor for the missions conference at church. Anyway, it'll be good for just the two of you to have some time. Maury and I can enjoy some girl time with you men gone."

Amos nodded absently, then grinned wryly. "Maybe I ought to tell him he *can't* go with me—that way he'd be sure to go. If I tell him he's got to go with me, he'll probably start bellowing 'No trip! No trip!'"

"I don't think so, dear," Rose said slowly. "He really admires you, but there's something in him that makes him dissatisfied. He just can't seem to find his way."

"Well, maybe we'll be able to talk it out. He did so poorly at college, I think he's determined not to go back. Hate to see him do something foolish," Amos said, "like joining the Foreign Legion."

"He won't do that," Rose laughed. "He'd have to obey too many orders. If they told him to march across the desert, I hardly think he'd get out of it by screaming, 'No march! No march!'"

Amos was pleasantly surprised by the easy camaraderie he and his son enjoyed on the train that took them from New York to Fort Smith. Jerry had accepted his invitation instantly, and the two of them had passed the hours of their journey talking and reading. Jerry had not been to the old home place for six years, but he still had good memories of the time he'd spent there.

When they got off the train at Fort Smith, he insisted on a quick visit to the gallows where Judge Isaac Parker had stretched the necks of almost a hundred desperadoes harvested from Indian Territory. As the two stood looking up at the gallows with five ropes swaying in the breeze, Amos smiled at a memory that came to him.

"When I was just a kid, we used to come to town about once a month. We never had any money to spend, so we used to come and visit the gallows. When I got mad at Owen or Lylah, I'd say, 'I hope you hang on Judge Parker's gallows!'"

"Don't guess any of you will be hanged." Jerry smiled at his father, adding, "Guess I'll be the one to do that. The rest of you are so respectable you won't eat an egg laid on Sunday."

Amos laughed aloud, amused by the wit that lay under

Jerry's demeanor. He slapped the broad shoulder of his son, saying, "You got that right. You're so cantankerous, if I threw you in the river, you'd float upstream! Come on, let's see if we can rent some kind of a car."

After a brief search, Amos found that a car could be rented from the local blacksmith. Jerry loved engines of all sorts and had a long talk with the burly man, whose name was Ty Stone. He had been a blacksmith in the same location for years, and he remembered Amos instantly. While Amos was giving him the deposit, he said, "Been reading them stories you write for the paper, Amos. Never would have thought the little feller who used to come and watch me shoe hosses would wind up a New York big shot!"

Amos smiled at the statement, then shook his head. "I'm no big shot, Ty. Just a plug of a newspaperman. Have you seen any of my family lately?"

"Shore, Amos. Your pa was in town last week. He brung your sister by. Her wheelchair got some kind of wallop that warped the wheel, so I fixed it fer her."

"How'd she seem to you?"

Stone wiped his balding head with a red handkerchief, then shook his head in wonder. "That gal's got more nerve than a bluetick hound, I tell you! Most young gals her age would have give up, but not Lenora Stuart! You heard about what she done with the young'uns up in the mountains?"

"No, what was that?"

"Why, she organized some kind of church school fer 'em. When crops was laid by, she had every shirttail young'un in Stone County comin' to the thing. Whole county was talkin' about it!"

"What sort of school?" Jerry inquired with interest.

"Sort of a Sunday school, but it lasted a month, and she got everybody involved. I reckon Reverend Satterfield got word around, and he helped teach the Bible to the kids—my grandkids went, and they can't stop talking about Sister Lenora. They both got saved, and so did about fifty others. Had a big baptizin' in the river, and the preacher's arm got sore from dippin' so many—and some of the parents got saved on the last night."

"I knew Lenora was doing some work with the poor kids, but she never told me about all this," Amos said.

"She's a daisy, Amos!" Ty Stone beamed, slapping one big fist into his palm. Then he asked, "Reckon you're going to Gavin's air circus ?"

"Sure, that's one reason I picked this time to come."

When they were on their way down the road that wound around toward the east, Jerry said, "I didn't know Uncle Gavin's show would be here." He was driving the car skillfully. He asked rather hesitantly, "Do you think he'd take me up for a ride?"

"I'll use my influence," Amos grinned. "But you couldn't get me in one of those things—not in a million years. If God had intended man to fly, he'd have given him wings!"

"Aw, Dad, that's not right!" Jerry protested. "If you really believed that, you'd say if God intended for man to ride in a car, he'd have given him wheels!"

The two argued for a time, but it was a playful banter with no angry words. They enjoyed the crisp November air, and once a small herd of deer were startled as they rounded a turn. Both men watched as the deer seemed to float in long jumps, clearing a rail fence, and disappearing into the dense first-growth timber that lined the dirt road.

They pulled up in front of the house just at noon and were greeted by Lenora and Christie, who were out of the house by the time the car stopped. Amos was watching as Lenora steered her wheelchair down a ramp that sloped from the porch to the ground, and it was to her he went first. Stooping over he put his arms around her and held her close. "How's my girl?" he whispered, aware of a tightness in his throat.

"Finer than peach fuzz!" Lenora laughed. She drew back, and Amos saw that she was tanned and fit. She was wearing a powder blue dress, and he noted that her arms were hard and swelled with muscle from pushing the chair. There was a peace in her face as she said, "Come on inside. Pa's gone hunting, but Christie and me will fix up something to eat."

Jerry felt awkward for a time, not knowing how to act toward a handicapped woman. But after the dinner, he went to the room that he was to share with Amos. "I don't see how she can be so happy, Dad," he said slowly. "She was always so active, wasn't she? I think I'd just give up if I had to live with something like that."

Amos gave Jerry a direct look. "That's the joy of the Lord you see in your aunt, Jerry. Nothing else it could be. She's always been a fine Christian, and now she's showing how God can give peace in a bad situation."

For the next two days, Jerry went fishing and hunting with his grandfather, and the two became fast friends. Will had aged, but Jerry remembered the days when the two of them had gone trapping in winter, and all the old affection came flooding back to him. He had difficulties with Agnes, but since he was not in the house a great deal, he managed to avoid any conflict with her.

On the third day, the whole family piled into the rented car and made the trip to town to see Gavin. Jerry tied Lenora's wheelchair to the rear bumper, and when they arrived at the fairgrounds, he unfastened it and then took her in his arms. She put her arms around his neck and teased him. "How many young girls would give their eyeteeth to get hugged by a handsome thing like you, Jerry!" She laughed in delight at his blush, and later when she and Amos were alone, said, "He's such a fine boy, Amos!"

"He's stubborn as a mule, Lenora!"

"He's a Stuart—and I can remember a time or two when Pa had some choice words about his oldest boy being stubborn. Give him time!"

"You're doing fine," Amos nodded. "I don't think I could handle it."

"God is greater than anything that comes into our lives,

Amos," Lenora said. "Whatever comes to us, it comes from his hand. I'm learning to thank him for everything."

"Even for being lame?"

"Not *for* that, I guess, but *in* my handicap I'm learning that God's grace is so much stronger than our weaknesses." She shook her head, adding, "It's Christie I'm worried about."

"What's wrong with Christie?"

"She's not happy, Amos." The fine hazel eyes clouded, and Lenora hesitated before saying, "I think she's mixed up with what it means to be a woman. She thinks she's failed, and I'm afraid she's going to be hurt."

"What about her and Mel Tolliver?"

"That's part of it. Christie thinks she has to stay with me all the time, and I feel that Mel resents it. Sooner or later he's going to tell her she's got to cut her ties with me—and if she doesn't, he'll cut and run."

"Might be the best thing for Christie," Amos frowned.

"Not in her mind. She feels like it's her last chance."

The conversation stayed with Amos, and as they moved toward the field where the planes were being serviced by the mechanics, he walked beside Christie. "Lenora's doing great," he said, then added, "Why don't you come to New York for a visit?"

"Oh, I couldn't leave her!"

Amos saw that he had touched a nerve but persisted, "She can take care of herself."

"I promised God I'd take care of her," Christie said, and there was something in her voice that told Amos that he could say nothing to change her mind. *She's got to learn the hard way— just like some of the rest of us.*

Gavin was surprised to see them, and when he had greeted them all, Amos said, "How about a ride for Jerry?"

Gavin smiled at once, nodding his head. "How about some acrobatics, Jerry? Front cockpit's empty."

Jerry's face lit up, and he exclaimed, "I'd like it fine, Uncle Gavin!"

"Come along and meet my people."

Jerry was ecstatic, and when he was introduced to Cara Gilmore he was stunned. Cara was wearing a close-fitting white flying suit that clung to her curves. She grinned at Gavin when he introduced them, saying, "You never told me you had such a good-looking nephew, Gavin." Then she went to Jerry, pressed herself against him, and whispered, "After the show, maybe you'd like to show me the town?"

"Well . . . sure," Jerry blurted. He was acutely aware of the firm curves of her body pressing against him, and he wondered if her lips were as soft as they appeared. When he was set in the cockpit, he asked, "Uncle Gavin, does Cara fly a plane?"

"She does anything she likes, Jerry," Gavin nodded. "Watch out for her. She *devours* nice-looking young fellows like you!"

Jerry soon had other things to think about. He was fascinated by the plane and asked, "Is this one like you flew in the war, Uncle Gavin?"

"Yep, it's a Sopwith Camel, Jerry. Sure glad to get it. Under the Wilson Act, fighter planes could be sold to civilians. Cost anywhere from three hundred dollars to five thousand." He revved the engine up, saying, "If you have to be sick, use the sack under your feet!"

As Gavin took off, he was thinking of the day when he'd gone for his first plane ride. It had been on this very field, and his brother Amos had talked Lincoln Beachey into taking him up. Beachey had been the premier acrobatic flier in the world, and Gavin remembered the plane he had gone in, strips of wood covered with fabric and held together by wire. He still remembered the loops and dives of that ride, mostly at a mere hundred feet above the ground. *Jerry looks just like I did, I guess,* he thought as he took the Camel up to five thousand feet. *All starry-eyed and excited.*

As for Jerry, he had never felt so free—never in his life! As Gavin made inside and outside loops, went into spins, rolled the Camel over and over through the clouds, he shouted for joy. Turning around he grinned wildly, shouting, "Uncle Gavin—this is better than anything in the world!"

When the plane landed, Gavin waited until his nephew was on the ground and Cara had climbed into the cockpit—after she managed to stop and give Jerry a hug—then he took off again. Jerry made his way to the stands, where Amos asked, "Well, how was it? Make you sick?"

Jerry could still feel the freedom of the rolls and spins. He stood there looking up into the sky as Cara crawled out on the wing and stood with her arms uplifted as Gavin brought the Camel roaring by the stands. The wind plastered the white silk fabric of her coveralls to her body, stressing the taut curves.

Amos caught the look, then asked, "Did you like it, Son?"

Jerry turned toward his father, and with the same stubborn look on his face that Amos had seen when he was two, crying "No bip! No bip!" he said, "It's what I'm going to do, Dad."

Amos's heart sank, and he knew instantly that no persuasion would change the mind of this strong-willed young man. *He's not going to listen to me—or to anyone,* he thought leadenly.

Later that afternoon Amos and Jerry met with Gavin, and Jerry said, "Uncle Gavin, I'll clean up the planes and do any dirty work. I don't want any salary except for a place to sleep and something to eat—but I've got to do it! I've got to fly!"

Gavin argued against the thing, but he soon discovered that Jerry was going to fly—somehow. He said, "It's up to you, Amos. Some of the barnstormers are flying death traps. I'll take him on, but it's a dangerous business. It's your decision."

Amos glanced at Jerry, whose face was tight with strain. *If I say no, he'll hate me forever.* Then he said, "I don't think it's wise, Son, but I can see you're set on it. I'll have to agree."

Jerry expelled his breath and threw his arms around his father—for the first time since he had become a man.

"Oh, Dad!" he muttered, drawing back with some embarrassment. "I'll never forget this!"

"Neither will I, Son," Amos said wryly. "Your mother will see to that!"

6

RUNNING WILD

A re you sure you want to do this, Jerry?"
The show had come to Chicago, and Gavin had stepped up beside Jerry, a troubled frown on his face. "It's pretty soon for you to be tackling a stunt."

It was not Jerry who answered, but Cara Gilmore. She had come up to put her arm through that of the younger man, and now she pouted, "You never tried to get *me* to back off from a stunt, Gavin."

Jerry grinned at the girl and then nodded at Gavin. "It'll be a piece of cake." But as soon as he spoke, he saw pain leap into his uncle's eyes. "What's wrong, Gavin?"

The answer was slow in coming, and when Gavin did speak it was without a touch of his usual humor. "My best friend in the war was a young fellow about your age. His name was Edmund Genet. He and I were about the only ones left of the original bunch. He was like . . . like a younger brother to me."

When Gavin paused, Jerry finally glanced at Cara, who was watching the older man carefully. "What happened, Gavin?"

"We were all worn out—making too many flights. But the order came, and Edmund insisted on taking it. He said, 'I'll do it. You old fellows take a nap and let us youngsters take care of the fighting.'" He closed his eyes and leaned back against the plane, then added softly, "He didn't look a day over sixteen, had a peach-bloom complexion and a stubby nose. Always an expression of pleased surprise in his blue eyes." Then Gavin jerked away from the plane, and his lips were drawn into a tight line. "He said, 'It'll be a piece of cake,' and then he took off. And he never came back. Got hit by a shell, and his plane hit nose into the ground at full speed. We didn't open the coffin at his funeral."

Jerry had never seen this side of his uncle, and now he said, "I'm sorry, Gavin. I didn't mean . . ."

"Not your fault," Gavin said roughly. "But you can get killed doing this stunt, Jerry. Why don't you wait for awhile?"

Jerry had been faithful to his promise to Gavin. He'd worked hard cleaning and servicing the planes, doing the hard, dirty, grinding labor that was necessary to keep the show going. Gavin had given him lessons in the air, and he reveled in those. But he craved action, and when one of the stunt-men hurt his back, Jerry had persuaded Gavin to let him do the stunt.

"It's not too dangerous, Gavin," he said quickly. "Nobody ever got hurt doing this one."

The stunt was simple enough. It consisted of one of the stuntmen—or the stuntwoman, when Cara did it—climbing out on the wing and standing braced against the wind. The wingwalker, wearing no parachute, at the right time allowed himself to be swept backward. The crowd always fell for it, but of course the stuntman wore a rope attached to a special leather harness, and the rope was tied to the plane. Every person in the stands leaped to his or her feet uttering screams as the body fell toward the earth. It was a crowd pleaser, and Gavin hated to leave it out of the program, so he had consented to Jerry's importunate pleas.

Now, however, he stared at the eager face of the boy and wished he'd never promised. "That rope could get wound around your neck and kill you," he said. "Let Cara do it."

"No, you promised, Gavin," Jerry said. "I'll be all right."

"Sure he will," Cara grinned. "Let him do it, Gavin."

Finally Gavin nodded, saying shortly, "All right, let's do it."

Cara pulled Jerry's head down and kissed him, letting her lips fall open. "I'll give you a *real* reward tonight, Jerry."

"Sure, Cara." Jerry was never certain how free with her favors Cara was. She *talked* roughly about sex a lot, but so far he'd never done more than kiss her a few times. She drank a lot, and now as he turned to go get into the plane, he had the sudden thought, *If I get killed doing this—I'll never know about her.*

But he scrambled into the plane as Gavin growled, "Fasten that rope *now*—and make certain it's tied right!"

"Right!" Jerry tied the rope and then rose to show his handiwork to Gavin. The pilot nodded, then took off. As they gained altitude Jerry thought of what would happen if the rope broke, but he was one of those fortunate souls who has no fear at all of heights, and he'd seen the stunt performed successfully many times. If it had been a pass—moving from one plane to another at full speed—that would have been different. Those stunts required perfect timing and total concentration.

Why, anybody can fall off a wing, he thought, and grinned at himself. *If I do this right, Gavin will let me do more stuff—maybe get an act with Cara like she's been talking about.*

Finally they achieved the height Gavin wanted, close enough to the ground to give the crowd a good view. "All right—do your stuff, Jerry!" he yelled, and gave a thumbs-up sign when the boy looked around.

Jerry returned the signal and stood up in the cockpit. The wind tore at his dark green coveralls, and he was careful to see that the rope didn't get tangled. He put one foot on the edge of the cockpit and grasped the trailing edge of the wing, holding to a handle covered with tape for that purpose. Then he heaved himself upward and sprawled on the surface of the upper wing. *Old Gavin's keeping this ship as steady as an ocean liner!* he thought. Then he collected himself and in one smooth motion stood to his feet. He leaned forward to compensate for the rush of wind that pushed against him, caught his balance, and flashed a thumbs-up sign at Gavin.

Carefully he made his way to the center of the wing, locked his feet in the leather stirrups, then waved at Gavin. That was the sign for some fancy flying—a little showing off for the crowd. The crowd below was a rectangle of colors, and Jerry waved as Gavin sent the ship by the grandstands several times, rocking from side to side, or up and down. The wind was cold, making his hands numb, but he didn't have to grasp anything.

Suddenly Gavin made a turn, then came roaring down the field. *Wait now*, Jerry thought, his whole being intent on what was to come. *Don't go off too soon—wait—Now!*

He shoved himself backward and fancied he could hear the screams of the crowd as he fell through space. The drop was not far, only fifteen or twenty feet—but it seemed to go on forever.

A thought raced through him like a scream—*The rope—it's slipped free!* But then there was a tremendous jerk that took the breath from his body—and he was swinging from beneath the plane. Gavin was leaning over the edge of the cockpit, and Jerry waved at him merrily. Gavin grinned and motioned for him to come up.

Climbing back was the most difficult part of the stunt, especially in cold weather. But Cara had devised nooses in the rope so that now Jerry was able to use them as a ladder of sorts. He got back on the axle between the two wheels, pulled himself onto the upper section of the lower wing, then climbed into the front cockpit.

"You did fine, Jerry!" Gavin shouted above the roar of the engine.

"How about next time *I* fly—and you do the drop?" Jerry hollered back. Gavin grinned and shook his head, then turned the plane back toward the field.

When they landed, Cara came to him at once, hugging him. "Tonight we celebrate your not getting killed," she nodded. "Don't tell Father Gavin."

"Why not?"

"Because he's the man who says, 'Find out who's having fun—and make them stop!'" Then she laughed with delight and pulled a soft leather helmet over her hair. "See you after it gets good and dark—that way nobody can see us!"

Cara stepped out of the tub, admired herself in the mirror, then dried with a fluffy pink towel. She sat down at the vanity and made up her face, then rose and moved to her bed where she'd laid out her outfit for her outing with Jerry. She wore mannish clothing most of the time, but there was nothing masculine about these garments she picked up. First she slipped into a pair of pink silk knickers, then pulled a sheer chemise over her head. Sitting down on the bed, she drew on a pair of sheer flesh-colored hose, then deliberately rolled them down. Rising again, she picked up the dress and slipped it over her head. It was tea rose in color and consisted of a georgette petal skirt with a satin bow. The neckline of the dress was very low, and the back dipped dangerously close to illegal limits. Somehow female beauty had been redefined, so that the bosom was bound and the back was bared. The ideal woman's figure was thin, no hips, no bust. Some women even wore undergarments called "flatteners" compassing the bosom to achieve the ideal "no shape" shape. But Cara laughed at such fashions, saying often, "A man wants a woman to have a few curves!"

When she was dressed, she moved to stand before the mirror and smiled at her image. "That ought to do him," she murmured. She opened a purse and checked the contents, which included rouge, cigarettes, and a silver flask of hooch that she'd bought from the bellboy when taking the room.

A knock at the door caused her to turn around, a smile on her rosebud lips. When she opened it, she was pleased at the startled look Jerry gave her. "Come in," she smiled, stepping back. "You're right on time."

Jerry was surprised at the transformation in the girl. The clinging overalls she wore were tantalizing, but there was something provocative about the manner of Cara's dress. "You look swell," he nodded. "New dress?"

"Yes. Designed by Schiaparelli. You really like it?"

"I'd be a fool not to!"

Cara laughed and moved to put a cloche hat over her cropped hair. She then allowed him to hold the black fur coat, with white trim at the collar and cuffs, for her. Turning, she pulled his head down and kissed him lingeringly. "We're going to have a good time tonight, Honey!"

"Where would you like to go? To a play?"

"Not likely! In Chicago you go where the action is—jazz! I love it!" Then she laughed and took his arm. "Come on, Jerry, I'll show you what music *really* is!"

They caught a cab, and the cabdriver grinned when Cara said, "Take us to Lincoln Gardens—and step on it!"

Historians of jazz usually designate New Orleans as the birthplace of that music, but jazz had moved upriver and now was heard mainly in the Negro dance halls in Harlem and Chicago. The records of the early jazz musicians were labeled "race records" and were sold only in black neighborhoods. Paul Whiteman, a tubby orchestra leader, was idolized as *the* jazz musician of the country, but the real greats, such as Bix Beiderbecke and others, tooted their horns for pocket change in third-rate dance bands.

As the cab threaded its way down the streets of the South Side of Chicago, Cara gave Jerry a glowing account of the music of the best jazzman of all. "King Oliver's Creole Jazz Band—it's the hottest thing going," she nodded. "He's got the best, no question. He's got Johnny Dodds on clarinet and his brother, Baby, on drums. Lil Hardin pounds the ivories, and of course, Joe Oliver—he's the greatest!"

"I never heard of any of them," Jerry confessed. "I don't know a thing about jazz. Never really listened to it."

Cara pressed close to him, her perfume exciting and bold. "I'll teach you, Jerry!" she whispered, and her words seemed to go beyond music.

The Lincoln Gardens was a dirty place, as Jerry saw when they entered. It was dingy and needed paint, and the paper decorations and faded flowers hanging from the walls added nothing.

They sat down at a small table, and Cara winked at the waiter, saying, "Bring me something nice to drink." When he took their order, Cara suddenly said, "Look over there, Jerry—"

Jerry turned to see a group of men wearing dark suits sitting at a table. "Who's that? They all look like gangsters."

"Jerry—they *are* gangsters!" Cara giggled and put her hand on his arm. "You're such a baby!"

Jerry studied the men, who were all smoking black cigars and drinking as they talked. One of them looked vaguely familiar, and he asked, "Who's that big man?"

"That's Big Jim Colosimo with his bodyguards. And the other two are Johnny Torrio and Al Capone."

Jerry stared at her. "How in the world do you know all those men?"

"I read the papers, silly! They're famous!"

"They look like they'd kill their own mother for a dollar bill!"

"I guess so—but they're exciting," Cara shrugged. A band came out and took its station, and Cara said, "That's King Oliver—the big strong-looking man. You listen now!"

Jerry was nearly bowled over by the sound that the group poured out. It was raw and loud and somehow animalistic. It had the power to stir him, and he realized for the first time what his father had meant when he'd written, "Jazz is a combination of nervousness, lawlessness, primitive and savage animalism, and lasciviousness."

It was all of those things, and by the time the couple had listened to the music for an hour, Jerry was caught up in it. Once when Oliver was taking the roof off, Cara shouted over the music, "Now you'll get a chance to see Papa Joe's red underwear!" And as the big man continued to lift the notes, his stiff shirtfront popped open, and his red undershirt was exposed.

Finally Cara persuaded Jerry to dance, and he proved to be an apt pupil. The Charleston he had heard of but had never seen. He was feeling the effect of the "nice"—and il-legal—drinks the waiter had brought, so he threw himself into it.

"You're a real sheik, Jerry," Cara laughed, holding on to him as they moved back to the table. A black man carrying a gleaming golden trumpet encountered them and smiled. "You folks dance good," he said with a gravelly voice. "Ought to get paid for it."

Cara laughed and asked, "Are you with the band?"

"I sometimes plays when Papa Joe ain't tootin his horn." He grinned and said, "My name's Louis Armstrong, but folks calls me 'Papa Dip.'"

"Why do they call you that?" Jerry asked.

Armstrong laughed and touched his lower lip. "Cause of this. I was called 'Dippermouth' for a long time, but I guess I got some respect now. Well, Papa Dip, he's got to play for the folks. Enjoy the show."

The two of them listened with awe as Armstrong made the room vibrate with a great soaring solo, and Cara said rever-ently, "He's the best there is, Jerry."

"You said that about Oliver."

"That was before I heard Papa Dip," she retorted. She leaned forward, but whatever she was going to say was drowned out by a voice that proposed, "How about a dance, Sweetheart?"

Both Jerry and Cara looked up to see a man who had come to stand beside their table. He was, Jerry noted instantly, one of the men Cara had pointed out—the one called Johnny Tor-rio. He was not a tall man, but there was some sort of primi-tive power in his gaze. Jerry said, "Not tonight—sorry."

"I guess I'll have to insist."

"Insist all you want," Jerry shrugged. "But you'll have to find another partner."

Cara was pale and said nervously, "Jerry, it's all right."

But Jerry was in one of his "no" moods. He stood up and faced Torrio, saying, "She's not dancing with you, and that's the last time I want to say it."

Torrio looked startled. He had steady brown eyes, and there was something in the scene that amused him. "Do you know who I am?"

"Johnny Torrio," Jerry said. He was nervous and noted that the music was muted and that everybody in the club was watching. "Do you know who I am?"

"No."

"I'm Jerry Stuart."

"Never heard of you."

"You will when I get to be famous. Look, I'm getting tired of this. Why don't you go back to your table before somebody gets hurt."

"Jerry!" Cara stood up and took his arm. She gave Torrio a steady look, then said, "Find another girl, Mr. Torrio."

Torrio was enjoying the spotlight. "I like you," he said. "Just one dance. I can't let a baby like this push me around."

And then another man suddenly appeared, one who had sat at the table with Torrio. He was trim and had dark hair and eyes. "You any relation to the preacher, Owen Stuart?" he asked.

Jerry was startled and gave the man a close look. "My uncle," he nodded. "You know him?"

"Do I know him?" The sleek man laughed silently. "Sure I know him—Amos must be your dad. I'm Eddy Castellano. Amos lived at our house when I was a kid. And Owen saved my life over in France. You hear about that?"

"Yes, I've heard him talk about you—Dad, too. He sends your mother flowers every time she has a birthday."

Castellano smiled. "Sure. He's a straight-up guy, and so is Owen."

Torrio was staring at Castellano strangely. "This kid's dad and uncle is friends of yours? One of them a preacher?"

"That's right, Mr. Torrio." Castellano turned to face the

gangleader, his right hand held loosely at his side. "Like I say, I owe a lot to the kid's uncle. He came across a field where me and the rest of the outfit was pinned down by the Krauts. They blew his hand off—but he got up and kept coming. Him and a baby-faced kid set up the machine gun and stopped the charge. If they hadn't I wouldn't be here."

"And you're telling me not to bother this punk?"

Eddy Castellano's voice was smooth as velvet, but there was no mistaking the threat in his body. "I'm saying that my brother Nick wouldn't like it if anyone bothered this kid. And you know what a pest Nick can be when he gets his back up, Mr. Torrio. He just goes crazy." Eddy was aware that several of Torrio's men, including Al Capone, were edging around behind their boss. It was Capone who said, "Want us to take him out, Johnny?"

The silence in the room was heavy, so heavy it seemed to press down on Torrio. He was a man who was accustomed to being obeyed, and the impulse to kill was in him. Still—he saw that Eddy was ready to pull his gun. Torrio knew that Nick Castellano was a fierce enemy—one he didn't need. He had enough trouble with the Castellanos already, now that they had moved in from New York.

"Why, I didn't mean to be rude," Torrio said, smiling with his lips, though it never reached his eyes. "I gotta' lot of respect for men like your uncle, Stuart—war heroes. They kept this country from getting whipped. No hard feelings?"

"Not at all," Jerry swallowed.

"Swell—and don't pay for nothin', it's all on Torrio."

When Johnny Torrio turned and walked away, Eddy smiled queerly at Jerry. "Well, Kid, you'll never come as close to shutting it down as you just did."

Jerry stared at the slender face of the gangster. "I'll tell Owen what you did. Dad, too." He shook his head, adding, "I was a goner. Thanks a lot, Mr. Castellano."

Eddy stared at the open face of the young man. "Tell Owen—maybe this will make up for some things—"

Then he turned and left. Jerry said, "Let's get out of here, Cara."

"All right."

As they rose to leave the band struck up, and they heard Armstrong's golden trumpet playing a quick-paced solo. Cara began to sing the words as they left:

Runnin' wild, lost control,
Runnin' wild, mighty bold,
Feelin' gay, reckless too—

Later Jerry would remember that night as the beginning of some sort of wild journey—and he never heard the song without feeling a touch of sadness.

That was the night he became part of what a young writer, F. Scott Fitzgerald, called the "lost generation."

It was the night he began his first affair.

And it was the night he left the way of his fathers to begin a slow journey into shame.

Part 2
WINGS

7

LENORA

ot to get these peanuts while the weather's still hot," Will said. He came to stand beside Lenora and Christie, who had come to watch the harvest. He glanced down at Lenora's chair, which the blacksmith had equipped with large thick bicycle tires for outside use. The first wheels had cut into the ground, making progress hard in the fields, but Lenora had come up with the idea, and now she went everywhere.

Christie looked over to the thresher that had come down the road and watched as the owner, a neighbor named John DeForge, attached a steel blade to the feet of the cultivator. She looked down at Lenora, thinking of how well her sister had adjusted to her limitations. She was not able to ride her horse, of course, but she collected eggs, milked the cow by slipping out of her chair onto a low stool that Will had built, and even managed to pick tomatoes and other vegetables in the garden. *She never complains*, Christie marveled. *If I was tied to that wheelchair, I'd be terrible!*

Lenora turned her head to smile, saying, "Remember how we used to have to dig peanuts by hand, Christie? I think we all hated that job worse than any other chore on the farm."

"Yes. Owen threatened once to run away from home if he had to dig another peanut!"

"He hated it, all right, and so did I," Will put in. He glanced over toward the cultivator, adding, "Some of the newfangled inventions they come up with I could do without, but this one suits me fine."

They watched as the cultivator began to move. Up the row it went, the steel blade slicing under the rows, loosening the dirt, and cutting the taproots of the peanut vines. As DeForge urged the team of mules forward, a cloud of dust rose, and Will and Christie followed, picking up the vines and shaking the dirt free. The hired man came after them, loading the vines into a wheelbarrow and hauling them to the wagon. When the wagon was filled, he drove it to a clear spot and unloaded them into a pile.

Lenora was sitting beside the pile when the thresher came, driven by DeForge's oldest boy, Denton. As he set up the thresher, attaching it to the small gasoline engine, Lenora said, "Remember you promised me you'd come to the revival tonight, Dent."

The young man was thin as a rail and tough as a boot. He had a shock of black hair, piercing black eyes—and a bad reputation in the community. Now he paused and looked up at her, a gleam of humor in his dark eyes. "Did I really promise that, Lenora?"

"Yes, you did—and I'm holding you to it."

"Aw, I guess I did—but the roof would fall in if I came to meet'n!" he grinned. "Why don't me and you go out and watch the moon come up at Spangler's Point?" This particular location was where young lovers parked in their cars and buggies, and the idea tickled young DeForge. "Tell you what, Lenora, you go to Spangler's Point with me—and I'll go to the revival with you."

Lenora was accustomed to Dent's teasing. He had tried to court her for years, though he was ten years younger. "Never mind Spangler's Point—you gave your word, so I'll see you tonight."

DeForge shrugged, giving up. "All right, I'll be there. But I'm sitting on the back row."

"Better get there early then, Dent," Lenora said, the corners of her lips turning upward in a smile. "All the real bad

sinners want those seats. They don't last long. Why don't you
sing in the choir with me? Plenty of seats there."

"Now that'd be something for folks to talk about, wouldn't
it?" The idea tickled the young man, but he shook his head.
"The songs I know can't be sung in church, Lenora. But I'll
be on that back row."

Christie and Will came to lift the peanuts on pitchforks
and piled them into the hopper. The peanuts came out of one
spout, the leaves and vines out of another. Then the sacks of
peanuts had to be stacked, and the thrashed-out vines loaded
on the wagon for hay.

All afternoon the engine made a noisy cadence—Clap!
Clap! Clap!—that echoed on the hot, dusty air. All of them
were covered with a fine dust that clogged the nose and
burned the eyes. Hour after hour it went on, and the pile of
peanuts grew higher and higher.

"Never *seen* so many peanuts!" Dent DeForge groaned.
"Where you going to put 'em all, Mr. Stuart?"

"Don't know," Will admitted. "Didn't bring near enough
sacks, and we can't leave 'em out in the weather. Might rain
and that would be a mess."

"We got plenty of sacks. I'll ride over and get some."

"That'll answer, Dent," Will nodded. "Christie, you go
with Dent. Stop by the house and get what sacks we got left,
and bring something to eat and some fresh water."

"All right, Pa." Christie got into the wagon with young De-
Forge, and he spoke to the team. The Stuarts' house was only
half a mile away, and the DeForges' place wasn't far down
the road. They went to the DeForge place, collected a mountain of sacks, then went back up the road. Dent lolled in the
kitchen while Christie got fresh water in gallon jugs and made
a quick lunch. He was watching her carefully and without
warning came over and put his arm around her.

Christie gasped and struggled to get away, but he held her
with an easy strength. His eyes danced, and he said, "Hate
to see a woman wasted—especially a good-looking one like

you!" He ignored her protests and kissed her. Christie was like a child, and as he ran his hand down her back, she found herself stirred—as she never had been with Mel Tolliver. The touch of DeForge's lean, strong body pressing against her suddenly aroused some emotion that both frightened and excited her. His lips were firm, and he pulled her even closer—and then something like fear came to her and she wrenched herself away.

"Denton DeForge . . . you ought to be ashamed!" she said, her voice unsteady and her breast heaving.

"Of what, Christie? Of being a man?" DeForge had been surprised by the return his kiss had brought. He had admired Christie's trim figure and clean features for a long time—but she had never given him any encouragement. Now he said, "Mel doesn't kiss you like that, does he?"

Christie's face flamed, and she snapped, "That's none of your business! Now, leave me alone, Dent!"

"Sure. Never force myself on a woman." Dent spoke the truth, for there were enough women to satisfy him who didn't fight. He accompanied her out to the wagon, and when they were halfway back to the peanut fields, he said impassively, "Sorry if I acted wrong, Christie. But a man needs a woman—and a woman needs a man." When she didn't answer, he urged, "Don't you think so, Christie? I mean—it's the way God made us, ain't it?"

"That . . . that's for married people!"

Her answer intrigued the young man, and he thought of it as the mules plodded along, their hooves lifting small clouds of dust. The sun was hot, and the sky was decked with thin streamers of clouds. He studied them for a time, then turned to her, curiosity in his eyes. "But don't you *like* being kissed? I mean, there ain't no *magic* in a wedding, Christie. A man and a woman, they got their cravings *before* they stand up before a preacher, don't they?"

"I don't want to talk about it, Dent. It's not proper."

DeForge was young, but he had learned a great deal about

women. They had been, more or less, the major study of his life since he had passed his middle teens. He had seen all kinds of girls and now quickly categorized Christie: *She's afraid of men, I reckon. Seen a few like that. Never seen one this good-lookin' who was so skeered though.* He cut his eyes around, admiring the firm lines of Christie's body and noting the smooth texture of her skin. *But somehow I think she's about as skeered of herself as she is of men. I got the feelin' when I was kissin' her that she really wanted to let go—but was afraid of what she might do if she cut loose.*

And then they were back beside the thresher. DeForge reached up to help Christie down, but she ignored his hand, stepping to the ground herself. This little action was noted by Lenora, and when Christie had helped unload the sacks and came to bring her some fresh water, she asked abruptly, "Dent try to get you, Christie?" And when Christie stared at her with a reddened face, she said, "Don't be embarrassed. That's the way he is, you know." She took a sip of the cool water, then lowered the glass. "Did he kiss you?"

"Yes—but I fought him off!"

"He's a fine-looking fellow. Did you enjoy it?"

"No!"

Lenora lifted her eyebrows. "Why are you so mad? Don't you enjoy flirting a little?"

"Lenora!" Christie was shocked. "I can't believe you'd take up for him."

"He's a fine young man—a little wild, of course. But God will take care of him pretty soon."

"He drinks, and he . . . he's been with every floozie in the county!"

Lenora unknowingly echoed Dent's words. "He's a man, Christie. A hot-blooded young man, true, but he'll make a good husband when God gets through with him." She was troubled by the incident and not for the first time felt that there was something not quite normal about the way Christie stood aloof from men. She had tried to get the younger woman to talk, but there was a wall between the two—at least on this one subject. *She's not going to be happy with Tolliver.* The thought touched her, as it had before, and she began to pray as Christie went back to work. *Lord, give her whatever love she needs, because she's headed for some kind of bitterness if she doesn't have it!*

"Wish we had time to make a brush arbor," Will said regretfully. He had appeared in a clean pair of overalls and a white shirt that Christie had pressed carefully for him, and now as he lifted Lenora into the wagon, he shook his head, adding, "Don't seem like a *real* meet'n just having preaching at night."

He put the wheelchair into the bed of the wagon, took his seat between Lenora and Christie, and when he spoke to the horses, sending them into a brisk trot, he added, "It's pretty hot, but I like a meet'n to go all day. This once a night—why, it just won't hardly do."

Lenora thought of all the years her father had refused to go to church and now leaned over and squeezed his arm. "I'd like it, too, Pa, but God will use what we have. Brother McGee is a fine evangelist. There's already been eleven saved—and lots of stumps blasted."

"You're right, Daughter, and I'm grateful for what God's done." He thought of his wife and was saddened by the knowledge that she had no use for religion—not in any form. He'd tried to get her to attend, but she'd refused. Now he shook off the thought and said, "You're right about that young preacher—he is a man of God."

They arrived at the church a little late. By the time Lenora had been placed in her chair, they could hear the choir singing a familiar old song:

I will arise and go to Jesus,
He will embrace me in His arms;
In the arms of my dear Savior,
Oh, there are ten thousand charms.

The three of them made their way into the crowded church, and Will pushed Lenora's chair right past the platform as the choir leader gave them a welcome smile. The Stuarts were the backbone of brother Ed Sanders's small choir, and as soon as they joined in, he sighed with relief. Will was an accomplished musician with a fine tenor voice. Lenora sang a clear alto, and Christie had a strong, vibrant soprano.

At the end of the song, Sanders said, "We'll be favored with a song from Sister Lenora." He nodded at Lenora, and when Will moved to the piano and struck a chord, she lifted her head and began to sing:

Life is like a mountain railway,
With an engineer that's brave;
You must make the road successful
From the cradle to the grave.
Watch the turns, the grades, the tunnels,
Never falter, never fail—
Keep your hand upon the throttle
And your eye upon the rail . . .

There were many amens and at Sanders's request, she sang another—this one about heaven.

Oh, think of the home over there
Beyond the portals of light
Where the saints all immortal and fair
Are robed in their garments of white . . .

Her rich alto filled the church, and her face was suffused with such joy that many in the congregation began to pull out handkerchiefs. When the song was ended, the minister stood up and said, "It's a glorious thing to be blessed with such a voice as this dear sister—but it is far more wonderful to be blessed with the Spirit of the Lord that flows out of her. Let

us thank God for our blessings and ask him to save every man,
woman, boy, or girl in this building who know not Jesus Christ
as Savior!"

The service was long, but the preacher was inspired. He
preached on a short text, "In him there is life," and for over
an hour he moved through the Bible, reading verse after
verse that pointed to Jesus Christ as the source of all life. He
was a strongly built man of thirty with pale blue eyes and a
shock of dark brown hair. His voice was clear, and his manner was proof that he believed what he was saying with all
his heart.

When he came to the end, he said, "Who in this building
wants life—not just existence, for animals have that! But who
wants the best, the finest, the most exciting life that a human
being can have? I know the pleasures of the world are strong,
but they pass like the grass of the field! But Jesus is the same,
always the same. In him is life, and you will either live in him,
or you will die. Some of you have been dead for years, filling
your life with empty pleasures, but you're not satisfied, are
you? When you're alone, there's an emptiness in you that
nothing has been able to fill."

As the minister spoke his urgent plea, Lenora's eyes were
fixed on the face of Denton DeForge. True to his word, he
had come and managed to find a seat in the very back. He
had been uncomfortable at first and, as the preacher had read
the Scripture and preached the gospel, he had dropped his
head. More than once he'd made a move as though he intended to rise and flee, but he had not.

Now the choir began to sing,

Come home, come home,
Ye who are weary come home.
Softly and tenderly Jesus is calling,
Calling, "Oh, sinner, come home."

Two young women rose at once, coming to fall at the altar,

weeping audibly. They were followed by others, and soon the minister and the deacons were praying with those who came. But Lenora saw that Denton was gripping the back of the pine bench in front of him. His face was pale, and his features twisted in what seemed to be agony.

Go to him!

The words came to Lenora's spirit as clearly as if they'd been spoken aloud. At once she put down her hymnbook and wheeled her way from where the choir stood singing. She had to thread her way through the congregation, but she managed to get to the aisle. Every eye was on her as she rolled the chair to the last seat. She stopped and looked up at young DeForge, who was trembling. "Denton, Jesus loves you," she said quietly.

At those simple words, tears flooded the eyes of the young man. He put out his hand, groping for hers, and when she grasped it, he stepped out into the aisle. The two made their way forward, and as he knelt, she began to pray, holding his hand with both of hers. "Denton's coming home, Father," she said softly, and there was a great victory in her face. "Receive him as your beloved child."

Christie had been touched by the conversion of young Dent DeForge. After the revival she seemed thoughtful, more so than usual. She had gone about her work with her usual thoroughness, but both her father and Lenora recognized that she was troubled.

"I think she's worried about getting married and leaving me, Pa," Lenora said one evening. Mel Tolliver had come to take Christie to a pie social, and Will and Lenora were alone on the front porch. Lightning bugs were making their tiny flecks of yellow fire in the darkness, and the crickets made their monotonous chant, broken at intervals by the hoarse bellow of a bullfrog.

"Appears that might be, Daughter." Will rocked steadily for a time, then said, "I don't feel good about her marryin'

Mel." He had spoken of this to Lenora before, and now he shook his head sadly. "She ain't happy, Lenora. A girl about to get married ought to be happy, shouldn't she?"

"I think so, Pa."

The two of them sat on the porch letting the stillness flow over them. They spoke of the family, mostly of the letter from Amos. He'd expressed his concern for his son Jerry. They'd gotten a letter from Gavin the previous day in which he'd said, "I'm worried about Jerry. He's running with a wild young woman, and he's drinking. I can't talk to him. He's stubborn as a mule!"

"Jerry's in poor shape," Will said. He went on to speak of how his own boys had some problems, then they went inside to avoid the whining mosquitoes. Two hours later Christie came in, and they both saw at once that there was something disturbing her. Her face was flushed, and she spoke in a high unnatural voice.

"Pa—and you, too, Lenora," she said abruptly. "I've got something to ask you." She bit her lips nervously, then seemed to stiffen her back. "Mel thinks it might be good for me to work some. And he's got a job for me."

"Work? Why, you work all the time, Christie," her father said in surprise. "What sorta job is Mel talkin' about?"

"He thinks after we're married that I could help him with the hardware store, doing some of the book work. And he asked Mr. Stevenson if he'd let me work for him—and he said yes."

"Clyde Stevenson over at Mountain View—runs the general store?" Will asked.

"Yes. I could still live at home. It would only be part-time, Pa. I could learn how to keep books, and I could make some money to help out at home."

"Don't need to do that," Will protested. "But if it's what you want to do, it might be good."

Lenora had thought rapidly, and now she said, "It might

be better if you get some experience, Christie. Do you really want to do it?"

"I . . . I think I do. But can you get along without me?"

Both her father and her sister made it clear that they could, and finally Christie said, "Well, I'll do it then. It'll be nice to be able to help with the hardware store."

The following day Christie hitched the buggy and drove to Mountain View. She returned that afternoon saying that she liked the work and that Mr. Stevenson was a nice man. She added with less certainty, "His wife is a little sharp, but I won't see her too much, I don't guess."

Three weeks passed, and Christie went to her job three days each week. She said little of her work to her father or Lenora, but both of them discerned that Mrs. Stevenson was hard to deal with. One night at supper, Lenora asked her pointedly, "Is Mrs. Stevenson giving you a hard time, Christie?"

"Well, she's older than her husband," Christie said. "She's very jealous of any woman her husband sees. That's what everyone says. But I won't be there too long—and I'm learning a lot about how to keep books."

Lenora studied her younger sister, saying no more of the matter. But, after they were finished and were drinking coffee, Lenora said suddenly, "I've got an announcement to make." When they looked up at her with surprise, she said, "I've been accepted in the Salvation Army." She laughed at their stunned expressions, and she then reached over and patted her father's hand. "You know I've always wanted to be a missionary. Well, I won't be going to Africa, but I'll be going someplace that's even more in need of the gospel."

"Where's that?" Will demanded.

"Chicago," Lenora said. "Here, let me read you the letter from Major Hastings—he's in charge of the Army there." She pulled a letter from her pocket and read aloud. It said that she had been accepted and would begin her service by the first of the new year. Folding the letter, she returned it to her pocket, then laughed aloud at the expressions on their faces.

"For once I've shocked you," she said, then grew serious. "I've been writing to Major Hastings for several weeks. And it's of God, my going there. I've been fasting and praying, and I know God wants me to go serve him."

"But who'll take care of you?" Christie blurted out.

"God will take care of me, as he always has."

"But you've never been away from home in your life, Lenora!" Will Stuart was as shocked as a man could be. He'd pondered over what Lenora would do with herself—but never once had a thing like this occurred to him. "What kinda out-fit is this Salvation Army?" he demanded.

"It was founded by William Booth over in England, Pa," Lenora said. "He wanted to reach poor people with the gospel. And that's what it does. Oh, it takes care of people who are down and out, but basically it tries to get people saved."

For the rest of the evening, until nearly ten, Lenora spoke of how the Army was the most powerful force for evangelism in the world. Finally she took a deep breath, and a beautiful smile touched her lips.

"And God's going to let me be a part of it! Isn't that won-derful, Pa?"

Will felt a sudden surge of gratitude to God. *He's done this for her—given her what she wanted more than anything else!* And then he went to her and put his arms around her.

"I always thought you'd be a missionary, Daughter, but I thought it'd be in China or some other far-off place. I'm proud of you!"

"Christie, why don't you come with me when I go—just for a visit?"

"When are you leaving?"

"Oh, not until the first of the year. But when I go, I'd like for us to go together." The thought had been with her that if Christie saw Chicago, she might be persuaded to stay for a long visit—and she might meet someone who would cause her to change her mind about marrying Mel. She said none of this, however, but left the door open. "We'll see when it's time, Christie," Lenora said.

"All right—but I don't think so. Mel wants to get married before then." She did not see the look that her father and sister exchanged, but there was a thoughtful look on her face that revealed her interest in such a trip.

8

JERRY TAKES A WALK

T he biplane dived out of the cumulus cloud, leaving a cool moisture on Jerry's face. For some reason he thought, *It's the tenth of May—Uncle Pete's birthday.* There was no reason for him to think of that, but he had discovered that when he was about to do a jump or a stunt of any kind, random thoughts seemed to race through his mind. He'd been with the show long enough to get most of the stunts down, the nonflying ones, of course. Gavin had finally admitted that he was getting good enough at flying to even do a few of those—something he longed for desperately.

Leaning out of the front of the cockpit, he saw Tony Pasco's ship. He could even make out the brilliant green scarf that Cara wore. A thump came from behind, and he looked around to see Gavin give him a nod. He climbed out of the cockpit thinking of how scared he'd been the first time he'd performed this stunt. Now it was just another job. He'd never been afraid of heights and had a veiled contempt for those who were. Another random thought flashed through his mind—more of an image, really. He saw a scene he'd thought of often. He was standing by a creek with Uncle Owen, and a cottonmouth appeared at his ankle. As always, time seemed to stand still, and he could see the snake's white mouth coming toward his bare leg. He could not seem to move, but Owen had stooped down and grabbed the snake by the tail and sent it sailing through the air.

I never teased Uncle Owen about being afraid of high places after that, Jerry thought as he placed his feet on the footwalk that covered the fabric where the lower wing joined the fuselage. *I wouldn't touch a snake for a million dollars—and he tossed it like it was a piece of rope!*

He made his way down until he could sit comfortably on the spreader bar between the landing wheels. Ignoring the ground that lay spread out like a large quilt a thousand feet below, he pulled rosin from his side pocket, took a pinch, and applied it to his hands. He felt the Standard dip as Gavin closed the gap between the two planes, and now he was close enough to see Cara grinning at him as she stood on the upper wing.

Jerry swung down and hung by his knees, as unconcerned as if he were hanging five feet from the earth. Upside down, he saw Cara coming toward him and held his hands down. The ships moved slowly together, and Cara stretched her arms high. Their fingertips touched, and just as they swept by the stands, their hands slapped firmly, Jerry's hands closing like vises on Cara's slender wrists.

As Pasco's plane fell away, Jerry pulled Cara up until her face was inches away from his.

"Hi, good-looking," he said. "How about some loving?"

Cara's upside-down face grinned. "I prefer sailors," she said, "but I don't see any around here." She kissed him, their noses bumping, and then they both giggled wildly. As Jerry pulled her up, she lifted one hand and quickly grasped the spar, then pulled herself to sit on it. When Jerry came swinging up to sit beside her, he put his arm around her, and they kissed again. She pulled back finally, gasping, "You can pick the most interesting places to kiss me!"

"Any place is interesting with you," Jerry teased. "Why don't we do a double parachute jump and kiss all the way down?"

"You're crazy!"

Cara climbed up the side of the plane and crawled into the cockpit. Soon Jerry plopped down beside her. Gavin brought the plane in, and the two piled out. Gavin cut the engine, but he didn't get out at once. He was watching the pair as they crossed the field, holding tightly to one another.

I don't like it, he thought grimly. *They're going to get killed fooling around. Neither of them has a lick of sense!*

He climbed out of the Standard and went through the tedious procedure of wrapping up the show and making all the decisions for the following day. When he left the field he was tired to the bone, and the steps that led up to the room he and Heather had rented seemed two feet high.

Heather met him as he entered, noting the fatigue that etched small lines across his face. She took his kiss, held him tightly for a moment, then said, "You go take a good hot bath. I've got a surprise for supper."

"I may fall asleep and drown."

"Go on," she smiled. "Be sure you wash behind your ears."

"Us Arkansas hillbillies never wash that part," he grinned. He went at once to the bathroom, stripped off his dirty clothes, and soaked in water as hot as he could stand it for twenty minutes. It took an effort to get out of the tub, and he wanted nothing so much as to go to bed. "Getting old," he muttered, pulling on a clean undershirt. "I can remember when I'd put in a day plowing behind a blue-nosed mule from sunup till dark, then ride twenty miles and dance until dawn."

When he came out of the bedroom, Heather said, "Sit down. You've always wanted me to call you Lord Gavin and treat you like a king—well, this is your night, Lord Gavin!"

As he slipped his legs under the small oak dining table, Gavin grinned. "You must want something to be this nice to me."

"No, I'm just naturally sweet and thoughtful."

"All you English people think that about yourselves."

"And you Americans love us for it."

The table was set with fine china, for no matter how much they traveled, Heather insisted on eating like nobility. "I don't care so much what's on the plate," she often said, "but I will *not* eat on one of those awful plates!"

Now Gavin leaned back and looked over the fine white linen cloth with matching napkins, the sparkling crystal glasses, the heavy silver service, and nodded. "It does make a difference. I guess you've made an English snob out of me."

"You're a very nice snob," Heather nodded firmly as she brought a silver tureen and set it on the table. "Mock turtle soup," she said. "And the rest of the menu includes chops and shepherd's pie." She sat down, and as they bowed their heads, Gavin asked the blessing. He had been converted while serving as a fighter pilot in France, and since their marriage they had grown very close to God.

Heather filled his bowl with soup, and as he ate, she asked, "Did things go well today?"

"A good crowd," he nodded. "But we're going to have to spend some money on aircraft. The Standard has about done its duty."

They talked as they ate leisurely, and finally Heather asked, "Is something wrong, dear?"

Gavin glanced up quickly, a smile pulling at his wide mouth. "I might as well be married to a private detective," he said. "You know too much about me."

"What is it?"

"Well, it's Jerry." He toyed with his teacup, stared down into it, then lifted troubled eyes to her. "It's Cara," he said finally.

Heather nodded slowly. They had talked of this before, but now she saw that Gavin was more troubled than he had been earlier. "They're having an affair, I take it."

"You know Cara," Gavin shrugged. "She has the morals of an alley cat. Makes no secret of it."

"What about Jerry?"

"Oh, he's flattered, of course. What young man wouldn't be? She's beautiful, famous in a way—and Jerry's had no experience with her kind."

"Have you talked to him?"

"About Cara? Sure. Might as well be talking into the wind."

"Do you think Amos knows?"

"I don't know. Think I ought to tell him?"

Heather was a thoughtful woman, tactful and highly sensitive to the moods of people. She let the silence run on, then shook her head. "I don't think so. That would make you a snitch—and nobody likes one of those. Jerry would never trust you again."

"I can't let it go on much longer," Gavin said heavily. "The affair—well, they would say it's their business. But up in the air flying like we do, everyone has to have his mind on the job—all the time. Just one careless slip, and somebody gets killed."

"Yes, I know."

Gavin saw that his words had struck Heather, and he regretted them. "I'm very careful, and so is the rest of the team. But Jerry's cocky, and Cara's crazy. That's a bad combination." He leaned back in his chair, thinking hard. Finally he nodded, "I'll have to talk to him."

"What will you say, Gavin?"

"That who he beds down with is his business—but if it affects his performance, I'll have to let him go!"

"He'll listen to you, I'm sure," Heather said quickly. "He really loves you, Gavin—and he respects you."

Heather knew Gavin was very troubled, so she gave him an engaging smile. Gavin's worry about the show evaporated. He came up out of his seat, pulled her up, and held her tightly.

He kissed her, and she gave herself to his embrace, happy that she was able to provide the love and assurance this man of hers needed. As they moved toward the bedroom, she thought, *I hope Jerry has more sense than to trade in what he values most for what he can get from that little tramp!*

Jerry came into the hangar, his head aching and his mouth dry. He moved to the locker that held his flying suit and began to pull off his shirt. The door opened, and Gavin walked in. "Oh, hi, Gavin," Jerry mumbled. Yanking off the shirt, he threw it into the bottom of the locker. As he pulled on a fresh one, he glanced up to catch a quick expression on Gavin's face. "Something wrong?" he asked.

"What time did you get to bed last night—or this morning?"

Jerry blinked his eyes in surprise and licked his lips. Gavin usually wore a pleasant expression, but now he was stern and forbidding. "Why, I don't know exactly—"

"It was exactly 4:30," Gavin snapped.

Jerry reddened. He had gone with Cara to a series of jazz joints, and they had drunk far too much. He remembered vaguely getting stopped by a policeman and being warned that if he got stopped again, it'd be jail. He had taken Cara to her hotel, then stumbled into his room and fallen across the bed fully dressed. "Did that two-bit clerk tip you off?" he demanded angrily.

"Doesn't matter *how* I found out, what counts is that you're not fit to go up today."

Jerry glared at Gavin angrily. "That's not so!"

"You think so?" Gavin demanded. "Your reflexes are all right?"

"Sure!"

"Let's see if they are."

Gavin put his hands out, palms up. Jerry stared at them, then put his own hands, palms down, on Gavin's. It was a game they often played. The one who had his hands on the bottom tried to jerk them out and slap the hands of the other. If he connected, he got another try, and if he missed, it was the other's turn to try and slap him. Jerry enjoyed the game, for he usually won—even with Gavin. His reflexes were amazingly fast, and he had no trouble winning over and over.

"All right," he said defiantly, with his hands over Gavin's. He waited for the twitch of Gavin's hands, for that was the signal to jerk his own away. He grinned despite his headache, for he knew he was much faster than Gavin. *I'll give him a few extra-hard slaps just to teach him to show more respect for his nephew,* he thought.

Then Gavin's hands moved, and Jerry yanked his own—but Gavin's hands came down on his with a loud slapping noise. Jerry stopped grinning, for Gavin had slapped him so hard that the back of one hand was red. Angrily he put his hands back over Gavin's, who was staring at him, and said, "Go on, try it!"

But before he could finish, Gavin had slapped his hands again with a stinging blow. Jerry winced but then gritted his teeth. He carefully put his hands back and for the next three minutes endured the shame of having Gavin slap his hands repeatedly. He cursed the drinking that had robbed him of his coordination, and he desperately tried to anticipate the lightning blows that Gavin rained on him.

Finally Gavin said, "Want to tell me again how great your reflexes are?"

Gavin's sarcasm caused Jerry to flush. "I may not be at my best—"

"Best? You're moving like you're underwater, Jerry!" Gavin shook his head, his eyes filled with anger. "How many times have you heard me say that when you go up, you need all the stuff you've got? If you don't care anything about yourself, you ought to care about the people who trust you."

Jerry stood there, miserably aware that Gavin was right. But something in him rebelled, and he finally blurted out, "You're not my father, Gavin. I took enough of this when I was living at home!"

"You should have listened to him!" Gavin snapped.

"I can take care of myself!"

Gavin had braced himself for this, had dreaded it. Now he knew he had no choice. "No need getting dressed, Jerry. You're grounded."

"Gavin—you can't do that to me!"

"You did it to yourself, Jerry."

"Look, I'm a little slow, but—"

"You're not going up until you prove that your job is better than getting drunk and rolling in the dirt with Cara."

Jerry's face flamed, and he dropped his head. Silence fell over the room, and finally he forced himself to ask, "Am I fired?"

"No, you're grounded. Help Al take care of the planes. When you prove to me you're serious, we'll talk again."

Gavin turned and walked out of the room, leaving Jerry to stare at the door. He stood there for a moment, then turned and rammed his fist against the steel door of the locker. He wanted to walk out, but he knew he had to fly. Slowly he put on old coveralls, shut the door, and went out to help Al service the planes. He knew the jibes he'd take from Cara, but he had no choice. He muttered to himself as he walked slowly toward the planes, *All right, Gavin, all right. I've got to do what you say. But someday I'll show you something! I'll make you and everybody else see that I'm the best!*

Jerry stayed grounded only for a week, but that seemed like an eternity. Every time a plane took off, his heart went with it.

All summer long he labored, determined to show Gavin that he was to be trusted. Cara taunted him, for though he still went out dancing with her, he was careful to be in at an early hour, and he drank very little. "You're no man!" she jibed time and again, but Jerry knew he had no chance to learn to fly unless he met Gavin's terms.

After that first week, Gavin came to him as he was washing down one of the planes. He put out his hands, saying, "All right, let's see about this."

Jerry at once put his hands on top of Gavin's, and there was no contest. Gavin was far too slow for him, and when it was Jerry's turn to try to hit the tops of his uncle's hands, he slapped them sharply five times in a row.

"All right, get ready to fly."

Jerry swallowed, nodded, and ran to get ready. He knew that Gavin was watching him like a hawk, and for weeks he did exactly as Gavin demanded. Finally he saw that he had

won back the ground he'd lost—or most of it. He flew with
Gavin constantly, learning the skills that a first-rate pilot had
to master, and he was grateful for the chance to learn from
such a man.

Still, there was a sharp-edged memory of the humiliation
he'd endured, and he determined to prove to Gavin that he
was able to fly as well as most, or even better.

One day in St. Louis, he came in feeling reckless. He was
touchy, for Cara had stood him up. When she came over to
the plane, he demanded, "Where were you last night?"

She looked up at him defiantly. "I had a date with Red Toffler." Toffler was a pilot who flew with another air circus. Cara
had mentioned his name more than once, and Jerry suspected
the two of them had been lovers. Now he saw that she was
waiting for him to begin a quarrel. It was, he discovered, the
sort of thing Cara liked—to get men into fights for her favors.

If he had been older or wiser, he would have dropped the
matter, but instead he said bitterly, "He's too old for you."

"He's not a mama's boy. We had a good time—like we used
to have, Jerry, before you joined the choir."

"You know I can't go carousing all night! Gavin would fire
me!"

"If you want me, Jerry, come along. If not, let's hang it up."

Indecision broke through, and Jerry stared down at her cur-
vaceous body. He knew he was weak and despised himself
for it, but it seemed she had some sort of power to make him
follow her. "All right, we'll go out tonight—but we'll have to
be sure Gavin doesn't find out."

A smile came to her red lips instantly. She pressed herself
against him and whispered, "There's my Jerry!" Then she
was gone, leaving him to wonder how he could pull it off.

He finished the show, then said to Gavin, "I'd like to look
around St. Louis. Want to come along?"

"I've seen it, Jerry. You go on."

"Sure. Oh, I'll probably be late. Maybe I'll get a room

downtown—but I'll be back in time to go over the program with you at the field."

"All right. Have a good time, Jerry."

Elated by his easy success, Jerry left at once. He met Cara at a bar they'd agreed on, and they launched themselves into a night of wild revelry. Cara had been in St. Louis before and knew all the speakeasies.

By the time they got to Madge's Place, Jerry was fairly well drunk. It was a Negro club on the fringe of the city. The two of them walked down a flight of stairs and passed into a room so low-ceilinged that Jerry felt the roof was falling in. As soon as they sat down, the waiter whispered, "Keep your bottle in your pocket, don't put it on the floor."

"This is a high class joint," Cara laughed. She was wearing a dress with a hem so high that when she crossed her legs her undergarments were visible. "Come on, let's dance," she demanded.

They moved around the crowded dance floor, the smell of perfume, whiskey, and sweat forming a canopy over the room. When they sat down, Jerry felt slightly sick. He had been off liquor most of the summer, and it hit him hard.

"Look—that's the one we came to hear," Cara said. Jerry followed her gesture to see a rotund black man sit down at the piano. "That's Fats Waller!"

The name meant nothing to Jerry, who had to excuse himself. He threw up in the men's room and wanted to leave, but Cara was taken with the singing of Waller. She kept demanding whiskey, and when they finally left the club it was after three in the morning. They made their way, moving drunkenly to a cab that deposited them in front of a dilapidated hotel. Jerry made it to the room, but as soon as he was inside, he fell on the bed and passed out.

When he awoke, the light was streaming in through the dirty window. He groaned, looked around, and saw no sign of Cara. He came to his feet, stopping to let the pains in his head

subside. Then he looked at his watch—and the room seemed
to sway.

"Twelve-thirty!" he gasped. Knowing he had to be at the
field by one, he ran down the stairs, paid his bill, caught a taxi,
and urged the driver to break the law getting him to the field.
When he got out, he shoved some bills into the driver's hands
and ran to the hangar. His head was throbbing, and he knew
if Gavin saw him, he was lost.

He managed to get into the hangar, which was empty. Outside he heard the planes revving up. Frantically he donned
his flying clothes and raced out on the field. He saw Gavin
and went up to him, saying, "Sorry to be late—"

Gavin took in the red-rimmed eyes and caught the smell
of whiskey. He shook his head sadly. "You never learn, do
you?" he murmured.

"I'm all right!"

Gavin put his hands out, palms up. "Let's see if you are."

Jerry blinked but knew he had no choice. He tried hard,
but Gavin beat the backs of his hands five times, then said in
disgust, "Go put your overalls on, Jerry. I can't trust you in
the air. A man who can't keep a few rules on the ground can't
fly for me."

"I won't go back to being a janitor!"

"Then you'd better go someplace and grow up, Jerry,"
Gavin said. "I hate to do this. You've got more natural ability
than most men, but I can't let you fly. I could never face Amos
if you got killed flying drunk."

"I'm sacked?"

"Until you learn to give me your best, you're not flying."

Jerry stared at Gavin, then said, "All right—that's it!"

He moved away, collected his things, and left the hangar.
Later that day he found Cara and told her the story.

"What are you going to do, Honey?" she asked.

"I'm going to fly."

"Yeah, I think you will. You've got it in your blood." Then

a soft light came into her eyes. She put her hands on his face, saying, "I'm sorry about this, Jerry. It was all my fault!"

He looked at her quickly and saw that the hard look was gone. Cara looked tired, and he said quickly, "Nobody made me do anything, Cara." He tried to speak with assurance, adding, "Look, I'll get a job flying with somebody else. And you know we've always talked about getting an act together? Well, we'll do it! And we'll make Father Gavin take notice!"

Cara bit her lip, then brightened. "I've got an offer to do a distance flight. Going to fly across the ocean or something. It'll mean big money, and maybe I'll get enough attention to get into the movies or something."

"Hey, that's great!" Jerry managed a smile and kissed her. "You go do your flying, and I'll think about our act. Hey, my aunt's in the movies. Maybe we can get parts as fliers!"

They talked for a time, then Jerry said, "Well, I'll be seeing you, Cara. Don't forget me."

And then she was gone. Jerry left St. Louis, buying a bus ticket to Detroit where he thought he could get a job with Bix Tolbert's Air Circus. It was a crummy outfit, but at least it would be flying! As the bus left the city, he looked up and saw a biplane skimming the clouds. It was Gavin, and Jerry whispered, "Well, Father Gavin, you old son-of-a-gun, I'll show you something one of these days!"

The plane dipped its wings, then soared up to disappear in the clouds. Jerry put his head back and dozed, thinking of what a fool he'd been. The bus lumbered over the potholes in the highway, swerving from time to time to dodge them. Finally he fell asleep and dreamed of being in the air, touching the clouds.

9

A JOB IN FORT SMITH

Amos arrived at the farm driving a large yellow car with an open top and a spare tire mounted in matching yellow on the rear. He sprang out and made a sweeping bow to the wide-eyed members of his family, grinning broadly.

"Here it is, your chariot to Chicago. How do you like it, Sis?"

Lenora rolled her chair forward until she could run her palm over the brightly painted metal. "Amos—is this yours?"

"Not likely," Amos laughed. "I'm just a lowly reporter. This is the pride and joy of my boss, Mr. Hearst. He's letting me use it now that he's sent me to Chicago to work on the *Examiner.* Rose and Maury like it, too."

"It ain't no Ford, is it, Amos?"

"Mr. Hearst wouldn't go to his own funeral in a Ford, Pa. This is a brand-new Pierce-Arrow two-passenger runabout." He spieled off the virtues of the car rapidly. "Got a six-cylinder dual-valve engine, a power-driven pump for inflating the tires, an inspection lamp, and a grease gun for greasing the running gear."

"How much does a thing like that cost?" Will demanded.

"A little over seven thousand dollars."

"Jumpin' Jehoshaphat!" Will Stuart exclaimed. "Why, you can buy a pretty fair farm for that much!"

"Don't guess William Randolph Hearst needs a farm," Amos grinned. Turning to Christie, he said, "I'd planned to get a bigger car, but when you said you couldn't come, I figured this would do me. Mr. Hearst said he didn't want any of his reporters looking shabby, so he insisted on my driving this little hummer."

"A little bit swanky for a Salvation Army lassie," Lenora smiled. "You'll have to let me out down the street so they won't think the queen of England's come to join the Army."

"Got some belated presents for all of you," Amos said. As he moved to the rear of the low-slung car and opened the trunk, he talked rapidly. "I had to get old 1921 out of the way and get the new year in. Stayed pretty busy—but better late than never." He piled packages into Lenora's lap, then loaded Will and Christie down with more. "Let's get inside," he said, "My hands are frozen solid. I wish they'd found a way to put a stove in this thing! Guess they will someday."

When they stepped inside the house, Amos looked around, asking, "Where's Agnes, Pa?"

"She's over at Rogers. She wanted to see her folks this Christmas."

Amos sat them down, and they all began opening the presents he had brought. He enjoyed the cries of joy from his sisters as they opened their gifts—mostly clothing that Rose had selected and wrapped. When his father opened a large box and stared at it, Amos said, "It's a wireless set, Pa. They're broadcasting ball games now. I think you'll be able to hear the Cardinal games from St. Louis."

Will ran his fingers over the smooth walnut sides of the case and said softly, "Son, I can't think of anything I'd of wanted more."

"Well, now you can catch up on some of this modern jazz the country's going mad about."

"Humph!" Will snorted. "I'd just as soon listen to a pack of wild monkeys as listen to that—that stuff!" He loved music, mountain music, but he hated the jazz movement fiercely. "But that would be *something* to hear a ball game." He shook his head sadly, adding, "I give up on baseball after the White Sox sold out the Series in 1919—but I guess a few bad apples

didn't spoil the whole barrel." He stroked the sides of the
radio, adding, "Gets a little lonesome out in these hills, Son.
Guess you know that. This here wireless will sort of bring the
world in, won't it, Christie?"

"Sure will, Pa." Christie had opened another large heavy
box and cried out when she saw the contents, "Oh, Amos, it's
a phonograph player!" She looked up at Amos with a brilliant
smile. "How did you know I wanted this?"

"Just a wild guess." Amos gave Lenora a sly wink, for she
had written him suggestions of what to get the family for presents. "And this is for you, Lenora—" He bent over and
opened a large box, then lifted out a typewriter. "Guess this
might help you do some of your correspondence when you
get to Chicago."

"Why, Amos, how nice!"

"And that's not all." He picked up a smaller package, and
when she opened it she stared at him in bewilderment. He
smiled. "I notice Salvation Army bands playing on the street.
Got this little gem for you so you could join the band."

Lenora took the shining brass trumpet out of the case and
held it reverently. She was very musical, as were all the Stuarts, and had learned to play a little on a trumpet that a neigh-
boring youth used in the high school band. Her eyes sparkled
as she lifted the trumpet to her lips, then made the room fairly
quake with a tremendous blast.

"Holy smoke!" Amos cried, putting his hands over his ears.
"I hope you don't toot that thing all the way back to Chicago!"
He looked around at the small mountain of gifts and said sud-
denly, "Wish all the family were here, Pa."

"Don't guess the room would hold 'em all now, Amos." He
looked sad for a moment, then managed a smile. "I'm about
to run out of young'uns—and now you go taking another one
off the farm."

"You've still got me, Pa," Christie said quickly. "And even
after I'm married, I'll just be over at Mountain View. I wish
you'd come and live there with Mel and me."

They all knew that their father would never leave the farm, and he said quietly, "No, guess I'll stay here. I wouldn't feel like myself anywhere except this place."

Amos knew how his father felt and said only, "Well, we've got to get an early start in the morning, Lenora."

"I'll be ready by sunup!"

Later that night Amos had a chance to talk with his father. "How's Christie doing, Pa? She still working in Mountain View?"

"Yup, she goes in three or four days a week."

"She likes it, does she?"

"Can't say, Amos." Will ran his hand over his hair, a puzzled look in his eyes. "She don't seem happy to me. Can't say she's not—but me and Lenora have been uneasy about her."

"You don't like Mel Tolliver, do you?"

"Nope."

"What's wrong with him, Pa?"

"Oh, he's got his good points, Amos. Works hard, got ambition—maybe too much of it. Seems like all he thinks about is having the biggest store in the state. Everything comes second to that."

"Not a very good prospect for Christie," Amos frowned. He had learned from their letters that his father and Lenora were not satisfied with Christie's engagement. "I wish she'd wait. I asked her to come and visit Rose and me in Chicago. She might find someone there."

"She's got her mind set, I reckon."

The next morning at dawn, Amos lifted Lenora into the car, then stepped back as his father and Christie came to kiss her. "Be sure to write," Christie begged, then she turned to hug Amos. "I wish you didn't have to go," she whispered.

Amos held her tightly as his father said his good-bye to Lenora and whispered, "Christie—don't go too fast, will you?"

Christie blinked back the tears, knowing instantly what he meant. She knew that none of her family approved of her engagement, but she had made up her mind. "I'll be fine, Amos," she said brightly.

Amos wanted to say more, but he knew it was useless. He got into the car and sent it out of the yard with a muffled roar. "Why do we all have to be so blasted stubborn, Lenora?" he said. "All stubborn as mules!"

"You mean Christie?"

"Yes. She shouldn't marry that fellow!"

The yellow Pierce-Arrow flew down the winding mountain road, a plume of white dust billowing up behind it. The cold wintry air leaked into the car, and the two inside wrapped in heavy robes to keep off the chill. As they sped along, Lenora said softly, "I've prayed for Christie, Amos—that God will keep her from making a ruin out of her life."

Amos thought about that, then shook his head. "God gave us the power to choose, Lenora. He even lets us choose the wrong way—as I well know from hard experience."

"Yes, he does. But I'm praying that God will do whatever he has to—even if it hurts Christie for a time." She snuggled down into the heavy wool coat, adding, "I'd rather Christie were hurt for a little while than to be miserable for a lifetime."

Fort Smith, Arkansas, was not overcrowded with private detectives. Lorene Stevenson knew practically everyone in town and finally failed to find even one of this species. She did, however, have an old acquaintance in Dallas, Nancy Henderson, who worked in a minor position in city government.

One afternoon Nancy opened a letter, noting that it was from Lorene. The two had kept in touch, seeing each other every two years when the Stevensons came to Dallas to visit Lorene's family. Prepared to read the usual boring sort of letter that Lorene wrote, Nancy read carelessly at first—then her eyes narrowed. Carefully she read the letter, then smiled bitterly. "So Lorene is ready to dump her hubby," she murmured. "I always knew it would come to that."

She thought about the letter from time to time as she

worked, and by the time she left the office she knew what to do. She got into her Ford and went to a seedy section of town. Parking the car, she entered a shabby two-story office building and climbed to the second floor. The corridor was dimly lighted, so she had to peer at the names until she found the one she sought: Ralph Vallentine. Opening the door she found herself in a tiny outer office with a small desk and several chairs. The door to another office stood open, and a heavy-set man with a crop of thick black hair turned from the window.

"Why, Nancy," he said, a smile creasing his rather thick lips. He came to her at once and squeezed her upper arms with his massive hands. "Been thinking about you," he said.

"I'll bet," Nancy said cynically. "My phone's been ringing off the hook." She drew away from his grip, saying coldly, "This is business, Ralph—get that straight."

Vallentine was an olive-skinned man with dark moody eyes and heavy jowls. He had been trim and handsome when the two of them had been lovers, but now he had gone to seed. "Business?" he asked. "I could use some. Sit down, Nancy." He waited until she sat down in one of the two chairs in front of his desk, then sat down on the edge of the desk looking down at her. *She still looks good,* he thought.

Nancy knew Vallentine well enough to read his thoughts, and she shook her head with distaste, "Business, Ralph—and that's all."

"Sure, sure," Vallentine nodded. "If you want to change the rules, let me know. We had some good times together, didn't we, Sweetheart?"

"Peachy. Now here's the job. I have an old friend who lives in the sticks of Arkansas. Her name is Lorene Stevenson. She's married to a wealthy man named Clyde Stevenson."

"Where'd he get his money?"

"Timber at first, and he owns several stores. He's got the money all right."

"And what's the play, Nancy?"

A rather cruel smile twisted Nancy's lips. "She always put me down because she married a rich man—and I didn't. Oh, not really mean, Ralph, but she never let me forget that she was in the money and I wasn't." Nancy pulled a cigarette case from her purse, extracted one, and leaned forward as Vallentine pulled out a lighter and held it. Blowing a plume of smoke into the air, she leaned back and studied the big man. "She wants out, Ralph."

"Dump the husband?"

"That's it."

Vallentine rose and went to sit in his chair. He'd been on the police force in Detroit until he was fired for taking kickbacks. Now he made ends meet by doing a little private investigating and doing whatever the big oilmen needed done. Some of it was illegal, and he was interested in any scheme that involved money.

"What's her problem?" he asked softly.

"The guy's a real straight arrow, Ralph. Goes to church, doesn't drink—and won't even look at another woman."

"She better hang on to him."

"That's what I thought—but she's going crazy in that hick town, and he won't move to the big city."

Vallentine leaned back, hunching his big shoulders together. "What's the law on divorce in Arkansas?"

Nancy blew a puff of smoke toward the ceiling. "You have to prove adultery," she said evenly.

"And the husband ain't going to give her that kind of grounds?"

"No, he's not. He's kind of a nice guy—but he's always been dull. Lorene says she's got to get out of the backwoods or she'll go crazy. But he won't give her money, and he's too clean for her to get a divorce."

Silence fell over the room. Vallentine looked over Nancy's head at a picture on the wall. It was an English hunting scene filled with dogs and horses crazy to jump over fences. He hated the picture and resolved for the hundredth time to throw it into the trash can. But his mind was working with the information Nancy had given him. He had no illusions about what the job would be, and he made up his mind at once.

"I got nothing big going here. How much will she pay?"

"She's got a thousand squirreled away—but she could pay big if she gets the kind of settlement she wants—maybe two, three thousand more."

Vallentine grinned. "Maybe if I could squeeze her after she gets the dough, me and you could take a trip to the coast, Nancy. Remember those warm nights down there?"

Nancy smiled suddenly. "You get the money and we'll talk about it, Ralph. But be careful. Those hicks sometimes can be pretty tough if they catch a city man fooling with them." She puffed on the cigarette, leaned back, and murmured, "Those were pretty good times, Ralph. I think about that white sand and blue water sometimes."

Vallentine came and put his heavy hand on her shoulder, caressing it. "We'll be there before you know it, Sweetheart!"

Christie had never liked the idea of going to the Stevenson home to work on the books, but Clyde had several ventures and had made himself an office in a small room off the back of the house. As they approached the house, she listened as her employer explained how the new bookkeeping system would work.

"The old system was all right when I had just two or three operations," Stevenson shrugged as he drove down the road that went by his house, "but I've got so many things going now, Christie, that we've got to step things up."

"I'm not sure I can do it, Mr. Stevenson," Christie said nervously. "Don't you think you ought to get a regular bookkeeper to do the changeover?"

"No, you and I can handle it."

Stevenson was a good businessman and a good husband—but his wife was difficult. The one time Stevenson had

brought Christie to his home—just to get some papers—
Lorene Stevenson had been insolent to her. And now as they
pulled into the driveway to the big house that lay far back off
the main road, Christie dreaded the visit. She had tried to get
out of it, but Stevenson had insisted.

He stopped the car, got out, and came to open the door for
her. "We'll work for awhile, and then Lorene will fix us something to eat."

The two went inside, and Lorene came to meet them. She
was wearing a pink organdy dress trimmed in matching velvet ribbons on the skirt and poufed sleeves. To Christie's surprise, Lorene greeted her rather warmly. "Good to see you
again, Miss Stuart." She turned to her husband, saying, "I let
the servants go for the day, Clyde. But I'll have a good meal
when you two are ready."

"Why, that's wonderful, Lorene!" Stevenson went to his
wife and kissed her, then said, "We'll be in the office. Call us
when dinner's ready."

"I will. You two work up an appetite."

Christie followed Stevenson to the office, and the two of
them went to work at once. The room grew cold, and he made
a fire in the wood-burning stove. Christie felt the pressure of
learning the new method, but Stevenson went over it slowly
and methodically.

Finally they looked up to see Lorene put her head in.
"Dinner's ready," she said. As the two rose and followed her,
she seemed nervous, Christie thought. She talked rapidly in
an artificial voice, and her hands fluttered as she sat them
down.

"Looks good," Stevenson nodded. "You cook all this
yourself?"

"Not the roast. Millie did that—but I did the rest of it. And
I got a bottle of that wine you like so much, Clyde."

"Fine!"

The meal went well enough, though Christie felt ill at ease.
She ate enough of the roast and vegetables to satisfy appear-

ances and commented on how good it was to Mrs. Stevenson. She noted again how nervous her employer's wife seemed to be and was puzzled. *Why would she care what I think? She's used to entertaining lots of people.*

But Clyde did not appear to notice his wife's nervousness. He ate a huge meal and drank liberally from the bottle of wine that sat beside him. "Better try some of this, Miss Stuart," he urged.

"No, I'd rather not," Christie said quickly.

"Oh, you must!" Mrs. Stevenson urged. "I can't drink it myself, but you must try it."

But all her urging was to no avail, and Christie saw that she was angry. "I just don't drink—not ever, Mrs. Stevenson," Christie finally explained. "You'll just have to excuse me."

The apology did not seem to soothe the woman, and after the meal, she said, "Well, you might as well finish the bottle, Clyde."

But Stevenson shook his head. "I guess I've had enough," he said, a queer look on his face. "Matter of fact—I think I've had *too* much. Didn't ever get woozy with this stuff before!"

"Do you feel bad, dear?" Lorene gave her husband a sudden look. "There's some sort of flu going around. I hope you're not getting that."

"No, no! I'm just dizzy and a bit warm. Too much wine."

"Go lie down while Miss Stuart and I do the dishes. You'll feel better."

"Guess maybe I better."

As Stevenson, removing his shirt, moved slowly out of the dining room, Christie said, "Let me do the dishes, Mrs. Stevenson. I don't mind."

"Well, if you don't mind. I have to go check on my greenhouse. The temperature's dropping, and I wouldn't want to lose any of my flowers."

"Glad to have something to do," Christie said reassuringly. "Just show me where the dishes go."

For the next thirty minutes Christie cleaned the table and

washed the dishes. She once thought she heard a voice calling, but when she listened carefully, she didn't hear it again.
She was just putting the glasses back on the shelf when she
heard a car start, then leave the driveway. *Who could that be?*
she wondered. She ran from the kitchen to look out of the
front window. But darkness had fallen, and she saw only the
twin red taillights disappearing into the night.

The front door opened and she turned, expecting to see
Mrs. Stevenson, but she found herself looking at a burly man
wearing a dark suit and a fedora. Christie had never seen him
before and asked, "Do you want to see Mr. Stevenson?"

"I guess so, girlie."

Something about the big man was threatening, and Christie
said hastily, "He's lying down—but Mrs. Stevenson is in the
greenhouse—"

She broke off, for the big man came toward her, moving
deliberately. "What do you want?" she demanded, fear now
threading her voice.

"I got a job to do, girlie," he said. "It's not a nice job, but
you can make it easy—or hard."

"What . . . what do you want?" Christie asked again. She
tried to turn and run, but he moved swiftly, capturing her arm
with a terrible strength. "Let me go!" she cried. "I'll scream!"

"Won't do you any good. Come on—"

Christie did scream, but she knew it was hopeless. She
tried to fight, but the grip on her arm was paralyzing. When
the intruder pulled her down the hall, she cried, "Mr.
Stevenson—"

But then she was taken into the bedroom and saw that
Clyde Stevenson was stretched face down across the bed.
"He's out," the man said. A tough grin crossed his lips, and
he shook his head. "Too much wine, I guess."

Christie's mind was reeling, and she stared down at the still
figure of her employer. "Is he . . . dead?"

"Dead? Why, no, he's just drugged." He looked down at

her and said, "Look, I'm not gonna' hurt you, girlie. But I've got a job to do. Make it easy on yourself, why don't you?"

"What kind of a . . . job?"

"I've got to get you drunk—and then get some pictures of you." He nodded at the helpless form of Stevenson, adding, "Got to get shots of the two of you in bed."

Revulsion came to Christie, and she understood at once what was happening. "You'll never get away with it. Even with a picture!"

"Oh, I guess I will. You see, Mrs. Stevenson, she ain't been here. She's gone to see a friend way across town. The friend will swear to that. So you and Stevenson came to the house for some loving. Happens all the time! Now, pretty soon there's going to be some people coming to take pictures. But you've got to be drinking to make it look good. Now—drink this down."

Christie stared at the dark bottle the man produced with his free hand. "I won't do it!"

"Sure, you will—one way or another." He suddenly released her arm, caught the back of her neck and after pulling the cork free with his teeth, forced the bottle between her teeth.

Christie gagged and fought but had no chance at all. The raw odor of whiskey filled her nose, and she gagged as she tried to escape. Despite her struggle, the whiskey went down her throat, burning rankly.

"Don't fight it, Sweetie," the big man said, almost gently. "We all have to take what comes—so just ride with it."

Christie fought, but her captor relentlessly funneled the liquor down her throat. Soon she got dizzy, then sick, but he kept on until she passed out.

He looked down at the limp form, and disgust came to him. "There's gotta be a better way of making a living than this!" he muttered. He put the whiskey bottle on the bedside table, then placed Christie on the bed next to Stevenson and left the room. He went at once to a telephone, and when he got

his party, said roughly, "All right, come and get the shots—
and have witnesses. The front door won't be locked."

Slamming the phone on the hook, Vallentine gave one look
toward the bedroom, then left the house. He got into his car,
and when a dark sedan came roaring out of the darkness to
stop in front of the house, he watched carefully. When three
men went inside, one of them carrying a camera, he started
the engine and pulled out of the shadows.

"A shame to pull a stunt like that on a sweet kid." He grew
angry and spoke into the darkness. "Now, then, Mrs. Lorene
Stevenson, you can dish it out—let's see if you can take it. I
figure about five grand would be a nice round fee for a private detective."

10

LYLAH AND THE BURGLAR

A keen March wind holding a tang of winter cold blew across Lake Michigan, riffling the dark gray water into small whitecaps. It snatched up a sheaf of newspaper, scattering the pages across the park with a prodigal hand. One of the pages fluttered wildly as if trying to escape, then surrendered. It rose high into the air, rolling with the current of air, then suddenly dropped, falling on the lap of the man who sat staring out at the cold waters.

"What?—" Jerry started, then grabbed the paper and stared at it. "Front page," he muttered. "Won't have any good news, though." Straightening it out, he let his gaze trace the stories, reading aloud with numbed lips.

"Lee De Forest announces invention of motion picture device containing photoplay and voice on same film." He grinned and shook his head. "Talking pictures? I guess Aunt Lylah will like that—if it works." He lowered his eyes and noted that Annie Oakley had broken the world's trapshooting record by breaking ninety-eight out of one hundred clay pigeons in Pinehurst, North Carolina. A new magazine, the *Reader's Digest*, had been founded, and the new pope took the name of Pius XI. Turning the page he saw an incriminating story about Fatty Arbuckle, the actor. "Lylah said she knew him," he muttered.

Jerry tossed the paper down with distaste, rose, and walked along the lake. "Don't see why Lylah wants to get involved with people like that," he muttered. Then he thought of his own life and shook his head. "I'm a fine one to criticize her—lost everything I really wanted, and for what?"

He had failed to get a flying job, for there were still plenty of pilots who'd flown in the war. For weeks he'd followed every air show he could find, but none of the owners would even talk to him. He'd worked for three weeks for one of them cleaning and servicing planes, but it had gone bankrupt, and he'd used his last few dollars to take a bus to Chicago.

Now as he moved slowly around the lake he thought of going home. His parents would accept him, he knew that. But stubbornly he refused to give in. "Got to be *some* kind of flying job," he muttered. The sky was growing dark, and he tried to think of a place to stay. *Grew up in a big city like this and can't find a place to sleep!* he thought morbidly.

Actually he had several good friends who would have been happy to take him in—one or two on a long-term basis. But he couldn't make himself go to them. He'd left town bragging about how he was going to be a hotshot pilot in an air show, and now to go back broke and out of work was something he couldn't face.

He felt the stirrings of hunger pangs, and after counting the last of his money, he decided to have a meal. By the time he got to the South Side where he knew several good restaurants, he was famished. He ordered a big meal, ate it hungrily, then left his last dollar as a tip for the waitress. It was a gesture he felt he had to make—besides, one dollar wouldn't help him.

He walked the streets for an hour, his mind fluttering like a bird in a cage, seeking for some answer. He had no skill save for flying—and even that was not marketable. He thought of the newly born airmail service but knew they demanded many more hours than he had.

The thought of flying drew him to the airport, and as darkness began to close in, he stood on the edge of the field watching the planes land and take off. He saw no one he knew and finally realized he had no options. *Got to go home—and I'd rather die almost!*

Wearily he turned, wondering if he had enough change to take a cab, but he knew he didn't. It was a long walk all the way across town to his parents' home, and he hated to ask for rides.

As he passed the hangar he was aware of a man dressed in a long black overcoat and a derby who was talking with one of the mechanics. He looked vaguely familiar, but Jerry couldn't remember where he'd seen him. He passed by the two, and when he was a few steps away, he heard someone call, "Hey—Stuart—that you?"

Jerry turned quickly, and the man in the overcoat came toward him. "I'm Stuart," he nodded, then he recognized Eddy Castellano. "How are you, Mr. Castellano?"

"Hey, you got a good memory, Kid," Castellano nodded.

"I don't forget favors," Jerry said. "After we left the club, I found out who it was I was about to get into a fight with. I don't think I'd have lasted long against Johnny Torrio and his men."

"It was a pretty close thing," Eddy nodded. "I got letters from Amos and Owen thanking me for stepping in. You must have told them I was quite a fellow."

"Well, it was good of you to take my troubles." Jerry hesitated then asked, "You're . . . sort of in business with them, aren't you?"

Castellano laughed and slapped Jerry on the shoulder. "I guess 'sort of' describes it pretty well. We're competitors, you might say." He looked up at the sky and said abruptly, "I gotta' run, Jerry. Give you a ride someplace?"

"Well, I'm headed for Kenwood to Dad's house—but that's out of your way—"

"No problem, Kid! I got me a new car. Come along and see what you think of it." He led Jerry to the parking lot where he pointed with pride to a huge Packard. "Still got the new smell," Eddy nodded. "Ever drive one of these?"

"No, I never did."

"Get behind the wheel. You can be the chauffeur."

Jerry nodded eagerly. He started the big car and drove it smoothly out of the parking lot, turning east. He drove with verve and assurance, and Eddy said, "Hey, you're quite a driver, Kid! Ever think of giving Barney Oldsfield a run for his money?"

"Never driven a racing car, but they can't be as tricky as a plane."

Eddy twisted his head and regarded Jerry with surprise. "You a pilot, Jerry?"

"I've been flying some for my uncle, Gavin Stuart. He's a younger brother of Dad's and Uncle Owen's." Jerry nodded. "He's about the best pilot there is, I think."

Eddy fell silent, and when Jerry glanced at him he saw that the owner of the car was in some kind of deep study. Finally Eddy asked, "You still working for your uncle?"

"Well . . . no, I'm not." Jerry squirmed and finally admitted, "I got out of line, and he laid me off. I've been knocking around trying to find another job, but I don't have as much experience as lots of the older pilots."

"Kid, I want you to have supper with me. You don't have to be home right away, do you?"

"No, not really."

"Good! Take a turn and head for the levee. You know it?"

"Sure. It's a pretty tough part of town, Mr. Castellano."

"Yeah, it is. But I'm meet'n my brother Nick. He'll be glad to see you. Thinks the world of your dad and your uncle Owen."

Jerry followed Eddy's instructions, pulling up finally before a cafe with the name Dutch's Place on the front. "Come on, Kid. We'll get something good to eat. The Dutchman is the best cook in Little Italy."

Jerry followed Eddy inside, glancing around at the dimly lighted interior. It was a nicer place than the exterior had implied—tables covered with red and white tablecloths, expensive chandeliers, waiters wearing black suits and gleaming white shirts. One of them, an older man with silver hair and bright black eyes came to say, "Ah, Mister Castellano! Your brother is here. Come with me, please."

Eddy motioned to Jerry, and the two of them followed the head waiter to a table set off in an alcove. Eddy said at once, "Nick, this is Jerry Stuart—the kid I told you about."

Nick Castellano was not the lean, hard young man that Amos had described to Jerry. He was only forty-five, but he was too heavy. He had swarthy skin and regular features, but his lustrous black hair was going gray. However, his eyes were warm, and he put out his hand at once, "Hey, you're the image of your old man!" he said. "Sit down—I'll order you something really great." Turning to the waiter, he said, "Leon, bring this young fellow one of them good steaks, the special kind, you know?"

"Of course, Mr. Castellano—and some of your special wine?"

"Why not?" Nick waited until the two were seated then grinned at Jerry. "First time I seen your old man, he looked like a puppy somebody had thrown in the river. But so did I, come to think of it. We were all half-starved in those days. He ever tell you about when he stayed in our house in New York?"

"Yes, he did. He's never forgotten how kind you were to him. I think he looks on your mother as sort of a second mother."

"Sure, he still sends her flowers on her birthday—even after all these years." He nodded at Jerry, saying, "That's a good old man you got—and your mother, she's turned out real good. Hope you appreciate them."

"I . . . guess I haven't been as good to them as my sister," Jerry said. "She's the good one."

"Hey, you gotta' show respect, Kid!" Nick scolded. "Ain't that right, Eddy?"

"Sure, Jerry. Family—that's everything. The country

comes and goes—so does everything else. But the family, that's where the roots are. That's why Nick brought us with him when he moved his operation to Chicago a couple of years ago."

"Eddy's right," Nick nodded. "I read every word your old man writes. He's smart—a little old fashioned, but there ain't no man I respect more than I do Amos Stuart. Bet you got a good education, too, ain't you?"

"I got through some college, but I haven't finished."

"Go back and get all the education you can."

Jerry smiled at him, saying, "You're doing all right, Mr. Castellano. Missing out on college didn't hurt you any."

Nick glanced at Eddy, then smiled broadly. "You're a pretty up-front young fellow. Just like your dad!"

"Nick, Jerry's a pilot. Been flying with his uncle, Amos's brother."

Nick stared at Jerry, finding the statement interesting. "Is that right? How'd that happen?"

Jerry stumbled through his history, not sparing himself when he came to the story of how he'd left the show. "It wasn't Uncle Gavin's fault," he said quickly. "I'm just too much of a maverick I guess."

"Sounds like I found a winner, don't it, Nick," Eddy grinned. "Talk about pennies from heaven!"

Nick nodded slowly but waited until the meal came before he said, "Buck into that slab of meat, Jerry." He himself ate heartily, drinking liberally of the red wine. He talked about the early days, when he and Amos had scraped by doing whatever they could find. Relating the history of those days pleased him, and he finally said, "They were hard times— but a few of us survived. Me and Amos and Owen. Lots of fellows just didn't make it." He leaned back and said abruptly, "Tell me about the flying you do."

Jerry began to speak, and the two men listened carefully. Finally he laughed, "I've been talking too much—but flying's all I want to do."

"But you can't get a job, you say?" Nick prompted.

"Not so far. But I'll keep on trying."

Nick exchanged glances with Eddy, who nodded at him. Leaning forward with his smoldering dark eyes on the young man, Nick said, "Jerry, I'm a businessman. You pretty well know what it is, I guess. You've read it in the paper, or maybe your old man told you."

"I guess you're in the liquor business."

"Sure. Everybody calls me a racketeer. I call myself a businessman. When I sell liquor, it's bootlegging. When the people I sell it to serve it on a silver tray on Lakeshore Drive, it's hospitality." He spoke for some time on the injustice of prohibition, then asked abruptly, "You ever hear of a fellow called Ben Howard?"

"I don't think so."

"He designs airplanes—a real special kind." Nick grinned and blew on his cigar tip. "The kind he designs are built to haul liquor, not passengers. He's been selling them to fellows who fly liquor across the Canadian and Mexican borders."

"And we've just bought one of his planes, Kid," Eddy spoke up. "That's what I was doing at the airport—trying to make a connection with a pilot." He grinned, adding, "And here I bump into you—a flier without a job who wants to get rich—and the son of an old friend of the family. If I believed in miracles, I'd say this is one of them."

"Well, what do you say?" Nick demanded. "We'll pay you twice what you were making with that air show—with a bonus every time you take a load."

When Jerry hesitated, Eddy said smoothly, "I know your family won't like this—but a man's got to look out for himself. Stay with us for awhile, Kid, and you'll be able to buy your own plane—write your own ticket."

Jerry sat bolt upright, his brain racing. *I can't go home broke and whipped! But if I do this job—just for awhile—I'll make enough dough to get on my own.*

The light of the yellow candle flame reflected in Nick's

and Eddy's eyes, giving them a wolfish appearance. But Jerry was seeing the money that lay ahead of him—not the men who would provide it, not the dangers he would have to face to get it.

"I'll do it, Mr. Castellano—until I get enough money to go on my own."

The brothers smiled, and Eddy patted Jerry on the back. "Now you're being smart, Kid! We're gonna' make a pile of money!"

Lylah took the note from the man, asking, "You say it's from Bonnie Hart?"

"Yes, ma'am. I live down the road from her a ways. She flagged me down and gave me a dollar to bring it to you." He was a moon-faced man of around thirty with a terrible complexion. "You want me to take her an answer?"

"Let me read it." She took out the slip of paper and read the brief message:

> *Miss Stuart,*
>   *I hurt my ankle and won't be able to come to work for awhile. I'm so sorry! If you could bring Adam here, I could keep him while you work.*
>   *Bonnie*

Looking up, Lylah said impulsively, "I need to see Bonnie. Wait until I get my little boy ready, and you can ride back in a taxi with us." She hurried inside and found Adam playing on the floor. "We're going to see Bonnie, Adam. You'll have to get dressed."

Thirty minutes later the cab stopped in front of a house set back from the main road. "That's it, ma'am," the moon-faced messenger nodded.

"Thanks for showing it to me." Lylah gave him two dollars, then said to the driver, "I'll be a few minutes. Wait for me." She bundled up the large sack filled with Adam's clothes and a few toys. Going up to the front door, she pushed the bell, then waited. The house was a low ranch-style affair, made of white stucco. It was shaded by large trees, and flowers grew luxuriously. The door opened, and Bonnie, balancing on one foot, stared at her visitors.

"Why—I didn't expect you so soon, Miss Stuart!" She gasped as Adam held his arms up, begging to be taken up. "I can't hold you, Sweetheart," Bonnie said. "Come on in, and I'll fix you something good to eat."

"I'm going to take you up on your offer to keep Adam," Lylah said as soon as she had put down the bulky sack. "If you feel like it?"

"Oh, I'm fine—just twisted my ankle." Bonnie pointed to her left ankle, which was obviously swollen. "Adam won't be any problem—but it's a long way for you to bring him."

"I'd rather you kept him, Bonnie." Lylah smiled and patted the girl on the shoulder. "You've become indispensable to Adam and me. Well, the taxi's waiting. I'll be back as soon as I can."

"Don't worry if you're late," Bonnie said as Lylah left the house. "Adam and I will be fine!"

Lylah got into the cab, saying, "Take me to the Triangle Pictures studio. Do you know where it is?"

"Sure do!"

Lylah sat back, relieved that she had solved the problem of taking care of Adam—at least for a time. All day as she worked, she went over in her mind what she might do with him until Bonnie was fit. But by the time she left the studio and got into a taxi, she was no closer to a solution.

When the taxi pulled up in front of the house, she said, "Wait for me, please." When she entered the house she found that Bonnie had fixed supper. "Why, how did you do this on that bad ankle?" she scolded. "You're supposed to stay off of it."

Bonnie smiled engagingly. "It wasn't hard. You can cook

sitting down," she said. "Send the cab away. We can't waste all this food."

The meal was excellent—chops and fresh vegetables well-cooked and seasoned just right. "This is a luxury for me, Bonnie," Lylah said as they finished. "Sometimes I'm so tired when I get home, it's all I can do to open a can of soup for Adam."

"You work so hard," Bonnie said. "People don't have any idea what an awful lot of work it is to make a movie."

"No, but I like it." Lylah got up, insisting, "Now, *I* do the dishes. You read a book to Adam. He's about to go to sleep."

"Not sleepy!" Adam protested. He continued to protest, but by the time the dishes were done, he was lying on the couch, fast asleep.

"It's a shame to wake him," Bonnie said. "Why don't you two stay here tonight?"

"Oh, we couldn't do that!"

"Why not, Miss Stuart? There're three bedrooms. It'll be late by the time you get home, then you'll have to come all the way back here to leave him. It seems a waste."

Lylah *was* very tired. The thought of the long trip, and the idea of getting Adam there, then putting him to bed again seemed monumental. "Well—if you're sure it won't be too much trouble, I think we will stay."

"Fine! We can put Adam in the small bedroom, next to mine. You can take the large one at the end of the hall. There's plenty of soap and towels in the bathroom. You can sleep in one of my nightgowns. I think I'll go to bed myself—but I'll be up to fix your breakfast in the morning."

Lylah felt a surge of affection for the young woman. "Thank you, Bonnie." But the words seemed inadequate, so she went over and hugged the girl. "I haven't met too many like you! I don't know what Adam and I would have done if you hadn't come along."

Bonnie looked embarrassed, then said, "Good night, Miss Stuart."

"Oh, call me Lylah, for heaven's sake!"

"Well, good night, Lylah." She hopped out of the room, and her door closed softly.

Lylah quickly put Adam's pajamas on him, then tucked him in bed. She kissed his forehead, whispered, "Good night, Sweetheart," then left, closing the door softly.

She took a hot bath, then put on the nightgown that Bonnie had laid out. When she looked in the closet filled with men's clothes she remembered that Bonnie had a brother who was out of the country. She found a blue cotton robe and slipped it on. It was far too big for her, but there was no one to see. She lay down on the bed but had to study her lines for the next day's shooting, so she opened the small case and took out the notebook.

She lay there, her lips moving as she went over the lines for an hour. Then she suddenly jerked upright and realized that she had nodded off.

"This won't do!" She got out of bed and made her way to the kitchen. The coffeepot was still half-filled so she turned on the gas and waited for it to heat. As she stood there, still mouthing lines, she suddenly heard a noise and turned quickly to see a shadowy figure at the window.

Her heart seemed to freeze, for someone was forcing the window open!

A burglar! Lylah had steady nerves, but she'd never been in a position like this. She thought of Adam, helpless in his bed—and of Bonnie. The window gave a creaking noise, then slowly began to open.

I've got to do something! Desperately she tried to think of a weapon, but nothing came to mind. The house was isolated, well off the road, and there were no houses on either side for several hundred yards.

As the window rose stealthily, she saw the large *olla*, a clay water pot, beside the door. It was filled with flowers, but she knew that it must be very heavy. Quickly she moved to pick it up and was gratified by the weight of the jar.

The window uttered one final groan, then a leg was thrown over the sill. Lylah moved in the shadows, holding the heavy *olla* over her head. She was breathing in short gasps, and when the man came over the sill, she brought the jar down directly on his head.

He uttered a slight cry, then collapsed on the floor. At once Lylah turned to throw the switch. He was a tall man with a short beard and a square face. His forehead was bleeding, but he was still conscious. Lylah took only one glance, then grabbed a lamp from a table, smashed it, and using the lamp cord, tied the man's hands behind his back.

When she was finished, the man gave a groan, then rolled over on his back and opened his eyes. He was confused and stared up at her. "What? . . ."

"Just lie still," Lylah commanded. "I'm calling the police, but if you try to get loose, I'll break another pot over your head!"

"Who . . . are you?" The burglar had brown eyes and crisp brown hair, slightly curly. "Why did you hit me?"

"You're a burglar. Now, be still or I'll have to hit you again!" She moved to pick up another table lamp and held it as a weapon. Picking up the phone, she asked for the police—but at that moment, Bonnie came through the door, her eyes wide with alarm. "Don't be afraid, Bonnie," Lylah said briskly. "A burglar broke in, but I'm calling—"

But Bonnie cried out, "Jesse!" Then she hobbled across the room to drop beside the prone figure. "Jesse—you're hurt!"

Lylah stared at the two—and a horrible thought came to her. "Jesse? Bonnie . . . this isn't your brother?"

But Bonnie was weeping as she tried to untie the lamp cord. "Jesse, are you all right?"

Lylah slowly replaced the phone. She had never felt like such a fool in her life. *Idiot!—you could have killed him!* Taking a deep breath, she moved over to say, "Let me untie that, Bonnie." She freed his hands and then pulled the man into an upright position. "Let me see that cut—" She put her hands on his forehead, then drew a sigh of relief. "It's not too bad," she said. "No stitches."

Jesse Hart had a broad mouth, and it suddenly turned upward into a smile. "My name's Jesse," he said. "Glad to make your acquaintance."

Lylah stared at him in shock. Most men would have been raging at her, but his brown eyes were calm. "I . . . I'm so sorry," she murmured. "Does your head hurt much?"

Jesse got to his feet, and she was surprised at how tall he was. He touched his head, then said, "Not too much."

"Let me wash it out. Bonnie, do you have any antiseptic?"

Soon Lylah was bending over Jesse, carefully cleaning out the ragged gash. He sat very still, listening as Bonnie explained how Lylah had happened to be there. When she finished, he looked up, and Lylah's face was very close to his. "Why, you have violet eyes," he said with interest. "I never saw eyes like that."

"Didn't you?"

"Nope." He studied her carefully, then said, "Well, if a fellow's going to get his brains scrambled, he might as well have the job done by a beautiful woman with violet eyes."

Lylah couldn't help smiling at his strange statement. "I've got your bed and your robe, too. But I'll sleep with Adam."

Getting the bed situation straight took some time, but when Lylah finally lay beside Adam, she thought for a long time about Jesse Hart. *I wonder how old he is?* She decided he was in his late thirties, a little younger than she was. *I'm glad I didn't hurt him any worse,* she thought drowsily. Then she dropped off into a deep sleep and dreamed of something she could never remember afterward.

11

JERRY TO THE RESCUE

B ingo—stop chewing that rug!"

Jesse Hart had been telling Lylah and Bonnie how he'd been thrown in jail for vagrancy in Salt Lake City. When Bonnie mentioned that the huge St. Bernard that Jesse had picked up on his travels was chewing the rug to shreds, he gave a sharp command.

"He doesn't mind very well, does he?" Lylah observed.

Jesse said loudly, "Bingo, keep on chewing the rug!" When the dog continued, Jesse nodded. "See how he minds?"

"I see. He minds when he wants to," Lylah smiled.

"Exactly. He's no slave to authority." He rose and went over and smacked the dog on the head with a rolled up magazine. Bingo gave him a reproachful look, uttered a deep *wuff*, then rose and walked away, insult in every move of his massive body.

"You hurt his feelings, Jesse," Bonnie grinned. "I'll go feed him. That always makes him feel better."

After Bonnie left, Jesse returned to where he'd been lying on the floor and stretched out. "Where was I? Oh, yes, in jail in Salt Lake City . . ."

As Jesse rambled on giving the details of his adventure, Lylah leaned back in the overstuffed chair and watched him. During the two months he'd been in town, she'd come to know him very well. He was in the habit, she had discovered, of rambling over the country collecting facts about different places and unusual people—and then coming home to write it up. He didn't make a great deal of money, he freely admitted, but it was an easy life. Now as she studied him, she knew suddenly why she found him so refreshing. *He's not tense like most people. I think he's the most relaxed human being I've ever seen.*

Suddenly she broke into his story, asking, "Don't you ever get anxious about what's going to happen, Jesse?" When he turned his head toward her, a quizzical look in his warm brown eyes, she spread her hands out and said with something like exasperation, "Will you make enough money to live on? What if you get sick and can't work? What's going to happen when you get old?"

"I am old," he said comfortably. "Did you know that in the Middle Ages the average life span of a person was twenty-six years. I've already lived eleven years longer than that. As for the rest, well, as they say in France, *pomme de terre.*"

"And what does *that* mean?"

"It means 'apple of the earth' or 'potato.'" He saw her look of bewilderment, then grinned. "I don't know much French." He rolled over on his stomach and did five one-arm push-ups. "Can you do this?"

"No."

"You can't?" He stopped and sat down, his brown hair falling over his forehead. He studied her carefully, noting the dressing gown she was wearing—it was made of purple flowered satin trimmed with fine lavender lace. He shook his head. "A chameleon would have a time if you stuck him on that coat of many colors. Why can't you do push-ups?"

Lylah threw up her hands in disgust. "You've got the mind of a fluttering butterfly!" she exclaimed. Drawing up her legs she hugged them and turned her head to one side in a critical glance. "Are all writers as wild as you, Jesse?"

"Only the good ones," he assured her solemnly. "The bad ones—the ones who make all the big money—they're all as boring as accountants." He came up from the floor in a smooth motion, sat down beside her, and studied her. "I've never known a big-time movie star. What's it like to be famous?"

"It feels tired," she said. The day had been long, and the klieg lights had singed her skin and made her eyes burn. Lylah liked his teasing. Most men were either intimidated by her position—or were convinced that all actresses were totally devoid of morals. Jesse Hart treated her exactly as he treated everybody else, and he had not made any advances in any way since he'd come home. "What does it feel like to be a writer?" Lylah countered.

"It feels poor."

"Don't you want to make a lot of money?" she asked curiously. "Everybody else does."

"Not everybody," he contradicted her. "Bingo doesn't, and he's happier than Douglas Fairbanks."

"How can you know that?"

"Look into Fairbanks's eyes sometime," Jesse nodded. "He smiles all the time, too much, I think. But when you look into his eyes you can see he's not happy. So that proves money doesn't bring happiness."

"And Bingo is happy?"

"Sure. He gets lots to eat, there's usually a nice female who comes along, and he's got me to take care of him. As the French put it, *chemain de fer.*"

"And what does *that* mean?"

"It means railroad. Road of iron, literally." He reached over and touched her nose, adding absently, "Your nose is too short."

Lylah laughed explosively, reached up, and captured his finger, bending it back sharply until he cried out, then released him. "Keep your hands off my nose!" It amused her that after so many years of hearing men tell her how beautiful she was that she could take pleasure in Jesse's manner of telling her she had flaws. "My nose *is* too short," she said, "but nobody seems to care."

"I don't either," Jesse shrugged. "Mine's too long, so I

guess we average out." He looked over at Adam who was asleep on the floor. Lylah had tried to put the boy to bed, but he'd begged to stay up and play with "Uncle Jesse." Jesse had added his plea, and now he said, "That's a fine boy, Lylah. Smart and good-looking." He leaned forward and studied Adam's face, then asked, "Does he look like his father?"

Lylah Stuart was not usually at a loss for words, but now she said shortly, "Yes, I suppose he does."

Her abrupt tone caused Jesse to turn to her. He was, Lylah had discovered, almost infallible at reading people. Now he studied her carefully, then offered, "You must love him very much." When she looked at him, he said, "When a woman reacts like you do she either hates or loves very much."

"He's dead."

"But love is stronger than the grave."

"I . . . don't want to talk about it, Jesse!"

"That's too bad—because I'm a good listener."

Lylah was more disturbed than she had ever been with Jesse. Almost angrily she said, "You're just like the rest—can't *wait* to find out all the juicy details!" Her violet eyes were filled with anger, and she shook her head, sending her rich crown of auburn hair in motion. "What do you want, more material for one of your stories? Are you writing something for one of those awful tabloid newspapers?"

Lylah rose at once, and Jesse stood up. "I guess you've got a right to think that, Lylah—but it's not true."

Lylah paused, turned, and stared into Jesse's eyes. He said nothing, merely stood waiting. Suddenly Lylah's eyes filled with tears. "I . . . I'm sorry, Jesse. I had no right to accuse you like that!" She struggled to keep the tears back, but the pressures of her job kept her on the edge. DeMille was a hard taskmaster, and she left the studio each day drained and empty.

But it was more than that, she knew. The mention of Adam's father had brought back bittersweet memories of the man she'd loved against all wisdom. She had only had him

with her for brief periods, but as she grew older she was aware
of a loneliness that she'd never known before. It was harder
to rear a small child, especially a boy, than she had ever
dreamed, and if it had not been for the Harts, she would have
been lost.

Unsteadily she said, "You've been so good for Adam, Jesse.
A boy needs a man. I'm the world's worst ingrate, screaming
at you. It's just that . . . that . . ."

And then to her dismay, she began to weep uncontrollably.
Her shoulders shook, and tears streamed down her face. Jesse
was shocked at the fear and strain he saw. It came close to
being as near bottomless despair as he had ever seen. He had
once been struck in the pit of the stomach so that he could
neither breathe nor speak, and this seemed to be something
like that. At once he stepped forward and put his arms around
her. "Maybe," he said gently, "I can help." As he pulled her
close, he felt the quick loosening of her body and heard the
sobs she could not control.

He said nothing but held her firmly. Her hair was rich and
sweet, her body full and firm against him. She had more than
the tawdry beauty so prized by many actresses. Her lips were
broad and full, and the planes of her face were gentle and
well formed.

And then the weight went from his arms. She gave him a
strange look, and he could not know that she was thinking, *I
was helpless—and he didn't take advantage—as most men would.*
Pulling a handkerchief from the pocket of her dressing gown,
she cleaned her face, then said, almost shyly, "Thanks, Jesse."

"Jesse Hart's comforting service—we never close," he said
easily, then turned, saying, "I'll put Adam to bed."

Lylah knew it was to give her time to collect herself that
he did this, and she went at once to wash her face. The phone
rang, and then Jesse called out, "Lylah, can you come to the
phone?"

"Yes."

Coming back into the living room, she noted that Bonnie

and Bingo had come back and were sitting on the floor. Taking the phone from Jesse, she said, "Hello?"

"Lylah?"

"Pa, is that you?" She had given her father the phone numbers at home, at the Harts', and at the studio, but he had never called her, not once. Sensing a tension in his voice, she asked, "Is something wrong?"

"Yes, there is." Anger colored the voice of Will Stuart, and he spoke almost harshly. "Lylah, we got to do something about Christie!"

Somehow Lylah had known that she would get a call like this. She had grieved over the terrible anguish that her gentle younger sister had gone through. More than once she had called to offer to come and help, but her father had said, "There ain't nothin' you can do here, Lylah. If it gets worse, maybe you can do somethin'."

"What is it, Pa?"

A slight hesitation occurred, then Will said, "It's bad, Lylah. You know how it is in a small place. Most people are kind, but some are hateful. It's got so bad that Christie won't go out of the house, and—"

When her father halted abruptly, Lylah said, "And Agnes won't let her alone when she's there—is that it?"

"Well, she's got to get away, Lylah."

"What about Mel Tolliver? But I don't have to ask about him! He dropped her, didn't he?"

"Yes, the low life! But anyways Christie won't be married to him, and I guess that's somethin'!"

"Do you want me to bring her out to California with me?"

"I don't think that would be the answer, Lylah. She's hurtin' bad, and she don't need that Hollywood bunch."

"I think that's right, Pa. But what?—"

"Lenora wrote a letter. She wants Christie to come and stay with her. They were always close."

"Is that all right with the Salvation Army people?"

"Yes. It's all fixed up—but I can't get Amos. He'd come

and get her, but him and Rose and Maury are gone on some kind of a trip. I don't know what to do. Don't even know if Christie would agree to go—but she's *got* to get away from here."

Desperation now threaded her father's voice, and Lylah said, "Don't worry, Pa. I'll take care of it. All right?"

"All right, Lylah. Good-bye, then."

Lylah hung up the phone and stood there, thinking furiously. She could not leave the picture, for it would tie up the whole company. She thought of Peter in Oklahoma, and Logan—but neither would be able to handle this. *Gavin could do it*, she thought, and then was aware that Jesse and Bonnie were watching her. "I've got to do a great deal of long distance calling," she said. "I can go home, but if you'll let me use your phone, I'll pay the charges."

"Of course," Jesse said, then turned to say, "Come on, Bonnie. We'll take a walk."

Grateful for his thoughtfulness, Lylah waited until the door closed, then at once began trying to trace Gavin. She didn't know his schedule, however, and Heather was not at home. Finally she dialed Amos's home, and the phone was answered by the maid. "Can you tell me how to reach Mr. Stuart, Emily?"

"No, Miss Lylah. They went in the car and said they were going to get away from telephones."

"Well, thanks—"

"Mr. Jerry called this afternoon. He's here in Chicago. Would you like his number?"

"Oh, yes, give it to me, please."

Lylah wrote down the number, thanked Emily, then dialed it. At once a voice said, "Hello?"

"Jerry?"

"Yes, this is Jerry."

"This is Aunt Lylah. Jerry, we've got a big problem. Can you reach your father?"

"Don't think so. What's up?"

Lylah hesitated. If it had been Maury, she would have tried to get her to help, but she was well aware of Jerry's record. "Oh, never mind, Jerry—"

"Wait a minute, Aunt Lylah! If there's a problem, I want to help."

"Well—it's your aunt Christie. You know about her trouble?"

"I know she didn't do what they say! She's not that kind. What's going on?"

"She's got to leave Arkansas, Jerry. Your grandfather called and asked me to help. But I can't leave. Is there any way you can go there and get her?"

"I can be there tomorrow! Where do you want me to take her?"

"Tomorrow? Why, it will take the train longer than that!"

"Won't take a plane longer, though. Now, tell me what to do, Aunt Lylah."

"All right. You'll have to be careful with her, Jerry. None of your jokes. She's badly broken up, and she doesn't need that sort of thing."

"All right, no jokes. Where do I take her?"

"Pa thinks she needs to go to be with Lenora."

"At the Salvation Army—here in Chicago?"

"You know it? Have you been there?"

"Sure—been in to see Aunt Lenora twice. She'll be good for Aunt Christie. Well, I'll call you when we get back."

"Do you need money?—"

"No, I've got plenty. And thanks for trusting me, Aunt Lylah. I won't let you down!"

Agnes came in from the garden, her face flushed from the heat of the sun. When she saw Christie sitting in the rocking chair staring out the window, she said sharply, "I told you to get those peas shelled. All you've done is sit and stare out that window!"

"I'm sorry, Agnes."

"Well, hurry up! I can't do all the work around here by my-

self." Agnes passed through the kitchen, moving into the bedroom where she washed her face in the basin on the oak wash-
stand, then laid down on the bed to rest. She had been pleased
at the accusations that had followed Christie's disgrace, as she
called it. For years her own affairs with men had been known
by most of the people in the county, and now she had stri-
dently said to her husband, "Well, she's no better than a
woman of the streets! It's a shame that we have to endure the
tongues of everybody in Stone County. You ought to run her
off the place, Will!"

Will had been shocked by the story, humiliated by the talk
that went around—but never once had he doubted the innocence of his daughter. He had put up with Agnes's nagging
for years, but her sharp tongue was destroying Christie. It was
for this reason that he had called Lylah, and now as he sat on
the porch, he wished he'd handled the matter differently.

Ought to have been man enough to make Agnes shut her mouth,
he thought. He was a weak man, and now he was so out of
the habit of asserting himself with the gross woman he had
married that he had tried to keep her pacified.

But he had heard her words when she'd come in from the
garden, and he rose and moved into the house, going to the
kitchen. He found Christie listlessly shelling peas and said,
"Lemme' help you with them peas, Daughter."

"You don't have to do that, Pa."

"Got my chores all done," he replied. He sat down and
with thick, work-blunted fingers began to shell the peas.
They sat there silently for a time, then Will said, "I talked to
Lylah yesterday."

This interested Christie, and she glanced at him. "You
went to the store to use the phone?" Her face was thinner,
for she had lost weight, and her eyes were tired. There was
a sadness about her that hurt her father's heart.

"Yep, I did." He ran his thumb down the inside of a pea,
and the small pellets drummed into the tin pan. "I told her
to get you away from here somehow."

Christie swallowed and nodded. "I know it's hard on you, Pa—"

"Me? Why, Daughter, I wasn't thinkin' about *me!*"

But Christie seemed not to hear him. Her lips were pale and trembling, and she whispered, "I'm so . . . so *ashamed*, Pa!"

Will at once put the pan on the worn table, reached over, and put his hand over hers. "You got no need of that," he said urgently. "You've done nothing—"

Suddenly he broke off and turned his head to one side. "What in tarnation?—"

And then the house seemed filled with a great roaring. Both of them thought it was an earthquake, and they leaped to their feet. Christie ran outside and looked up, crying, "Pa— it's a flying machine!"

"Must be Gavin," Will nodded with relief. "What's he doin' here?"

Up in the two-seater Jerry laughed as he saw the pair come flying out of the house. "That got their attention," he said. He pulled back on the stick, did an inside roll, then began to look for a place to land.

Guess that pasture's about as good a landing field as I'm likely to find. He throttled back, studied the field, then made his decision. He'd landed on smaller fields many times, but he was uncertain of how many hidden holes he might encounter in this one. But it was the only possibility, so he slowed the craft, keeping it barely at flying speed. When he was ten feet from the rail fence, he cut the power and drifted to the ground. The wheels hit, the plane bounced twice, then came to a stop forty feet from the line of timber. "Wish Gavin could have seen that!" he cried out, then climbed out of the plane.

He moved toward the house and was met by his grand-father and his aunt. "Why, you crazy lunatic!" Will exclaimed. "You could have broken your neck!"

"Didn't though. How are you, Grandpa?"

Will stared at his tall young grandson and beamed with pride. "Lylah send you?" he demanded.

"She called me yesterday," Jerry nodded. Then he turned to his aunt, who had said nothing. Smiling he said, "Well, what are you waiting for, Aunt Christie? We've got a long way to go."

Christie stared at him, not understanding. And then she knew. "I . . . I can't leave here," she murmured.

But Jerry went to her and put his arm around her. "Sure you can. I talked to Lenora before I left. She told me to tie you up and throw you into the plane if you wouldn't come on your own." He saw the distress in the young woman's eyes and said gently, "Honest, Aunt Lenora's excited about your coming. She said the two of you will have more fun than you can think of—but she said you'd have to work, too."

"Work?"

"Why, those Army people work to put a mule to shame! Feeding people, helping women and kids, all kinds of services on the streets! Never saw anything like it! And you know Lenora—she's about worn herself out. She really needs you, Aunt Christie."

It was this offer of a place to work—and the fact that Lenora needed help—that gave Christie the strength to make the plunge. "All right, I'll go get my suitcase packed."

As she turned and ran toward the house, Will said, "Son, you handled that *real* good! I been worried what to do if she wouldn't go."

Jerry reddened with the praise, then looked toward the house. "Going to be lonesome for you, isn't it, Grandpa?"

"I don't mind that. Reckon I'll go spend some time over at Logan's. He needs some help with that place of his."

Thirty minutes later Jerry had strapped Christie firmly into the front cockpit. He stepped to the ground and put his hand out, saying, "Take care of yourself, Grandpa."

"Sure. And don't kill yourself and my girl in this fool machine."

And then Jerry ran to climb into the cockpit. He started the engine, then said, "You scared, Aunt Christie?"

"No. I'm ready to go."

"Well—here we go, then."

Will Stuart watched as the plane roared from the field, clearing the fence by a matter of inches. He kept his eyes on it until it was a mere speck that finally disappeared. Then he turned and walked back toward the house, his shoulders stooped and loneliness etched into his features.

12

"HE DOESN'T LOOK LIKE A GANGSTER—"

C hristie kept her eyes closed while the plane took off, frightened more than she had admitted to Jerry. The engine directly in front of her roared hoarsely, and she was pressed downward into her seat as the two-seater pointed its nose into the air. Her fingers ached from clutching the edge of the seat, and she had to force herself to relax her jaws when they began to hurt.

As the plane banked sharply to her right, she heard Jerry yell, "Look, Aunt Christie—there's the home place!"

When Christie opened her eyes, she saw that the house looked like a dollhouse. Fascinated, she took in the barn, the stock in the corral—everything looked so tiny! Then Jerry turned the plane toward the west, and she eagerly searched the landscape. There was the creek she'd fished in all her life—but she'd never known how crooked it was! She searched the road that wound between the hills, naming off the houses, marveling at how different they looked from this vantage point.

"Pretty neat, isn't it, Aunt Christie?" Jerry yelled. She turned around, smiled at him, then swung back to watch the country flow by. *It's like flying over a big patchwork quilt*, she thought, noting how the fields were mostly laid out in geometrical patterns. Then Jerry gunned the engine, and the plane climbed upward. They were headed straight for a huge white cloud that looked solid as rock—but when they passed through it, she discovered that it was like flying through a white mist.

Then they popped out, and soon she was looking down on white clouds, flattened on top, and marveling at the immensity of the world. She'd been surrounded by trees and hills all her life, and only now did the grandeur of the world become obvious to her.

Hour after hour passed, then Jerry landed to refuel. As Christie got out and stretched, she wondered what sort of world she'd find in Chicago. She was an imaginative young woman, able to dream up scenarios almost like viewing a motion picture. Her life had been a nightmare since she had been thrown into the public eye, and no matter what came next, she didn't think it could be as bad as what had preceded. *At least I'll be with Lenora—and nobody will know about it . . . what's happened*, she thought.

Jerry exited the small building carrying a sack and two bottles. "Lunch," he grinned. "Not the Ritz, but it'll keep us from getting hungry. Think you can stand another few hours, Aunt Christie?"

"Oh, yes, Jerry! It's a wonderful way to travel!"

Jerry opened the sack and gave her a sandwich. "Well, if we get caught in a thunderstorm you might not think so." He bit into the sandwich, made a face, then chewed slowly. "I *hate* peanut butter!" he complained. Then looking up at the sky, he shook his head. "We're all right. Perfect weather for flying. We might have to lay over, though. But we'll be in Chicago tomorrow."

"Jerry—thanks for coming for me."

"Aw, it's a piece of cake. Be good to have you in Chicago. Now I can take the two best-looking women in the whole town out at the same time."

Christie saw that he was embarrassed at being thanked but put her hand on his arm. "It means a lot to me. You're like your dad—always ready to help others."

Jerry Stuart stared at this aunt of his, but he knew that she was wrong. "I wish you were right about that, Aunt Christie," he said almost bitterly, "but I've spent my life looking out for number one."

Christie was surprised at the unhappiness that her remark had brought to her nephew's face. She knew little about him—except that he'd been a problem to his parents for some time. Now she studied the clean-cut features, the coal black hair, and the strange-colored green eyes. *He's so fine looking,* she thought, *and he's troubled about himself. But he's good, no matter how much trouble he's been in.*

The two ate, then climbed back into the plane. Jerry kept in the air until dusk began to fall. They landed at a small airport and managed to find two cots in the hangar, where they lay down and went to sleep almost instantly. The last thing Christie thought before she drifted off was, *I'll see Lenora—and things will be different.*

"There it is, Aunt Christie—Chicago!"

At Jerry's loud cry, Christie stirred herself and peered out over the edge of the cockpit. The sight made her gasp, for she had never dreamed that men could make anything so impressive as the city that lay below her. People the size of ants were moving along the tiny streets, and the cars looked like toys. As they passed over the city, she noted that the skyscrapers were like mountains with the streets lying in valleys between them.

Jerry brought the small plane in, and when he taxied up to one of the hangars and cut the engine, he said, "All out for Chicago—" Christie descended, having an awkward time keeping her skirt down as she climbed down to the pavement.

Jerry got her suitcase and led her into the hangar. He was met by a man in greasy clothes who said, "Phone call for you, Jerry. Guy said to be sure and get to him."

Jerry took the slip of paper the mechanic handed him,

glanced at it, and nodded. "Got to make a call, Aunt Christie. Wait here, will you?"

"All right."

Christie stood beside her suitcase, watching the men at work on the planes for a few minutes, then Jerry was back. "Got to make one stop before I take you to the Salvation Army headquarters. Won't take too long. Okay?"

"Of course, Jerry."

He led her to a low, sleek car, stored her luggage in a compartment in the rear, then helped her in. When he got in, he said as he started the engine, "Got to go see my boss. You'll get to see a little of Chicago."

Jerry drove almost recklessly through the heavy traffic. He looped one arm out the window, letting his wrist drape over the wheel, and several times Christie gasped as he seemed to be unaware of escaping a collision by a fraction of an inch. He left a wake of honking cars and probably cursing drivers but chatted happily, pointing out the sights of the city.

"Look, here's the way the city's laid out," he told her. "The Chicago River runs straight east into Lake Michigan. And the other way, west, there's a fork, sort of like a Y. The city's divided into three main divisions—North Side and South Side, meaning north or south of the river, and the West Side, which is everything between the two branches of the Y."

As they moved along, he pointed out the Potter Palmer mansion, built in 1882, on north Lake Shore Drive. "This is the ritzy section, Aunt Christie," Jerry informed her. "All the swells live here."

They drove over a new bridge, and he informed her, "Michigan Avenue Bridge—just opened this month." A little later he pointed out the Loop and the Million Dollar Mile, then finally after what seemed like a long drive, pulled up in front of a brick building with "Colosimo's Cafe" on a sign over the door. "Come on inside," Jerry said. "Want you to meet my employers."

Christie walked with Jerry through the front door, and the

pair were met at once by a bulky man who eyed them suspiciously, then recognized Jerry. "You looking for Mr. Castellano? Come along."

"Not very busy right now," Jerry nodded at the ranks of empty tables, "but it's filled up every night."

"Right in there—better knock first," the burly man said, then turned and left them.

Jerry knocked twice and the door opened at once. "Well, come in, Kid," the swarthy-skinned man smiled. He stepped back, and when Jerry and Christie were inside, he said, "This must be your aunt, I guess?"

"Sure, this is Miss Christie Stuart," Jerry nodded. "This is Eddy Castellano—and this is his brother Nick."

Nick had been sitting behind a big desk, but he got up at once and came to smile at Christie. "Well, now, you better give them brothers of yours a hiding, Miss Stuart. Amos and Owen, they never told me what a fine-looking lady they had for a sister." He shook his head in admiration. "Come in, come in—we won't be long. Hey—this is my youngest brother, Mario," he nodded toward a young man just under six feet tall, with dark hair neatly cut and alert brown eyes. He was wearing an expensive suit and looked somehow more refined than his brothers.

"I'm pleased to meet you, Miss Stuart," he smiled. "Is this your first trip to Chicago?"

"Yes, it is."

"Well, I hope you'll let me show you around. I've heard so much about your family, it's a pleasure to meet one of the famous Stuarts."

Christie flushed, saying, "I'm not famous, Mr. Castellano—but thank you for your offer."

"Hey, Mario, why don't you show Miss Stuart the china—all the fancy dishes and stuff."

"Certainly. If you'll come with me, Miss Stuart—Mr. Colosimo has worked on it for a long time."

When the two were outside the room, Eddy turned to Jerry at once, saying, "Well, I'm glad you're back, Kid."

"Thanks for letting me use the plane, Eddy. My aunt—well, she really needed a helping hand."

"Sure, glad to be of help." Eddy tilted his head to one side. "What's she going to do in Chicago?"

Jerry shrugged. "She'll be with the Salvation Army, I guess. With my aunt Lenora."

The Castellano brothers gave each other an unbelieving glance, and then both smiled. "I thought all those women had to be old and plain," Nick observed. "Sure don't seem like much of a life for a woman—but if that's what she wants to do . . ." He puffed on his cigar, then changed the subject abruptly. "Got a job for you."

"Today?"

"Naw, tomorrow. You rest up tonight, but tomorrow I want you to fly to Detroit. When you get there, call this number." He turned to his desk, picked up a pencil and jotted a number on a slip of paper. "Ask for Mr. Smith. Tell him to come to the airport."

"No first name?"

Nick hesitated, then nodded. "John Smith. Bring him here. When you get back, call Eddy and he'll come out and get the guy."

"Sure, Nick."

"And, Jerry—don't talk to the guy."

"What if he talks to me?"

"He won't." The flat statement hung in the air, and Nick added, "It's a business deal, Jerry. The less said the better, okay?"

"Okay by me. I'll call as soon as we get back. Now I better get my aunt to the Salvation Army depot." He hesitated, then said, "I never knew you had a younger brother."

"He's in college," Nick said, pride in his dark eyes. "Gonna be a first-rate lawyer one of these days!"

Eddy grinned, "Saves money, having a lawyer in the business. He's a good kid—reminds me of you, Jerry."

"Deliver me from being a lawyer—but to each his own.
Well, I'll call when I get in—may be late, though."

"Makes no difference, call even if it's past midnight." Eddy
eyed Jerry, then asked, "How can you see to fly a plane at
night?"

"Lights from towns—and when the moon is full and there's
not many clouds, you can see the rivers and lakes. Really a
pretty sight. You want to come along, Eddy?"

"Not me!"

Jerry laughed and turned to leave the room. He found
Christie and Mario in the collection room and said, "Hate to
break up the lecture, but we've got to go."

"Sure," Mario smiled. "Next time, I'll show you the rest,
Miss Stuart."

"That would be nice."

"A pleasure to meet you."

When they were in the car driving away, Christie said,
"He's very nice. What does he do?"

Jerry hesitated, then shrugged. "He's a gangster, Aunt
Christie."

Christie turned instantly to stare at him. "I can't believe
that!"

"He's a Castellano. They're all gangsters. Haven't you ever
heard Amos talk about them? Or Owen?"

"Well, yes, but he seems—different."

"He's the baby brother. I'd guess Nick's made up his mind
to buy some respectability. Mario looks pretty much like a
successful young college man, but he's a Castellano. That
makes him different. That restaurant? Colosimo? He was one
of the bosses, ran gambling and bootlegging. A gangster
named Johnny Torrio had him killed just a few months ago.
That's the kind of world the Castellano family lives in."

Christie said no more until Jerry pulled up in front of a
large three-story building with SALVATION ARMY painted

on the front. When he shut off the engine, she said, "He doesn't look like a gangster."

Jerry walked around and opened the door. As Christie got out, he said, "No, he doesn't. Maybe I'm wrong—but I don't think so." Then he nodded toward the door, "Come on, Aunt Lenora's probably anxious about you."

As they entered the building, Christie looked around curiously. There was nothing fancy about the place, rather it was plain and unadorned. Along the walls were tables piled high with old clothes, and several women wearing uniforms were sorting them. "Where will we find Miss Lenora?" Jerry asked one of them.

"She's working in the kitchen."

"I know where that is," Jerry nodded. He led the way down a long hall, and when he opened a door, Christie stepped into a long rectangular room filled with tables. Men sat on benches, and it was obvious that they had arrived at mealtime. The men all wore rough, ragged clothing, and most of them needed shaves and haircuts. "There she is—" Jerry said, nodding toward the back of the room.

Christie saw Lenora at once. Her sister was wheeling down between two rows of tables, a large basket of bread in her lap. As Christie watched, she saw Lenora stop, put loaves on a table, say a word to the men, then wheel on. She stopped at another table, then looked up and saw the two.

"Christie!" she cried out and spun the wheels so rapidly that the bread went flying. Ignoring the fallen loaves, she scooted down the aisle, slammed on the brakes, and held up her arms. Her face was glowing with pleasure, and when Christie bent over, she found herself grabbed so hard that she lost her breath.

"Praise God, you're here!" Lenora said, then after a quick squeeze, released her sister and winked at Jerry. "Well, you didn't waste any time did you? How's Pa?" But before either could answer, she shook her head. "Never mind, we'll have

all kinds of time to talk, Christie. Now, you two sit down, and
we'll have a good dinner."

"Oh, I've got to run—"

"Hush and sit down, Jerry Stuart. You're too skinny.
There—right over by the wall—see? Go sit down, and I'll get
us something to eat. You can tell me about the trip."

"She's something, isn't she?" Jerry said as the two sat down
at one of the tables.

"She always has been," Christie said softly. They waited
for a short time, and then Lenora returned with a tall man in
an Army uniform. "This is Major Hastings. Major, my sister
Christie, and my nephew Jerry Stuart."

The major was a wiry man, taller than most, with a craggy
face and clear gray eyes. When Jerry shook hands with him,
it was, he told Christie later, "like shaking hands with a Stil-
son wrench!" He had red hair and many freckles and was
homely as a plowed field, but his eyes were kind. "We've
been making big plans for you, Miss Christie," he nodded.
"I won't tell you all of them, but your sister tells me you're a
musician. What instruments can you play?"

"Any of them, Major," Lenora answered quickly. "She's
like my pa. He can play anything."

Major Hastings looked at Jerry and asked, "I don't suppose you can play a tuba?"

Jerry thought that was amusing and laughed outright. "Not
me, Major. Maybe I could pound on a big drum, but that's
all."

The four of them had a good meal of rich stew and vegetables, then Jerry rose. "Thanks for the meal. I've got to fly
early, but I'll be checking on you two."

"Thank you, Jerry," Christie said. "You came at just the
right time."

Jerry nodded, turned, and left with a jaunty step. "Now
then, come along and we'll get you settled," Lenora said
firmly. "And don't let Major Hastings talk you into going out
on the street with a band tonight."

"I had no such intentions!"

"Don't believe him, Christie," Lenora smiled. "He's an evangelist and will stop at nothing to get a service out of us. Come along now—" She led Christie to a room with a single bed and one chest. It was clean, but very small. "We'll fix it up nice," Lenora said. She put her arms up, and Christie came to her. The tension seemed to flow from her as her older sister held her tightly. "I've been so unhappy, Lenora!" she whispered.

"I know. But the good Lord has brought you here—and in his presence is fullness of joy!"

"You Mr. John Smith?"

The short, squat man who had stepped out of the taxi peered at Jerry with slate-colored eyes. "Yeah, I'm Smith. You the pilot?"

"Yes. Can I help you with your suitcase?" Jerry reached for a short, blunt leather suitcase, but Smith forestalled him. "I'll take this one. You can get that one there."

"Sure." Jerry picked up the shiny new black leather suitcase, saying, "You ready to go now? Weather's good enough for a nice flight."

The chunky man nodded, and Jerry noticed he had a wicked-looking scar that ran from his forehead down his cheek, turning outward to draw the lips into a grimace. *Looks like he nearly lost an eye in whatever did that*, Jerry thought. He realized that his passenger was not going to give him any small talk, so he loaded the suitcase into the small compartment and watched as Smith carefully put the smaller one beside it. Jerry shut the door, locked it, then nodded at the front cockpit. "You ever fly before?"

"No."

"Well, it'll be an easy flight." He showed the passenger how to get up to the seat, then reached over and fastened his safety belt. He noticed when he leaned over that Mr. Smith carried a gun but said only, "All right, I guess we're ready."

It was an easy flight, and when they reached Chicago, Smith said not one word until Eddy came and picked him up.

"Good job, Kid," Eddy nodded to Jerry. He gave him an envelope, saying, "Little bonus there."

"Thanks, Eddy."

Jerry went to his room, took a bath, and went to bed at once. He was tired and slept dreamlessly. The next day he went to the Salvation Army headquarters and visited with his aunts. He saw at once that Christie was more relaxed. The lines of tension were easing, and Jerry said to Lenora when he got her alone, "She's feeling better, isn't she?"

"Yes, much better. She won't talk much about what happened, but time helps."

"Will she join the Army like you?"

Lenora was wearing the black uniform and bonnet that women in the Army all wore. She touched her lapel tentatively, then said quietly, "It's too soon to tell, Jerry. For now she needs a place where she'll be loved and accepted—and where she'll have plenty to do. That's what we can give her with the Army. Later on she may decide to do something else. People don't always stay with the Army."

"No?"

"Oh, it's a hard, demanding life, Jerry," Lenora answered. "We work hard and have little, and people make fun of us."

Jerry grinned, making a fetching appearance. "Better not while I'm around. I'll teach them better manners!"

Lenora laughed at his threat. "Come along and beat the big bass drum for us tonight. We've got a service in Little Sicily."

"Hey, that's the roughest section of Chicago."

"That's where they need God, Jerry."

"I . . . I guess so. Well, I've got to run. Be back when I can. I promised to take you and Aunt Christie out for a fancy meal."

"That would be nice."

Jerry left the headquarters and went by Nick's office to get his instructions. Nick looked worried. "Glad to see you, Jerry. You ready to fly?"

"Always ready, Nick."

Nick grinned with relief. "Mr. Smith's in the Beverly Hotel over on Washington Street. Pick him up and take him back to Detroit, okay?"

"Sure, Nick. When do you want me to fly him there?"

"Right now!"

Jerry saw the tension on Nick's face, but he'd made up his mind to ask no questions. "On my way."

He found Smith waiting, and on the trip back to Detroit, the two of them barely spoke. When Smith got out of the plane, he grabbed his two suitcases and hurried off the field.

"You're welcome!" Jerry called after him, but the squat man didn't look around.

Jerry made the trip back uneventfully, went to bed, and slept hard. The next morning he ate breakfast at Buddy's Grill, and as he ate the eggs and ham, the proprietor himself came over to say, "Hey, Jerry, you been gone?"

"Made a short trip, Buddy."

"You hear about the big score?"

Jerry gave the pale-faced man a puzzled look, asking, "What's that?"

"Why, somebody took out Ace Tanhauser and two of his men." Tanhauser, Jerry knew, was a fairly big-time bootlegger. He had been with Torrio but had set up his own organization. "Look at the picture," Buddy urged, shoving a paper under Jerry's nose.

The picture was gruesome. It showed three men lying in stiff, awkward positions, obviously riddled with bullets. One of them held his arm up in a mute, eloquent gesture.

"Who did it?"

"Aw, who knows—or cares?" Buddy took the paper, adding, "I wish they'd all kill each other off—Capone, Torrio, Castellano." He looked at the paper and shrugged. "The cops are looking for some guy who they think might have done it." He read aloud, "'Police are looking for a suspect named Hymie Holtzman. Holtzman, a notorious gunman wanted by the police, was reportedly named by one of the dying victims. Holtzman is thirty-two years old, short and muscular and has a scar on the left side of his face. He is armed and dangerous, and police captain Lofton Edge warns that no citizen should try to apprehend him.'"

Jerry took the paper, staring at it incredulously. His face turned pale, and he got up at once, putting two bills on the bar. When he was going out the door, Buddy called out, "Hey, don't you want the rest of your breakfast, Jerry?"

Then he stared at the picture on the front page of the paper and said in disgust, "What kind of a jerk am I—showing a customer who's havin' his breakfast this kind of garbage?"

Jerry walked stiffly down the street, unaware of anything except the picture in the paper—and the description of Hymie Holtzman.

"It was Smith—" he muttered, and startled at the sound of his own voice, clamped his lips shut. His hands were trembling, and as he walked toward his car, he thought, *I've got to get out of this—I've got to!*

The pigeons overhead circled and cooed, coming down to light on the sidewalk. They walked with nodding heads, their soft voices a contrast to the raucous vehicles that passed, cars jostling each other. Finally a small boy came racing out of a doorway, waving a stick, and yelling at them. They rose with a flutter, circled once, then flew to the top of a dirty building and lined up on the edge of the roof.

But Jerry Stuart paid the birds no heed. He got into his car, drove away, and over and over he kept saying to himself, *I can't stay in this thing—I've got to get out!*

Part 3
AIRMAIL

13

MARIO

illiam "Big Bill" Thompson was probably one of the most corrupt politicians who ever filled the office of mayor of Chicago—which is quite a record, considering the competition. Under his look-the-other-way policy, prostitution, gambling, and bootlegging flourished.

Chicago, under Big Bill's rule, imported a small army of hardened criminals, many of them serving as thugs in the newspaper circulation war. The principal battles between Hearst's *Chicago Examiner* and the thugs of the *Chicago Tribune* were pitched battles, intimidating truck drivers, news dealers, and even paperboys.

In 1923, Big Bill was succeeded by an honest man, Judge William E. Dever. The new mayor closed so many speakeasies that Torrio, Capone, and Castellano moved the mob operations to Cicero, just west of Chicago. That unfortunate small town would have been better off if a tornado had hit, for Capone, using goons and thugs, influenced the Cicero municipal election so that only candidates favorable to a wide-open town were elected. Almost overnight more than 150 speakeasies mushroomed, and vice abounded.

Jerry Stuart inhabited this jungle, his nerves constantly alert, hating every minute of it. He was well paid, and he told himself this justified what he did—but deep down he knew that he had joined himself to a world of predators killing for profit.

As he drove down the streets of Cicero to the Castellano

headquarters, Jerry noted that the stores were decorated for George Washington's birthday. "Wonder what the father of our country would think of this if he came back?" he muttered. "Probably say it wasn't worth men going through Valley Forge to make men like Torrio and Capone rich."

He pulled his Stutz Bearcat into a narrow parking space in front of a gray stone building, entered, and as he passed by the two men who sat watching the entrance, he said, "Don't shoot, guys, it's only me."

"Hi, Jerry," one of them grunted. "How's the weather up there?"

"Rotten. Got caught in a thunderstorm."

"Yeah? Well, watch out for Nick. He's a bear with a sore tail today."

"What's wrong?"

"Dunno—but he just bawled me out for nothin'." The speaker was a tall, lanky individual named Bones Moreland. He carried three guns that Jerry knew of, and probably more. Now he glanced down at a paper in his hand and shook his head. "Competition is gettin' fierce. Lots of amateurs settin' up for themselves. Look at this, Jerry."

Taking the paper, Jerry ran his eyes down the list, which was apparently an offer for services to be rendered:

Punching	$ 2
Both eyes blacked	4
Nose and jaw broke	10
Blackjacked	15
Ear chawed off	15
Leg or arm broke	19
Shot in leg	25
Stabbed	25
Doing the big job	100

Jerry handed the paper back, saying with a straight face, "The business is going downhill, Bones. I think you fellows ought to start a union."

The thick-bodied man on the right, a former prizefighter named Sailor Harrelson, laughed aloud. "That's a hot one! A union!"

Bones snorted slightly. "We got ways of cuttin' down on the competition without startin' no union. Better get in there—but watch out for Nick. Like I say, he's in a bad mood."

"I'll watch myself, Bones."

The house had been a mansion once, and it still had traces of grandeur. Jerry climbed the spiral staircase, admiring as always the fine woodwork, burl-walnut panels that gleamed richly under the crystal chandelier. He smiled faintly at the eclectic collection of paintings on the wall. Those left by the original owner were staid landscapes painted by English masters. Nick kept them but had added cheap prints of famous actresses in various stages of undress. One print caught Jerry's eye, and he paused to examine it. It was a picture of Lillian Russell, the singer and actress whose torrid romance with Diamond Jim Brady had shocked the respectable world. Jerry studied the classic face and forthright eyes of the actress, then muttered, "You'd be right at home here, Lillian." Then he remembered that Lillian Russell had died the previous year, 1922, and was ashamed of speaking ill of the dead.

At the top of the stairs he turned to the left, then knocked on the massive, solid walnut door. When a voice said gruffly, "Come in," he stepped inside and found Nick Castellano talking with an older man. "This is Walt Stevens," Nick said shortly. "My pilot, Jerry Stuart. Sit over there, Jerry."

Jerry returned the polite greeting of Stevens, who at the advanced age of fifty-four was the dean of Chicago's gunmen, then took a seat on a Queen Anne sofa. As Nick spoke with Stevens, Jerry studied him carefully. He'd seen him twice but had never met the man. Now he thought of the strange incongruities that seemed to surround the killer. He was a cold-blooded murderer, yet he had adored his wife, nursing her for twenty years through a long illness until she died. He was

an educated man, his favorite authors being Robert Burns
and Jack London. And he had a strange puritanical streak.
He never touched a drop of liquor and forbade his adopted
daughters to wear short skirts or use cosmetics. Jerry had
heard that before he allowed them to read the classics, he ex-
cised any passages he considered indecent. He constantly
preached old-fashioned morality and idealism and denounced
the "flaming youth" of the era, typified by Clara Bow, Hollywood's "It" girl.

Jerry's attention was sharpened when Stevens said, "I've
got some new arms to show you, Nick." He turned to pick up
a brown leather case, and Jerry saw that it was the same shape
as the case Hymie Holtzman had brought on the plane. The
memory was still bitter in him, and he had kept up with the
matter. Holtzman had provided an ironclad alibi, and no one
had ever been arrested for the murder of Ace Tanhauser.

Stevens pulled a gun from the case, saying in the manner
of a college professor lecturing on the history of Rome, "This
is the highest-powered instrument of destruction ever developed, Nick—a Thompson submachine gun."

Jerry had heard of the machine gun, and he saw that it was
in effect a rifle with a circular drum to hold the ammunition.
"Weighs only eight and a half pounds," Stevens went on.
"Can fire up to a thousand .45 caliber pistol cartridges a
minute and penetrate a pine board three inches thick at five
hundred yards."

"Yeah? Lemme' see it." Nick took the machine gun and
held it as he asked, "Are these things hard to get? They must
cost a bundle."

Stevens shook his head. "That one you're holding costs
$175," he said. "A fifty-cartridge drum costs $21. They're not
hard to get right now." A frosty smile touched his thin lips.
"The Sullivan Law they passed in 1911 prohibits possession
of small firearms, but it puts no restrictions on guns like this.
Anybody can buy as many as he likes. Just have to give your
name and address."

"Better buy up an arsenal of these, Walt," Nick said, handing the gun back. "The Feds will get a law passed to keep these things under control."

"How many?"

"Better get twenty or so, I guess." Nick looked tired and irritable. "Get with Eddy on it. Better stock up on ammunition, too."

Stevens had pale blue eyes that seemed to have a hard surface. "Some trouble coming up, Nick?" he asked softly.

Castellano moved back to his chair, nodded, and lit up a cigar. "Get on with it, Walt. I'll get back with you tomorrow." He waited until the gunman left the room, then swiveled around to face Jerry. He had an angry expression on his face and said abruptly, "What's with this aunt of yours—Christie?"

Jerry stared at the man, not understanding the question. "Don't know what you're talking about, Nick."

"I'm talking about *this!*" Nick reached into his desk drawer, yanked out a newspaper, and threw it on the desk. He leaned back and watched as Jerry scanned the front page of the paper, his eyes hard and watchful.

Jerry saw that it was an old copy of the *Fort Smith Tribune*—and the story on the front page carried a picture of Christie and the headline, "Local Businessman Caught with Mistress." Jerry tossed the paper down and faced Castellano. "Christie was set up, Nick. The guy's wife wanted a divorce and he wouldn't give her one—so she hired a guy to frame this thing."

"It don't look good."

Jerry felt a stab of anger, his green eyes suddenly flashing. "You say that? Nick Castellano—the gangster?"

"Watch your mouth, Stuart!"

"You watch yours, Nick!" Jerry stood to his feet angrily. "I'm not afraid of you or your thugs! Don't talk about my family or I'll bust you!"

The threat seemed to amuse Nick, for he felt exactly the

same way about his own family. He stood up to say, "Don't fly off the handle, Jerry. I just wanted to know about the girl."

"What do you care about her?"

Nick stared at him, doubt in his eyes. "She ain't told you about Mario?"

"What about Mario?"

The question seemed to ease Nick's anger, and he said, "Why, he's been seeing her. I thought you knew that."

Jerry was stunned. "She never said a word to me, Nick. Neither has Aunt Lenora."

"That's the older sister? Well, maybe Christie don't tell her everything."

Jerry was disturbed about the thing. He shook his head, saying, "I'll have a talk with her, Nick. She doesn't need to be seeing Mario."

"Why not?" Nick's temper was as volatile as a man's could be. He'd been angry that his brother was seeing Christie— now he demanded, "He's not good enough for her? Is that it?"

Knowing that he was on dangerous ground, Jerry said carefully, "They're from different worlds, Nick. She's never been out of the hills until now. She's had a hard time, and she's confused. She doesn't need a slick city man like Mario. And he doesn't need her, either."

Nick nodded slowly. "I think you got it right." He went back to sit down and puffed slowly on the big cigar. He was silent for a time, then leaned forward to say, "Look, maybe I can explain. I know what kind of a guy I am. Me and Eddy came up rough. Owen knows about that. Okay, so we're a couple of hoods—that's the way it is. But we want something better for Mario." Nick was not a man who explained himself often, and now he seemed awkward and nervous. "We keep the kid out of the rough stuff. He's got his own law office—and I hope he don't ever want to work for us. I want him to make it in the kind of world your father is in—I want him to be respectable. You see how it is, Jerry?"

Jerry nodded slowly. He was seeing a side of Nick Castellano he'd never seen, and he liked the man for it. "Sure, I think that's great, Nick. Your mother would like it, wouldn't she?"

"That's right. The kid's the apple of her eye, and I'm going to see to it that nothin' stops Mario! He's got to go all the way."

"I hope he does, Nick."

"Somebody sent me this paper—don't know who. It scared me a little bit, Jerry. Takes a lot to do that to old Nick, hey?"

"Scared you how?"

"Why, I seen many a good man get taken down by a woman. When I seen the story, I thought it was so. I don't know your aunt, and there's lots of women out there who ain't straight."

"If you knew Christie, you'd know she's not one of them. Ask Dad or Uncle Owen if you don't believe me."

Nick hesitated. "I don't want to do that, Jerry, not if I don't have to."

"Why not?"

"Those two guys—I admire them. I don't want to do nothin' to mess up our friendship." Nick sat watching the young man, his mind working rapidly. Finally he said, "Look, Jerry, you're a smart guy. You and me, we can handle this. Like you say, your aunt don't need a guy like Mario—and he don't need her. In the first place, we're Catholic and your aunt ain't. That's trouble right there, Jerry!"

"Yes, it is—but I can't think they're serious, Nick." Jerry bit his lip, trying to think. He knew that if his dad or his uncle Owen found out about this, they would be terribly disturbed. "Let me talk to her, Nick. We're pretty close, and I think she'll tell me what's going on. And as soon as I get the word, I'll get right back to you."

Relief washed over the face of Nick Castellano. "Hey, that's great, Jerry. You do that! How about if you get right on it? We can fix it so you don't have no trips until this is settled."

"I'll go right over to see her, Nick." He turned at once, then halted. Swinging back toward Nick, he said, "Might be good if you talked to Mario, wouldn't it?"

Nick looked down at the desk for a moment. When he looked up he was troubled. "You know, Jerry, me and Eddy can talk about anything. But with Mario, it's different. He's been sort of sheltered, and he's educated. Somehow I can't get him to see what life is like. He—kind of looks down on the business. But I'll give it a shot. I may be way out of line on this thing," he added hopefully. "They may not be thinkin' of anything serious."

"I'll get back to you as soon as I can, Nick."

For some reason walking along in the falling snow beside a young woman wearing the sober dress of a Salvation Army lassie tickled the fancy of Mario Castellano. A pale sun burned in the gray sky, and he enjoyed the sight of millions of flakes falling across the path in front of them. They bit at his face, burning like icy fire, and he said, "Are you warm enough, Christie?"

"Yes. Except for my nose and my ears."

"Mine too—but I love the snow. Come on, let's make a snowman!"

The two of them had been walking down one of the aisles of Lincoln Park, but now they stopped and Christie smiled at his remark. "I don't think it would look good, would it? A Chicago lawyer and a Salvation Army lassie making a snowman in the park?"

Mario was wearing a long black overcoat and a felt derby. His dark eyes laughed with amusement, and he shrugged. "Who's to see? All the serious people are inside. Come on, I haven't made a snowman in years."

"All right, I'll help you." Christie stooped and began to form a snowball, saying, "When I was a little girl and we made a snowman, I cried because they wouldn't let me bring it in the house at night. I used to cry thinking of how lonely he must be out by himself in the dark."

"Here, let me get this ball started—" Mario took the snowball from her, placed it in the snow, and began to roll it along the layer of fresh snow. "If I'd been there," he said as the ball grew larger, "I'd have brought it in for you."

"He'd have melted, and then I'd have cried even more. Be careful, you're getting it lopsided!"

"Woman, you're talking to the snowman-making champion of the city of Chicago!"

Christie laughed, and the two of them worked to create first one ball, two feet in diameter, then another. "Now, you make a head while I put him together," Mario commanded. Bending over, he picked up the second ball, set it on top of the first, then cemented the middle with handfuls of the damp snow. Christie made a smaller ball and stuck it on the body.

"There you are," she nodded. "But you've got no eyes or nose or teeth. I wish we had some buttons for eyes, Mario—and a carrot for a nose."

Mario at once ripped two buttons from his coat and handed them to her. "Eyes—and how's this for a mouth?" He broke a branch from an overhanging oak, then snapped a curving piece out and stuck it on the head of the snowman. Taking his pen from his pocket he stuck it deep into the ball, just under the eyes. "A fine nose!"

Christie looked at him, wondering at the streak of fun that ran in him. She'd not seen any sign of this in his brothers, though, according to Amos, Mario's mother, Anna, had a trace of it. *Odd how we've gotten to be friends*, she thought as they laughed and worked to complete their snowman. *He's about the last person in the whole city of Chicago I'd have thought I'd get close to.*

Mario had come by headquarters unexpectedly just three days after she'd met him. Christie had been flustered at his appearance and thought he'd be totally out of place. He wore a diamond ring on his finger and an expensive suit that set him apart from the roughly dressed inhabitants of the establishment, but he had a way of making friends, she soon discovered. She caught him giving money to a poor woman with two children who'd been evicted, and he seemed embarrassed by the incident. Major Hastings told her some time later, "He's a generous man, Christie. He gave me an envelope filled with bills and mumbled that he was behind with his Christmas giving—told me not to let it get out."

At first Lenora was amused by Mario, who came back to visit at least once a week. But when Christie had started going out for dinner with him, then for walks, she watched the thing carefully. She had said once to Christie, "Be careful, Christie. He's a worldly man, and you don't need to get involved with him."

Christie had merely agreed, but now as they laughed and worked on the snowman, she was suddenly aware that times like these with Mario had become very important to her. She had been happy with the Army, but she missed her home— the old days, not those of recent times. Lenora was a dear, and the two had grown even closer. But Lenora had been given more and more responsibility so that she had little time to spend with Christie.

Thus it was that the visits of the lawyer came to be more and more welcome to Christie. She knew that they were from different worlds, but somehow his wit and gentleness filled a place in her heart. She had grown up in the midst of brothers and missed the male companionship she'd enjoyed with them.

Now as the two laughed at the comic features of their creation, she said, "At home we always got old clothes and put them on our snowman."

At once Mario plucked off his expensive derby and set it in place. Laughing, he took a cigar from his pocket and stuck it in the snowman's face, saying, "There now, you look like a Chicago alderman!"

"Mario—you'll freeze without your hat!" Christie removed the hat, then reached up to brush the snow from his dark hair. She scolded him, but after she replaced the hat, he suddenly reached up and took her hand.

"Your hands are like ice!" he said. "Let me warm them."

"Oh—they're all right," Christie said quickly. But he held her hands, lifted them to his lips, and blew on them. She was shocked by the gesture and lifted her face to him. Her dark blue eyes grew large, and the snow left tiny flakes in her long lashes. As he continued to blow on her hands, she grew uncomfortable for some reason, and then when he suddenly kissed her hands, she whispered, "Don't . . . don't do that!"

"Why not?" Mario looked at her with surprise. He was twenty-eight and had known women. They had come to him easily enough—so easily that he had begun to wonder if he had any quality except money to draw a woman. Most of those he'd known had been experienced—and hard. It was the gentleness of Christie Stuart that had caught his attention, and when he had visited her once and found out that she had wit as well, he was drawn to her. Now as he saw the frightened expression on her face, he was startled. Never had he known a woman who was so fragile, and he said quietly, "You don't have to be afraid of me, Christie."

She saw something in his dark eyes that drove the fear away. "I . . . I'm silly, aren't I, Mario?"

"You're very lovely," he replied. "And I wish you'd trust me. I'd never do anything to hurt you."

"I don't think you would."

He still held her hands, which had grown warmer, and he was suddenly very much aware of the feminine grace of her features. He drew her to him gently, ready to release her at the first protest, but she made none. Her eyes grew wider, and when he bent and kissed her, he was shocked at the feeling that ran through him at the touch of her soft lips. He was accustomed to women who met him hungrily, but there was an innocence in Christie that was like nothing he'd ever seen in a woman. She was very still, but there was a pressure in her lips that made him think that beneath the stillness of her demeanor lay a passion that had never been touched.

He lifted his head, smiled at her, then said quietly, "I like you very much, Christie. There's a . . . a sweetness in you that's very rare."

Christie could not speak, for she was shocked at herself. She was shocked that she'd let him kiss her—and even more alarmed at the pleasure that had come with his caress. It frightened her, and she dropped her gaze to the ground. "I think we'd better go, Mario," she said quietly.

"All right."

The two walked through the slanting lines of white, and finally Mario stopped and drew her around. "Look, I don't know how to act with you. Are you angry with me?"

"No, I'm not angry—but I think we shouldn't see each other for awhile."

"You're wrong," he said, and then he took her hands again. "I'm not used to a woman like you—but don't shut me out, Christie." He was utterly serious, and his eyes were intent. "These times with you—well, they've come to be important to me. I don't want to lose them."

"They . . . they're important to me, too, Mario," Christie said. But there was a tremulous note in her voice as she met his eyes honestly. "I can't let myself like you too much. We're too far apart."

"Sure—but we can be friends?"

"Y-yes, I think so."

"Good! I'd hate to lose my best snowman-making helper!" He was happy that the crisis had passed. Later he would try to understand why it was that the thought of not seeing this woman again was something that alarmed him greatly. "Come on, let's go to the street meeting. Lenora's been trying to get me to one of those for weeks."

The anxiety left her, and a droll thought came to her. "I'm

going to play the trumpet with the band. But we need more
than that. Can you play an instrument?"

"Why—as a matter of fact I play sax with a little band—
just for kicks. But I can't . . ."

"Oh, Mario! You're an answer to prayer! Come on, we've
got to hurry."

Mario protested, but when they got to where the service
was to be held, he found himself standing between Christie
and Major Hastings, feeling like an utter fool. He didn't know
any of the songs, but he was very good, and after hearing a
song only once, could stumble along.

As he played "When the Saints Go Marching In," he
thought suddenly what it would be like if one of his clients—
or Nick—came by and saw him. The thought amused him,
and when Major Hastings asked him what was funny, he said,
"Just thinking how I've never played with a better band,
Major."

Lenora was in front of them, the snow making her dark cap
white. She heard the remark and turned to look at the three.
She caught the eye of Major Hastings and winked, then when
the song was over, she lifted her voice, saying, "Now, let me
tell you about Jesus—God's Christmas present to the world!"

14

SNOWBOUND

lthough Jerry left Nick's office firmly determined to go right to his aunt and find out what was going on with Mario Castellano, by the time he had driven a few blocks, he began to have second thoughts. Dodging a horse-drawn wagon skillfully—and ignoring the shaken fist of the driver—he began to hum a few bars of "Yes, We Have No Bananas." It was the only song he knew all the words to, and he drove people crazy singing it years after everyone else had forgotten it.

Speaking aloud, he said, "I can't go read the riot act to Aunt Christie. She's my *aunt*, for crying out loud! And who am I to be giving advice to anyone? After the mess I've made of my own life, nobody's going to listen to me."

He drove aimlessly around the Loop, then finally thought, *I'll have to go to one of Aunt Christie's brothers. Uncle Owen and Dad know how dangerous it is to get close to the Castellano family. They can tell her.*

But Owen was in California, and Amos was in bed with the flu. *Well, that leaves Uncle Gavin,* Jerry thought, and at once went to his uncle's apartment. He found Heather, who said, "He's out at the airport, Jerry." She seemed to be discouraged but smiled and said, "Go see him. You two need to spend more time together."

"Sure, I'll do that, Aunt Heather."

Jerry drove to the airport, and when he found Gavin, he knew at once that something was wrong. Gavin was talking

180

with a tall, portly man, and as Jerry waited until he finished, he noted that his uncle's face was drawn. Gavin had been serious, but he was not gloomy, and when he turned and walked away from the big man, Jerry stepped forward. "Hello, Uncle Gavin."

"Hello, Jerry. What are you doing out here?"

The words were terse, and Jerry's first thought was, *He's still sore at me for messing up with the show.* But then Gavin managed a grin that made his eyes crinkle. "Didn't mean to bite your head off, Jerry. Come on, let's get some coffee."

The two of them made their way to the Dew Drop Inn and soon were sipping blistering hot black coffee. Gavin had been silent, and finally Jerry asked, "What's the matter?"

"Is it that obvious?" Gavin asked with surprise. "Well, I guess I won't ever make a good poker player." He took a swig of the coffee, blinked at the bite of it, then lowered the cup. "I just sold the show, Jerry." He saw the surprise in the young man's eyes and said, "I've seen it coming for a long time. The public's gotten tired of air shows. They were great after the war, but now it takes more than an outside loop in a Jenny to get the people out."

"I didn't know you were in trouble. Guess having clods like me working for you didn't help any."

"Don't give yourself any credit for this, Jerry," Gavin said quickly. "Like I said, I've seen it coming a long time. I was lucky to sell out at a good price to McGovern."

"What will you do now?"

Gavin shot a speculative glance at his nephew. "Going to work for the government."

"Flying the mail, I'll bet!"

"That's right."

Having forgotten his reason for visiting his uncle, Jerry, young and impulsive, spoke his thought even as it came to his mind. "I'm going with you, Uncle Gavin!" He saw the amused surprise on Gavin's face and flushed. "I'm sick of my job. Got to get out of it."

"I think that's good. Your dad is sick about it, and your mother, too." Gavin leaned forward and put his elbows on the table, examining the smooth face of his nephew. "Why'd you ever get involved in such a fool thing? You could get killed—or go to jail for a long time."

Jerry shrugged his shoulders wearily. "Ask me why I did a hundred other stupid things, Uncle Gavin," he muttered. He sipped the coffee, then nodded. "I don't blame you for thinking I'm crazy. I think so myself. But I want to fly, and this is about all I can think of."

"You're a great pilot, Jerry," Gavin said. "You have more coordination and better hands than most pilots. But this isn't like flying with the show. It isn't like anything else."

"Why not?"

"I guess because it's never been done before." Gavin toyed with his cup, then demanded, "How much do you know about how the airmail service started?"

"Not a lot."

"Well, it got off to a rough start. On the very first flight, a Washington–New York run, the plane started to take off, then stopped. Someone had forgotten to fill the fuel tank."

"Sounds like something I'd do," Jerry grinned. "Did he make it?"

"No, he got lost and landed in Maryland." Gavin had to smile, then said, "Things are a little better now, but there's no radio on the planes, and few navigational instruments." A sober look washed across his face, and he said quietly, "Thirty-one of the first forty pilots to fly the mail from New York to Chicago were killed."

Jerry stared at Gavin's grim face and sobered instantly. "And yet you're going to fly the airmail?"

"Yes, but you don't have to. It takes all a man's got, Jerry. Back in February of '21 a friend of mine, Jack Knight, landed in Omaha after a 248-mile flight from North Platte, Nebraska. It was one leg of the first transcontinental day-and-night delivery. Jack was just about dead for sleep when he landed—

and he found out that no pilot was available for the next leg, a four-hundred-mile flight to Chicago."

"What happened?"

"Jack knew that Congress would be voting the next day on the mail appropriation, so he climbed back into his plane and made the flight through heavy snow. He was in that open plane for ten hours, Jerry. I'm telling you the truth. You need to cut your ties with Castellano—but I'd hate to see you get killed flying the mail."

Despite his differences with his uncle, Jerry admired him tremendously. "I guess it's time to find out if I'm good for anything," he said. "Will you help me get a job?"

Gavin hesitated, then nodded. "Yes. And I'll kick your tail all over the landing strip if you don't come through!" Then he smiled and slapped the young flier on the shoulder. "It's a big thing, nephew—and we're going to be a part of it!"

Lylah came home from the studio perplexed and weary. She had shot the last scene at two, and now she went into the letdown that always came to her when a play or a movie was finished. The weather was frightful, snow falling and the temperature dropping. She took a long, hot bath, then dressed and got ready to go pick up Adam. She was reaching for her coat when a knock at the door startled her. When she opened it, Jerry grinned at her. "Hello, Aunt Lylah!"

"Jerry! What in the world are you doing in California?" She pulled him inside and at once began to pepper him with questions.

"Hey, not so fast!" Jerry protested. "I'll answer one question, then we go eat. I'm here to pick up a plane and fly it back to Chicago."

"For the airmail service?" she asked.

"Sure. Now, I'm starved. Let's go eat."

"I've got to go across town and pick up Adam."

"I've got a car. Belongs to a fellow who works at the aircraft factory. Let's go."

Lylah pulled on her heavy coat, and the two left the house. As Jerry followed her directions, he brought her up to date on the family. When he mentioned Christie, Lylah gave him a direct look. "Is she still seeing Mario Castellano?"

"Yeah, I guess so—but she says they're just friends. How'd you know about that?"

"Lenora calls me quite often. She's really worried about Christie—and your parents are worried about you. Do you *have* to fly, Jerry? It's so dangerous—even Gavin says so."

"It's a piece of cake," Jerry grinned. "Don't worry about me, Auntie." He slammed on the brakes, and the car skidded on the snow, stopping inches short of a black car. "You going to introduce me to Clara Bow while I'm here?"

"You wouldn't like her. She hasn't a brain in her head."

"Not her *head* I'm interested in, Auntie," Jerry grinned.

"That's all this family needs," Lylah said. "Christie running around with a gangster and you chasing after a Hollywood sex symbol."

"Is she honestly that?" Jerry demanded. "I really should meet her."

They joked until finally they arrived at the Hart house. When they got out of the car, Jerry looked up at the dark skies. Snow was falling heavily, some of the flakes as large as quarters. "No flying tonight—and driving a car's going to be pretty hard."

When they stepped into the warmth of the big room, Lylah snatched up Adam, who came running to her, flinging himself into her arms. "There's my boy!" She hugged him, then nodded to Jerry. "This is your cousin Jerry. He flies airplanes."

"Can I go with you?"

Jerry laughed at the solemn question, then reached out and took the boy in his arms. "Sure you can—if it ever stops snowing."

"This is my nephew Jerry," Lylah said. "My brother Amos's son. Jerry, this is Bonnie Hart—who has saved my life."

Jerry took in the beauty of the girl who smiled at him, noting the straight black hair and the almond-shaped dark blue eyes. "Always glad to meet a lady who saves the life of my aunt. Did you pull her out of the way of a train?"

Bonnie shook her head. At that moment Jesse Hart came into the room through a side door, carrying a huge load of split wood for the fireplace. "Oh, this is my brother, Jesse, Mr. Stuart."

"My father is Mr. Stuart—I'm Jerry. Glad to meet you, Jesse."

Jesse tossed the wood into the woodbox and came to offer his hand. "Hello. How'd you get in through the snow?"

"Well, it wasn't easy. I thought California was the land of sunshine."

"Usually it is. The wireless says it's a freak storm."

"I've got dinner almost ready," Bonnie said. "As soon as I set the table, we'll eat."

"I'm the best table-setter in the conference," Jerry volunteered. "Just show me the plates and the table."

Jesse moved forward, saying, "Let me take your coat, Lylah. Go sit down by the fire and thaw out." He shook the snow from her mink coat, studied it, then shook his head. "You died in a good cause, mink—to keep a lady warm."

Lylah had gone to spread her hands to the fire that crackled cheerfully in the fireplace. At his words she turned to shake her head at Jesse. "You have the oddest mind, Jesse. I've had that coat for two years—and I never *once* thought of where the fur came from."

"He hath put all things in subject to man," Jesse said, coming over to stand by her. "I guess that means minks, too."

Lylah hesitated, asking, "Is that from the Bible?"

"Yes, Hebrews 1, verse 8."

"You know the Bible better than anyone I've ever known. It seems like you have a verse to fit anything that happens."

The fire threw a flickering reflection in Jesse's clear brown eyes. "We had a preacher when I was a boy. He was that way, always quoting Scripture for anything that happened. One

Sunday morning when he was preaching, he opened his
mouth, and a big black bug flew right in!"

"How awful! What did he do?"

"Well, he had to either spit it out and make a real scene—
or swallow it. So he decided just to swallow it." Jesse's square
face looked bland, but his eyes gleamed with humor. "After
the service one of the deacons went to him. He said, 'Well,
preacher, you've always got a verse to fit anything that happens. What verse fits that bug?'"

Jesse stopped and picked up a log, tossing it on the fire.
He watched the myriads of yellow sparks fly upward, and
Lylah asked impertinently, "Well, what did he say?"

"The preacher? Oh, he shot right back, 'That bug—well,
he was a stranger and I took him in!'"

Lylah found this irresistibly funny. She had a good strong
laugh, deep and husky. Now she laughed so hard that she fell
against Jesse, holding to him. "You made that up!" she gasped.
And then she realized that he had put his arms around her.

Looking up, she saw that his eyes were fixed on her in a
straight gaze. She'd seen him look at things like that many
times, for he was an observing man. Now that she was the ob-
ject of this gaze, she grew quiet, submitting to his embrace
and his searching glance. The fire sputtered, and from the
dining room came the sounds of voices and clattering dishes.
Lylah was aware of the lean strength of his body, the masculine smell of his clothing. She expected him to kiss her—most
men would—and she wondered what it would be like.

But Jesse said, "You're troubled, Lylah. What's the matter?"

Lylah was taken by surprise. He was always doing that to
her. She had expected him to kiss her; instead he'd come up
with one of those uncanny observations of his. She drew back
and leaned against the mantel, asking, "What makes you
think anything's wrong?"

"What is it?"

Lylah turned to face him, her face glowing from the heat
of the blaze. Her eyes were filled with wonder, and she said,

"I'm not much of an actress, am I? Not with you, anyway." She bit her lip, then shook her head slightly. "I'm at a fork in the road, Jesse. Got to make a decision, and I don't want to."

"Want to tell me about it?"

"Oh, it's my work. I finished the last picture under my contract, and now I've got to decide what to do."

"Does DeMille want you to do more pictures?"

"Yes—but I'm not sure I want to." She moved restlessly, her long hair catching the warm tints of the yellow fire. She still had the figure and grace of a much younger woman, and now as she turned to face him, Jesse admired the strong features of her face. "I've got an idea, but it's so crazy I haven't had the nerve to tell anyone."

"Tell me," Jesse offered. "I've heard a crazier one, I'll bet. Probably I've even had one that's worse."

Lylah hesitated, then said, "I want to get into the *making* of movies, Jesse. My days as a leading lady are over. The public wants either 'little girl' roles such as Mary Pickford plays, or 'vamps,' sex symbols, like Clara Bow. I can't do either of those. It'll be character roles from now on."

"Some pretty good ones around," Jesse shrugged.

"Oh, yes, and I'll be acting," Lylah said quickly. "But I want the best for Adam. I want him to go to the finest schools, to have the best of things."

Jesse shook his head in a mild reproof. "Not sure about that," he said quietly. "I see rich kids going to the devil all the time. Money's not the answer."

Lylah studied the tall man carefully. He reminded her suddenly of Don Satterfield, the steady minister from Bible school days. The two men looked nothing alike, for Don was plain, and Jesse, while not handsome, was quite attractive to women. No, it was the *solid* quality Jesse had that reminded her of Satterfield. *He'd never change—always be the same, just like Don*, Lylah thought.

"You're right," Lylah admitted. "But I've got to take care of him, and I only know one thing—the theater."

"I'm surprised you never married."

Lylah looked up, startled. "I've had chances," she nodded. "Men are drawn to actresses—mostly for the wrong reasons." She hesitated, then said, "I'm not a good judge of men, I guess. I've been a fool more than once."

"Join the club," Jesse said wryly. "I've made a specialty of throwing myself at the wrong women—well, *one* woman, actually."

"You were married?"

"No, thank God, it didn't get that far." Pain touched his fine eyes, and he tried a smile that failed. "I loved her more than I loved life, Lylah."

When he said no more, Lylah whispered, "What happened, Jesse?"

"She—found somebody else." It was a brief, clipped statement, but it told Lylah more about Jesse than if he'd spoken volumes. The pain in his face was the result of a misery that had cut him so deeply he couldn't even bear to speak of it. Lylah knew that women felt like that, but for the first time she understood that a man could suffer in the same way.

"I'm sorry, Jesse," she said quietly.

"Ancient history. Shouldn't have mentioned it."

"Yes, you should." Lylah put her hand out and he took it. "We're friends aren't we?"

Jesse held her hand, and somehow the warmth in her eyes drove away the shadows of old grief. "Can't think when I've ever had a better one," he said simply. And then he asked, "Don't you think friends should express their feelings in a physical manner at times like this?"

Lylah's eyes crinkled with amusement. "I've never had a man try to get a kiss with such a line. You're something, Jesse Hart—and yes, I do think a physical demonstration of our friendship is in order." She came into his arms and lifted her face. His lips were firm but gentle, and when she drew back, her eyes were glistening with tears. "You're quite a fellow, Jesse Hart!"

"You make a great cup of hot chocolate, Bonnie."

The snow had fallen so fast that by the time dinner was over, Jesse had proclaimed that it was too late for the visitors to go home. "We've got beds, cots, and can make Baptist pallets," he'd said firmly.

After a flurry of arranging, it had been settled. Now all were asleep except Bonnie and Jerry. They were sitting on the sofa in front of the fire, and Jerry tasted the steaming chocolate carefully, then nodded critically. "Yep, you can't get good stuff like this at Mom's Cafe."

Bonnie had pulled her legs up under her. She had listened to Jerry's stories of his time in the air circus for two hours, and now she said, "Tell me another story about the circus."

Jerry was amused at the girl. "It's late for little girls to be up."

"I'm not a little girl!" Bonnie said indignantly. "I'll be eighteen next month."

"But what big eyes you have, Grandma!" Jerry laughed at the indignation that came at once. "Don't try to grow up so fast," he advised. "Enjoy your childhood."

"I am *not* a child!" Bonnie's dark eyes flashed, and she suddenly unlimbered her leg and kicked out. When he grunted, she smiled and said smugly, "You can't strike me. I'm just a child."

"Why, you little brat!" Jerry rubbed his leg, but then laughed at her. "I give up! You're not a child. You are, in fact, a very charming young lady."

"Good! Now tell me about the circus. Did you ever jump out of a plane in a parachute?"

"Yes, a few times. But it was mostly a young woman who did that stunt."

"What was her name?"

"Cara Gilmore."

Something about the tone of Jerry's voice caught Bonnie's attention. She turned to face him, a curious light in her dark blue eyes. She studied the long form of the young man, then asked, "Did you know her very well?"

Jerry stirred restlessly. "Getting colder," he observed, then when he met her curious gaze, nodded reluctantly. "Yes, I knew her pretty well."

"Tell me about her. Was she pretty?"

"She was good-looking," Jerry responded shortly. "She's getting to be famous. Saw a story in a magazine about a long-distance flight she did last month." Jerry got up and went to stare out of the window. "Snow in California!" he exclaimed in disgust. "Trust me to hit the beach in the middle of a blizzard! Do you and Jesse go fishing much?"

But Bonnie demanded, "Were you in love with her?"

"Great Scott!" Jerry exclaimed, whirling around to stare at the girl. "Don't you do anything but ask questions?"

"I'll bet you were," Bonnie persisted. "You get all nervous when you talk about her. Did you break up?"

Jerry glared at Bonnie almost angrily. "You're not grown up at all! You're a nagging pest!"

Bonnie saw that she'd gone too far. Quickly she came off the sofa and stood facing him. "I'm sorry, Jerry," she whispered contritely. "Jesse scolds me all the time for being so nosy. He says my spiritual gift is meddling."

The sight of the young woman's woeful face drove the anger out of Jerry. He had not been able to think about Cara rationally since their last meeting. He had not seen her recently, but he knew in his heart that all she had to do was give him one look, and he'd go to her at once.

But then he saw that Bonnie's lower lip was trembling, and his irritation fled. "I was in love with her," he said slowly. "But it's all over. She's famous, and I'm only a humble airmail pilot."

"I . . . didn't mean to pry," Bonnie said, and Jerry was shocked to see tears in her eyes. "I'm sorry."

"Hey, it's not that bad!" Jerry exclaimed. He reached into his pocket and pulled out a handkerchief. "Here, let me take care of this—" He dabbed at the tears, then awkwardly patted her on the shoulder. "I'm just an old bear," he said gently. "Look, sit down and I'll have one more cup of this great chocolate—and I'll tell you about how I did my first outside loop, okay?"

"Okay."

Jerry sat down and told the story, but he was watching the face of the young woman. *Never saw a girl so sensitive—crying like that over nothing!*

Then the clock struck one time, and Jerry exclaimed, "One o'clock! I can't believe it!"

Bonnie rose and took his cup. "Thanks for telling me about the air circus."

"Good night, Bonnie. See you in the morning. Maybe we can have a snowball fight with Adam."

"That would be fun. I put an extra blanket out for you. Good night." She turned to leave, but a thought came to her. She hesitated, then turned to say, "Your work is very dangerous, isn't it?"

"Yes, I guess so."

"I'll pray for you."

She whirled, embarrassed by her remark, afraid that he'd be offended. When she was in bed with Lylah, Bonnie lay awake a long time thinking of the stories Jerry had told her. But just as she drifted off, she thought of his expression when he spoke of Cara Gilmore.

He's still in love with her, she thought. *I could see it in his face— I wonder if she's older than Jerry?* And then she thought illogically, *I'm almost eighteen—and he's twenty-three. That's not much difference.*

15

INTO THE DARKNESS

For several days after Jerry flew back to Chicago Lylah spent most of her time with Adam. More often than not when she took him to various places, Jesse and Bonnie accompanied them. Jesse had acquired a Ford—the survivor of a collision. After he put it back together, it ran, after a fashion. The weather changed abruptly, the snow melted, and the four of them explored the countryside of southern California.

One of Adam's favorite places was the beach. He loved to dig in the sand, and he made the sand fly with the toy shovel Jesse bought for him. One Thursday afternoon, Lylah and Jesse were sitting on a blanket watching him burrow like a mole. They were back from the edge of the surf and could hear the boy's excited treble voice as he explained to Bonnie what he was doing.

"Wish everyone was as easy to please as Adam," Jesse said lazily. He had been up all night working on a story, and his eyes were half-lidded. He wore a pair of faded khaki pants and a blue sweater over a white shirt. *Somehow no matter how old his clothes are,* Lylah thought, *he makes them look good. Some men can put on a brand-new suit, and it looks like it came from a secondhand sale.*

"I guess most kids are easily pleased," she said.

"Nope. Most of 'em are unhappy. The 'Golden Years of Youth' are a fable." Jesse picked up a shell, examined it carefully, then said idly, "Look at this, Lylah—how intricate it is!"

192

Lylah obediently looked at the shell, but her mind was elsewhere. "I guess you're right—about some kids. I was mostly miserable growing up." Picking up a handful of sand, she let it filter through her fingers, then shook her head. "To tell the truth, things haven't been so great *since* I grew up."

Dropping the shell, Jesse twisted around to face her. "You're still worried about what to do, aren't you?"

"Oh, I'm spoiled, I suppose. About twenty million women would like to be in the movies. And all I've done is mope and feel sorry for myself."

"Have you talked to anyone about your idea?"

"No, not yet. What would I say? Everyone in charge of making movies is a man who looks on movie stars—especially women—as bodies without a brain. If I went to a producer and told him I wanted to *make* a movie, he'd pat me on the head and say, 'Run along now, dear, and let the *men* who know how make the movies.'"

Jesse nodded. "That's pretty well true in most businesses, I guess. Women have made some gains—who would have believed twenty years ago that women would be able to vote today? It'll be different someday."

"When? Jesse, I'm worried about *now*—that's all the time I have! And it's moving past me." She gave him a look filled with doubt and then said, "I don't even know what *kind* of movie I'd like to make. But so many *bad* films are rolling out of the studios, I'd like to do something *good*."

The two of them sat on the sand watching Adam and Bonnie dig in the sand. Overhead the gulls were uttering their harsh cries, circling in eccentric patterns, their cold eyes glittering. The waves rolled in, completing their journey of thousands of miles, their roar making a final crescendo of broken white water on the beach. Overhead the sky arched like a blue dome, dotted by rounded humps of thick clouds that bowled along over the horizon.

Jesse listened as Lylah spoke of her dream, and he traced the unhappiness in her voice. She was approaching a fork in the road and was uncertain which direction to take. Now as she sat hugging her knees he saw that there was a tension in her that had not been there when they first met. Her deep-set violet eyes, usually brilliant and clear, looked tired and filled with doubt. *She's running out of time—so she thinks. That's the worst time to make decisions.*

"Lylah," he said slowly, "I've been pretty critical of the whole movie industry. I'm a book man, and I wouldn't give one page of Dickens for all the movies ever made. But when I met you, well, I began to think about films. What is bad about them—what is good—"

Lylah listened carefully as Jesse spoke. She knew he was a fine writer, for she'd read his pieces. She knew also that he was fiercely independent and highly creative. None of the things he'd written had been the usual sort of writing—and publishers were beginning to come to him, asking for more. Now as he spoke of how silly some of the movies were, how far from human experience, she said, "Why, that's what *I've* always thought of the movies, Jesse!"

"You're a smart woman, Lylah. The question is—how does anyone make the things better? We've got Keystone Cops chasing people, Harold Lloyd hanging from buildings, Chaplin's Little Tramp, and Theda Bara, the female vamp. But not much in the way of good solid drama."

Lylah was intrigued at Jesse's knowledge of her profession. "I don't know if the public would go to see a fine movie, Jesse," she said at last. "I've seen bad plays become huge successes, while good ones played to empty theaters."

"I guess America has plenty of bad taste," Jesse admitted, "but I've got the idea that if you took a contemporary subject—something everyone's interested in—and did something *different* with the camera, they'd come to see it."

Instantly Lylah looked at Jesse. "I have the feeling you've got something along that line in your head. Let's have it."

"Well, I feel foolish, getting involved in a form I know so little about—but I've been tinkering around with an idea for a movie. I've got a little of it on paper, but I don't know enough about how to put things on the screen to really write it."

"Well, *I* do," Lylah nodded. "Tell me about it."

"All right, here it is. What's everybody interested in? Criminals, Chicago criminals. The public can't get enough of them! Every day they read stories in the newspapers about the Torrios and the Capones. Everybody knows they're evil men, but people are fascinated with them." He shook his head ruefully. "I think evil has a fascination of its own that virtue doesn't have."

"Shakespeare is like that. The really great villains in his plays are the meatiest roles—Richard III, Lady Macbeth."

"Exactly! And the hero of this movie I've dreamed up will have a dark side like those great characters. He will be a young man who rises to power in the criminal world until he becomes a famous man with power so great that his word is like a king's! Somebody like Al Capone or Johnny Torrio—" He spoke rapidly, using his hands to shape out his ideas.

When he finally stopped, Lylah asked, "What about different kinds of camera work?"

"Most movies are filmed from one level and from one distance. It's like the camera is nailed to the spot, and the viewer gets one point of view. But that's not the way life is, Lylah. We get all sorts of views. Why not take the camera off the tripod and put it on the floor, pointed up. Say you want to stress how strong and powerful a man is. From that low point of view, he'd look like a giant! And why does a close-up always have to be of a *face?* In your last film, in the scene where you learn you're going to die, the camera was glued to your face. That's all right, but it's done *every time!*"

"What else could you do?"

"Why, show your *hands!*" Jesse said at once. He picked up one of her hands and held it up. "Your hands clenching as you learn that the end has come! Or have a symbol, a leaf falling from a tree—*anything* to break the same old pattern!" He suddenly blinked and uttered an embarrassed laugh. "Well, here's the great expert. Never been on a movie set, and here I am telling the people who do know how they should do it!"

Lylah's face had become intent as Jesse had outlined his idea. Now she exclaimed, "It's *wonderful*, Jesse! Nothing like it has ever been done! How soon can you have the screenplay ready?"

"What?—"

"As soon as you have it, I'll take it to Carl Thomas. He's a small-time producer, but he's not lackluster like most of them. What we have to do—"

"Wait a minute!" Jesse protested. "I just told you, Lylah, I don't know how to write a screenplay. It's not at all like writing an article or a novel."

Lylah took his hand in hers. "We'll do it together, Jesse," she said simply. Her smile was warm, and excitement brightened her eyes. "You and I—we'll do this thing together!"

Jesse thought for a brief moment of the one time in his life he'd put his trust in a woman. The bitterness and pain of that experience still rankled inside, and for one instant he drew back. Then he took a deep breath and squeezed her hand.

"Yes—together we can do it, Lylah!"

The mechanic admired the pilot's clothes. "You look good, Jerry . . . wisht I could wear duds like that!"

Jerry still wore the same outfit he'd worn while working the air show: twill trousers tight at the calf, flaring at the knee; highly polished boots of cordovan leather; a crimson silk scarf around his neck; and goggles raised on his leather helmet.

But Jerry felt the bite of the wintry breath and shook his head. "Got to bundle up, Mack." He walked back to his locker and began gearing up. He had already put on the heaviest winter underwear he could buy and had bought a leather face mask. He donned two heavy wool sweaters, a pair of coveralls, and a heavy fleece-lined jacket. When he finally pulled on his parachute, he felt like a ball, and he knew that he'd have to squeeze himself into the cockpit.

When he got back to where Mack was waiting, the mechanic handed him a pistol in a black leather holster. Taking the gun he grimaced. "Who am I supposed to shoot?"

"Dunno, but it's gov'ment regulations."

Jerry grunted. Then the mail truck came. Two men climbed out and began loading the mail into the Pitcairn, placing it in the compartment just in front of the cockpit. As they loaded it, Jerry studied the craft, passing his hand over the fuselage. He caressed it as he might the shoulder of a beautiful woman, noting the way the rudder fin curved up from the fuselage. He studied the name on the rudder—*Pitcairn Mailwing.*

Walking around the plane, he came to the engine, a Wright J–5 Whirlwind, the finest and most powerful he'd ever flown behind. It swung a new type of propeller made of metal, not the old wooden variety. It was painted black to protect the pilot's eyes against the glare that came like a sword through the sunshine.

He studied the gentle symmetrical twist of the blade, glanced at the words on the side, U.S. AIRMAIL, then climbed into the cockpit, his parachute banging awkwardly at the back of his legs. He reached forward and touched the controls. Gently he moved the rudder pedals back and forth, looking over his shoulder to watch the rudder swing from side to side. Grasping the control stick, he moved it forward, then backward, watching the elevator flippers rise and fall. He was listening and touching the machine reverently, gently, knowing that it held his life.

He studied the instruments before him carefully. A compass, a turn-and-bank instrument, which he didn't trust, an airspeed gauge, an altimeter, a tachometer, and oil pressure and fuel gauges. They were more precious to him than any books ever written, for they guided him through the blackness of space, the wild storms that tossed the plane like a ship caught in a hurricane. When his senses failed, he had to trust in these bits of metal and glass.

"Sign here." Jerry signed the slip, handed it back, then looked down at the mechanic who had come to stand in front of the propeller.

"Ready, Jerry?"

"Sure."

He fastened his safety belt and slipped on his gloves. Then the mechanic asked, "Off?"

"Off."

Jerry put the magneto switch in the off position. The mechanic stepped forward and pulled the propeller through a few turns, then stepped back.

"Contact!"

"Contact."

Jerry pumped the primer four times, then pressed the inertia starter switch and listened as a low whine came from the engine and then rose in pitch. When it reached its highest note and held, he pulled the mesh lever. The gears squealed shrilly, then the propeller turned very slowly. Jerry switched the magneto to "both." Smoke came pouring out of the exhaust ports. The engine fired, then coughed, and settled to an even, flat roar as he advanced the throttle.

Methodically he went through the process of getting the plane ready to leave the ground—checking the oil pressure, adjusting the small light over the instrument panel. Then when the tachometer wound to 1950 revolutions per minute, the ship shook with a kind of taut fury.

"Chocks out!"

The mechanic ducked beneath the wing and pulled out the wooden blocks, and Jerry gave the engine a burst of power. The wheels rolled over the cinders, and he checked the time—2:30 A.M.

Winter chilled the land with an iron breath. Now as Jerry flew through the thick layers of stratus clouds that covered huge areas, he felt the weight of them. He could fly on top if he had the will, skimming along the swells of a gentle aerial ocean with the sunshine on his shoulders. Or he could fly between layers with sometimes a portion of the earth visible through a small hole in the clouds. But the clouds were ever changing, so that finding such a hole became a critical necessity. And the treacherous winds could slyly pull a plane off course, which meant that fuel would become more precious than gold.

When he reached a thousand feet, he moved the controls, swinging the Pitcairn into a dizzy sweeping movement. Then he grinned as he thought of how different pilots flew their planes. Uncle Gavin flew his ship carefully, keeping all the rules, flying with perfect mechanical precision.

Jerry loved the fancy moves, the fortissimos of flying, and was quickly bored with routine. On the long, monotonous flights between cities, he would sometimes perform an inside loop, or even put the plane into a spin just for the joy of it. It was an overflow of the exuberant spirit that was his, and he knew that he was being foolish.

But there was no stunting this day, for the winter sky was dark and brooding. Jerry watched it as he would watch a wild beast, knowing that it could reach out and slap him down to earth with a cruel stroke.

As the hours passed, he grew numb, and his reactions, he knew, were slowed. The visibility was poor, less than a mile, but there was a wild beauty in the snow streaking through the wings in spitting, horizontal streams. He kept careful watch on the dark and brooding bank of mountains on his left, and his compass remained gently rocking in the soft glow of its filmy light to guide him.

Finally he reached Albany, eased his ship over toward the east bank of the Hudson, and worked the rudder slightly left and right. Despite the snow that stung his eyelids, he pushed his goggles up. He slowed the plane to a minimum speed and glided down into the snow.

He got out of the plane stiffly, and the mechanic refueled

the ship. Jerry went inside to warm himself, and as he downed the boiling black coffee that burned his throat, he wondered what lay ahead. The mechanic, an older man named Kellerman, came inside, shaking his head. "You want to go on through this?"

"Sure."

Kellerman looked gloomy, giving Jerry a hard look. "It's getting worse, the radio says. Better lay over till it clears up."

Jerry thought with longing of lying down on a cot with warm blankets—then decided against it. "I'll make it all right."

"Should have stayed over!"

Jerry's lips were so numb he could hardly move them to speak, and he wiped at his goggles futilely. The snow whirled around him so thickly he could not see the nose of the Pitcairn. The wind screamed at him fiercely, and the cold closed around him like an iron fist.

He cut the throttle and pushed the nose down, applying the left rudder. The Pitcairn's engine coughed and sputtered, and Jerry cleared it with a quick burst of the throttle—and then a hill suddenly reared itself in front of him!

Jerry hauled back on the stick, kicked at the controls, and held his breath. *Shouldn't be a hill around here!* his mind cried out. He almost felt the mass of the earth as the plane was thrown into a wild turn—but then he saw the hill falling away until the snow closed it to his vision.

Fear came then, freezing his mind as the wind froze his body. He knew he was hopelessly lost, and finding his way was impossible. Instruments were useless, except to show him how high he was. But his fuel was low, and he knew he'd have to find a hole in the clouds, a break in the storm, or go down blindly.

He tried to think, but even as his mind raced wildly, he felt the plane vibrate. Looking out to the flying wires that stretched between the wings, he saw that the leading edges of the wings were encrusted with a thin white line of ice.

I'll have to jump, he thought numbly. But Jerry hated to lose a plane. When a plane crashed it was like losing a friend, the twisted broken longerons and spars like broken bones. It was a matter of pride, and pride ran strongly in Jerry Stuart. He had vowed that he'd make good on this job, and now he determined to ride the plane down.

He kept the ship on an even keel, fighting the winds, hoping to find a clearing in the storm. The Pitcairn was tossed like a toy, but he took satisfaction in holding it as steady as possible.

As he flew on, he had no illusions about his chances. He'd heard of too many good pilots who'd gone to their deaths, mangled so badly that the funerals had been held with closed caskets. He'd always counted on his considerable flying skills to keep him from dying, and now these were almost useless. No pilot, he knew, could do more than he was doing—and he knew he was a dead man if he didn't find a break in the clouds and a field flat enough to land on.

Death had been an abstraction to him—something you read about or that happened to someone else. Always it had been a theory, not a living fact.

Now as he tore along through the madness of the storm, he looked at his hands encased in heavy gloves and thought, *If I die, my fingernails and my hair will keep on growing for a few days—but I'll be dead.* He'd heard this and had only half believed it, but now it seemed to be very important.

What will it be like . . . to be dead?

Instantly he thought of the many sermons he'd heard while growing up—some of them on the subject of hell. One evangelist had painted a vivid picture: *Imagine a blast furnace glowing white with heat. Imagine putting only your hand into that terrible searing heat for just one minute—and then think of the incredible pain of having your entire body in raging flames—forever! No hope of relief—pain forever!*

Jerry had not been affected by the sermon, not nearly so much as he'd been frightened by a calm sermon by the pastor of the church a year later. As the Pitcairn bucked the winds, he could hear the words almost as clearly as if they were spoken—

Hell is separation from all that's good—which is to say, separation from God. God cannot bear evil, and he will not have heaven contaminated with it. Hell is the penitentiary where all who will not come to Jesus Christ will be confined. If they were permitted to enter heaven, the evil in them would spread like leaven. If your sins are not forgiven in this life, you will endure them forever—cut off from saved parents, from those who know the Lord. This is worse, I think, than all the physical pain that hell might contain. It was to bring you to himself that God sent his Son to die. He longs for each of you to be with him. But it is only through the cross of Jesus that you can come. There is no other way!

Jerry seemed to see the face of his mother. She'd bent over his bed once when he was having a nightmare and whispered, "Jesus casts out fear, Jerry. Perfect love casts out fear—"

Now as fear ran along the nerves of the pilot, he knew that his whole life was a waste. *If I die, there'll be nothing left of me on earth!*

And then he thought of the face of Bonnie Hart—of her last words to him:

I'll pray for you, Jerry!

A sudden gust of gritty snow blinded him, and panic came. But as he held desperately to the controls, he came as close to having a vision as ever before in his life.

Her face was innocent and her dark eyes were warm. Like a cascade her straight black hair flowed down her back, and there was a vulnerability in her soft youthful lips.

I'll pray for you, Jerry!

As he felt the plane cough and sputter, he knew the last of his fuel was gone—and he cried out, "Oh, God—don't let me die!"

He raked the back of his gloves across his face, then

blinked fiercely. The driving snow rushed toward him—but as the Pitcairn dropped heavily, his heart leaped as he caught a glimpse of light.

He broke through the clouds, and there in front of him lay a large field of some kind, filled with stubble piercing the snow. He used the last of the power to pull the nose of the plane up, and then the wheels struck, bounced, and then came down hard. He fought for control, and finally the plane came to a shuddering halt.

Jerry Stuart sat in the cockpit, trembling and still not able to believe that he was on solid ground. Slowly he crawled out of the airplane, falling to the snow on numbed feet. He pulled himself upright, then looked up into the leaden sky filled with large flakes.

"Thank you, God!" he whispered. Then he thought again of the vision he'd had of Bonnie Hart, and wonder came to him.

He stood quietly for a time, thinking hard, then slapped the side of the plane and turned to walk through the deep snow.

16

JERRY GETS A WARNING

C hristie had been delighted when Mario showed some interest in the work of the Army. The moment they'd had in the park had never left her, and she wondered if he thought about it. Somehow that time had fixed itself in her so firmly that she wondered if she was falling in love with him.

Mario had been more affected by Christie's kiss than he wanted to admit. He found himself thinking of her during business hours and making excuses to go by and see her. He had a streak of humor, and somehow the incongruity of a wealthy lawyer spending time with "a bunch of fanatics," as Nick called the members of the Salvation Army, amused him.

One evening after a hard day in court, he found himself pulling up in his Packard in front of the large building that housed the Army, and when he killed the engine, he sat in the big car thinking, *What am I doing here? I must be losing my mind!* He knew that Nick and Eddy were concerned about him, but he shook off that problem. He was worried about *himself*, and he almost drove off without getting out. But he had no plans, and his apartment seemed suddenly very lonely.

"Just find out if there's anything I can do," he muttered. When he got inside the building, he saw Jerry Stuart at once. The young pilot had been short with him on the few occasions they had met, and now as Mario stopped to say, "Hello, Jerry," he saw a look of dislike come to the pilot's eyes.

"Hello."

"I dropped by to see your aunts," Mario said, ignoring the curtness of Jerry's greeting. "Haven't seen you lately. Been flying lots of hours?"

"Yes, I have." Jerry nodded toward the inner door, saying, "Lenora's in her office."

The hint was plain, but Mario said easily, "I'll stop and say hello to her. Good to see you again."

Jerry watched as the trim young lawyer moved away, then chewed his lower lip nervously. He knew he had to talk to Christie now. Abruptly Jerry whirled and went to the storage room where he found Christie sorting clothing. "Gotta talk to you, Aunt Christie," he said at once.

Christie looked up, startled, then put down a shirt to say, "All right. Do you want to go outside?"

"Okay." Jerry followed her through a side door and found himself standing inside a loading dock. It was not occupied, and he said, "Aunt Christie, I've got to talk to you—about Mario."

Christie nodded. "All right, Jerry. What about Mario?"

"Well, I think you're seeing too much of him."

"Do you? Why is that?"

Jerry was awkward and embarrassed. He pulled off his hat and ran his fingers through his black hair. "I wish you'd listen to Lenora. She's talked to you about him, hasn't she?"

"Yes, she has."

"Well, can't you see how—how wrong it is?"

Christie had been expecting Jerry to come to her with this. She knew that he felt responsible for the friendship between her and Mario, and she tried to tell him it wasn't his fault. "We're just good friends, Jerry. There's nothing wrong with that."

Jerry felt that there *was* something wrong, but he felt he wasn't the one to say so. Still, he *had* been responsible for bringing Mario into his aunt's life, so he pressed on despite his awkwardness. "Look, I don't think there's anything going on between you two—I know you better than that. But, Aunt

Christie, you've been brought up in a world that's as different from his as Chicago is from Africa! He's a rich, good-looking guy, and I guess almost any girl would be flattered to have him hanging around. But what's going to come of it? He'll never marry you."

"I . . . never thought of that."

"Why, you *must* have, Aunt Christie!" Jerry protested. "It'd be the thing any woman would think of. But you don't know how tight these Italian families are! I mean, they're like little *kingdoms*—and nobody outside the kingdom is going to get inside!"

"We don't talk about that, Jerry."

A lassie came bustling out, stopped abruptly, then said, "Excuse me—did Major Hastings come out here?"

"No, I haven't seen him, Irene." Christie gave Jerry an odd look as the woman turned and left. "Don't worry about me, Jerry! I . . . I'll be all right."

But Jerry was unhappy with her. He felt more than a little like a blundering young fool but knew he had to be plainer. "Look, if he's not going to marry you, there's only one other thing that *could* be on his mind, Aunt Christie!"

At once Christie caught his meaning. Her face reddened, and she lifted her head to look into her nephew's eyes. "He's never tried to—to do anything that wasn't right!" A streak of anger ran through her, and she said sharply, "Jerry, has it ever occurred to you that I'm *responsible* for Mario, for his soul, I mean?"

Jerry stared at her blankly. "No, I never thought of that."

"He doesn't know God—and I'm praying that he'll be saved. Now I wish you'd not come to me again with this!"

Jerry felt crushed. "All right, Aunt Christie. I just . . . well, I don't want anything bad to happen to you, that's all."

"That's sweet of you, Jerry," Christie said, softening and patting his arm. "And I'm praying for you, too. You need God as much as Mario does."

Jerry flushed, for since his perilous landing he'd spent

many hours thinking of God. But he said only, "I guess I do—but watch yourself with him, Aunt Christie."

Mario found her and asked at once, "How about I take you to meet my mother, Christie? Give you a real Italian dinner!"

"Why, I'd like very much to meet her."

Christie went to change, and a knock at her door caused her to turn and open it. Major Hastings said, "Christie, are you going out with Mr. Castellano?"

"Why, yes I am. He wants me to meet his mother."

"Are you sure that's wise?" Major Hastings had nothing but praise for Christie, but now his thin face was tense with apprehension. "As your superior I feel I must give you at least a warning about your friendship with him . . ."

Christie listened as the major spoke of his doubts. When he finished, she said, "I'm grateful for your concern, and of course I want to do what's right. He asked me to meet his mother, and I've agreed." She liked the man very much and said quietly, "Perhaps we can talk about this later?"

"Yes, I think we might." Hastings grew thoughtful and said slowly, "We in the Army reach out to the poor and helpless. Not often do we help the rich and powerful. Sometimes I think we should do more of that—but we'll speak of it later."

After Christie got into Mario's car and the two drove away, Jerry said, "Aunt Lenora, I've got to do something." He'd been standing at her window looking down on the street, and now his face was set. "It's not right, her seeing him."

"What can you do, Jerry?"

"For one thing I can put it to Mario that he needs to stop seeing her."

Lenora was having difficulty over Christie's behavior, and a troubled look came to her face. "I don't know, Jerry. Sometimes doing a thing like that just makes things worse. Maybe if we just wait—"

"That's no good! The longer he keeps seeing her the more

likely she is to fall for the guy. No, I'm going to have it out with him!"

Jerry decided to see Nick before confronting Mario. *It'd be better if he did it,* was his thought. *Mario's not likely to listen to me, but he might pay attention to his brother.*

He found Bones propped up in a chair outside Nick's office. "Nick in?" he asked.

"No, he ain't. He's on a business trip. Eddy's here, though."

Jerry hesitated, then said, "Guess I'll talk to him."

"He's got company—might not have time for you."

"I'll wait."

Jerry sat down and read an old copy of the *Police Gazette.* Finally the door opened, and Eddy came out to say, "Bones, go get us some steaks." Then he saw Jerry and said with surprise, "Hey, Kid, how are you?"

"All right, Eddy. Need to see you for a few minutes."

"Sure—come on in."

Jerry walked into the office and stopped dead still when he saw Hymie Holtzman sitting in a chair, and directly across from him the slight figure of Walter Stevens. Something about the pale blue eyes of Stevens chilled him, and he merely nodded when Eddy said, "You remember Jerry, Walt."

"Yes, I do."

Hymie Holtzman didn't speak at all, but his agate eyes were fixed on Jerry. Jerry ignored him and said, "Eddy, this is a little personal. Can we talk privately?"

"Oh, we'll step outside." Walt Stevens rose and left the room followed by Holtzman. As soon as they were outside, Holtzman said, "That's bad news."

"What is?"

"That guy—the pilot. He's the one who flew me in from Detroit when I did the number on Ace Tanhauser." His lips grew thin, and he looked toward the door. "He can put the finger on me, Walt. I'd better take care of him."

"No reason for him to," Stevens said slowly. He thought

hard, then shook his head. "No, you'd better not hit him, Hymie. He's the son of Amos Stuart—and you know how funny Nick is about that guy—him and that preacher brother of his."

Holtzman said nothing, but a stubborn light fired his eyes. "All right, I'll go easy on him. But I'll send Tonk and Griffin around to give him a *warning*."

Stevens shrugged. "Better make it clear that's what it is, Hymie. Not a bad idea to watch yourself in these things— and a kid like that might need to be shook a little."

Inside the office Jerry found a ready listener in Eddy. When he had explained the situation, Eddy said, "Hey, Kid, I'm glad you're leveling with me and Nick. I'll have a talk with Mario. Him and me—we hit it off pretty good sometimes. I think he'll listen to me."

Relief washed over Jerry, and he said, "I hope so, Eddy. Nothing against your brother—but it wouldn't be good for him or my aunt."

"Yeah, well, give me a shot at it, Kid. And keep in touch."

"Right. Tell Nick I came by, will you?"

Jerry took Eddy's clap on the shoulder and left the office. As he passed down the hall he met the eyes of Hymie Holtzman and had to restrain a shiver that went over him. There was a reptilian look about the man's eyes, and the merciless mouth told him that Holtzman was thinking of the flight they'd made together. However, the squat killer merely followed Stevens into the office, and Jerry released a sigh of relief.

Holtzman waited until the meeting was over, then went at once to a back room where he found a poker game in progress. "Tonk—you and Griffin come with me."

A burly man with a beetling brow looked up and groaned, "Aw, Hymie, I'm losing. Gimme a chance to catch up."

"Shut up and come on, Tonk," Holtzman grunted. He left the room, led the pair to an empty table in the bar, and said, "I got a job for you. Guy named Jerry Stuart . . ."

The pair listened carefully, then the taller of the two said, "What you want us to do? Ace him?"

"No, nothin' like that, Griffin. Just rough him up a little, then tell him if he ever gets any ideas of remembering a little plane ride we took together, he'll get worse." He pulled some bills out of his pocket and handed them to the pair. "Don't kill him—but rough him up pretty good."

"Sure, Hymie," Tonk grinned. He counted the bills, then stuck them into his pocket. "Where can we find him, Hymie?"

"He's got an apartment someplace. Check at the airport. He flies the mail. They'll give you his address. Remember, don't rub him out or Nick will step on you." The reptilian eyes were flat and seemed to have nothing behind the surface, and as tough as Tonk and Griffin were, they seemed to find something else to look at.

"Yeah, sure, Hymie," Griffin said quickly. "We'll do it right."

As soon as Owen looked at Amos, he knew there was trouble. Owen had come to Chicago to speak at the Moody Bible Institute and had gotten a message that said, "Come to the paper. Amos."

"What's wrong, Amos?" Owen said. He'd found his brother behind his desk staring at the wall, but he knew this man. Behind the calm exterior he knew Amos was boiling with anger.

"It's Jerry," he said slowly, as if keeping a check on his temper. "He got beat up last night—and Christie got in on it."

"What!" Owen had expected anything but this, and his eyes narrowed. "Tell me," he said evenly. "What happened?"

"I wrote you about Christie seeing Mario Castellano. Well, Jerry feels responsible because he introduced them. He's been stewing about it, so he finally went to talk to Nick and Eddy about it."

"What did they say?"

"They don't like it, Owen. You know how the Castellanos are about their family. They said they'd talk to Mario—but somehow it didn't work."

"You don't mean to tell me Nick sent some thugs around to beat Jerry up?"

"Jerry says it wasn't them. Says he talked to both of them, and they weren't sore."

"Who was it then?"

Amos lifted his eyebrows and said, "Two guys who do a little leg-breaking for the loan sharks. They work for Nick sometimes. Small-time hoods, but they did a first-class job on Jerry."

"He's hurt bad?"

"Couple of broken ribs and lots of cuts and bruises. He was taking Christie to the circus when the two of them got jumped." Amos got to his feet and went to peer out the window thinking hard. "There's something Jerry isn't telling me, Owen. Those two guys don't do things like this unless somebody pays them. Jerry got evasive when I tried to pump him."

Owen bit his lip, disturbed by the thing. "I guess it has something to do with the time he flew booze for Nick."

Amos nodded his agreement. "That's my idea. But I'm worried that they might do something worse."

"Did Jerry know them?"

"Sure, they work for Nick and Eddy. Their names are Tonk Denaro and Lew Griffin."

Owen stared at his brother hard, then nodded. "I move we pay them a visit, Amos."

Amos lifted an eyebrow cautiously. "They're pretty rough boys, Owen. Maybe we should let the police handle it."

"It's family, Amos."

Amos grinned widely. "All right, Reverend Stuart." He opened his desk drawer and pulled out a pistol. He checked the loads, gave the cylinder a spin, then got up and stuck it in his waistband. "Let's have a nice chat with Mr. Denaro and Mr. Griffin."

"Hey, Amos—and Owen!" Nick's face broke into a smile as the two men walked into the room. He would not have smiled if it had been anyone else, for he was meeting with a roomful of his men. But he came at once to shake the hands of both men, turning to say, "Eddy, we got some company. Don't be a stranger!"

Eddy had seen the faces of the two men and came slowly to greet them. "Hello, Owen," he said quietly. "Good to see you. Amos—how you been?"

Amos had been sweeping the room with his eyes, and he spotted at once the two men Jerry had described. He glanced at Owen and saw that he'd discovered them, too. "Nick— we've got a beef with a couple of your boys."

A bewildered look swept Nick's face. "A beef with my boys? What's the trouble?"

Owen moved quickly to stand in front of Tonk, who stood up at once. He was a brute of a man with bulging arms and the misshapen ears of a prizefighter. "I'm going to have to put you down, Tonk," Owen said pleasantly.

The silence that dropped over the room was thick enough to cut with a knife. Tonk blinked with surprise, then said, "I don't have no squawk with you."

"You broke my nephew's ribs. I've come to talk to you about that."

Nick burst out, "Owen, you're wrong!"

But Owen had already moved. He had only one hand, but when he moved his left it blurred so fast it caught Tonk in the mouth and drove him backward. He hit the wall, careened off it, then came roaring back, all his old prizefighting instinct aroused.

Owen ducked the thunderous right hand that Tonk threw at him and from a crouch, unleashed every bit of strength into a left that started in his right foot, ran through his body, and exploded in Tonk's side. The blow made a muffled *thud*, and Tonk cried out and fell to the floor gasping with pain.

"Hold it, Griffin!"

Owen turned to find Amos holding a gun on the tall form of Griffin who had a pistol half pulled from a shoulder holster. Amos said gently, "It's not a good idea, Griffin." He waited until the man's face turned pale, and he held his hands away from the gun. "Second thoughts are usually best," Amos said quietly.

Eddy said immediately, "Let's get easy here—no trouble!" He had seen several of his men reaching for their guns, but his command steadied them. Turning to Amos and Owen he shook his head. "This is nothing to do with Nick and me. Whatever those two did, they didn't get any orders from us."

Nick stared at Tonk, who was getting slowly to his feet. Then he said, "Everybody out—except Tonk and Griffin."

At once the other men left the room, and Nick moved over to stand in front of the two men. Both of them were wide-eyed with fear, and Tonk gasped, "It wasn't our fault, Nick."

"How come you roughed up the kid?" Eddy broke in. Anger drew him up stiffly, and he came to put his face inches away from that of Tonk. "Who paid you, Tonk?"

Tonk was afraid of Nick and Eddy—but he was even more afraid of Hymie Holtzman. "I . . . I can't say, Nick—not with them two in the room."

"It was a private beef, Eddy," Griffin said quickly. "We thought you knew about it."

"Who ordered the hit?" Nick grated, and when the two hesitated, he stepped forward and struck Tonk a powerful blow in the side. Tonk screamed and fell to the floor, and Nick pulled a gun from his pocket and held it to the temple of Griffin. "Tell it—or die!" he grunted.

"It was Hymie!" Griffin cried. "Don't shoot, Nick!"

"Hymie?" Nick asked. He lowered the gun and stared at the pair. "Get out of here," he snapped. He waited until Griffin pulled Tonk to his feet gasping with pain and left the room.

Then he replaced the gun and turned to face Owen and Amos.

"I swear I didn't know anything about this, Amos," he said. "I like Jerry, always have."

Eddy nodded quickly. "Let us work on it. Whatever it was, we'll see to it that Jerry won't be touched again."

Owen said slowly, "Eddy, you and I went through a war together. You give me your word you had nothing to do with this?"

"You got my word!"

"Amos, we been friends a long time," Nick said slowly. "I know we ain't got the same ideas—but I always respected you. And I'm tellin' you I had no idea that a thing like this was happening. I'd have squashed those two like bugs if I'd got a hint of it."

"What about this fellow named Hymie?" Amos asked.

"I'll take care of him," Nick said grimly. "Let me pump him. I'll find out what's in his craw. And I'll see to it that he don't ever touch any of you again."

It was a tense moment, but finally Amos relaxed. "Your word's good enough for me, Nick."

Relief came to the lips of Nick Castellano, and he took out a handkerchief and mopped his brow. His hands were not steady, and he stared at them. "Look at that!" he exclaimed. "I didn't think there was anything in the world could make me do that!"

Owen stood solidly, watching the two men. "Nick, I remember the time you saved Allie's life."

Nick flushed, but he had pride in that one thing. "She's a fine lady, Owen, that wife of yours."

"She prays for you every day."

Nick dropped his head and seemed struck dumb. The silence ran on, and finally he lifted his eyes. "I guess I can use it more than most, Owen. My thanks to her."

Amos spoke up. "This is bad, Nick. I don't believe you and Eddy were involved—but look at what happened. Two of your men hurt a boy who's trying hard to find his way. I love my son just as you love Mario. Think how you'd feel if he got hurt."

"I'm sorry, Amos."

"I know you are—but it happened. And our sister, even she got a bruise or two trying to help Jerry. I remember when I came to live with your family, the first thing you ever said to me was, 'Don't do anything to my sister or I'll lay you out!' Remember that?"

Nick stared at his friend. "I remember, Amos—and I'm shamed that your sister got hurt. I'll see that it don't happen again."

"But that's just what you *can't* promise, Nick," Amos said, sadness in his tone. "You've got money and power, but you live by violence. And you can't contain violence. It's impossible!"

"Amos is right, Nick," Owen nodded. "Look, you're one of the smartest men I ever knew—you, too, Eddy. You two would be successful at anything you tried. Why don't you just walk away from all this? It's only going to make you miserable."

Nick stared at the tall minister. "It's not that easy, Owen." He seemed to search for words, failed, then shook his head. "I'm sorry it happened."

"Sure. Come on, Amos."

When the two men left the office, Eddy said thoughtfully, "Do you think we could make it on the outside—go legit?"

Nick stared at Eddy and shook his head. "We got to go on, Eddy. No way out for us." Then anger touched his eyes. "Go see Hymie, Eddy. And if he gives you any trouble, write him off!"

17

LAST PASSAGE

H ello?"

"Lylah, this is Amos—" Instantly Lylah knew that something was wrong. Amos's voice was thick, and he said, "It's Pa—he's had a heart attack."

Coldness closed like a fist around Lylah's heart, and she asked, "How is he?"

"He . . . can't make it. Logan just called. He said if we wanted to get there before Pa died, we'd have to get there right away. It's a long way for you—"

"I'll fly out as soon as I can get someone to make the flight." Her voice broke, and she said, "If I don't get there in time, tell Pa I love him."

"I'll tell him, Lylah . . ."

"There it is—right over there."

Jed Hoskins looked over the cockpit at the weather-beaten house, then searched for a field or a road to land on. He spotted a field—the same one that Jerry had chosen when he'd come for Christie. "Hang on, lady—this might be a little rough!"

Lylah shouted back, "I'm okay," then watched as the earth tilted up. Hoskins made his turn, cut the engine back, and brought the small plane in for a perfect landing. He hopped out of the plane and reached up to help the woman down. When she came to stand in front of him, he said, "You're a good passenger, Miss Stuart. That was a pretty hard flight."

Lylah put her hand out and smiled briefly. "I needed your help, Jed. I'll never forget it."

"Sorry about your dad. Hope he makes it. I'll go into Fort Smith. When you're ready to go back, leave word at the airport."

He pulled Lylah's luggage out of the plane and looked up to see two men coming across the field. "Guess your menfolks will take care of these."

"Yes, thank you, Jed." She handed him an envelope, saying, "There's a bonus in there—and I'll pay you for the time you spend here."

"Thanks, Miss Stuart."

The pilot climbed into the plane and waved, then swung the plane around and took off. Lylah turned to meet Amos and Logan. Both of them embraced her, and then she asked, "How is he?"

Logan shook his head. "He's just barely making it, Lylah. I think he's holding on just to see you and Owen. He's already said good-bye to the rest of us."

Amos picked up the suitcase, then took Lylah's arm. "Come on. You need to go to him."

The three made their way back to the house, and as they approached, Lylah looked around. "I couldn't wait to get away from here once—now I can think of all the good times we had together."

"Always like that," Logan nodded. "Why do we have to get older before we learn that?"

Lylah entered the house and met Agnes, who had come out of the kitchen. "Hello, Agnes," Lylah said. She had never liked the woman, for Agnes had not made life easy for her father—nor for any of them. Just how much love Agnes had for her father Lylah didn't know, but it was not a time to quarrel. "It's a bad time. How is he?"

Agnes gave Lylah a nervous look, as if expecting to be blamed for Will's illness—but when she saw there was no malice in her stepdaughter, she seemed relieved. "He's been feeling bad for a month—or longer. But he wouldn't go to the doctor." Her face worked, and she added, "He went out to do the milking Tuesday morning, and when he stayed so long, I went to see about him." Twisting her hands together, she hesitated, then whispered, "He was laying on the floor, and I thought he was gone. But he came out of it, and I got him to the house. But when Doc Smith came, he said it wasn't no use. I . . . I did the best I could, Lylah!"

Lylah touched the woman's shoulder, the first time she'd ever done such a thing, and said, "I'm sure you did, Agnes." She saw the gratitude in the woman's eyes and said, "I'd better go see him."

"He's been asking for you. Go on in, and I'll fix something to eat."

Lylah paused to greet Peter, who'd just arrived from Oklahoma, and Gavin. He'd hired a plane and flown Christie and Lenora in from Chicago, along with his wife and new son, Phillip. "Owen's on his way," Gavin said, after embracing Lylah. "Go on and see Pa."

"All right, Gavin."

She entered the room and found her father awake. He was propped up in bed against a bank of pillows, and his eyes lit up when he saw her. "Daughter!" he whispered, and she ran to fall into his arms. He held her as she fought back the tears, her face pressed against his cheek. When she drew back, her tears ran down her cheeks.

"Glad you made it, Lylah," Will said, his voice thin and reedy. "Wasn't sure I could wait."

"Owen's coming, Pa," Lylah said. Her throat was so tightly constricted that she had trouble speaking.

Will Stuart had always been a fine-looking man, and he still had traces of those looks. His eyes were clear and his hair was silver, but his face was pinched and drawn. It hurt Lylah to see the weakness, for he'd been a man proud of his strength.

"Maybe the doctor can do something, Pa."

Shaking his head, Will answered, "No, it's my time. And I'm ready, Lylah." He reached out and touched her cheek, marveling at the smoothness of it. "You look like your ma—didn't remember how much. But I've been thinking of her a lot, laying here . . ."

Lylah sat beside him for half an hour as he talked, then when he dropped off to sleep, she rose and went back into the crowded living room. "He's asleep," she said. "What does Dr. Smith say?"

"He could go anytime," Pete said. "Owen just called from Fort Smith. He'll be here pretty soon."

Agnes appeared at the door, saying, "We've got food. The neighbors have been bringing it in till there's no place to put it."

"We've got to eat," Lenora said. She wheeled her chair out of the living room, and soon they were all gathered around the table. It was Christie who said gently, "Agnes, come and sit down. You've been working all day."

Her invitation brought a flush to Agnes's face. Memories of how badly she'd treated this young woman flooded her, and she stumbled, "No . . . I don't . . . I don't think I should."

But Christie rose and went to Agnes. She pressed her into a chair, saying, "Sit down and eat something. We've got to take care of each other in this."

Suddenly Agnes began to weep, and Logan, who sat beside her, patted her shoulder. "Don't feel bad, Agnes." He had suffered at this woman's hands as had all the rest of them, but now kindness came to his warm brown eyes. "Families have to stick together."

After that, Agnes managed to control herself, and the family ate what they could. Afterward, the long wait began, that time when minutes seem to drag by on leaden feet. There was nothing to do, and talk seemed foolish and awkward somehow. From time to time one of them would go sit beside the dying man, but the others wandered around the yard, talking in small groups and trying to entertain the children.

"Look at the mob of kids," Logan said to Pete. "We got enough for a baseball team!"

And indeed there were enough—and more—for that. Logan's four—Helen, Ray, Violet, and the youngest, Clinton; Pete's son and daughter, Stephen and Mona; Gavin's brand-new son Phillip; and Owen's three, William Lee, Woody, and Wendy.

Pete grinned and shook his head. "Looks like the crops of Stuarts have been right good, don't it, now?" He asked suddenly, "Logan, how you making out—on your farm, I mean?"

"Ain't missed a meal—but we had to postpone a few, I reckon. How about you, Pete? Workin' in the oil fields, that's rough, ain't it?"

"Pretty rough," Pete admitted. "Don't know as I'd want to do it the rest of my life." He drew a barlow knife from his pocket, picked up a piece of cedar from the ground, and began to shave long, curling shavings from it. "Guess it's a good thing Amos and Owen and Lylah are doing good. You and me sure ain't set no records."

Logan had no answer, for he'd thought the same thing. The two men stood there talking. The children played, their voices shrill on the afternoon air. "Glad Owen got here," Logan nodded. "Pa sure was anxious—" He broke off, for Amos had appeared, calling urgently, "Logan, you and Pete—hurry!"

Both men hurried toward the house, and Amos said, "He's going—come on!"

They all crowded into the small room, and when Will opened his eyes and looked around, he whispered, "All here? All the children?"

"We're all here, Pa," Lylah whispered. Her face was pale and her lips trembled. "We love you, Pa!"

Will's eyes closed and they thought he was gone, but then he opened them and his lips moved slightly. "I'll see your ma . . . tell her about all . . . of you . . ." His eyes moved from face to face, and he called their names—"Christie . . . Lenora . . . and Lylah . . . all my . . . good girls!" He looked at the tall sons, whispering, "Amos—my first boy . . . and Owen, my preacher boy . . . Pete and Gavin and you, Logan . . . what good sons—God blessed me and your ma!"

He heard the sound of weeping and looked up to Agnes. "Don't cry," he murmured. He reached out and took her hand, squeezing it, which caused her to turn and leave the room.

"Take care of her." Will nodded. He lay still, and silence filled the room. He lay that way for perhaps two minutes, then his chest lifted and his eyes flew open. He cried out in a stronger voice—"Marian!—" And then he smiled. It was a peaceful smile, and the lines of his face seemed to fade.

He took one look around the room, at the beloved faces of his children. "I'll wait . . . for you!" he whispered, and then his voice became so soft they barely heard it.

"Lord Jesus—I'm coming . . ."

And then he was gone. Lenora picked up the still hand, kissed it, then put it on his breast. "He's gone," she said, but though there were tears in her eyes, there was victory, too. "Gone to be with the Lord. One day we'll see him again—him and Ma."

Don Satterfield preached the funeral, and it was a simple sermon. The church was filled to overflowing, neighbors coming from miles away.

They buried their father in the ancient cemetery beside his first wife, Marian. The stone they put at the head of the grave gave his name and the dates of his life. And one verse was carved into the white granite—"The Dead in Christ Shall Rise First."

Afterward there was the usual time when no one knows what to do. The neighbors left, promising to return, and then the family was alone.

It was Amos, the oldest, who did the necessary things. Calling them all together, he said, "Pa wanted Agnes to be taken care of." He turned to Agnes, saying, "Do you want to try to hire a man to work the farm, Agnes?"

"No, I can't do that. I'll move to town."

"I think that might be best. Here's what I think. Pa left you some money from his insurance and half of the farm. The other half he left to the children. I'd like to see you come back and take over the place, Logan."

"Why—I'd like that, Amos!"

"Fine. Now, we'll pay you for your half of the farm in a lump sum, Agnes. Is that all right?"

Agnes nodded, then said, "I . . . I wish I'd been different! I could've made things easier for him!"

Finally the arrangements were made, and the children of Will Stuart sat together talking about their lives. "We'll be pretty well scattered over the country," Gavin said finally. "But I want us to come back to this place once a year—bring all the kids. Make a tradition of it."

"I like that idea," Amos replied instantly. "I wanted to keep the old home place—and now with Logan here, we'll always be able to bring our kids and grandkids here. Let's promise each other that once a year we all come to Stone County, to this house."

Everyone vowed to return, and the next morning when they all left to go back to their homes and their lives, Owen said to Lylah, "I'll see you sooner than next year. I've got a meeting in Los Angeles. Will you come?"

Lylah nodded, then smiled. "I'll come. I might even be one of those who hit the sawdust trail."

"I wish you would put God in your life, Lylah. It's what I want—and what Pa wanted most of all."

"I . . . I have a friend now," Lylah said, her face showing something that Owen hadn't seen for a long time. "A man who knows God." She hesitated, then smiled. "He's become very important to me and Adam. I want you to meet him."

Owen lifted an eyebrow. "I'll look forward to meeting him. Is he an actor?"

"No!" Lylah said instantly. "He's a writer."

Owen studied his sister's face, which was glowing with a radiance that made her look younger. He saw in her a hope that he'd seen when she was a young girl but which had been in her only rarely in her later years.

"Well," he said quietly, a smile coming to his broad lips. "He must be something to make you light up like that!"

"Oh, I just like him, Owen," Lylah said quickly. "And he's been good for Adam."

"He's been good for Lylah, too, I think." Placing his good arm around her, he drew her close and whispered, "Don't let him get away!"

18

A GATHERING OF STUARTS

C arl Thomas had been a successful tractor salesman, and he still retained some of the rural quality that had made that possible. He'd been able to sell a tractor to a farmer but had quickly learned how to sell *thousands* of them by organizing his own company. He was what some have called "country smart," with little formal education but an enormous fund of native wit and a sense of timing.

He'd been one of the first to see the potential of Thomas Edison's invention, the kinetoscope. Edison did not actually invent the motion picture camera. Most of the credit for that should go to a French scientist named Etienne Jules Aarey. This pioneer laid the foundation for a British-born American photographer, Eadweard Muybridge, to develop a method employing a camera house for a battery of twelve electrically operated cameras and a specially marked fence. With this he was able to take a series of still photographs of a trotting horse that proved all four of its feet were off the ground at one phase of the trot. In 1879, he developed a machine called a zoopraxiscope that would project the images on a large-size screen.

Edison was an inventor, an entertainer, and an entrepreneur. He laid claims to every device he could imagine and managed to produce most of these devices. And he contributed the one necessary element of motion picture photography—the perforation of the film strip at equidistant intervals so that the film would run smoothly past the lens.

The practical—that is, the economic—end of all of this was the nickelodeon. These were machines that an individual could peer into to view a fifteen-minute film. Beginning in 1893, these devices spread all over the country, and the next step was the full-sized screen where an audience could collect. The vaudeville theaters were waiting. In 1905, the first neighborhood storefront theater in America was opened in McKeesport, Pennsylvania. The rest, as they say, is history.

Carl Thomas was tired of selling tractors. He sold out, put his money into a studio, and began making films. He didn't know much about such things, but neither did anyone else. It didn't matter, for audiences were so enthralled that they would pay to see practically anything on the screen.

He made a great deal of money—and by failing to keep up with new techniques, managed to lose most of it. However, he still owned equipment and had close ties with theater owners all over the country—and this was why Lylah was sitting in his office one morning.

"Carl, I want you to help me make a film," she'd said as soon as he'd greeted her warmly and asked her to sit down.

Her request caught him off guard, and he stood staring at her. He was a short man, not over five feet, five inches tall, who always wore the finest and most fashionable suits. He had a thin mustache, a full head of black hair, and bulging eyes. He was rarely taken off guard, for he was a shrewd man.

"Why, my dear Lylah, why in the world would we want to do that? Don't you know how many men have lost their shirts trying to make pictures?"

"Tell me, Carl," Lylah said, leaning forward. "Tell me everything that can go wrong." Then she sat back, and for the next hour the dapper producer outlined the pitfalls of the film business.

When he had finished, he spread his small hands out saying earnestly, "So you see, my dear, it's not what you might call a good, sound risk. Have nothing to do with it! I'm getting out, myself."

"Would you sell me your equipment—on credit?" she demanded at once. "And would you help make the film—and then help distribute it?"

For two days the two were locked in a struggle, but finally Thomas said, "All right, Lylah! If you're determined to lose everything you have, I'll help you do it. But you'll have to raise a great deal of money. The kind of picture you want to make will be expensive—and as much as I like you, my dear, I'm not going to go broke with you!"

They had shaken hands on the deal, and Lylah left at once, determined to raise the money. For a week she visited banks and quickly discovered that they were not interested. "Why don't you take up horse racing, Miss Stuart?" one of the loan officers asked her. "Compared to making movies, that's a sound, solid, conservative business."

She arrived at Jesse's house late one afternoon, and after greeting Adam with a hug, fell on the couch. She kicked off her shoes and put her head back on the couch. "Jesse, there's no hope!" she moaned. "I've been to every bank in town, and they all just laugh at me!"

Jesse sat down beside her and lifted her feet onto his lap. He began to massage one, asking sympathetically, "What do they really say?"

"Oh, that feels good! Why, they say that I've got no track record, that they have a duty to their depositors, and that there's no way the thing will ever find a backer."

Jesse remained silent, rubbing her arches for a few minutes. He looked out the window and saw Bonnie swinging Adam. The boy's squeals of pleasure came to them, and he smiled. "Bonnie's going to make a good wife—and mother. She dotes on Adam. And so do I."

Lylah opened her eyes and smiled despite her weariness. "You've been so good for him, Jesse."

For one moment Jesse gazed at her, then said abruptly, "I'd like to apply for a full-time job at it."

Lylah blinked in surprise. "Job? What kind of job?"

"At being Adam's dad." He reached over and pulled her up into his arms, adding, "And I guess you go with the territory." Then he kissed her, a long kiss that stirred her. He whispered, "I love you, Lylah. I want to marry you."

Lylah had known for weeks that she loved him. But now she drew back. "I've never told you about Adam's father," she said quietly. "He was Baron Manfred von Richthofen."

Jesse sat quietly holding her hand as she told of her mad affair with the German ace. Finally she ended by saying, "Some people still hate the Germans. I had to tell you."

Jesse kissed her hand, then said, "Adam's father was a man of courage and honor. And if you loved him, Lylah, he must have had other good qualities. Do you love me? That's the only question."

Lylah's eyes brimmed with tears, and her throat was so full she could scarcely say, "Oh, yes, Jesse!"

When Bonnie came inside with Adam, Jesse called her. She came at once to the two, and Jesse said, "How would you like a sister-in-law?"

Bonnie's eyes flew open, and then she released Adam and flew to hug them both. Later she told Jesse, "I knew you were going to marry her. I'm so glad!"

She said the same thing to Jerry, who came to pick up another mail plane. He arrived unexpectedly, and he took her out for a long walk after supper. She was shy with him, and finally he said, "I've got something to tell you, Bonnie—"

Bonnie's heart sank. *He's going to marry that flier, that Cara Gilmore!* She swallowed hard, then asked, "What is it, Jerry?"

He stopped, saying, "Let's sit down. It's kind of a long story." The two of them sat down, and he told her of his close call. She sat beside him, riveted by his story. Finally he said, "It was all up with me, Bonnie. No way out but to go down. Out of gas and no place to land." He turned to her with an odd expression and looked at her heart-shaped face. "And then I remembered the last thing you said to me. Remember what it was?"

"I . . . think I said I'd pray for you."

"That's right—and I swear, Bonnie, as I was freezing and going down, I could *see* you—as clearly as I can right now!"

"Jerry!"

"And I could hear you saying 'I'll pray for you, Jerry!'"

His hands took hers, and he whispered, "Bonnie, it was so real! And then I asked God to get me down safe—and right then a hole in the clouds opened—and there was a field."

"How wonderful!" Bonnie said, enthralled—and very aware of her hands in his. He was squeezing them so hard they hurt, but she didn't care. "I'm so glad!"

Jerry suddenly leaned over and kissed her cheek. "You're a fine girl, Bonnie Hart! I've got to find out more about God, and I'm counting on you to help me. Will you?"

"I don't know much, Jerry, but I know Jesus Christ is the only one who can save us!"

"Tell me—how did you find him?"

The two of them talked for a long time, and when they got back to the house, Jerry grinned. "I guess you and I are sort of related now."

"No, we're not!"

Jerry stared at her in surprise. "All I meant was, my aunt is marrying your brother, so that's—"

"We're not related," Bonnie said more firmly than necessary. "Don't talk so silly!"

The two of them had a fine time, but Jerry was aware that Lylah was tense. He finally asked her on the night before he left, "What's wrong, Aunt Lylah?" He listened carefully as she told him her problem, how she wanted to make a film and couldn't get backing.

"Don't worry about it, Jerry," she said. "Some things we just can't do."

"Well, I guess God can do about anything he wants to, can't he?"

Lylah stared at him. "You sound like Owen—and like your father, and Lenora."

"Pretty good company," Jerry said with a grin. "You better get Bonnie to pray for you. She did a number on me . . ." He related his close brush with death, then nodded, "I'd say that young lady has a pretty close connection—and so has Jesse."

When he left the next morning, his parting words to Lylah were, "Don't give up, Lylah." Then he was gone, a smile on his lips.

"A fine young man," Jesse nodded. He looked at Bonnie with a mischievous light in his eyes. "Don't you agree, Bonnie?"

Bonnie gave him a steady look, then turned and walked away. Jesse smiled, then said, "Well, let's go to some more banks. There's got to be at least one willing to take a chance."

But Lylah was not smiling. "We've tried them all, Jesse. There's got to be some other way."

Two weeks after Jerry left, Lylah was in her kitchen drinking coffee. She dreaded going to the studio, for this was the day she had to sign the contract to do three more pictures— and she disliked the thought of it. She felt drained and tired, and she wished she didn't have to tell Jesse that there would be no movie. It had become a real thing in his life, for he'd thrown himself into writing the script with passion. When Lylah had tried to warn him that it might never be filmed, he'd merely said, "We've got to do it, Lylah!"

A knock came at her door and she got up, expecting it was the milkman. It was his morning to collect, and she got the money to pay him, then went to the door. Opening it, she said, "You're early—" and then broke off in astonishment.

"Hello, Sis!" Amos stepped in, hugged her, then stepped back. "You fellas take your turn—but hurry up, I'm starving!"

Lylah was overwhelmed as Gavin and Owen stepped in, kissed her, then stood there grinning.

"What in the world are you three doing here?"

Owen waved his steel hook in the air. "Came for breakfast."

"And after that," Gavin said, "we're going to have a talk with this fellow Jesse Hart. See if his intentions are honorable."

"And after that—" Amos smiled, his eyes sparkling, "we're gonna make a movie!"

Lylah looked from one grinning face to another, mystified. "I think you've all gone crazy," she announced. "Now, tell me what this is all about."

"All right, Lylah," Amos said. "Jerry came to me as soon as he got back to Chicago. He told me all about your plan to make a movie. Did you get the funds yet?"

"No, Amos."

"Well, I guess it's going to have to be a family affair. Tell her, Owen."

Owen shook his head in wonder. "Never thought I'd get involved with anything like this, but Jerry convinced us all. He says you want to make a movie that's *good*—and we're going to help you do it."

"But . . . it takes an enormous amount of money to make a movie!" Lylah protested. "You don't have it!"

"Wrong!" Amos shook his head. "I've been squirreling away money, and so have these two. We've got enough to get started." He pulled out a check and handed it to her. "This enough for that?"

Lylah stared at the check, then shook her head. "I can't let you risk your life savings!" she protested. Her eyes began to glow, and she suddenly threw herself into Amos's arms, then attacked Gavin and Owen, laughing and crying.

"Logan and Pete said they'd come in a flash if you need them," Amos finally said. He paused, then said, "I guess this family can do just about anything it sets its mind to."

"It's all set then," Gavin nodded. "You'll have to move to Chicago—and I think it's time we met the future bridegroom. See if he's good enough for you, Sis!"

Lylah looked around at the three strong faces. "I'm not good enough for him—or for you three either!" Then she laughed, and it made her look very young. "Come on—I'm anxious to see how Jesse will stand up to the three of you. He'll probably take off running when he sees what a family he's getting into!"

Owen shook his head, smiling at her. "I don't think so, Sis. I think a man would have to be crazy to give up a woman like you!"

Part 4
CHICAGO

19

A LITTLE WARNING

On January 1, 1925, Notre Dame defeated Stanford 27 to 10 in the Rose Bowl.

But Lylah Stuart was not there to see the game as she had planned. She was walking the streets of Little Italy on Chicago's West Side. A sharp, chilling wind whipped her skirts and caught at her hat, and she shivered as she said, "I miss the sunshine in California, Amos."

Amos had been absently humming "I'm Forever Blowing Bubbles," but at her comment, he took his eyes from the grubby buildings that lined the street. "Could be worse," he shrugged. He noted her outfit, a plain black overcoat and a cloche hat, plus a pair of sensible-looking and very plain black shoes. "You don't look much like a movie star," he commented. "Nobody's recognized you."

"Good! I hope it stays that way," Lylah nodded. She glanced around at a group of boys playing some sort of game, hitting a can with sticks. "It all looks pretty dirty, Amos. We grew up poor, but at least we had a place to play. We could go fishing or trapping. Those kids have no place but the street."

"They've got the factories," Amos responded bitterly. He drew the collar of his overcoat tighter, adding, "Child-labor abuse is a long way from dead. We've got kids twelve or thirteen years old working twelve-hour days—and women, too." He nodded toward a group of young men lounging outside a pool hall, matching pennies. "You need to get shots of things like that," he commented. "It's the sort of background that

235

Capone grew up in. But matching pennies was too tame for Al. He graduated to armed robbery and worse before he was out of his teens."

The movie that Lylah had come to Chicago to make was to be based on the life of Al Capone, the most flamboyant of the Chicago gangsters. Amos had volunteered to do the research on Capone, and he fed the information to Jesse, who wrote it into the script. Jesse and Bonnie had come to Chicago with Lylah, and they threw themselves into the making of the film with great enthusiasm.

Lylah listened carefully as Amos related the history of the mob, and later he pointed to a flower shop. "See that flower shop—right there across the street from the Holy Name Cathedral?"

"What about it, Amos?"

"It belonged to a man named Dion O'Banion. A gangster, grew up right here in Chicago." Amos stared at the shop carefully, adding, "He was one of Capone's competitors. Last year he tapped the police, and Johnny Torrio and Capone were caught."

"I didn't read about them going to jail."

"Because they didn't. Some money changed hands—and they walked out of court without being charged. Capone's got more lawyers on his payroll than they've got in Harvard Law School."

The two of them walked toward the flower shop, and Amos noted the blood red roses in the window. "Wait a minute—" he said, then darted into the shop. Lylah peered through the window but could see little. When Amos came out, he had a single long-stemmed rose in his hand. "Here—" he broke the stem short and pinned it to the lapel of Lylah's coat. "To celebrate your new career."

Lylah smiled and lowered her head to smell the rose. "Beautiful! Thank you, Amos." She took her glove off and touched the delicate flower, then looked up. "The gangster—he owns a flower shop? The two don't seem to go together."

"All Dion O'Banion owns now is six feet of ground."

"He's dead?"

"Sure. I wrote the story. Got some of it here in my briefcase for Jesse."

"How did he die, Amos?"

"He was right in the back of the shop, clipping some chrysanthemums," Amos related. "A dark blue, nickel-trimmed Jewett sedan pulled up in front of the cathedral, and three men got out and went into the shop. An eleven-year-old schoolboy was playing in the street. He told the police that two of them were dark and looked like foreigners, and he said the other man had a light complexion. A Negro porter named Crutchfield was sweeping the floor. He said at the hearing that O'Banion walked toward the men. Crutchfield left the room, and as soon as he did, the shooting started."

Amos looked with distaste at the flower shop, adding, "When he went back in, he found O'Banion dead in the middle of a lot of crushed flowers—he'd knocked over some containers of carnations and lilies. Crutchfield told me O'Banion's blood dyed some white peonies red. For some reason I can remember the lab report word for word: 'Two bullets passed through the victim's chest, the third through the right cheek, the fourth and fifth through his larynx. The sixth was fired into his brain at such close range the powder scorched his skin.' "

"How dreadful!"

"Typical gangster killing, Lylah. They shot him through the larynx so if he failed to die immediately he wouldn't be able to speak." In disgust he swept the street with an impetuous gesture. "This place is worse than Verdun back in the war! And my boss makes a fortune off it!" He suddenly fumbled in his briefcase, found a paper, then thrust it toward Lylah. "That's the account of the funeral that came out in the paper I work for! Read it!"

Lylah read the account, which said:

The casket of the deceased was purchased from a Philadel-

phia firm and rushed to Chicago in a special express freight
car carrying no other cargo. It was equipped with solid silver
and bronze double walls, inner sealed and air tight, with a
heavy plate glass above and a couch of white satin below, with
a tufted cushion extra for his left hand to rest on.

At the corners of the casket are solid silver posts, carved in
wonderful designs. Modest is the dignified silver gray of the
casket, content with the austere glory of the carved silver posts
at its corners, and broken only by a line across one side that
reads "Dion O'Banion, 1892–1924."

Silver angels stood at the head and feet with their heads
bowed in the light of ten candles that burned in the solid
golden candlesticks they held in their hands, and over it all
the perfume of flowers.

But, vying with that perfume was the fragrance of per-
fumed women, wrapped in furs from ears to ankles, who tip-
toed down the aisle, escorted by soft-stepping, tailored gentlemen with black, shining pompadours.

And also treading, deftly changing places, were more well-
formed gentlemen in tailored garments, with square, blue
steel jaws and shifting glances.

In the soft light of the candles at the head of the $10,000
casket sat Mrs. O'Banion, a picture of patient sorrow.

"They live like animals—no—worse!" Amos said grimly.
"But when they die they want to be buried like Roman
emperors!"

Lylah handed the clipping back to Amos. As he shoved it
back into his briefcase, she said, "You hate all of this, don't
you, Amos?"

"Yes! It's not what we fought a war for! I thought we were
fighting for freedom, but these thugs are worse than any enemies we had in France!" As the two moved toward his car,
he tried to find words to explain it to Lylah. When they were
in it and had left Little Italy, he sighed heavily. "I love this
country, Lylah, and it's being torn apart. Capone and Torrio
and men like them are vermin—but the public heaps adula-

tion on them! They're as famous as . . . as movie stars! Kids who can't name the presidents of the United States can give you the names of every big-time racketeer in the country! And my boss has to answer for his part of that!"

"Why does he do it? And why do you keep on working for him if you feel that way?"

"He got his start with what's called 'yellow journalism,' which simply means, give the public all the garbage you can dredge up. He got rich and famous—and when I asked him why he didn't lift the standards of his newspapers, he said, 'We sell what they want.'" Amos swerved to miss a covey of nuns, saying with surprise, "They remind me of a flock of penguins!"

"Why do you stay with him?"

"Well, he pays well—" Amos grinned sourly. "But to tell the truth, I've thought of quitting. When I mentioned it to him, he got pretty upset."

"A fine compliment for you!"

"I guess so, Lylah. Why don't I leave? I guess I keep hoping he'll change. And he did give me the go-ahead for doing a series of stories on the mob here in Chicago—which will probably make a few more people go to see *The Gangster.*" This was the title Jesse had insisted on for the movie, and Amos noted, "That's a good title—short and blunt."

As they pulled up in front of the big barnlike structure Lylah had rented to use for a studio, she asked abruptly, "What about you, Amos? Won't it get you in trouble—writing an exposé of Capone?"

"I don't think Al will be pinning any medals on me. But I'd hate to think I'd do anything Capone would admire."

This was an element that Lylah had not considered, and as they got out of the car, she waited for him to come to stand beside her. "If he's as ruthless as everyone says, he might—"

"Have me bumped off?" Amos shrugged. "Always a chance of that when you're dealing with people like Capone. But they seem to handle the press pretty carefully. Don't worry about it, Sis."

Amos's answer did not completely satisfy Lylah, and she filed the thought for future reference. The door was locked, and when she rang a bell, they waited for some time before a hasp grated and they were admitted. Peter Stuart, wearing carpenter's overalls, closed the door behind them. "Just in time to stop a fight, Lylah," he grinned. "Jesse and that director fellow, Mr. Thomas, are just about to scalp each other."

The sight of her brother Peter gave Lylah a warm feeling. He'd dropped his job in the oil fields and come to Chicago, announcing he was going to be in show business. He'd brought his wife and two children along, and he had been a gift from heaven, or so Lylah said. The huge lot she'd leased had once housed a variety of businesses, but on a limited budget, she'd been baffled as to how to turn the structures into sets for the movie.

Pete had swarmed into the job, bossing the carpenters, plumbers, and the rest. He had been obliged to whip one hulking carpenter who jeered at his methods and his accent, but afterwards the two had become good friends. Now as Lylah looked around, she was pleased to see that the sets were all taking form.

"What's the argument about?" Lylah asked as she and Amos hurried to keep up with her long-legged brother.

"Got no idea," Pete shrugged. "Something about an ambulance."

"An *ambulance?*" Lylah stared at Pete. "We don't have an ambulance in the script, do we?" But Pete only shrugged and led her into one of the big frame buildings that had once housed a wagon wheel factory. When they were inside she was pleased to see that it had been transformed by Pete and his men into a fine restaurant. "Oh, Pete, this is a miracle!" She half ran into the midst of the tables set with red and white tablecloths, adorned with candles imbedded in wine bottles. It was a classic replica of a rather fancy Italian restaurant such as one might find in Little Italy. "Where did you get the props—the tablecloths and candles?"

"Bonnie and Jerry dug 'em up. Think they talked a friend of Gavin's out of the lot." Pete cast a professional eye on the set, then nodded. "When you get the restaurant shots done, I'll turn this into a speakeasy. Won't be hard."

Lylah pulled Pete's head down and kissed him on the cheek. "You're priceless! You'll never have to go back to roughneck work in the oil fields!"

"Ah, shoot, Lylah, this ain't my style. But I couldn't miss out on this picture making! Why, you got almost the whole family working on it!" Then he nodded toward the end of the large room. "You hear 'em, Lylah?"

Lylah could hear Jesse and Carl arguing before she saw them. As she and Amos moved down the set, they heard Carl's high-pitched voice protesting strenuously, then Jesse's lower baritone answering. They found them in a room still filled with some of the equipment used to make wheels, standing over a door that had been placed on two sawhorses, on which were spread several large drawings.

"What's this about an ambulance?" Lylah broke into the argument. "I don't remember any ambulance in the script, Jesse."

"Ambulance?" Jesse turned to her, his eyes lighting as they always did when she came to him. "Who said anything about an ambulance?" He was wearing a pair of twill pants and a white shirt under a brown pullover sweater. His eyes were red, for he slept little since the project had started. All day long he raced from one set to another, then dashed away to get a taste of some portion of Chicago's high-crime section. Then he would stay up most of the night working on the script. He had become an expert scriptwriter by sheer determination, but he and Carl were constantly at loggerheads.

Carl was wearing a pair of gray flannel slacks, an immaculate white shirt, a colorful tie, and a carefully tailored navy blue coat. His face was red, and he said loudly, "Ambulance? Where did you hear that?"

"Pete said you were arguing about an ambulance."

Suddenly Jesse laughed, his eyes crinkling. "I know what it was. He was working close to us, and Carl kept trying to tell me that the *ambiance* of the gangster's room was wrong. *Ambiance*, not *ambulance!*"

Lylah laughed, saying, "Well, he said the way the two of you were fighting, one of you would *need* an ambulance!"

Thomas's eyes bulged out, and his tiny chest swelled with anger. "Look at this, Lylah—just look! It's all wrong!"

"No, it's all *right!*" Jesse protested. "Look, Carl, this is the room of a *gangster*, not an art collector!" He turned to Lylah, his brown eyes snapping. "Carl wants to put the *Mona Lisa* on the wall—and I keep telling him a tough like Capone would be more likely to have a picture of Clara Bow on his wall."

"No, he would not!" The short man stood on tiptoe to emphasize his words. "These gangsters, they are uncouth, but they are rich. I have been in the home of Big Jim Colosimo— and I tell you he had *masterpieces* on the walls! Right out of museums. They want to *buy* respectability."

Amos nodded at once. "I'm afraid Carl's right, Jesse. These killers surround themselves with symbols of culture. They buy the best in art, just like they buy the best in guns."

Jesse soaked up information like a sponge, and when Amos finished, said instantly, "You're right, then, Carl."

"Of course I'm right!"

Jesse grinned at the pout of the small man who'd taken the job as director of the picture. "But how about this—" he said quickly. "We show one of the great works of art in the gangster's room, then we shift from that to a close-up of his gun— show that despite his collection of fine art, he still lives by the gun. How about that?"

Carl stared at the younger man. He'd been insulted when Lylah told him he'd have to work with Jesse Hart—a man who'd never even *seen* a picture made. He'd privately felt that Hart was Lylah's "pet," and that it was a mistake to use him on the picture. He'd been stiff and unyielding for the first few days, but he soon discovered that Hart was a man who wanted to learn—and also a man with creative juices. He saw at once the greatness of the shot and nodded, "Now, that's a great idea." He turned his head, winked slyly at Amos, and nodded, saying loudly, "I'm glad I thought of it!"

Jesse grinned, but he knew this man. Carl Thomas knew as much as any man alive about making a movie, and Jesse paid him the compliment of seeking him out and listening to him for hours.

The four stood there talking, and it was Carl who brought up the subject of Capone. "We can call the main character of *The Gangster* any name we please—but we won't fool anybody. Everybody who buys a ticket will know it's Capone we're putting on the scene."

"And you're afraid he'll get tough?" Jesse asked idly. "If he does, it'll mean we did a good job."

"It could also mean we'll be *dead!*" Carl snapped. "You don't know these people, Jesse. They put no value on human life."

"That's why we're making the film, isn't it?" Amos asked quietly. "To show what Capone and his sort are like?"

"They're too busy making bootleg whiskey to pay attention to us," Jesse stated flatly. "Now, let's talk about this idea of yours to show the gangster meeting the president, Amos."

Jesse for all his astuteness had misjudged the nature of the lords of Chicago. On the same day he'd shrugged off any possibility of the criminal element paying attention to a mere movie, a meeting was taking place that would have changed his mind.

"I thought we were supposed to meet Al at Lindy's place," Eddy complained. He was driving the heavy Packard, but be-

fore they'd gone more than a block, Nick told him to go across
town to the old Hotel Lexington.

"You know Capone," Nick shrugged. "He don't like to be
regular with his appointments."

Eddy nodded slowly, thinking of how Al Capone spent a
fortune protecting himself. He'd bought a $30,000 custom-
built Cadillac limousine, which weighed seven tons and had
a steel armor-plated body, a steel-hooded gas tank, bullet-
proof windows half an inch thick, and a movable window en-
abling passengers to fire at pursuers. Even with this vehicle,
Capone always kept a small scout car ahead and a touring car
full of sharpshooters behind.

"What's this meet'n about, Nick?" Eddy inquired, his eyes
moving restlessly.

"He didn't say." He shifted in his seat restlessly, then
added, "He's more cautious than ever. Won't cross a sidewalk
without his bodyguards. Guess Torrio's close call shook him
up." Both men thought of how Johnny Torrio had been
gunned down and almost killed. Since his recovery he'd been
in hiding, and Capone ran the city in his stead.

The two spoke of business briefly, then Eddy said, "Here
we are, Nick." The two got out and walked up the steps of
the Hotel Lexington. They were greeted in the lobby by two
of Capone's bodyguards, who pleasantly reminded them to
check their guns. After this bit of formality they were taken
upstairs to room 430, a six-room suite that was the nerve center of Capone's activities, where they found Capone having
his dinner. He looked up and asked, "You wanna' eat? This
is pretty good stuff."

"Naw, I gotta' take the wife out later," Nick said. He sat
down at Capone's gesture, and Eddy took another chair.
Capone was eating spaghetti, and he ate like a starved wolf.
He could not seem to get the long strands into his mouth
quickly enough, and eager grunting sounds erupted as he
crammed the food down. From time to time he would choke,
whereupon he would snatch up a glass of Chianti and wash

the spaghetti down. He seemed to have forgotten his visitors, but when he finally shoved the plate away, he looked at them with a sharp light in his eyes.

Eddy had met only twice with the leader of the Chicago underworld, and he paid him careful attention. Capone was a little over five feet, ten inches tall and had a rock-hard body just beginning to put on fat. His shoulders were meaty, and his big round head sat on a short, thick neck. His hair was dark brown, his eyes light gray under thick, shaggy eyebrows. A scar ran along his left cheek from ear to jaw, and he was touchy about it. He always presented his right side to news photographers, and he hated the sobriquet the press had given him—Scarface.

He was wearing a lemon yellow, custom-made suit from Marshall Field that cost $135, with the right pocket reinforced to bear the width of a revolver. On his middle finger he wore a flawless, eleven-carat, blue white diamond that had cost him $50,000.

Eddy's study of Capone was cut short when Capone said, "I hear bad things, Nick."

Carefully Nick asked, "What kind of bad things, Al? More trouble from Weiss?"

"Nah, not him. I can take care of that." Capone pulled a monogrammed silk handkerchief from his breast pocket and wiped his meaty lips. "This is about your friend Amos Stuart."

At once alarms ran through Nick's nerves. He stiffened and then tried to look calm. "Them stories he writes about you? Who cares, Al." Nick forced a laugh and spread his hands wide. "Well, we grew up together—in my mama's house— and you should see what he writes about *me!*"

Capone picked up a knife, ran the edge of it along his palm, then shook his head. "Times are changin', Nick. The Feds are breathin' down my neck. I don't need no hassle from him. Tell him that."

"I'll tell him, Al."

Capone frowned and threw the knife down. "It ain't just

his stories, Nick. They're making a movie about me. The way
I hear it, that sister of his, the actress, she's set up here in
Chicago over on the North Side. She's gonna make a movie
that'll show the world what an animal I am." His eyes turned
flat and hard. "I want you to stop it, Nick. These people,
they're friends of yours, ain't they?"

"Well, sure, but—"

"Then you be a friend to them!" Capone's mouth twisted
cruelly, and he turned his eyes full on Nick Castellano. "I'm
givin' them a break, Nick, on account of you. Tell that
woman—and Amos Stuart—if they think they can make a
movie showing me like I was some kind of monster, they'd
better think again."

Nick sat very still, his mind racing. He knew Capone would
never have called him and Eddy to talk to them unless he
was serious—and to Capone being serious could be a killing
matter.

Finally Capone laughed, but the laughter didn't reach his
eyes. "You tell 'em just to go easy on ol' Al, Nick. I got people
who know watchin' 'em. I don't mind bein' in the movies—
but it's gotta be *right*. You tell 'em that, Nick—and make sure
they understand it."

That concluded the interview. Capone waved them out of
the room, and as soon as they were in the car, Eddy groaned,
"Nick, this is *bad!* You know how Capone is about things like
this! Remember that reporter—what's his name? Tibbets?
Yeah, that's it. Remember how he got smashed up so bad he
was never right? And it was Capone that got the job done."

Nick shook his head silently. He was feeling sick, for he
knew as well as Eddy what Capone was capable of. "Go get
ahold of Amos, Eddy. We gotta talk to him!"

Eddy said gloomily, "You ever know Amos to back off from
anybody, Nick?"

"I'm hoping this time he will, Eddy." Nick bit his lip nervously, then shook his head. "We got to show them how it is,
Eddy. We *got* to!"

20

CAPONE STRIKES

That won't do, Emory—we'll just have to shoot it again." A groan rose from the lips of Emory Jannings. Turning to face Carl Thomas he complained, "What's *wrong* with the scene, Carl? We've shot it five times."

Carl hesitated, then came to stand before the tall actor who had been chosen to play the lead in *The Gangster.* Carl had disapproved strongly the choice and had protested to Lylah, "He's a pretty dull fellow—on the screen at least. Whatever makes the people who buy tickets sit up, well, he just doesn't have it." But Lylah had answered, "He's the best I can get, Carl. We'll just have to wring a good performance out of him."

But as Carl stood before the actor, he realized that he was asking the impossible. *What's wrong with the scene?* he asked himself with frustration running through him. *You're what's wrong with it!* But he sighed, then said patiently, "I want to try *one* more time, Emory. In this scene you've got to let the audience know that you've decided to get what you want out of life—no matter *what* you have to do. They've got to see in your face you're ready to *kill* to get your way. Understand?"

"Sure, Carl." Emory went back to his place and did his best. When the scene was shot, Carl said heavily, "All right, that's a take. Everyone get ready to go to the street scene."

As the cast and crew hastily loaded into vehicles to go to Little Italy for a scene, Carl went to Lylah's office where he found her with Jesse going over the script for the next day's shooting. "How did it go, Carl?" she asked. She played the

247

role of a policeman's wife in the film and was wearing a gray dress for the scene.

"Lylah, I just don't know," Carl scowled. Since the picture had started, he had thrown himself into it with gusto, but now he looked tired. He threw himself down on a chair and brooded, "Emory *tries*, but he just can't give me what he hasn't got."

Jesse and Lylah exchanged glances, for they both felt the same way. Jesse said, "Well, we'll just have to make up for his performance in other ways—camera angles and good performances by the rest of the cast."

Lylah knew this was not the answer, but she said nothing. Emory *looked* the part, and she had been with him in several plays. He was a good actor—but only for certain parts. *The Gangster* was one of those dramas that had to be carried by the star, and Lylah knew that Emory just wasn't strong enough to pull it off. "You're doing a fine job, Carl," she said and went to give him a hug. "Nobody could do better." Almost desperately she summoned a smile, adding, "We've got the best script and the best director in Hollywood—so let's go with it!"

Carl stared at her shrewdly. He knew the burden that lay on Lylah, that she was gambling everything on the success of this picture. He had grown very fond of the entire family, and he had been accepted into the circle as a trusted friend. He was a kindly man, and this endeavor had gotten to be the biggest thing in his life. But he knew the business, and a heaviness had come to him. *We're not going to make it*, he thought as he left the office to get into the car. *Emory just can't put the fire into it.*

Jesse turned to Lylah and saw the doubt in her eyes. He moved to her, putting his arms around her. She leaned against him, putting her face against his chest. Lylah was a strong woman, but the pressure of this production was far more intense than she had dreamed. Always before she had been able to concentrate on her own performance while others did the necessary work of getting the production into gear. Now she worked all day shooting, and at night she and Jesse worked over the script, or she and Carl planned the shooting schedule. Weariness had drained her, and she gave in to it as Jesse put his arms around her.

"When this is over, we get married," Jesse said gently. They had agreed that it would be best if they waited until the picture was finished before they married. Now Jesse stroked her hair and whispered, "Did you know that in the Old Testament times when a man got married, he quit work for a year."

"To do what?"

"Why, he did nothing but please his wife. How about that?"

Lylah lifted her head, a smile turning the corners of her lips up. "I think it's a good idea." She took his kiss, clinging to him almost fiercely. She was not in her first youth and had known other men, but her love for Jesse had come with a shocking passion. Finally she pulled back and said breathlessly, "Don't tease an old woman like that, Jesse!" Looking up, she studied the clean cut of his jaw and the steady brown eyes and said, "I can't believe the way I feel—like I'm sixteen."

Jesse kissed her again, then said, "Whoso findeth a wife findeth a good thing, and obtaineth favour of the Lord."

"Is that in the Bible?"

"Sure, it's in Proverbs 18," he nodded. "That's why I'm marrying you, really. The Lord favors married men, and I don't want to miss out on that."

The two of them laughed, and Lylah's eyes lost some of the heaviness that he'd seen in them. As they talked of timing, Jesse noted that it was the first of March. He calculated the scenes to be shot, balancing it against the money in the bank and the work he had to do on the script. They were speaking of this when the door opened and Amos came in, accompanied by Jerry.

"I thought you two were making movies," Amos grinned.
"Looks to me more like making whoopee!"

"It's her fault, Amos," Jesse drawled. "She just can't keep
her hands off me. Hello, Jerry." He shook hands with the
young pilot, asking, "When did you get in?"

Jerry looked tired, his eyes red from lack of sleep. "Just
a couple hours ago." He looked around and asked, "Where's
Bonnie?"

"Helping Sam with the developing." Lylah smiled as Jerry
immediately left the room. "He looks exhausted, Amos. Can
he fly like that?"

Amos shrugged, saying, "They fly in every condition, but
he's off for a week. Guess he'll be underfoot. I've got a project he's going to help me with."

An alert expression came to Jesse's face. "Something to do
with the series you're doing for the paper?" Amos was in the
middle of a series of stories laying bare the activities of the
Chicago criminal element. They were blunt and hard-hitting,
and the response to them had been tremendous. "Capone
and his bunch must be simmering!"

Lylah looked worried. Putting her hand on Amos's arm,
she protested, "You could get into trouble with them. I wish
you'd let off—at least for awhile."

"Not a chance, Sis," Amos shook his head firmly. He had
thrown himself into the battle with an energy that he hadn't
known he possessed. "If the newspaper business doesn't
speak out against Capone, who will? He can be hurt—but it's
going to have to be done the hard way."

"Had any more warnings from Nick?" Jesse asked.

"Sure. He's worried about me—about you, too, Lylah."

"You're the one hurting Capone most," Lylah argued. "He
wouldn't try to get at me. I doubt if he even knows what sort
of a picture we're making."

"You're wrong about that. Capone may be a monster, but
he's a crafty one. He's got somebody in your company, Lylah,

you can bet on it. And if he decides you're hurting him, he'll get at you."

"If he's that smart," Jesse said thoughtfully, "he may be likely to see the difference between a movie and a newspaper story. People who never read an editorial go to movies. Capone likes publicity, but he's sharp enough to see that if a movie came out showing him to be—well, what he *is*, it could hurt him. Maybe we'd better hire some security, Lylah."

"It would take too many to watch this whole operation." Lylah was more concerned about Amos. "But you be careful. Don't go into any dark alleys." The three of them stood there talking, but when Lylah asked what Jerry was going to do, Amos shook his head mysteriously. "Better you don't know," he said.

As soon as Jerry went into the developing room, he was greeted by Bonnie. She was wearing her favorite costume, a pair of riding pants and boots set off by a bright green silk shirt. Jerry grinned as he said, "Don't you have any other out-fits?" He admired the trim form set off by the garb, but he wouldn't dare say so. "How about something to eat?"

"Yes, I'm starved!"

The two left the lot, and ten minutes later they were sitting at a table in a small cafe close by. Jerry ate hungrily, listening as Bonnie told him how the picture was doing. She made a striking picture, her straight hair as black as hair can be, and her dark eyes flashing with excitement. *She doesn't know how pretty she is*, Jerry thought. *And how many girls are there as good as she is?* He had been out in the world enough to know that most young women boasted of their free ways. They drank and smoked and treated purity as if it were something to be ashamed of. Now as he munched his hamburger, he found himself comparing the sweetness of Bonnie's expression to the knowing light in the eyes of Cara Gilmore. He still remembered her, and he thought of her often. But when he looked at Bonnie, Cara's image faded.

"I'm getting into a new line of work," he announced. "Just for a few days."

"New line of work?"

"Sure, I'm going to be an undercover newspaperman." He picked up the glass of milk before him, drank it down, then grinned at her. "I'll be working for my dad."

"You have a milk mustache," Bonnie frowned. Picking up her napkin, she leaned across the table and patted his lips. "You are the messiest eater I've ever seen, Jerry—worse than Adam!"

"A neat person is ineffective."

"Who said that?"

"I did—just then." He leaned back and put his hands behind his head, relaxed as a cat. "Don't you want to hear about my new job?"

"You're kidding me, aren't you?"

"No, I'm going to dress up like a sheik and mooch around to get the background for the stuff Dad's writing for the *Examiner*." He closed his eyes, a smile on his wide mouth. "Dad was complaining because he didn't have some of the facts, so I volunteered to help until I go back to flying."

"What will you do?"

"Oh, I'll be a very wicked fellow!" Jerry opened his eyes and leaned forward. Her hands were on the table, and he suddenly picked them up. "You have nice hands, Bonnie. How do you keep your nails? I bite mine all the time."

Bonnie was stirred by the touch of his hands, and a slight flush came to her cheeks. She didn't try to pull her hands back but asked, "What do you mean, a wicked fellow? What exactly are you going to do, Jerry?"

"Oh, drift into some of the speakeasies Capone runs. Do some gambling and—other things."

Bonnie looked up instantly. "What does that mean—other things?"

Jerry shifted uncomfortably. Her hands were soft but firm, and he said, "I like it that you don't cut your hair. Most girls

look like plucked chickens!" Then when she kept her eyes
on him, he said, "I'll get the lowdown on the prostitution
racket. It's a big part of the mob's income. Dad thinks some
of the women are part of the white slave traffic—that they're
kept against their will."

"How . . . how will you do it?" Bonnie pulled her hands
back, and her dark blue eyes were fixed on his.

"Why, I haven't got it all figured out," Jerry said uncomfortably. "Have to see how it goes." He saw that she was disturbed and said quickly, "Don't worry, Bonnie."

But Bonnie didn't smile. "If they find out you're a spy,
they'll do something awful to you. Don't do it, Jerry!"

But Jerry had made up his mind. "It's a piece of cake!" he
said and changed the subject.

Jerry paused to study himself in the full length mirror before leaving his room. He admired his hair, which was plastered down with brilliantine and parted in the middle. It lay
as slick as that of Rudolph Valentino! He wore a suit with
wide checks, padded in the shoulders, a flower-figured neck-
tie, and pointed patent-leather shoes.

"What a piece of work you are, Stuart!" he whispered, and
then he picked up a pearl gray fedora and pulled it down over
his eyes, carefully creasing the brim to stand up on one side
in the fashion begun by Al Capone himself.

Finally, satisfied with his appearance, he left his room and
took a taxi to Cicero. He got out near the Hawthorne race-
track and made his way to an unpainted frame building two
stories high. His heart beat faster as he entered.

If I see some of Nick's gang here, they'll spot me even in this getup,
he thought. But he knew that Nick's boys usually left Cicero
for their revels.

He entered a large room with only one table and a miniature bar, sat down, and ordered some near beer. *Not a place
built for drinking*, he thought.

He studied the place, noting that a series of three doors

only a foot or two apart led out of the room. The first and third were hinged on the right, the middle one on the left. He sat nursing the beer, trying to fix it all in his memory. "I need details, Jerry," his father had instructed him. "Get all the little things down—it's what people need to make them interested."

A bouncer sat at a small table just inside the main entrance. Jerry soon figured out that the bartender was the "spotter." He controlled all three doors with electric buttons. He could let a client in through the first door, then lock all three electrically.

Jerry drank slowly, but finally the bartender gave him a hard look, and he moved to take a place with the other men seated on benches against the walls. The procedure was simple. A girl wearing only lingerie came down from upstairs, entered the waiting room through the third door, and made a slow circuit of the room, greeting the men with her painted smile. She would then go back upstairs through the first door, accompanied by one of the men.

Little conversation took place, and the traffic moved rapidly. It took about half an hour until Jerry was sitting on the end of the bench.

Finally a very young girl with dyed yellow hair came to him, smiling and asking, "You ready, Handsome?"

Jerry had never been as frightened, not in all his days of dangerous flying. There was something about the place that was ominous, and he had a sudden urge to flee. However, he followed the girl silently up the stairs. She led him to a room, opened the door, and stepped inside.

He had been curious about such things as this, but the room was totally unlovely, containing only a bed, a table, one chair, and a small closet. The air reeked with cheap perfume, sweat, and other rank odors he could not identify.

The girl was watching him with bored eyes. She seemed to be very young, but there was a hardness about her that no makeup could hide. She put her hands on her hips and cocked her head to one side. "You want a cigarette, Handsome?" When he shook his head, she moved to the table, picked up a cigarette, and as the smoke rose lazily, she turned and studied him.

Jerry grew nervous under her stare and said in a stumbling fashion, "I . . . how long have you been here?"

"Too long. What difference?"

"You . . . ah . . . do you like it here?"

A coarse laugh rose to her lips. She puffed on the cigarette, then said, "I love it! It was the dream of my life to wind up in a room like this!" She snuffed the cigarette out and turned to face him, saying, "You ain't got all day."

Jerry swallowed, then said, "To tell the truth, I . . . I'm not much in the mood for . . . anything." Her eyes hardened, and he said, "Look, would you just *talk* to me for a little while? I'll pay for your time."

The girl gave Jerry a curious stare, then shrugged. "Sure, what do you want me to talk about?" She moved to the bed and sat down. "Want a drink?"

"I don't think so . . . but you go ahead."

Reaching for the bottle on the table, the young woman unscrewed the cap, tilted the bottle, and took two quick swallows. She shuddered as the raw alcohol hit her throat, then asked wearily, "Talk about what?"

"Anything. What's your name? Where's your home—just talk."

The girl was reluctant, but the whiskey loosened her tongue. Jerry sat in the chair listening to her speak, feeling enormously sorry for her. She was cheap, coarse, profane— but still, as she lay back and closed her eyes wearily, there was at least a trace of something better than that in her.

She had something better than this once, Jerry thought. *She had parents who were proud of her—a mother who dreamed of a good life. She had friends and she wanted to be loved. Where did it all go?*

Finally the girl opened her eyes, and a hardness replaced

the expression that had been there. "Get outta here," she said angrily. "Go find somebody else to talk to."

Jerry rose hastily. Reaching into his pocket, he dropped some bills on the bed, then turned to leave. He stopped, then whirled to see her picking up the money. "Good luck," he said, feeling like a fool for saying anything so inane.

"Yeah, thanks," the woman nodded. There was an emptiness in her face and something in her eyes that reminded Jerry of death, and he fled the room as if it contained the plague.

Later, when he'd written down the details for his father, he thought of the girl with sadness. Amos read it, then said, "It's the sort of thing that Capone and his kind do to people. He leaves misery on every soul he touches."

"I felt sorry for her," Jerry muttered. "And I get mad when I think of something like that maybe happening to Bonnie."

"It does happen to girls like her. They don't mean to wind up in places like that—but somehow they do." Amos saw that the visit had disturbed Jerry. "You shouldn't have gone there, Son. Come on, I've got to go talk to Lylah."

Jerry brightened up, and on the way to the studio, his father asked suddenly, "You're very fond of Bonnie, aren't you?"

Flustered by the abruptness of the question, Jerry stammered, "Well—I guess so. She's a fine young woman."

Amos asked dryly, "How old is she?"

"Nineteen, I think."

"I met your mother when she was about that age."

The comment drew Jerry's gaze, and he seemed to be thinking deeply all the way across town.

When they reached the set of Monarch Pictures, the rather grandiose name Lylah and Jesse had chosen for the company, Amos led the way inside. They went to the room used for meetings of the cast and found Lylah, Jesse, and Carl together.

Amos took one look at their faces and demanded, "What's wrong?"

Lylah's face was pale, and she had trouble controlling her voice. "It's Emory, Amos."

"What happened? Is he sick?" Amos knew how serious such a thing was. "Did he have an accident?"

"An accident rigged by Al Capone!" It was Jesse who spoke, and Amos and Jerry saw that his face was angry. "Three of his goons caught Emory alone and broke his leg."

"It could have been worse—for Emory," Lylah said quietly.

"It couldn't have been worse for us!" Carl sat with his head in his hands. When he stood up, Amos saw misery on the small man's face. "We're out of business, Amos!"

"We'll get another actor," Amos said.

But Lylah seemed to be drained of all hope. "Get who?" she asked wearily. "It took all we had to get Emory. We can't just walk out on the street and get someone. And we don't have the money to go hire John Barrymore."

The room was silent, and it was Jesse who said slowly, "It looks bad—but God's not dead. With God all things are possible."

Lylah stared at him, then rose, and her lips trembled as she said, "I don't have any right to ask God for favors, Jesse." She walked slowly out of the room, and the men knew that Lylah Stuart had come to the end of herself.

21

A FAMILY ARGUMENT

How do you like your new apartment, Ma?"
Anna Castellano looked across the table, giving her oldest son a direct stare. "It's fine," she said, setting a heaping plateful of pasta on the table. "It costa too much, I bet!"
Nick shook his head, and when his mother came around the table to fill his wineglass, he grabbed her around the waist and squeezed her so hard she grunted. "Ain't nothin' costs too much for you, Ma!" he said fondly. "Ain't that right, you guys?"

Mario and Eddy made up the rest of the guests, and both of them grinned and nodded. "Nick's right, Ma," Eddy answered. He looked around the spacious dining room decorated with the best furniture money could buy and laughed shortly. "Not like the old days in New York, is it? Remember how the plumbing never worked right?"

"And we had to fight the rats all the time," Nick nodded. "And the wind whistled through the cracks—boy, that old rooming house was pretty grim!"

Anna Castellano pulled herself upright and glared at Nick. She was showing her age—her body was thickening and she had heart trouble—but her spirit still fired up from time to time. "That place was good enough for your papa and me—good enough for you, too!" She slammed down the loaf of bread she was cutting with a long knife, adding, "We never took no charity—and I never had to worry about what my boys were doing!"

Nick shifted uncomfortably and gave Eddy a wry glance. "Now, Ma, don't start again. Let's just have a nice dinner, okay?"

"Sure, Ma," Eddy put in quickly. "You got two girls married to nice fellas and four grandbabies. And your three sons are all successful businessmen—even if one of 'em *is* a lawyer!" He reached over and tapped Mario on the shoulder fondly. "Hey, Counselor, why don't you speak up? Tell Ma how happy she ought to be—three good-looking rich fellas like us!"

Mario had said little, and now he managed a smile. "I can't remember much about the old house," he murmured.

"Better you don't," Nick shrugged. "It ain't no virtue, bein' poor." He poked at his pasta with a fork, and a thoughtful look came to his dark eyes. "When I was ten years old I vowed I was going to get our family out of that dump. It took a little while, but look at us now!" He gave his mother a look that was a plea. "Ma, ain't you even a *little* happy we got out of there?"

Anna sat down heavily, but she managed a smile for Nick. "I know you mean well, Nicky," she said slowly, "But I'm alla time afraid for you."

Mario glanced at her and said without thinking, "And you're ashamed of us, too, aren't you, Mama?"

"Ashamed?" Nick grunted, displeasure on his face. He let anger creep into his tone, and he glared at Mario. "Why should she be ashamed? We work hard for our money! And you didn't turn it down when we sent you to law school, did you?"

Mario put his fork down, his face tense. "No, I didn't, Nick. I took it, just like Mama and the rest of the family take your money. And every time you break the law to make the money, I've got a hand in it."

Eddy grew nervous, for he knew that Nick had a volatile temper. "Look, Mario," he put in quickly, "this prohibition, it's no good. Everybody is saying it won't work. Everybody breaks that law. The rest of them are just hypocrites!"

Mario had gone over this in his mind for years. He was ashamed that he'd built his own success on money that came from booze and prostitution. The guilt from this knowledge burned in him—had for a long time. He had racked his brain trying to find a way to cut his ties—but the fact remained that he owed his success to Nick's money.

"What about Amos?" Anna demanded. "And what about Owen? Are they hypocrites, Nick?"

"They're different!"

"They're honest, that'sa why they're different," Anna said.

Nick lost his temper, almost shouting, "I tell you, Ma, I'm just a businessman!"

Anna turned her old eyes on him and asked quietly, "What kind of businessman breaks the leg of an innocent man?"

All three of the men stared at her, and it was Mario who asked, "What's that, Mama?" He knew that much worse than leg-breaking went on in the family business, and he wondered why the item had moved his mother. "Who got his leg broken?"

"The actor, that's who!" Anna shook her head, sorrow etching her lined face. "Amos, he call me today. He tell me about his sister, the one who's making a movie. And he say there ain't gonna be no movie now."

"Ma, I don't know nothing about this!" Nick protested.

Anna examined his face, then shook her head. "Amos say it's bad for them—all the Stuarts. They got all their money in this movie."

Mario asked harshly, "Nick, what's this all about?"

"Don't you start on me, Mario!"

"I'll start on you if you had anything to do with stopping the film! Did Capone tell you to stop it that way? Everybody knows he's tried to block the picture!"

Nick was beleaguered by the questions. He threw his napkin down, and his face reddened. "I'm telling you both, me and Eddy had nothin' to do with this. I didn't even know about it till just now!"

"That's straight, Mario," Eddy put in quickly. "Capone asked us to give Lylah a warnin' to let up on making him look like a monkey. But that's all we done!"

Mario's face had grown pale. He got up at once, saying, "All right, I believe you. Capone was behind it." He moved around the table, kissed his mother, then stepped to the door.

"Where you goin'?" Nick demanded. "Don't get mixed up in this! I know you're sweet on that sister of Amos's—but stay clear of it, Mario."

"I think I'll have a talk with Mr. Alfonse Capone," Mario said, his lips drawn tight.

"Hey, you can't do that!" Eddy almost shouted.

"Why not? He's a respectable businessman, isn't he?" Mario moved through the door, and they heard the door slam.

"Go after him, Eddy!" Nick said. "Don't let him do nothin' crazy."

"Right!"

Eddy dashed out, calling, "Hey, Mario, wait for me!"

Anna sat quietly watching the face of her son. "You see how it is?" she asked. "You're afraid of that man."

"Sure, I am! He's crazy, Ma!"

"What'sa difference between him and you?" Anna asked. "You think I don't hear about what you and Eddy do?" She suddenly put her face in her hands and began to weep. "Oh, Nicky! Nicky!"

Nick got up and awkwardly tried to comfort his mother. He loved her with all his heart, but he knew she was right. He was not a stupid man, and he had known for a long time that he was selling out all that was good in him for money and power. But like a man who's entangled in a snare, he could not free himself from the life he'd built. He patted his mother's heaving shoulders and thought, *I gotta do something! Capone will step on Mario like a bug if he sees trouble in him!*

Mario finally managed to get rid of Eddy by promising him to stay away from Capone. The two stood beside Mario's car arguing for ten minutes, and at last Mario said grimly, "All right, Eddy, I won't go to him—at least for *now*."

Eddy showed a great deal of relief, and as soon as he left, Mario got into his car and drove to the Salvation Army headquarters. It was only a little after eight, and he expected to find Christie there. But Major Hastings met him as he entered, saying, "Hello, Mr. Castellano. You've come to see Christie, I suppose."

"Yes, I have."

"She's not here. She and Lenora went over to that place where the movie's being shot. They should be back any time."

"Well, I'll try to catch them. Maybe I can give them a ride back."

Mario drove at once to the Monarch lot. He found Christie alone outside the main building, sitting on a bench and staring up at the sky. It was warm, and overhead the sky was lit by millions of tiny points of light. Mario saw that Christie was deep in thought, and he spoke to her as he was approaching, "Lots of them, aren't there?"

Christie was startled, and when he saw her face, he knew that she was troubled. He came to where she sat, then asked, "Mind if I sit down?"

"No, sit down, Mario."

He eased himself down carefully, then said, "I just heard the bad news—some of it. What's the whole story?"

Christie began to speak, her voice filled with sadness. When she ended, she shook her head. "It's bad, Mario. Amos and Lylah and Owen—they put all they had into this."

A hammer-headed, yellow tomcat strolled out of a crate. He came to stare at the pair, insolence in his face, then moved away. Mario watched him go, then said, "I guess the Castellanos aren't very popular around here right now."

"Oh, Mario, nobody blames *you!*"

"What about Nick?"

"Amos said it had to be Capone."

Mario relaxed. "I'm glad to hear that. Nick said he had nothing to do with it—and he never lies to me."

Overhead, bats began tumbling in the still air, fluttering in that almost frightening way they have. A bulb over the door of a building gave off an amber light that diffused slowly, melding into the darkness. Mario asked finally, "What happens now, Christie?"

"To the picture? It doesn't get made."

"But they haven't shot much of it, have they? I mean, can't they get another actor and redo what's been done with Jannings?"

Christie had been with the family for hours. She smiled faintly at Mario, saying, "It's not that easy, I'm afraid. In the first place, there's no money. And even if there was, it would be impossible to get a good actor to come and take over. Word is out about what happened to Emory, and it would take nerve for anyone to chance that." She leaned back, and the lines of her trim figure were revealed in the action. Shaking her head, she added, "It could happen again, Mario. You know it could."

"We could get bodyguards," Mario argued. "I could go to Capone and warn him to lay off."

Christie twisted to stare at him. "*We* could get bodyguards?" she asked with surprise.

Mario blinked, then laughed abruptly. "Guess I'm getting involved in the Stuart family. But I could go see Capone."

"Would he listen to you because of your brothers?"

"No, not really. He's too powerful to mind another enemy or two—especially one like me." Mario's lips twisted into a parody of a grin. "I never stood up to anyone else! How could I stand up to a man like Al Capone?"

Christie felt a surge of pity for his confession. She reached out and took his hand, noting the surprise that came to his features. "It's nice of you to want to help," she said quietly. "I know it's hard for you. You're caught in the middle."

Mario nodded, his eyes bitter. "I should have stood up for

what was right a long time ago. I knew where the money was coming from—but I was too much of a coward to say no."

"You're not a coward!"

Mario was warmed by her exclamation. He studied her face in the moonlight and said quietly, "I don't know whether I am or not, Christie. I've never had to prove anything. Nick paid for my education and set me up in my law office. He steered business to me, and to give him credit, he never wanted me involved in what he and Eddy do."

The two sat there talking, and finally Mario said, "I'll do anything I can, Christie, but Capone's done a pretty good number on your family. Isn't there *any* way out?"

"None of us have been able to find one."

Mario fell silent, then said, "I've been listening to the preaching at the meetings. Lots of things I don't understand. But I keep hearing Lenora and Major Hastings say that God takes care of his people. I always thought people had to take care of themselves."

"But what do you do when something happens that you *can't* handle?" Christie asked. "Sometimes only God can help."

"Did you ever ask God for anything—something impossible and get it?"

Surprise crossed Christie's face, and she said softly, "I never told you how I came to be in Chicago. Did you hear about what happened to me?"

"Why, no, I haven't."

Christie began to speak, and it was difficult. She told the entire story about the episode that had ruined her life back home. Finally she said, "I hit bottom, Mario. I was so sure that life was over. But one day I asked God to do something. And then Jerry came and took me out of all of it. I know it was God who did it—and I thank him for it."

Mario nodded. "That was a rough deal, Christie." He sat silently for a time, then asked curiously, "I don't know God—

not like you and Lenora do. But if I did—I guess I'd ask God
to do something."

Christie stared at him. "Oh, Mario, that's what we *have* to
do! All of us have been so shocked, I guess we've been acting like people who don't have God to help!" She smiled and
said with trembling lips, "Thanks for reminding me of God,
Mario! Now I know what to do!"

"You're going to do—*what!*"

Christie had taken Mario's suggestion seriously, and for
three days she'd fasted and prayed. Now as she saw the shock
in the faces of those before her, she almost lost hope.

Lylah, Jesse, and Carl had listened to her as she told them
how Mario had brought her to realize that doubt had paralyzed them. She'd taken a deep breath and then said, "I—
think I've got direction. I think we should go to Rudolph
Valentino and ask him to star in the picture."

It was Lylah who had burst out her doubts, and she shook
her head, adding, "He's the biggest star in Hollywood,
Christie. He wouldn't even listen to a proposition like this."

"Of course not!" Carl said. He was not a man of God and
added, "Besides, as the Bible says, 'God helps those who help
themselves.'"

Jesse frowned. "That's not in the Bible, Carl. It's in *Aesop's
Fables*." He turned to Christie, saying, "Do you think God
has told you this will happen?"

"Oh, no!" Christie answered quickly. "But it keeps coming to me over and over—and Owen says that's the way God
lets people know what to do."

But Lylah said in a kindly fashion, "I know you want to
help, Honey, but it's just not possible."

"With God all things are possible," Jesse said at once. But
he was ignored, and Christie left feeling depressed. She went
about her work, and the next afternoon, she called Mario. "I
want to do something crazy," she said. "Will you help me?"

"Sure. I'll be right over."

When he arrived, Christie met him with a smile. "It did me so much good—the way you agreed to help me without even knowing what it was I wanted." She bit her lip, then took a deep breath. "I want you to help me get an interview with Rudolph Valentino."

Mario did not reveal his surprise by one lift of his eyebrow. "Is this something to do with the prayer thing?" He listened carefully as she explained, then said, "Where do we find him—Valentino?"

"In New York. He's there finishing up a picture. There was a story in the paper about it yesterday." Christie's face was anxious, and she said, "Jerry could fly us there, or Gavin. But how do we get in to see him?"

"One thing at a time," Mario nodded. "Give me Jerry's number. We'll figure out something when we get there."

Rudolph Valentino rose from his dressing table as the two visitors entered. There was a grace and ease with his body that came from his former profession as a dancer. "Come in," he said pleasantly. "Can I offer you something to drink?"

"Oh, no!" Christie said instantly.

Valentino smiled, his face more handsome off the screen than on. "No, I don't believe people in your profession drink, do they?" He stood watching them, and Mario thought of how this man had become an idol for millions—mostly women. He had played the part of Julio in *The Four Horsemen of the Apocalypse* and had gone on to fame such as no movie actor had ever achieved.

"How can I help you?" Valentino asked. "Are you taking donations for your organization?"

"No, Mr. Valentino," Mario said at once. "My name is Mario Castellano, and this young lady is Miss Christie Stuart. I believe you may have heard of her sister, Lylah Stuart."

Interest came to the dark eyes of the actor. "A fine actress," he said. "I saw her as Lady Macbeth. She was very good."

Christie knew that they had only a few moments to present their case, and she said, "Mr. Valentino, my sister is making a film in Chicago . . ." She quickly laid out the nature of *The Gangster*, stressing that it was to be a new sort of film. Then Christie said frankly, "The film is making some people very unhappy."

"Al Capone is the most unhappy of all," Mario nodded when Christie faltered. "He objects to the manner in which the film portrays his life. In fact, he sent his men to break the leg of the actor who was playing the lead—Emory Jannings."

Shock ran across the swarthy features of Valentino. "Al Capone had Emory's leg broken?"

"Yes, he did—though it would be hard to prove." Mario hesitated, then said, "I know this because my family is in business with Capone."

Again Valentino showed some degree of surprise. "I see." He studied the pair, then asked, "Why have you come to me with this?"

Christie swallowed, then produced a thick packet from a case she'd brought with her. "I know you are a very busy man, Mr. Valentino, but if you could just read this script—"

Valentino was accustomed to being asked to take parts, but always by men who offered him fabulous sums. He was not a humorous man, but the situation amused him. He riffled the pages of the script, then smiled at Christie. "Let me see, you want me to do this part for very little money, I suppose, and risk getting my leg broken by a vicious criminal?"

"Yes, Mr. Valentino, that's what we'd like."

Her seriousness caught at the actor. He stared at her, then asked, "And why should I do such a thing?"

"Because it's a *good* thing to do," Christie said boldly. "It's the responsibility of decent men to stand against evil. You have great influence, and you could help those who believe that life in America means more than that."

With his smoldering eyes on Christie, finally he said, "I will read it, Miss Stuart."

"Thank you!" Christie burst out, her eyes thanking him.

But Mario said, "It could be dangerous. You are a very influential man, but Al Capone will kill when he sees a threat to his kingdom."

Valentino stared at him. "I will read the script. I make no promises to either of you—but I tell you now that Al Capone will not make my decision!"

When they were outside, Christie said, "He's a fiery man, isn't he?"

Mario nodded slowly. Taking her arm, he said, "Better not tell Lylah about this—no sense raising false hopes."

"No, I won't say anything." But she took his arm, pulled him around and to his complete shock, pulled his head down and kissed him. "There—now I'll have to explain that to the Army! They don't permit their young women to kiss dark handsome men on the street!"

The two of them laughed and made their way arm in arm back to the airport where Jerry waited for them. He listened to their story, then whistled, "Wow! The Sheik himself! Can't do better than that!" He looked at the pair of them, then grinned, "I feel like I'm contributing to the delinquency of minors! You two look happy enough to be a couple of teenagers on their first date!"

As they took off, Mario said over the roar of the engine, "If this works, I'll have to give this prayer thing a lot more attention!" He looked out at the skyline of New York, admiring the tall buildings, then thought, *Al Capone—here we come!*

22

"IT'S WHAT I'VE BEEN LOOKING FOR ALL MY LIFE!"

As soon as Lylah looked up and saw Milton Sanderson come through the door, her heart sank. Sanderson, the president of the First National Bank, had a kindly face, but something in his expression revealed his purpose.

"Am I interrupting anything, Miss Stuart?" he asked, taking off his black derby. He was a tall, portly man with a ruddy face and a shock of salt-and-pepper hair. Lylah thought he looked more like a lumberman than a banker with his massive shoulders and huge hands.

She had been sitting behind her small desk staring at the wall, exhausted from wrestling with the decisions that had to be made. "No, not at all, Mr. Sanderson. Sit down."

Sanderson took a seat and looked straight at Lylah. He had been tempted to put his bad news in a letter, but he was the sort of man who faced up to trouble, and now he said at once, "I wish I had better news for you, Miss Stuart."

Lylah summoned a smile, saying quietly, "I've been bracing myself for bad news. You can't lend us the money, can you?"

Sanderson admired courage, and he saw it in the violet eyes of the woman in front of him. He'd spent considerable time with her, coming to visit the set after she'd applied for a loan. He knew little about the motion picture business, but he had assistants who could give him the facts. And the facts had been that a loan to Monarch Pictures would be a high risk. His vice president, Asa Thornton, had come to him shaking his head. "It won't do, Milt. The odds are just too great. Turn her down."

But Sanderson liked Lylah Stuart from the moment she'd come into his office. He had never seen her on the screen, but her beauty impressed him. And she was honest—in Sanderson's experience a rare thing for someone who wanted to borrow money. As he looked at Lylah, he remembered her first words: "I want a lot of money, Mr. Sanderson, and it'll be a high-risk loan."

Now as he studied the woman who sat watching him, he wished there were some way he could let her have the money she'd asked for. But he had struggled with the application, and now he knew what he had to do. Shaking his head, he said, "I respect what you're trying to do, Miss Stuart, but it's just not the sort of thing a bank can lend money on."

"I understand, Mr. Sanderson."

Her calm answer disturbed the banker, for he was fairly certain that he represented the last hope for her fledgling company. "I've tried to find a way to make the loan, but it's just too risky. Even if I recommend it, the committee will never approve it." He leaned forward, and a puzzled expression crossed his face. "You're successful in your career. You can go back to that, I hope."

Lylah didn't mention that she and her brothers had sunk every dime they had into the venture. She had learned not to cry over her losses, and so she merely said, "It's nice of you to be concerned, Mr. Sanderson. I appreciate the personal attention you've put into my application."

Sanderson sighed, his face turning heavy. "Being a banker is not a great deal of pleasure at times like this." He got to his feet, and when Lylah rose and put her hand out, he took it, saying, "I wish it could be different, Miss Stuart. But investors are cautious people, afraid to take risks like this."

"I understand. Please don't feel bad about this. I knew

there was little hope for a loan, but I had to try." Summoning a smile, she said, "Perhaps the next time I ask for money, I'll have a nice safe venture—like a race horse."

Again Sanderson was filled with admiration for the courage of Lylah Stuart. He left the set, and when he got back to his office, he was out of sorts for several days. "Watch out for the old man," his vice president whispered. "Somebody's stepped on his toe!"

After Sanderson left her office, Lylah went back to her chair and sat down. She stared at the walls across from her, which were almost covered with pictures of famous actors and actresses posing with her—Bernhardt, Ellen Terry, several of the Barrymores, Lily Langtry. These were from her days on the stage. Other faces from the world of movies were fresher—Charlie Chaplin, Doug Fairbanks and Mary Pickford, Buster Keaton.

She thought briefly of asking some of these people for help but could not bring herself to do it. Closing her eyes, she tried to stifle the problems that swarmed her. Always before when she'd had financial problems, it had been very personal—but now she grieved over dragging her family into the whirlpool that was pulling them all deeper toward what seemed to be certain destruction. *Owen and Amos—they should never have put all they had into this thing!* The thought grieved her, and she rose and walked the floor, back and forth, trying to find a way out.

The door burst open, and Adam bolted into the room. "Mum—come and play!"

Lylah knelt and hugged the boy, then asked, "Play what?"

"Cowboys—with Jesse and me!"

"Yes, come on and play." Lylah looked up to see Jesse enter, and she burst out laughing. "You idiot! Where did you get that outfit?"

"Found it in a trunk." Jesse was wearing a pair of enormous furry chaps, two guns in holsters, and a hideous yellow shirt. A huge white Stetson came down over his eyes, and he peered from underneath it at Lylah. "Look to your laurels, Tom Mix!" he exclaimed. "Tex Hart, King of the Cowboys, is on the loose!"

Adam tugged at one of the pistols. "He's going to let me shoot it, Mum! Come on, Uncle Jesse!"

Lylah watched as Jesse teased the boy, then she said, "Are those things loaded?"

"I have no idea." Yanking one of the large revolvers from the holster, Jesse peered down the muzzle. "Doesn't seem to be—can't see any bullets."

"Jesse—you'll blow your head off!"

"Let me see!" Adam cried eagerly, reaching up for the pistol.

Seeing the alarm in Lylah's face, Jesse said, "Well, I guess not, Son. Tell you what, these are a mite big for you. Why don't we go down to the toy store and buy some just for you?"

Lylah relaxed as Jesse awkwardly replaced the pistol, promising Adam that they would go soon. "You go tell Bonnie what we're going to do." When Adam ran out of the office, he said thoughtfully, "I never had an outfit like this when I was growing up, so I thought I'd redeem the time. What sort of dress did you want when you were a little girl? I'll bet we can find it in one of those costume trunks."

"I've been playing dress-up for years, Jesse," Lylah said. "That's part of being an actress." She smiled and came to take off his hat. "You look ridiculous in that thing."

Jesse saw the trouble in her eyes and grew sober. "I saw the banker come by. No good news?"

"I wasn't really expecting any."

"We'll just have to keep on without their help."

"Oh, Jesse, it's hopeless!" Lylah had managed to keep her emotions hidden in front of Sanderson, but now she let her guard down. "There's no use kidding ourselves. It was a fine idea—but it's just not going to work."

As Lylah went to stand in front of the window, Jesse was aware that she'd reached the end of her hopes. "Let me go get dressed," he said quietly. "We'll buy Adam a toy gun, then we'll take him for a walk in the park." He left without waiting for an answer, and Lylah didn't move. *Owen told me once about when he got wounded in the war. He said he hardly felt it— but later when the action was over, the pain was terrible. I guess that's what's happened to me. As long as I had hope and something to fight for, I didn't have time to feel much—but now it's killing me!*

She stood there, the fear of the future immobilizing her nerves. The thoughts of a thousand bleak tomorrows were specters that jeered at her, and only by a direct act of will did she keep her back straight and hold back the tears. Finally she heard voices and turned quickly as Jesse opened the door to say, "Come on, we're ready."

As they drove to the store, Jesse and Adam chatted, but Lylah's heart was so heavy that she had to force herself to smile and say a word now and then. *I'm glad Jesse's here—I'd be poor company for Adam,* was her thought.

The three of them got out of the car, went inside a shop, and twenty minutes later came out with a tiny gunbelt, complete with toy gun, around Adam's waist. On his head perched a miniature cowboy hat, and around his neck he wore a bright red bandanna.

"Get in there, Cowboy," Jesse said, as Adam climbed into the car. "Be careful with that gun, now! Don't shoot anybody who don't need it." He drove to the park, and the three of them found a shady spot under a grove of trees. For two hours Jesse played with Adam while Lylah sat and watched.

Finally Adam began to tire, and Jesse came to say, "I'm about ready to drop! I thought he'd never run down. Come on, we'll take him home for his nap." Adam fell asleep on the way home, and Jesse carried him inside. Lylah turned down the covers and tried to take the gunbelt off, but Adam clutched it firmly and shook his head. She smiled and kissed him, then she and Jesse left the room.

"Wish I had his stamina," Jesse grinned. "He's got the drive of a locomotive."

"I guess we all do when we're young," Lylah said. She was suddenly close to tears, and she didn't want him to see her cry. "I think I'll take a nap myself. Do you mind, Jesse?"

"Yes, I do mind."

She blinked, thinking he had misunderstood her. "I said—"

"I know, you want to curl up in your bed and cry. Sorry, I can't permit that."

Her temper flared. "I'm *not* your little girl! You can baby Adam, but I don't need any of your sympathy!"

Jesse took her by the arm, pulled her to the sofa, and forced her to sit down. "Time for us to talk," he said, sitting down beside her. He made no attempt to touch her, but his eyes were alert, and there was an odd expression of expectation on his face. "And don't tell me you don't need sympathy, because I know better."

Lylah stared at him, then said wearily, "I'm so tired! And you're right—I was going to curl up and cry!"

"No wonder," Jesse said quietly. "And no shame to it, either. It's okay to cry. I do it myself sometimes."

"Not really?" she said, surprised by his words.

"Why not? You think women have a monopoly on crying?"

"Well, most men think it's a . . . a weakness."

"They're wrong if they think that." The light from outside filtered through the window, laying its golden bars across the carpet and highlighting the regular planes of Jesse's face. There was a toughness in his features, in the strong cheekbones and firm mouth. He could be hard, Lylah had discovered, and yet there was a tenderness in him that she'd never seen in a man before. For a time she'd considered that a weakness, but she'd learned that it was that very element that drew her to him. "All the great warriors blubbered like babies—David, Beowulf, Ulysses. They didn't *care* what people thought of them."

"That's right. I never thought of that," she murmured.

Jesse sat quietly for a moment, then said, "I think men who are afraid to cry—or afraid to do 'woman's work'—are afraid of their own masculinity. If a man's really strong, he doesn't need to prove it every ten minutes."

Lylah sat listening, wondering how this man had learned so much. He knew people better than anyone she'd ever known. When he paused, she said, "I suppose that's right, Jesse. But I'm a woman, and I've hit the end of the line. I'll cry when you leave, but it won't do any good, will it? To-morrow I'll wake up with the same old problems, and then what? Cry again? I can't spend my life wallowing in self-pity!"

"No, and that's what I want to talk to you about, Lylah," Jesse said. "You're headed for trouble, and you've got to find a way to handle it."

"*Headed* for trouble?" she laughed shortly. "I'm not *headed* for it, Jesse—I'm right in the *middle* of it!"

"You mean the problems with the picture?"

"Of course!"

"Lylah, you've got to understand that your financial troubles are not your problem. The problem I'm talking about is the one *inside* you," Jesse said. "What do you think, that you're going to get to some point in your life where there *isn't* any trouble?"

"Why, I suppose that's what—"

"You should be smarter than that," Jesse interrupted. "There's no place like that. The Bible says that the rich man's wealth is his strong tower, but towers fall; and what good did all of Diamond Jim Brady's money do him after he died? It was all gone then, and he had only what he took with him when he stood before God."

She stared at him, struck by the total seriousness in his face. "You're talking about religion, aren't you, Jesse?"

"No, I'm not, Lylah. Religion can be whatever a person makes his god. I had 'religion' for years and wasn't ready to meet God. I'm talking about the *only* thing that can help you have a victorious life—and that's in the Lord Jesus Christ. I know you've heard this before. You've heard it from Amos and Owen and Gavin—from Lenora and Christie. You also heard it from your dad, I expect."

She nodded slowly. "Yes, they're all good people—"

"No, they're *godly* people, Lylah. The Bible says 'All have sinned and come short of the glory of God.' That means that every one of us has failed—that we're cut off from God."

"I know I'm a sinner," she said stiffly. "I have been all my life. You don't have to convince me of that, Jesse!"

He nodded, saying, "That's good, because I think many die and go to hell because they won't admit that one thing."

She suddenly was flooded with memories—ugly memories of things she'd done—and had thought were safely buried. They came trooping before her, like corpses rising out of secret graves, accusing her, and she began to tremble. "It's—it's too late for me, Jesse," she said, her voice uneven. "You don't know the things I've done!"

"No, and I don't need to," Jesse agreed. "But God knows them. Did you know, Dearest, we can never disappoint God?"

"Oh, yes we can! I've done it a thousand times!"

"No, you haven't—because to disappoint means that something expected doesn't happen. I can be disappointed with you, but God *knows* the future. He knows not only what you *have* done and what you're doing right now—but he also knows what you're going to do in the future. You see, God is timeless—the past and the present and the future are all *now* with him. That's what he meant when he told Moses his name—*I Am*. Not, I will be, or, I was—but simply, I Am."

"That's too difficult for me!"

"Sure, for me, too. But there's one part about God's time that's always given me hope. The Bible says that Jesus is the Lamb slain. Let me read it to you." He pulled out a small, worn New Testament and leafed though the pages. "Right here in Revelation 13 it says that Jesus is the Lamb slain before the foundation of the world."

She saw that his eyes were soft and yet excited. "But— what does that *mean*, Jesse?"

"You've read about how the Jews sacrificed animals? Sheep and goats and rams? Well, the Book of Hebrews, the ninth chapter and the twenty-second verse says, 'Without shedding of blood is no remission.' But what blood? God says that the blood of goats and sheep could not take away sin." He turned back a page, then held his place, "Lylah, I'm going to read you a few verses. I want you to listen carefully. This is the heart of what I believe, and I think the heart of Christianity. It says:

> Neither by the blood of goats and calves, but by his own blood he entered in once into the holy place, having obtained eternal redemption for us.
> For if the blood of bulls and of goats, and the ashes of an heifer sprinkling the unclean, sanctifieth to the purifying of the flesh:
> How much more shall the blood of Christ, who through the eternal Spirit offered himself without spot to God, purge your conscience from dead works to serve the living God.

"And at the end of this wonderful passage, in verses 27 and 28, it says, 'And as it is appointed unto men once to die, but after this the judgment: So Christ was once offered to bear the sins of many; and unto them that look for him shall he appear the second time without sin unto salvation.'"

Jesse said quietly, "It's all there, Lylah. You are going to die and face judgment—as we all are. But you don't have to be afraid, for as this same book says 'For by one offering, he hath perfected forever them that are sanctified.' That's what the cross was. It was Jesus, the Lamb of God, dying so that all of us might live!"

Lylah began to tremble. Somehow the words, "Jesus, the Lamb of God," struck a chord in her heart and spirit. Fear came, but as Jesse continued to speak of Jesus and of the cross, she knew that there was hope. Tears came welling up, overflowed her eyes, and ran down her cheeks. She uttered

278 A Time to Laugh

a soft cry and then choked out the words, "Oh, Jesse! I need
. . . Jesus!"

Jesse at once said, "He's come for you, Lylah. Tell him you
want to turn from all that's wrong—and then ask him to for-
give you."

"I . . . can't!" she sobbed. "I'm so rotten!"

"Jesus died for you, God sent him to die, and now the Holy
Ghost is striving to get you to open your heart. When Adam
calls to you in fear, you always answer. And right now Jesus
Christ is waiting for you to call. Do it now, Lylah!"

Jesse heard her broken cries fill the room, and then after a
time, he felt her weeping in a different manner. She suddenly
lifted her hands, and there was a peace in her countenance
he'd never seen there. He took her in his arms, and she whispered, "Oh, Jesse—I feel so filled with peace. It's what I've
been looking for all my life!" Then she drew back and said,
"Whatever happens, I can face it now—as long as I have this!"

"It's just beginning," Jesse smiled. "One day you'll be with
him, but until he comes, every day you'll be learning to live
by his strength. You see, Lylah, the trouble with the picture?
It's *his* problem now. You're not alone. Let's ask him right now
to take care of it—whatever he wants to do with it. All right?"

"Yes, Jesse, let's ask him!"

23

THE ANSWER

I don't like the look of this fellow Hitler over in Germany." Amos Stuart lowered the newspaper he was reading, a frown on his face.

"I thought they put him in jail." Owen was sitting across the table from Amos, looking around at the crowd that had gathered to eat what was probably the final meal at Monarch Pictures. "The man's a maniac."

"He got out two months ago," Amos shrugged. "He's pulling his old organization together into something he calls the German National Socialist Workers Party." Disgust swept him, and he muttered, "You'd think the German people would have had enough of Hitler's sort after the war."

"I hope our boys never have to fight in another war. I thought the last one was called 'the war to end all wars,' but that'll never be—not until the Lord comes back."

Amos nodded, then said, "There comes Lylah." The two men watched as Lylah came out of a side door accompanied by Jesse and Adam. Amos said softly, "She's a different woman since she found Christ, isn't she, Owen?"

"A new creature," Owen agreed, pleasure on his face. "We've got us a fine brother-in-law, Amos—or will have when they get married."

"They were waiting to finish the picture, but I guess there's no point in waiting now," Amos sighed. "Too bad! It would have been a great blow against crime in this country."

"Lylah's worried about the money we lost—but it's worth everything to see her so full of joy," Owen remarked. "Well, it was a good idea, but it just didn't work. Look—I think she's going to make a speech."

"Farewell address, I guess. Everybody's ready for it."

Amos was correct, for the cast and crew had seen the end coming. Now as they gathered at Lylah's behest they all were subdued, nobody wanting to mention the failure of Monarch.

Jerry was seated between Bonnie and Gavin, and looking at the food that covered the table, said, "Well, the condemned man ate a hearty meal."

"Jerry, don't talk like that!" Bonnie nudged him with her elbow.

Gavin gave his nephew a dour look. "It's pretty bad, Jerry. We've got our flying to fall back on, but it's sort of the end for Lylah."

"No, it's not!"

Christie was sitting across from Gavin, next to Mario Castellano, who had crashed the party. Mario had been withdrawn, and now as Christie spoke up, he gave her a curious look. The two of them had sworn Jerry to secrecy about their flight to see Valentino. Now he was glad of it. Two weeks had gone by, and he had given up hope.

But Christie said with spirit, "God won't let us down, Gavin. You'll see!"

Owen and Pete looked up, surprise in both their faces. They had talked cautiously between themselves, agreeing sadly that the future looked pretty grim. Now they stared at Christie, who caught their looks. "We give up on God too quickly," she protested. She was very much aware that Mario had made this matter a test case, though she'd warned him against such a thing. Every day she'd prayed that God would save the company, and now as Lylah rose and caught their attention, she was dismayed.

"I don't have a long speech to make," Lylah said quietly, "just a few words." She looked over the crowd fondly. She knew the name of every member of the crew, and the cast had come to be very close during the days of shooting. "I've been in show business since I was a very young woman—I won't tell you exactly *how* many years—" She smiled at the wave of laughter, then went on, "But I will tell you that in all those years I've never had a better cast or a better crew to work with! You are beautiful—and I've learned to love you all."

Carl Thomas sat beside Lenora, anger and disappointment in his face. He whispered, "She's holding up well. I broke the furniture when I heard the bad news!"

Lenora had invited Major Hastings to the dinner. She glanced at him, then said, "I expect she would have done the same—but she's had a great change in her life, Mr. Thomas."

Carl looked at her abruptly. "Yes, she has. Never did have much confidence in this kind of thing—but it's held Lylah together." He dropped his head, then muttered, "But it's not helping to get the picture finished!"

Lylah glanced at Carl, seeming to sense his anger. "You all know by now that we won't be able to finish *The Gangster.*" She waited until the groan that went up at her words faded, then said, "We're all disappointed. It was something we all longed to do—but now it appears as though we won't be able to do it."

"We can do it, Miss Stuart!" Art Blevins, one of the camera crew, spoke up loudly. "You don't have to pay us—we can wait!"

A chorus of agreement went up, but Lylah said, "That's sweet of all of you—just what I'd expect. But we don't have a star—and without one, we can't go on." She stood there, erect and with a gentle smile on her face. "Not long ago, I heard one of you say that it would take a miracle to save the picture. I thought so myself and still do. But though we haven't seen that miracle yet, I want to tell you about something that's come into my own life—something that's a miracle to me . . ."

For fifteen minutes Lylah spoke, giving a simple testi-

mony of her life. She didn't spare herself but freely confessed that she'd run from God for years. Then with a glowing face she told how Jesse had come to her and shared the
gospel. As she spoke of this, tears rose in her eyes—and not
in hers alone! She concluded by saying, "I don't know what
I'll do tomorrow—but I'm not afraid." She looked out over
the faces, saying, "If anyone had tried to tell me I could lose
the thing I wanted most—which was to do *The Gangster*—
and yet not grieve, I would not have believed him. But I've
discovered that when we lose something, Jesus Christ can
take away the pain. As long as I have him—why, I have
everything!"

"Amen!" Owen could contain himself no longer. He rose
and went to Lylah, crushing her in his arms. "Pa would have
been so *proud* to see this—and Ma, too!"

That was the end of the formal speeches. Everyone in
the room came to Lylah, many of them unable to hold back
their tears. She received them all, smiling, and Jesse was
right beside her, with Adam, who watched it all with enormous curiosity.

Carl came to say with a shaky voice, "Lylah—you're a gal-
lant lady!"

"No, Carl—I've got a great God," Lylah said, holding his
hand in both of hers. She had grown to love this little man
and now whispered, "You'll love him, too, one day—"

Then Jesse said, "Now, let's eat!"

Despite the sad occasion of the meal, they all seemed to
be hungry. They sat down and soon were busy with the food,
talking among themselves.

Christie toyed with her food and was surprised when one
of the crew came to say, "There's a fellow who's asking for
you, Miss Christie. I asked him to wait in Miss Stuart's office.
Wasn't sure you'd want him bustin' in on the dinner."

"Thank you, Perry," Christie said. She got to her feet, and
Mario rose to go with her. When they were outside the din-

ing area, Mario said, his face rather tense, "Any idea who it could be?"

"No, not at all."

Mario stopped and took her by the arm. "Let me go first, Christie."

Christie looked up at him with surprise, then suddenly understood his caution. "You think it might be trouble from Capone?"

"I don't think so—but it never hurts to be careful. Just let me go in first."

They moved to the door of Lylah's office, and Mario motioned for Christie to stand to one side. When she was clear of the door, he opened it and stepped in—then stopped abruptly. "I think it's all right for you to come in, Christie," he said in an odd tone of voice.

Christie stepped inside, and she too stopped dead still.

"Mr. Valentino . . ." she gasped, and could not say a word more.

Valentino was smiling at the two of them, his dark eyes filled with humor. "I apologize for coming without an invitation—but I had to come to Chicago, and I thought it would be a good time to talk with your sister. Is she here?"

"Oh, yes," Christie breathed. "I'll get her—don't go away, please, Mr. Valentino!"

As the young woman left the room, Valentino gazed at Mario. "I think you looked a little—vigilant, shall we say—when you came through the door." He pulled out a cigarette, lit it with a platinum lighter, then asked, "Were you expecting trouble?"

"Yes, I was."

"Your family—what do they think of Capone?"

"That he's a killer."

"So I hear." The handsome face of the actor grew tight, and he said no more. The two men stood there quietly, and then the door opened and Christy entered with three others.

"This is my sister Lylah, and her fiancé, Jesse Hart, and this is—"

"Hello, Carl. How are you?" Valentino nodded to Thomas, then shook hands with Jesse and finally bowed slightly to Lylah. "I've seen you on the stage, Miss Stuart—in *Macbeth*. Brilliant!"

Lylah said in a tone of astonishment, "Thank you, Mr. Valentino."

"I suppose you know why I'm here?"

"As a matter of fact, I don't," Lylah admitted.

Valentino glanced at Christie, who burst out, "Oh, Lylah, Mario and I got Jerry to fly us to New York. I showed Mr. Valentino the script of *The Gangster*, and I asked him to read it—and to do the part if he liked it!"

Jesse was staring with unbelief at the dark face of the most famous actor in the world—but Mario was staring at Christie. Finally Lylah said with a laugh, "Well, my sister is quite bold. I guess the Salvation Army does that to you." Then she asked directly, "Did you like the script, Mr. Valentino?"

Valentino puffed on his cigarette, holding everyone's attention. He loved attention and had all that one man could handle—still this little moment of drama revealed his delight in playing a role. He saw their faces fixed on him, and he knew that he held their future in his hands. Finally he nodded, "Yes—I thought it was a powerful piece of writing."

Lylah said quietly, "If you took the part, it might be dangerous."

"So this gentleman tells me," Valentino nodded. The thought seemed to please him, and he added, "I don't think that will be a factor."

"But money will be," Carl said. "We don't have the money you're accustomed to, Rudy."

"I understand that. Would you like to discuss a percentage of the profits—say 10 percent?"

It was a princely offer, for with Rudolph Valentino as the star, the success of *The Gangster* was a certainty.

"That's more than generous of you," Lylah said instantly. "I agree, of course. And I believe that this role will add another dimension to your career."

"That is why I came," Valentino nodded. "It's a bold attempt, and I'm tired of playing sheiks and Latin lovers." He glanced at Jesse, saying, "I understand you are the scriptwriter. I have a few suggestions—could we talk about them?"

"Name the time!"

"Ah, then tomorrow at ten. I'm staying at the Hotel Bel Aire." He smiled and bowed slightly, "Good night. I trust that we'll make a little history." He turned and smiled at Christie, saying, "I admire courage." Then he left.

As soon as the door shut, the room exploded in laughter; pandemonium reigned. Carl was jumping up and down, his eyes bugging even more than usual, and he was shouting, "I don't believe it!" shrilly.

"Come on, we've got to tell everybody," Jesse said, and he left the room at once with Lylah and Carl.

When they were gone, Mario turned to Christie, his face stiff. "Well, I'd be pretty dumb not to see God in this! Do you think Valentino knows he's an answer to prayer?"

"I don't know, Mario. God uses all sorts of men for his own purposes," Christie said. "But as long as *you* know it's God, I'm satisfied."

Mario said slowly, his eyes fixed on hers, "I guess you know I love you, Christie. And I know one more thing—you'll never marry any man who doesn't know God."

Christie whispered, "Mario, you're very close to God. I've prayed for you so hard! And the same God who saved Lylah after so many years—and the same God who brought Valentino here—he's going to find you!" She came to him, her face bright with promise as he held her close. "God will give us to each other," she said, nodding firmly. "He knows how much we love each other."

Mario held her, but his thoughts went to his family—and

he was also wondering what Al Capone would do when he discovered his plans to stop production on *The Gangster* had failed.

But Mario had seen God work, and now he knew that no matter what happened, he had to know this God who did such wonderful things.

24

LOVE AND ICE CREAM

C hicago was a difficult town to impress in 1925, but when the news broke that Rudolph Valentino was coming to star in a picture—the whole city was talking. The story broke in the *Examiner* and was written by Amos Stuart.

The response literally swamped the fledgling Monarch Pictures, so much so that Lylah said in mock despair, "It's going to be harder to finish the picture *with* Valentino than it was without him!" Crowds milled around at the gates, and Peter had to hire a security force to keep them from just walking into the lot. Reporters resorted to all sorts of stunts to gain access to the star—and to Lylah as well.

"I've always wanted to be married to a wealthy woman," Jesse grinned at her one day between takes. "One who could cater to my every whim and set me up in a mansion."

Lylah was made-up for her part, wearing a fashionable gown designed by Schiaparelli. It was a platinum silk crepe georgette, trimmed with metal bead embroidery and ostrich plumes. She had enjoyed working with Valentino, but the lights were so hot that she grew faint at times. "If you keep getting offers to write scripts from people like DeMille," she said tartly, "I'll quit and play with Adam all day—and spend your money."

The humor of the financial miracle that had taken place brought a sudden laugh from Jesse. "Funny, isn't it, Lylah. A week ago we couldn't afford a cab—now we've got bankers lining up trying to lend us money!"

"Did you know Milton Sanderson came to see me yesterday?" She smiled at the thought, then reaching up, ran her hand down his cheek. "I've never seen you without a beard. Why don't you ever shave?"

"I'm too handsome," Jesse shrugged. "My good looks have driven women mad. Some of them took to drink. Had to cover up to save them. What did Mr. Sanderson want?"

"He wanted to lend me a lot of money." Lylah smiled at the memory. "He was tickled to death, Jesse. Said his board came to him and *begged* him to get Monarch to take a loan with their bank. That was the same bunch that wouldn't let us have a penny last month!"

At that moment Carl appeared, his eyes bulging as usual. "Lylah, we're *waiting* for you!"

"All right, Carl," Lylah answered. She stopped, reached out, and touched Jesse's neat beard. "On our wedding day, I want you to shave." She gave him a seductive look, fluttered her eyelids, and said, "I've always wanted to be driven mad by a handsome man!"

"Well, if you insist—but you've been warned."

Lylah walked to where Valentino was waiting. He was wearing a powder blue suit with a matching tie. "Ready, Lylah?" he asked at once. He had been an easy man to work with, to Lylah's surprise. She'd had her experiences with famous actors—most of them not pleasant, but Valentino had been professional and very easy to get along with.

"Yes, let's do it."

Thomas gave them their instructions, and they did the scene with little difficulty. "That's a take!" Thomas shouted. "Everybody take a break."

"That was good, Rudy," Lylah nodded. "We're ahead of schedule."

Valentino lit a cigarette and looked closely at Pete Stuart, who was standing to one side. "Your brother, he's always very close." He puffed thoughtfully, then demanded, "That gun he's carrying, it's not a prop, is it?"

Lylah hesitated, then shook her head. "No, it's real."

"Ah! You're expecting trouble?"

"I hope not, but Mario tells us that Capone is furious about what we're doing."

"And you think we may have trouble with him?"

"I don't think so, Rudy. Amos says Capone is very sensitive to public opinion. It would make him look bad if anything happened to you." She covered a smile, adding, "He also said that as much as he admires you, it wouldn't be *all* bad if Capone did try to hurt you. If he did that, he'd have most of the women in America after him!"

Valentino found that amusing, and the two spoke of the scenes that were to be made. But later that afternoon, Pete brought a man dressed in a black suit to see the pair. "Says he's got a message he's got to give to Mr. Valentino in person."

"Yes, I'll take it." Valentino took the envelope the man extended, opened it, and scanned it. "It's a dinner invitation for you and me, Lylah."

"We don't have time, Rudy!"

"I think we'll take the time." He smiled at the messenger, a heavy-set individual with close-set eyes. "Tell Mr. Capone we'll be glad to accept his invitation."

"Yes, Mr. Valentino. There'll be a car to pick you up at seven, if that's okay."

As soon as the arrangements were made, Lylah exclaimed, "Rudy, you can't mean it! Dinner with Al Capone?"

Valentino ran his hand over his slick black hair. His eyes glowed with excitement as he nodded, "Yes, it should be an interesting evening. I'll venture we won't be bored with Mr. Capone!"

Valentino and Lylah got out of the black limousine in front of the Hotel Metropole at 2300 South Michigan Avenue. They were escorted to the fourth floor by two burly men with suspicious bulges under their coats. One of them was talkative and informed the pair, "Mr. Capone, he's always liked the Metropole—got maybe fifteen or twenty rooms here. Up on the seventh floor he's made a gym—punching bags, rowing machines, and weights."

"He likes to keep his men trim?" Valentino murmured.

"Yes, sure, Mr. Valentino." A lewd smile split the lips of the big man, and he winked at the actor. "Mr. Capone, he likes *real* men! You know how he tests his bodyguards?"

"No, I don't."

"Why, he throws good-looking broads at 'em! If they don't go after the women, Mr. Capone gets rid of them."

"Shut up, Willie!"

"I wuz just—"

"Close your mouth!" The second guard apologized, "Sorry, Miss Stuart. Willie got his brains scrambled too many times when he was in the ring." The elevator stopped, and he said, "Here we are, folks."

Two more guards outside a door turned to them at once. "Mr. Capone's expecting you," one said politely. He opened the door, and the guests entered. They found themselves in a room that could have been lifted from an Italian Renaissance setting: white marble underfoot, exquisitely carved cabinets filled with china and figurines along the walls, a chandelier of a thousand lights glittering overhead, and a servant in full dress bowing. "Mr. Valentino, Miss Stuart. I'll get Mr. Capone at once."

As the waiter disappeared through a massive oak door, Lylah glanced around at the opulent furniture. "He's got rich taste, hasn't he?"

"Yes, indeed." Valentino looked around, then shook his head. "I've been reading the stories Amos has been writing in the *Examiner*. They must have stung Capone—"

He broke off, for the door opened and Al Capone came into the room. Lylah was impressed by the sheer animal power that flowed from the man. She'd heard from Amos that Capone was capable of anything. Once he'd told her of how Capone had personally executed three of his enemies: "He invited them to dinner at his apartment, and after he fed them, he had his hoods tie them to chairs. Then he took a baseball bat and beat them to death—that's Capone!"

"Well, now, it's good to see you, Rudy," Capone said, using the first name of the famous actor in a familiar fashion. He was accustomed to mixing with celebrities. Eddy Cantor, George Jessel, Joe Lewis, and many others had visited the big-time gangster. He shook Valentino's hand, then turned to say, "And this is the little lady who's makin' a movie about Al?" He didn't offer his hand, but his eyes glittered as he smiled. "Like to hear about that, Miss Stuart, but first, we eat, eh?"

They sat down and waiters began bringing out the food. It was a feast fit for an emperor, but only Capone ate very much. He kept urging the food on them, all the while cramming his own mouth full and washing it down with wine. But he talked constantly as he ate, telling story after story of famous people he knew.

Finally he wiped his lips with a snow white napkin and put his fork down. "They all come to Al, all the big ones. Did I tell you I met the president? Sure, I did! Nice fellow, too."

Valentino asked, "What did he say about your—profession, Mr. Capone?"

"Hey, call me Al! Why, he didn't say nothing about it." Capone regarded the actor and shrugged his burly shoulders. "Look, I'm known all over the world as a criminal. I'm just a businessman, that's all! I've never been convicted of a crime and I never had anything to do with vice. None of my people ever burglarized any homes while they worked for me. They might have pulled a job like that before they joined up with me, but not by my orders . . ."

He went on for some time about himself, then looked at Lylah. "I been hearing bad things about this picture you're making, Miss Stuart. But I look on myself as a public bene-factor. Ninety percent of the people of Cook County drink and gamble, and I furnish them with those amusements. My booze has been good as have my games on the square—so why are you making me look like a gorilla in your picture?"

Lylah was convinced that the man was a monster. *He really believes all these things he's saying*, she thought. "What about all the men who've been killed in the gang wars, Mr. Capone? Don't you think murder is wrong?"

Capone gave her an angry look, one that had paralyzed many a strong man with fear. "Look, there's the law of self-defense. It means killing a man who'd kill you if he saw you. Maybe it means that—but you can't blame me for lookin' out for myself!"

Lylah and Valentino endured the man's huge ego for some time and then finally rose to leave. "We thank you for your hospitality, Mr. Capone," Valentino said, then smiled. "I hope you enjoy the film."

But it was to Lylah that Capone directed his parting words. "You're a fine lady—but I wish you'd change your mind about me. That movie could do me a lot of harm. Why don't you show my side of this thing?"

Lylah did not hesitate. "I think you're bad for the country, Mr. Capone. You stand for violence, and I can only make the film as honestly as possible."

Capone stared at her, then whispered, "Glad to meet you." He waited until the two were gone, then moved stiffly to the phone on the table. He dialed a number, waited, then said with a fury in his voice, "Hymie—you know who this is? Yeah. Listen, pack your gear and come to Chicago. I got a job for you!"

Mario had few connections with the family business. Nick had discouraged these and was pleased when his younger brother showed no inclination toward such things. He boasted of Mario's success to everyone, proud of the young lawyer who was making a name for himself in the legal world.

As a child Mario had a close friend named Tony Pappa. Tony was the son of one of Nick's lieutenants, and as the two families lived close, the two boys became firm friends. However, Ralph Pappa had left Nick to go to work for Capone, and Tony had gone the same way when he was nineteen. Tony and Mario had drifted apart as a result, but they still fished together once a year at least and talked about old times.

Mario hadn't thought about Tony for some time, so was surprised when Pappa walked into his office one Thursday afternoon. "Hey, Ton!" he greeted his friend. "Come in and take a load off your feet!"

"Gotta talk to you—private," Tony grunted. He had his hat pulled down over his eyes and seemed nervous.

"Why, sure, Tony. Come inside." As soon as Mario shut the door, he turned to ask, "What's wrong, Tony? You in some kind of trouble?" It was the first thing that came to him, for Tony had been in trouble with the law more than once.

"Naw, Mario—I'm okay." Tony bit his lip, then blurted out, "Look, I been walkin' my feet off, tryin' to decide what to do."

"What is it? Spill it, Tony!"

"Well, I ain't no squealer—you know what happens to a guy like that who works for Capone." He hesitated, then his eyes narrowed. "How tight are you with this picture makin' outfit, Mario?"

"Monarch? What's up, Tony?" When Pappa hesitated, Mario said quickly, "I'm going to marry Christie Stuart. She's the sister of the woman who owns Monarch."

"Sister to Lylah Stuart and Amos Stuart?"

"That's right." Mario stared at his friend. "Look, I don't want you to get in any trouble for me, Tony. But you know me. Whatever you say stops right here."

Tony Pappa took a deep breath, then nodded. "I ain't never done nothin' like this before, but you're my friend, Mario." He hesitated, then said, "Al's brought Hymie Holtzman in from Detroit. You know what that means!"

Mario had heard enough to know that Holtzman was a paid killer. A chill went through him, and he asked, "Who's he gunning for, Tony?"

"Amos Stuart. And that ain't all. If that don't stop his sister from making the picture, Holtzman will hit *her*, too!" Tony stared at Mario for a tense moment, then said, "You'd better hurry. I think Holtzman's going to do the job outside the studio. He knows Amos Stuart comes almost every day about noon." He clamped his lips together, then said, "Tell Stuart to get outta town—and that sister of his better shut down that picture! So long, Mario—and if you breathe a word of this, I'm dead!"

"Thanks, Tony. I won't forget it—but you know I won't talk!"

As soon as Tony left, Mario picked up the phone and tried to reach Amos. His secretary said brightly, "Mr. Stuart's gone to meet his sister."

Mario slammed the phone down, dashed out of the office, and leaped into his car. As he roared across town, he kept glancing at his watch. "Eleven forty-eight!" he muttered, and tromped down harder on the gas pedal.

He reached the studio just as Amos's car was pulling up to the curb, breathed "Thank God!" as he braked his car, and leaped out. He ran forward, but even as he did, he was aware that a man had gotten out of a car across the street. He'd never seen Hymie Holtzman but he saw the man pull a gun from his overcoat pocket.

"Amos!" Mario saw Amos turn to him, a startled look on his face.

"Mario—" Amos called out in alarm. He didn't see Holtzman, but glancing to his right saw that Pete had stepped outside the gate. Then he heard Mario cry out, "Amos—get down!"

Amos was in full view of Holtzman, Mario saw. Mario ran full speed, crying out a warning, but the gun in the killer's hand was rising, and Mario knew Amos was helpless. With a desperate burst of speed he threw himself forward, his body coming between Amos and Holtzman. He crashed into Amos, and at that instant he heard the explosion of a gun and a sliver of pure pain ran through his back. As he fell to the pavement, he heard gunfire, but as he tried to cry out, he was swallowed in a sea of blackness. He heard Amos cry out, "Mario—" and then he knew no more.

The blackness grew lighter, and Mario felt hands touching him. He struggled to open his eyes, and the pain in his back struck him like a blow. He moaned and heard a familiar voice cry out his name.

With an effort he opened his eyes—and the blurred faces that bent over him grew clear.

"Christie?" he whispered, and then he felt something hot touch his face. "What's . . . wrong?" he gasped. He lifted his hand, which seemed to weigh tons, and touched her damp cheeks. She seized his hand and bent and kissed him.

"Mario—are you all right?"

"Back hurts . . ." he said, then it all came back with a rush. He looked over to his right and saw Amos standing there. He blinked and managed to say, "Amos . . ." but then he couldn't say more. Amos took his other hand and said, "You're going to be all right, Mario." Amos seemed to have trouble speaking, but he finally said, "You took the bullet meant for me, Mario. Saved my life . . ."

Mario's head was clearing, and he saw that the room was full: Amos, Lylah and Jesse, Lenora, Owen, Jerry holding tightly to Bonnie, and Christie. He managed a smile, saying, "Looks like a family reunion."

"It is, I guess," Amos nodded. He squeezed Mario's hand, saying with a smile, "Welcome to the family."

Mario looked up at Christie who said, "You've got to marry me now. Amos insists on it after you saved his life." Then she said, "We're all so proud of you, Mario!"

"What happened after I went down?"

"Pete put Holtzman down with one shot," Jerry put in. "That one won't be doing any more killing!"

"And Capone is in the fire," Lylah added. "Amos called in

the federal agency, and they've got Capone on suspicion. He's going to be too busy to think about Monarch—"

The door burst open, and a large gray-haired nurse took one look around and said "All of you—out! You're breaking the rules!"

All except Christie allowed themselves to be herded out. She came over and put her cheek on Mario's, saying, "Get well, Dearest! I need you!"

"I've got a lot to learn," Mario Castellano said quietly. "But we'll be together, whatever it takes!"

Outside Lylah watched as Bonnie took Jerry's arm and led him firmly down the hall. "I think your sister's got her eye on my nephew," she murmured.

Jesse eyed the pair, then said, "Never mind about those babies. What about us?" He ignored the interns, nurses, and other visitors. Taking Lylah into his arms, he kissed her soundly, then said, "Come on. Let's go get an engagement ring."

"All right, Jesse—I don't want you to get away!"

They left the hospital at once. When they were outside, Jesse hurried to where Pete was playing ball with Adam on the grass. Picking Adam up, he turned to Lylah, saying, "This fellow is getting big!" He grinned at the boy, asking, "How would you like to have a dad to take you to ball games, Adam?"

"And buy me ice cream?"

"Yes! How about some right now?"

"Yes!"

As Lylah Stuart looked at the tall man holding her son, she was filled with a sense of peace and joy. Her life had been a hard journey, but she was aware that she had come into a safe harbor.

"I'll have an ice cream, too, Jesse," she said, and he turned and smiled at her.

"We'll have love and ice cream," he said, "every day of our lives!"